BLUE DESTINY

MATTHEW JENKINS

CENTAUR BOOKS
Chicago

BLUE DESTINY

MATTHEW JENKINS

This is a work of fiction. Names, characters, places, and incidents are the product of the author's imagination or have been used fictitiously. Any resemblance to actual persons, living or dead, events, locales or organizations is entirely coincidental.

Published by CENTAUR BOOKS
CentaurBooks.com

imprint of Joshua Tree Publishing
JoshuaTreePublishing.com
• Chicago •

All rights reserved. No part of this book may be reproduced or transmitted in any form or by any means, electronic or mechanical, including information storage and retrieval system without written permission from the publisher, except by a reviewer who may quote brief passages in a review.

ISBN 13-Digit: 978-1-941049-14-3

Copyright © 2014 Matthew Jenkins. All Rights Reserved.

Book Cover Design : Matthew Jenkins

Printed in the United States of America

DEDICATION

*Dedicated to the idea of eternal love and
to my wife who in life has shown me the greatest evidence
that true love can and does exists.*

*To all those that encouraged my writing endeavors,
without you this book would not be possible.*

And to the Men and Women of HSL-49.

*This book is also dedicated to the idea that Dolphins and
other forms of life are intelligent
and should be respected in all regards.*

*It is my hope that this book aids in the efforts
to preserve our oceans for all.*

Chapter 1

Beginnings

As I left the dark daylight of the Alaskan sky, I had a bit of remorse in leaving. For months, and even years, I had been planning my escape. But even now on the day of my departure, I still couldn't believe I was leaving. This place, as cold and dark as it may seem, had a certain nostalgia that I had grown to love. It was "a constant of my expectation" at least that was what I had written in one of my many papers. It was what I had known all of my life, and it was hard to leave. But I didn't care. I was going. I wore my heavy jacket for the last time. I was finally heading out of the cold of Alaska and into the warmth of California.

My mother was in complete tears as she drove me to the Fairbanks airport. She was so sad. She had been crying for weeks as she counted down the time before I left.

"Are you sure you have to leave?" she would ask me every other day, always having a look of hope that my answer might change.

"Nope. Don't even try mom. You know I'm going," I would always tell her back, and she always looked so surprised. She even went so far as to leave my favorite things around the house to remind me that I would miss home if I left. But none of her efforts had succeeded, and now we were on our way to the airport at last.

I had hated Alaska the last few years. When college application time came around, I knew I had to pick the farthest place I could think of to get away from all this cold. I chose almost the farthest away, the University of California. To my surprise, I got accepted. I had never left Alaska before now, but I had seen pictures of deep blue oceans ever since I had been a little girl. I had a longing for the warmth and for the beach.

As I grabbed my bags, I hugged and kissed my mom goodbye. My mom in her last attempt to keep me in Alaska cried and cried and cried. As the escalator moved me away from her, I could still see her crying. But after that, I had only the future on my mind. I was going. I was going to see California. I couldn't feel too bad for my mom. She still had my brothers to take care of. But I was her only "little girl." I think that's what made my leaving so hard.

I quickly got situated in my seat. I was so excited from the moment I sat down. I felt like I had made it out the gates. I was finally leaving this cold and awful place. As the plane took off, I had the strange feeling that I would never again be a part of this dark, cold place that I had dreaded for so long. This was the last time I would be in Alaska. As I opened my bag to find my itinerary, I found a note.

It was from my brother George. It said, "It's still not too late, come back now. We need you!!!!" I laughed and shook my head as I read it. I knew they would be fine without me, and they would probably come visit me soon. I appreciated the last little attempt by my brother to convince me to come back, but it didn't work. I am still going. I began to think about the plan I had set up for myself. The first thing I had to do when I landed was to meet with my Aunt Carrie who had lived in San Diego for a few years.

She never came to visit us in Alaska, but she called whenever she got the chance to talk with my mom. She was going to be picking me up when I landed in San Diego. I had talked with Aunt Carrie only a few times in my life. I was a little nervous when I found out I got accepted to the University of California, but my mom told me Aunt Carrie would take care of me. That made me a little less nervous about going to a new place so far away from home. It was nice to know that I would have family nearby in this new place, but I was still a little apprehensive about being picked up by someone I had never met before. I guess years ago, my Aunt Carrie had gotten sick of the cold like me and decided to never come back.

As the plane began to take off, I thought of the long plane ride ahead of me. This was a nonstop flight. I had been so excited the night before that I hadn't got any sleep. I knew that I should get some rest so I would have enough energy to walk around the campus. I debated for a moment: "Should I sleep or stay awake?" It really wasn't much of a debate—I was so exhausted. I laid my head back and tried the best I could to get some sleep. I had never been able to sleep in strange places before, and a plane was no exception. I tried to relax my body the best that I could.

Soon I found that utter sweet spot—the spot you always look for when you are trying to go to sleep but rarely find. I just closed my eyes and fell fast asleep.

As I slept, I quickly slipped into a dream in which I was flying over the water like Superwoman. As I glided through the air, I felt the absolute exhilaration of freedom. For some unknown reason, I then went straight into the water like I had crashed. I quickly woke up startled. I tried to catch my breath as my eyes stared straight ahead at the seat in front of me. The dream had seemed so real. I was startled because I thought the plane had crashed. The lady next to me turned toward me and was fixated on how startled I was.

"Are you alright?" she asked. I looked at her for a second. I was dumbfounded by the question.

"I'm fine, thank you. I just had a bad dream," I said smiling as though I was embarrassed. I turned to my side staring at the window. My response seemed to satisfy the woman's curiosity. She left me alone after that. I looked at my watch. It had only been ten minutes since we took off. I closed my eyes again. I shifted my body around searching for the sweet spot again. As soon as I had fallen asleep, the oddest thing happened. My dream started exactly where it had left off. I was in the water again. I struggled not to wake up. I knew it was a dream. As I relaxed in the dream, I heard a voice in the distance.

"Auuurrroorrah," the voice said in an echoing whisper.

I turned to see where the voice was calling me from. Before I could see where it was coming from, there was a sudden flash of light. I jumped as the light hit me. I woke up again just as startled as I had been the first time my dream had scared me. This time though, I woke up as the plane was landing. I quickly shook off the dream and stared out the window.

As the plane landed, I saw the most remarkable view I think you could see of any city. San Diego seemed so different somehow from what I was used to. I knew it was San Diego as soon as I saw the Coronado Bridge and the iconic metallic dome library that had just been built. It was so spectacular and so sunny outside of the window that I almost began to cry because it was so beautiful. The sun had just come up. It had been a twelve-hour flight altogether so I was happy to get up and stretch my legs. The dream I had bothered me a little, but I decided not to worry about it. It was just a dream after all. The plane seemed to land safe in San Diego without any problems.

I went down the escalator to get my bags at the baggage pickup. When I got down the escalator, I saw Aunt Carrie waiting for me. She looked just like the picture I had seen of her. She was my mom's older sister, but I guess people age better down here because she looked so much younger than my mom. Aunt Carrie knew who I was right away. She ran right over to me and gave me the hardest, longest hug I had ever gotten.

"I'm so glad that you're here," Aunt Carrie told me.

"I'm glad I'm here too, Aunt Carrie," I replied as we waited for my bags. I immediately liked my aunt. I had been a bit nervous about spending time with a relative I had never met. But I quickly forgot about all of that when Aunt Carrie and I started to talk. It was like we had known each other all of our lives. Aunt Carrie started talking about all the fun things to do in San Diego and how I was going to love college.

"It is so beautiful there and close to the water," she said. She was quickly interrupted when I began to point at my bag that was heading toward us.

"It's the ugly green one," I said as I continued to point at it. Aunt Carrie grabbed it. As my Aunt held the bag in her hand, she gave it a look of disillusionment as though she had never seen a bag in such bad shape. I had got it from my mom who wasn't up on the latest in fashion.

Aunt Carrie turned her head toward me and said, "What is the color of your other bags? Are they the same as this one?"

I cleared my throat and with an embarrassing tone I said, "Oh that's the only bag. Most of what I had at home doesn't match the climate here. There aren't any stores where I'm from that carry the kind of clothes I needed."

Aunt Carrie smiled and said, "Don't worry. I'll fix that. I'll take you shopping."

"Thank you. I would love that," I said and smiled.

On the way out of the airport, I took another look at my aunt. I hadn't noticed when I first saw her, but Aunt Carrie was stunning. She was wearing an outfit that before today I would have only seen in high-end magazines. My aunt had a certain pizzazz about her that I never thought existed in real life. She outshined everyone we passed from the way she dressed and presented herself, to the way she talked. She was the picture of beauty and elegance. I knew I could learn a lot from her.

We both got into my aunt's car and continued to talk all the way to the campus. We talked about everything, from my goals in life to why I chose to come to San Diego. When we arrived at the campus, my aunt pulled up to a drop-off point and let me out of the car. I grabbed my bag and then turned toward my aunt.

"Promise me that you will at least come and see me on the weekends. I know how busy things can get while you're in college, but I want to get to know you," Aunt Carrie said.

"Yes, of course," I said. Though she didn't mention how I was supposed to get around without a car. But I didn't want to bring it up. My aunt had already done so much for me by picking me up and dropping me off at the campus.

I think I can figure out how to get around San Diego on my own, I thought as I walked away from the car with my ugly bag.

My aunt yelled out her window to me, "Alright. Well, take care and call me if you need anything."

"Thank you. I will," I said back to my aunt. I turned around and faced the campus. When I finally started to walk away from the car, I got my first real glimpse of the campus. The campus was so immense that it seemed a little intimidating. I began to walk forward with caution. I was worried I was going to get lost in such a large place. Luckily, one of the first things that I saw was a sign for the main office. A feeling of relief quickly came over me and soon replaced all of my anxiety.

Soon after walking for a minute, I was left with a much better view of the campus. I finally saw the utter expanding scene that was the campus. Back home, things had never seemed as big or impressive as the campus that was in front of me. In Alaska, there is a lot of wilderness, but as far as where the population is centralized, things are much smaller. Here, the courtyard alone was the equivalent to the population of my hometown. The campus seemed so busy. Everyone here walked around with a purpose. This was the first sign for me that this was going to be completely different from high school.

I went through the front doors of the main office where there was a line of no less than twenty-five people waiting to be seen. I quickly stepped to the back of the line and began what I knew would be a long wait. After waiting a half an hour, I was finally seen by one of the staff members who kindly handed me a "welcome to our college" package. As I looked through it, I noticed that it had a map, a basic how-to-survive-on-this-campus booklet, and an "in college" manual along with a few other things.

I was then directed to walk toward another woman behind the desk who quickly asked, "What is your name?"

"Aurora Carr," I said with some enthusiasm together with a heavy layer of nervousness. The woman smiled at me and typed my name into the computer.

"Oh, Ms. Carr, yes, yes, indeed. We have been expecting you all the way from…Alaska. Wow!" She continued to read the screen in front of her.

"Okay, we are glad that you are here and are staying in a dorm. Yes and it will be12B. 12B is a very good room. And your schedule, your freshman schedule, very good, very good."

The woman then turned around and walked toward the printer as it began to spit out sheets of paper. She picked up the papers and walked toward me.

"Here you go," the woman said as she straightened out the printouts and handed them to me.

Then she pointed out the door and said, "Okay, so I'm going to walk you through this. When you walk out this door, you're going to take a left straight across that nice big field you saw as you came in here. Then take another left when you get to a sign that says 'Wilmington Hall,' walk down a long corridor, and then take a right and walk about thirty more feet. You will see a hallway, walk down that hallway, walk up the stairs, and then you will see your room 12b. Did you catch all that?"

It was at this point that I looked confused. I hadn't heard anything she had said past after "you walk out this door." The woman had spoken entirely too fast, and it was impossible to keep up. After looking around the office hoping that I could find someone else who could explain the directions with a tad bit more clarity, I noticed a very large cup of coffee.

The cup of coffee was empty. I realized that the reason this woman didn't make any sense was because she was full of caffeine. I grinned with what most people thought was my happy smile but in fact was my nervous smile. I hadn't seen anyone else that I could ask for better directions, and I didn't think I was ever going to figure out the directions that this woman had just given me. I was having my first dilemma, and I hadn't even been at college for an hour.

Just then something funny happened. I think sometimes in life the right thing happens at the right time. And at this moment, a figure popped out from the corner and gave me my "right time" kind of moment.

"Hold on Mrs. Degory. I will take her to her room," the figure from the background said. As she emerged, it became clearer how she looked. She was a tall, slender, blond-haired, blue-eyed supermodel-looking girl. She reminded me of a volleyball player for some reason.

She smiled at me as she looked me in the eyes and said, "Hi, I'm Julia." Julia then put out her hand to shake mine.

I returned the gesture with my hand and said, "Aurora, Aurora Carr."

"You're staying in 12B, and it just so happens that I live in a room close to that. Do you want to come with me so you don't get lost? I will give you a small tour on the way." I took a second look at Mrs. Degory and thought about how bad the first set of directions had been.

"Yes, and thank you." I picked up my bag and welcome package. And with that, we started walking out the door.

"Thanks Mrs. Degory," Julia said as we left the door.

"No problem and good luck," Mrs. Degory said as she waved goodbye.

"Thanks," I said and then we continued to walk as the door closed behind us.

"That's crazy, huh? I just came here for a pen, and then by chance, you should happen to need a tour of the campus," Julia said as she picked up a college pen. Julia waved the pen at me.

"They are free, you know, these pens. You never know when you need a pen. So I grab one every time I pass this office. That's just one of a lot of tricks I guess you learn after you have been in college a while," Julia said.

"Thanks." I managed to say in between Julia's constant talking. She didn't stop talking much and seemed extremely upbeat.

"Boy, you look exhausted. Where are you flying in from?"

"Alaska."

"Alaska!!!!!" Julia exclaimed. "Wow, welcome to America," she said with a laugh.

I returned a smile at the joke. *Ha ha ha*, I thought to myself. In a way though, Julia was right. Alaska was so far away and so different than what most people experience in normal America that it may as well be another country.

As we started walking, Julia began to point and go over a few things about campus life. She pointed out things like the good hangouts, where the good study spots were, how the professors are, and even how the campus cafeteria food is.

"It's not half bad if you try it," Julia said."Oh and let me warn you about these rooms, they are small. In fact, they are like a closet. This is probably going to be the smallest room that you have ever been in. And it's three to a room too. But you get used to it I guess. I just wanted to warn you early and get rid of any high expectations about getting your own room or sharing with only one other person. Freshmen always share three people to a room. That was probably the hardest part for me to get used to when I first got to college a couple years back. I always like to warn all the people that I see coming into college for the first time about the room size. My sister is starting school this year too and I told her all about how small the rooms are." Julia turned her head to see my reaction.

"That's okay. My room isn't very big back home. We only had a few rooms in the house, and I have three brothers. So since I was the only girl, I got the smallest room. But I think that helped me. I should be fine."

"Okay, but don't say I didn't warn you," Julia said again. We finally got to the room after a very long walk.

"Here is your room. It's 12B, right?" Julia asked.

"Yes, it is. Wow! I would have never made it here without your help. Mrs. Degory's directions were horrible. I'm glad that we made it. Thank you so much."

"No problem. I was glad to guide you. I didn't want to leave you in the hands of Mrs. Degory's bad directions. Do you have your key?" Julia asked.

I grabbed my welcome package that I had been carrying. I searched around in it and found a small bag.

"There, that's it," Julia said as she pointed at it. I picked up the key out of the bag. It was brass and looked brand new.

"Careful, sometimes the keys don't work, and then you will have to go all the way back to tell the front desk and talk to Mrs. Degory again. And then she will have to call someone to fix it," Julia said.

I cautiously picked up the key and stuck it in the keyhole. I turned the key trying to be careful not to make any sudden movements. Luckily, the key worked the first time. I opened up the door and prepared myself for the smallest room in the world. When I saw it though, I immediately thought that it doesn't look half bad. In fact, it was better than half bad. It was great. I loved it. I saw my roommates as the door opened and introduced myself.

"Hi! I'm your new roommate, Aurora."

Both of my new roommates looked straight at me with suspicious eyes as I entered the room.

I saw their stares and looked at myself to see what they were looking at. Their glances were in the direction of my old tore up bag. Oh great! Here comes another comment about my bag. But if they were thinking about my hideous bag, they never said anything—instead they introduced themselves. The one on the left stuck out her hand.

"Hi, I'm Stacey," she said with a cheery smile.

"I'm Aurora, nice to meet you."

Stacey turned around and went back to what she was doing before I had entered the room. The second roommate just gave a big, long stare. It wasn't a look of hate or disgust. It was as though she was looking me over to figure out what her first impression would be of me.

Okay, you're freaking me out, I thought and put my hand out.

"Hi, I'm Aurora, your new roommate and you are?"

This girl blinked once as though she was shocked and put her hand out toward mine and said, "I'm Jessica." She then turned back to the chair behind her, picked up her book, and went to her bed where she sat. I shook this off and didn't let it bother me. I wasn't used to meeting so many people, but I knew that not everyone is supposed to like you when you first meet them. But if you work at it, you can usually get them to at least get along with you. I put my bag on my bed and turned around to Julia.

"Thanks so much Julia. I really do appreciate you taking me to my room."

"No problem, new girl! I mean Aurora. We will have to hang out later. Let me know if you need any help with anything. I'm right across the hall. I'll talk to you later, have fun. "

"I will, thank you," I said as I let Julia out and then closed the door behind her. After that, I started to find places to put my clothes and looked at my schedule as I got ready for my first day of college. I hadn't even finished unpacking when I noticed something on my schedule that made me very nervous.

Chapter 2

Welcome Week

I hadn't really looked at my schedule when I first got it, but I soon realized that the first week wasn't classes at all. It was this thing called "Welcome Week." *What is Welcome Week?* I thought for a second about it. I turned toward my new roommates, but then that sudden feeling came over me—like when you enter a cave and there is that black endless alone feeling. I didn't know either one of these girls, but I needed an answer about what "Welcome Week" was. I quickly left the room to catch up with my one and only friend Julia.

"Julia!!! Julia!!!!" I yelled loudly. I finally caught up with her, still surprised she wasn't annoyed by me yet.

"Yes, Aurora, how might I help you?"

"What is Welcome Week?" I asked her, almost out of breath.

Julia gave a smirk like she had forgotten to mention it.

"Oh, Welcome Week, that will help you a lot. Didn't you read anything about college before you came? Welcome week is your first week at college. It is the week when you learn all about campus and what's here. You know, stuff you would find out anyway through necessity, like where the store is, where the library is, and where all the pools are. At least, that's the first day or two and each night and every day after that. You have a bunch of events to get you started on your college career. It's a lot of fun."

"Oh, I hadn't heard anything about any of that. I just focused on getting here," I said smiling. I felt a little embarrassed about forgetting to figure out my schedule. *I wish I had focused more on that before I left. Oh well, I can't go back now*, I thought as Julia went on and on about what was going to go on during Welcome Week.

"Oh, you're going to absolutely love this week. Some say it is the most fun you'll have the whole time that you're in college. I don't know too much about that though. I always have fun, but it will show you a lot of stuff and will give you a chance to meet people."

It won't matter if it's a week or a month. I probably won't meet anyone.

I had always had trouble making friends. It was probably because I haven't had the chance to meet a lot of new people, and on a day-to-day basis, I usually feel a little out of place. Now in this place, I feel even worse.

"Oh, goodie, I can't wait," I said.

"I know it is going to be so much fun. You are going to love it. I think you are a cool person. I can tell just by talking with you. You really will meet a lot of people. Remember you can network or not work. That's why I know everyone," Julia said with a smile and a grin.

It really did seem like she did. In the short time that I had known Julia, it seemed like she knew everyone on campus. Everyone was giving her nice hand gestures of hello and nods.

"Aurora, I have to go. I'm late for a date. Remember, take a deep breath and take a walk around. Go explore and always remember your way back. You don't want to get lost on your first night here. Are you good?" Julia asked.

"Yeah, I'm good."

"Okay, I'm taking off now or I really am going to be late for this date," Julia said as she took off.

I was on my own again. I thought about what Julia had said and decided I would take a walk around and maybe get some dinner. But first, I had to finish unpacking.

I went back to my ugly green bag and finished pulling out my small wardrobe. Then I set up my laptop, put a few pictures up, and even managed to put my favorite stuffed animal, Mr. Snookie, on the bed.

Me and you, go way back, I thought as I stared at Mr. Snookie. I felt more at home. Something about a few pictures and a stuffed animal can help someone feel right at home. I decided to brush my teeth and freshen up a little bit before I took a walk.

I combed my hair, brushed my teeth, washed my face, and put some perfume on. *There, I feel loads better*, I thought as I put everything away.

My two roommates were still in the room preoccupied with whatever it was they were doing. Neither one of them said a word to me as I left.

This is going to be a quite couple of years here if this is the way it is going to be. I guess we better get used to it, Mr. Snuggles.

I left the room with my handy student map and began my exploration of the campus.

As I walked out the door and down the corridor, I began to make a mental map of this place. I had the actual map in my hands, but one thing that I had learned from all of my years of walking around the woods is know your bearing. Never forget which way you came from. So I found on the map where I was and then I plotted where I was going. I know they say college is big, but this place was really immense. It was hard to get used to it at first, but soon I gathered my bearings.

I just couldn't believe I got into such a nice place, and that I was going to live here. I walked past the main gym, an art gallery, and a bunch of halls. Then I passed a research facility, onto a medical facility, to a biology lab, physics lab, marine biology lab, a massive oceanography lab, a math lab, and a concert hall. Then on to three pools, five more giant halls, and a couple of sports fields. I passed four parking structures until I reached the area I was really looking for, the food court. *Finally*, I thought with a big sigh. I then saw a really familiar sign, fast-food. I got my food and sat down.

I began to eat my burger which seemed like the best burger I had ever had. I knew this food couldn't be this good, but I guess anything is going to be good if you're really hungry. I hadn't eaten since I left Alaska. After a minute or two of enjoying the moment, I looked at my watch.

"Shoot!!!" I said aloud. It was 9:00 p.m., and I had promised my mom I would call her by 8:00 pm. It was a promise I had said I would keep. But with everything going on, I had neglected to glance at my watch. I pulled out my phone and pressed call.

My mom was of course the last one on the call list. It shows how few friends I really had. A worried voice answered on the other end.

"What happened to eight?" my mom asked.

"I'm sorry mom. I lost track of time. I went exploring the campus and just forgot to call."

"I've been worried sick. You're my only little girl. I don't ever want anything to happen to you. It's bad enough you had to move to the other side of the world. You had me worried sick!"

"I really am sorry mom. Please don't get hysterical."

After a minute of my mom freaking out, she calmed down a bit, but there was still a long pause before either of us could talk. I could still hear the frustration in my mom's breathing. "So how was your flight and did you meet your aunt?"

"Oh, yeah, mom, the flight went great. It was nice and smooth and on time. I met Aunt Carrie, and she is great. She made me promise to hang out. She seems really cool and absolutely fashionable. Aunt Carrie reminds me of a picture in a magazine. She was wearing this red dress with a one slip tie off. It was so pretty. She has even offered to take me shopping whenever we get the chance," I said with an absolute sound of enthusiasm in my voice.

"That's good. I'm glad she was there to pick you up, and you are getting along with her. I haven't seen her in a few years."

I sensed a bit of jealousy in my mom's voice that I had never heard before from my mom. I recognized it because of my three brothers and all of the sibling rivalries that had occurred over my childhood. But for the first time ever, I was hearing it in a slight undertone from my mom. My mom hid it well though. It was barely noticeable. But it was still there.

It was as though she was jealous that her sister had made it away from Alaska— and she had not. I had never noticed it before from my mom. For the first time in my life, I realized that maybe my mom wasn't as happy in Alaska as I had imagined, and maybe she didn't want to be there either.

"And what is college like?"

"Well, I don't know mom. I just got here. I haven't even gone to class yet. I haven't even really settled in yet. I just barely put my stuff away and met my roommates. "

"I know, Aurora. I mean, what does it feel like to actually be at college? You know we are all so proud of you for going to college and everything. I always knew from an early age that you were smart and now you get to expand your mind and see everything I had always hoped you would. I'm just so sorry that I couldn't come down there with you like most parents. I wanted to help you settle in, but I couldn't get off work for that long. I'm so sorry. But I know you will do alright. Are you settling in okay?" She started to cry again.

"Don't worry, mom. I won't let you down. I know what this means to you for me to be here, and I'm going to do my best. I'm going to stick to the plan, study hard, and get a good career. I'm going to follow my dreams, I promise."

"And then you'll be back, right? You're coming back to Alaska right?"

"Yes mom," I said, but I knew in my heart I wasn't coming back. I had decided not to tell my mom that I had no intention of going back. Any mention I had made about my distaste of Alaska and the bitter cold had always been in private. My mom, I had thought, loved Alaska. I knew that she wouldn't like my dislike of the whole state.

I knew in my heart that Alaska was not in my plans for the future. The battle to not go back would have to be fought at a later time. I think any mention of it right at this moment would put my mom over the edge. I mean, she was nearly there with her hysteria because I didn't call on time. But I would pick some day later to tell her.

My mom suddenly yawned. We had been talking for about an hour, and it was getting late.

"Alright, Aurora. I'm going to let you go for now. I want you to keep me posted on how things go—and stay away from boys for now. I know that love can happen anywhere. But you have to stay focused and study. I'm not saying don't fall in love. Just don't forget why you are in college. You have worked hard to get where you are. I want you to stay focused on that, okay?" My mom said this with a serious and heartfelt tone.

"Don't worry mom. It was never a problem before, and it won't be a problem now."

Boys have never been very attracted to me. I was never as beautiful as some. But that was okay because I felt lucky in a way. It helped me to focus on my school without all the distractions of dating and falling in love. That was the last thing that I needed right now. I had seen others around me who fell in love and then fallen away from their studies. I solely focused on school as graduation approached. I knew that going to college was my ticket out of Alaska. I saw it as my one and only chance to leave. And now, I was here in college. I was ready to succeed.

"Alright," my mom continued. "I love you. Be safe and get some rest."

"Love you too, mom."

And with that, my mom hung up. Sometimes it was a battle to see who was going to hang up the phone first. But in this case, my mom had ended the call with no contest, which told me that my mom was tired— and so was I. As I put the phone down, I found myself alone again in this strange new place. I think it's odd that for the hour that I was talking to my mom, I had felt like she was right down the corner. It was almost like I was in high school again talking to my mom as if she was right down the street. But I knew that my mom wasn't here and that made me feel a tangle of knots inside my stomach.

For the first time in my life, I had never felt so alone and so far away from everyone that I knew. An overwhelming feeling of doubt came over me. *Had I made a mistake? Had this been a horribly bad decision?* I maintained my composure. I didn't want to start crying right there in the food court. But I continued to feel like maybe this whole idea of college and moving away from home was just one giant mistake. The worst part was that classes hadn't even started yet.

I took a deep breath. After thinking about it for a few minutes, I began to take the long walk back to my room.

All I need to do is get some sleep and I will have new outlook on things.

I found my way back toward my room. As I walked, I could make out the details in the night sky that had just come out. It was the first absolutely familiar thing I had seen since I had arrived. I stared at it with its omniscient presence. I had no idea that the night sky would look so much alike here as it did in Alaska. I found a bench where I sat for a minute. The stars were all there. It wasn't as clear here as it was back home, but I could still make out some of my favorites. There was peace in the ever expanding view of the night sky.

"I will make it through this," I said aloud as I stared at the sky. After a moment of staring, things finally felt right. I took another deep breath and got up feeling a little better. I gathered my bearing again and continued on my journey toward my room. When I finally got to my room, I opened the door to a surprising scene. My new roommates were sitting on their beds and facing the door as though they had been waiting for me to walk in for some time.

Chapter 3

Ground Rules

Stacey asked as I walked into the room, "What was your name again?"

"It's Aurora. I hope I haven't interrupted anything," I said with an astounded voice as I was thrown off by the whole scene.

"Ahh, Aurora, what an unusual name! No, you're not interrupting anything. In fact, we have been waiting for you. Before another minute goes on, we must discuss something together as roommates. Would you mind if we discuss ground rules for being in this room?"

Ground rules! I thought as my two new roommates stood up from their beds. *Ground rules, really!*

It hasn't even been five minutes of me being here, and these two have already decided to create some rules that would be the foundation for the rest of my off time here at college.

Alright, let's hear it.

Stacey dashed across to her desk and grabbed an erasable marker. Like a pair of synchronized divers, Jessica grabbed a 4 by 5 ft. marker board and propped it up on an easel that was conveniently set up close by in the center of the room facing my bed. It was like I was watching a well-rehearsed play or something.

The top of the marker board was already labeled "ground rules"—I would presume in anticipation for the presentation I was about to receive on the ground rules. The look of astonishment and anger was in the glare of my eyes that I am sure Stacey and Jessica could see. I watched Stacey as she propped herself up on her bed and began to clear her throat. Stacey then began to speak with a hyper tone about the new rules.

"Okay, let's discuss ground rules for this room. Jessica and I have made up some rules that we need you to follow. These are general rules that we will follow as well. Since you are the new addition to this room, you will adhere to these rules from this day forward, as long as you are here in this room with us. We've dealt with enough dirty-smelling, vial people not to create these ground rules. I hope you understand." Stacey handed Jessica the marker and then continued to talk.

"Rule number one." Jessica began to write the number one on the board.

"Brush your teeth. This rule is extremely important. I can't have my roommates running around with bad teeth or bad breath. And this rule includes not leaving your toothpaste out or your toothbrush after you've brushed your teeth. Also don't touch my toothpaste or use my toothbrush, got it?"

"Yeah, don't touch my brush," Jessica said seriously and then wrote on the board "brush teeth."

"Rule number two: Wash your clothes. And when I say wash your clothes, I mean with a washer—with soap and water unless it's silk and it that case, you would dry clean it. Don't leave your clothes everywhere for days. In addition, the wash-your-clothes rule includes washing your towel." This statement by Stacey was followed by her apparent sidekick Jessica writing down "wash clothes."

Then Jessica stated in her serious voice again, "Don't touch my clothes." Now looking at Jessica's grunge-like rave outfit, I had to say it wasn't really my taste in clothing anyways so I wasn't too upset that we weren't sharing clothes, but I started to wonder where all these rules were coming from.

With a wink from Jessica, Stacey went on to the next all-important rule. "Buy your own food. This includes your own take out, your own milk, your own cereal, and your own granola bars. In this room, don't assume anything is yours and don't ask if you can have a little and assume that any positive response maintains its validity after we have left the room." Jessica then followed in tune with previous rules by writing "buy your own food" and then Jessica said in a gloomy tone, "Don't eat my bread."

As Stacey and her sidekick Jessica continued laying the law of the room, I just sat there listening to the whole thing without asking why. It really was too much fun to watch these two tell me basic things that I already knew. The feeling of anger slowly left me as Stacey and Jessica continued. I wasn't any of these things that these two seemed to be describing. I just think it's funny that both these girls would assume right off the bat that I would need this kind of strict layout of basic rules that any adult should know. It was like I was in kindergarten or something. I mean, after all, aren't we all adults? My mom had raised me right and I didn't really need this, but I let Stacey continue on.

And she really did. She continued adding rules about toilet paper rotating week by week, with each roommate buying rolls on a three-week cycle. I actually liked the idea of that. Then she continued on talking about not using the room phone because we all had cell phones anyways.

"I had disconnected it anyways, and it better not get connected again," Stacey said. Then she continued on by talking about vacuuming regularly and not eating fish in the room and then leaving half of the fish in the trash can. She finished this crazy long list of rules with one final rule about keeping boys out. This rule was funny because it made this place feel less like college and more like a girls-only tree house.

But why all these rules? I kept on asking myself as Jessica wrote the last rule. It then hit me like a rock on the head. The reason for all of these rules must be because of my hideous bag. It has to be that bag. It was the only thing that made sense. I knew they had noticed it when I came in and now these stupid rules. I can't believe all of this is happening because of this bag.

I knew it was a mistake to use that bag, I thought as I shook my head. *I had no choice but to use that bag. It was the only bag in the house that would fit everything. I was a simple girl anyhow, and it normally didn't matter to me about things like fashion and the latest bag. But now, I had to deal with this first impression thing, and it was a nightmare all because of this bag. The first thing I do after all of this is settled is get a new bag,*

Or maybe these rules were created because of my meek appearance when I came in. I wasn't cool enough. All of these thoughts ran through my head, and then I finally thought, *I'll ask why. I mean what it could hurt, right?*

So I began to muster up the courage to ask why, burying the knots in my stomach and then an odd feeling of confidence came over me as I began to interrupt Stacey and Jessica's display of dominance.

"Alright, alright, what is all of this about? I just got to this college today. And before you guys even got to know me, you have decided to impose all of these rules on me," I said in a louder voice than I had planned. It was only a mere reflection of my anger. Then I picked up my bag.

"What is it? Is it this bag? You guys are trying to make me feel like a little kid because of a bag. I just got here. I just came to this college and five minutes after arriving, you guys treat me like I'm a kid or something. I don't have to take this!!!!" I said shaking my head. I grabbed my hideous bag and carried it with me as I stomped out of the room. I wanted to make a statement and let them know I wasn't going to take this insult. Mind you, I didn't know where I was going, but I was too mad to think about it. I knew that I had to live in that room and probably would have to accept the new rules these two had come up with. But I started walking nonetheless.

Sometimes you just have to make a statement, and one of the best ways to make your statement heard is to just leave. At least that is what I had learned growing up. Of course, I had never left my house in Alaska while I was arguing with my mom or brothers, but sometimes I would leave the room while I was arguing. But now, I had just left the only home that I had here in San Diego after only being here a short time.

Maybe I should turn back," I thought as I started walking. *No, that would be a mistake. I think I will just wait a while and then try this whole thing over again, or maybe I can get a new room.*

I continued to walk down the hallway. Before I even turned the corner, Stacey had ran over to me and yelled my name, "Auroraaaaa!"

"Wait, we didn't mean anything by it, come back in and we will explain everything to you!!!!" Stacey yelled louder.

As I began to turn to see Stacey, I still had the feeling of anger. I didn't know that I was so upset. I hadn't noticed it until I felt the tear hit my arm.

Great, now they are going to think they got to me. No, Aurora, don't let them get to you. Not the first day.

I stopped in mid-turn and faced Stacey.

"Look, I'm sorry. We didn't mean to upset you," Stacey said.

I looked down the hallway and saw Jessica at the door giving me a hand gesture to come back. I stood there for a second, thinking.

"Come on, let us start over again," Stacey said, pleading with me.

I thought while she was talking, I should give them a second chance. After all, I didn't have anywhere else to go anyways, and I wasn't ready to give up. I wiped the tear from my eyes. Then I walked with Stacey toward the room. We both entered the room. Jessica was already sitting on her bed waiting for us. Somehow in the short time that I had been gone, the marker board had been put away. We all sat down and began to talk.

Stacey looked like she was going to start talking, but I was going to say the first words this time. I started talking.

"Look, you don't have to make up all of these rules for me. I'm an adult. You guys didn't even give me a chance. You just assumed based on my bag and other first impressions of me that you knew how I was—that I was just like your old roommate. Well, I'm not. I know how to be an adult. I know how to put my stuff away!" As I said this, I had started to calm down a bit, and then Stacey stopped me.

"Let me start off by saying that I'm sorry. We all started off on the wrong foot. But you have to understand something about Jessica and me. We have been roommates for a year now. The last roommate we had, who is the main reason that we came up with all of these rules for you, was not the most desirable of roommates.

"She made the room stink so bad and was always eating our food—and never replacing it. I felt like I could never bring anyone over to my room because of her. Every complaint that we made to the office was ignored because she was friends with all of the right people. The school always believed her over us. When she graduated, Jessica and I swore we would never go through another bad roommate situation again."

"She was vile and disgusting. We hated every second she was in the room with us. She made our lives a living nightmare," Jessica said in a very upset voice.

I could tell this was all very emotional for both of them. It even made me feel a little bad for them both to think that they had to go through a whole year with a roommate that matched the description Stacey and Jessica had described. It made me glad that I wasn't here for it.

"Now, I just want to make clear that we just made up these rules because of last year. To be honest with you, these rules had nothing to do with you. It's just that Jessica and I finally felt like we finally had it good. Jessica and I naively thought we had the room to ourselves. Then you showed up and surprised us both. The school hadn't even told us we were getting a roommate. When we settled in after summer break, we didn't see any sign of a roommate," Stacey continued.

"So when we saw you, it wasn't personal. It just took us by surprise. After you left, we thought we had to do something so we came up with the rules that we presented to you. I really hope that you do forgive us and will give us a second chance. Would you mind if we did introductions again?"

At that moment, Stacey seemed so different than the first impression that I had of her. Stacey was perky and kind at the same time. She seemed like a cheerleader and a grandma all rolled into one. I immediately began to like her. Even Jessica who at first had seemed very distant and dark now seemed to have a rather nice side to her, an almost sunshine quality.

Stacey began to speak with a nice smile.

"Alright, I will begin our reintroduction. I am Stacey, as I said before, and I am a sophomore. I have a dual major. I am studying hospitality and hotel management. And I hope to one day own my own successful chain of fabulous hotels. Jessica, do you want to go next?" Stacey gestured over to Jessica who was already preparing to talk.

It seemed hard to tell at first with her dark eyeliner and black lipstick what her mood was. But Jessica also appeared differently now than she had at first. She seemed more upbeat and friendly.

I had never seen anyone dress like Jessica did.

"I'm Jessica, and I was in a band called Dark Sunrise. I'm also a sophomore. And I'm now studying poetry and political science and have a plan to either be a desperate poet or a congressman. I'm still deciding which one is more of a statement," Jessica said.

Then they both looked at me, and I realized it was my turn to do my reintroduction. I was no good at introductions, but I knew an introduction was necessary to get along with my new roommates. At this point though, after making my statement and storming off in anger, I was over my shyness.

"Hi. I'm Aurora," I began and then took a pause to clear my throat.

Why is it right before I begin to talk, my throat will always close up?

"Like I said, my name is Aurora, and I'm from Alaska. I am a freshman and have a passion for biochemistry and oceanography. I hope to one day figure out how the ocean works. And this is my first time living away from home."

I waited for the look of confusion that I usually get when I tell people what I want to do with my life. Most people don't understand what I am talking about when I say that I want to figure out how the oceans work. My two roommates apparently didn't want to upset me anymore than they already had. There wasn't even a bat of an eye from either one of them when

I said what I wanted to do. They didn't seem shocked or bewildered. Stacey gave a big smile at me and then took back control of the conversation.

"That's great. Now we know each other, and really, my dear, don't worry about your bag. I don't think it looks..." Stacey took a second look at my bag again and then said, "Well, actually, I like you, but your bag is kind of out of style. But I can help you with that. We can go pick a new one for your next trip if you would like?" Stacey said.

"That would be nice," I said and took a big sigh of relief.

At least all of that was over.

"Well, let us know if you need anything," Stacey said.

"Yeah, we are here for you," Jessica said. Stacey then went toward the kitchen. Jessica followed suit and joined her at the refrigerator.

"Do you want to join us for dinner?" Stacey asked as she stared over at me as she stood in front of the refrigerator.

"No, I ate before I came here, but thank you," I said in return.

"Okay," Stacey said and went back to the refrigerator with Jessica. They began to pull food out and put it on the table.

"Well, let us know if you change your mind," Jessica said.

"Okay, I will, but I think I'm going to get some sleep," I said.

"Alright. We will talk to you later," Stacey said.

"Yep night," Jessica said.

I took a long yawn. "Night," I said as I turned toward my bed.

Finally, I began to get ready for bed. I searched through my newly organized stuff and found everything easily. I was determined to take it easy for the rest of the night. It seemed that the jetlag and all of the drama with my new roommates took all of the energy out of me. I felt the absolute feeling of being exhausted. It seemed like my roommates, and I were all getting along. I wasn't going to let anything else bother me for the rest of the night. I sat on my bed and relaxed for a minute.

"Finally, peace," I said in a whisper to myself as I looked at Mr. Snuggles. I soon forgot about everything that had happened as I sat there. I took deep breaths and closed my eyes for just a second, but the peace of the moment didn't last long. Soon I remembered something, and a sudden rush of nervousness and excitement hit me all at once. The feeling that hit me was represented by two simple words:

"Welcome Week."

Chapter 4

So This Is College

Most freshmen seemed to have a pretty good idea what was going on. At least that's how things appeared as I walked around during my first official day of college. There were a lot of people moving around the college, but none of them seemed to be as lost as I was. I think this is because most of the time parents and prospective students will fly out to visit campus before school starts. It gives both students and parents an opportunity to look at everything at the college and ask questions that they might have. In addition, the parents and the student are given a presentation about details for the first week and what to expect.

So already I seemed to be behind the power curve. It was one of the disadvantages of coming from Alaska—besides the fact that it was Alaska, and it is already so far away from everything. It made any opportunity to come out to San Diego with my parents before the school year started slim to none. At the time that acceptance letters came back, it was just enough to actually be accepted into college. But now that I am here at college about to experience Welcome Week, it made me a little sad that my mom hadn't got to see the campus or ask questions like some parents get to. It might have set my mom's mind at ease if she had actually got to walk around the campus. It might have also made me a little less nervous about everything.

I knew that there was going to be a lot to do during Welcome Week so I began my day with the expectation of experiencing a lot of new things. I didn't know if they were going to be fun things, or boring things, but I was bound and determined to give anything a try at least once. I walked over to the list of activities and began to give the list a look over. It was Sunday and there was apparently a whole week planned up until Saturday. All there was to do in Alaska was read and the occasional outdoor activities like hiking or maybe snowboarding. But within my first week here, I already had more options of fun things to do than I had ever had in my whole life in Alaska. I knew that all of these activities weren't something that the college was going to do all of the time. It's only supposed to last a week, and then things would probably be different. But I was excited.

I will enjoy it while it's here.

As I browsed through the list of activities, I looked over today's events. On top of the list was a mandatory orientation gathering to start the Welcome Week.

There was also a tour of the museum and a few other events as well as a group photo. The orientation gathering was supposed to start at 8:00 a.m. I glanced at my watch, and it was 7:45 a.m. I followed the map to where the orientation gathering was. I found the building and entered a large auditorium where the meeting was about to begin. I quickly found a seat.

Shortly after everyone had settled in, I glanced at my watch, and it was 8:00 a.m.

"Well, just in time," I said in a whisper as the orientation began.

"Welcome to Welcome Week, please enjoy this presentation," the first presenter said, and then a PowerPoint began. After staring at the large screen for a little while, I realized that this orientation thing was boring. There seemed to be a repetitive cycle of information intended to make even the most studious of people fall asleep. The video stopped, and the Dean talked for a moment.

"Hello new students. I am the Dean, and I'd like to welcome each and every one of you to our college. Please watch this next video. It may help you to succeed while you're with us at this college." The video talked about study habits and staying focused. It was all stuff that I had heard before, but I sat there and watched it anyways. Shortly after that video was completed, there was a series of other various presidents of the school giving the same brief introduction about themselves that the Dean had given, followed by a video of a new tip about how to succeed at college.

There was also a number of faculty that did similar things. It all didn't make much sense and was overall boring.

There was just no wow factor about the whole thing. It was, for the most part, boring and hard to follow from the beginning. I could tell why the school made attending orientation mandatory. If the school hadn't, no one would come. At least there were some helpful hints about the campus and ways to save time getting from place to place. There were also some good hints on how to stay focused in class and how to keep that focus when you were out of class. But all of the good information was so spread out over so many videos that I found it hard to follow at best. I wasn't usually a critic when it came to some things, but I would say that the whole orientation gathering was one of the most boring things ever created in the history of mankind.

What made things even worse was when I realized how boring my week was going to be. I looked again at my schedule when the mandatory orientation meeting had taken an intermission. I hadn't noticed it the first time that I looked at the schedule, but there was one of these mandatory orientation meetings every day this week. There was one from each major department. I could only imagine how different each one would attempt to be while still remaining the same. Just as I looked over the schedule and came to grips with just how boring my week was going to be, a friend dropped in next to me. It was Julia.

"Hey Aurora."

"Julia, how's it going?" I asked.

"I'm good, what cha doing?" Julia asked.

"I'm trying not to get bored and looking over my schedule. I'm trying to see what's going on this week. I think I'm done with all of these mandatory orientations. They are just too much. They are so boring. How can you stand them?"

"Don't worry. These orientations are always this boring, but you get used to them. Anyways, I saw that you were over here, and I wanted you to meet someone. I think you two might be able to help each other get through these orientation presentations."

A figure came up from behind Julia as she continued.

"This is my sister, Erica. I have told her about you, and I think you two are going to get along great. You two seem like you are a lot alike. Erica wants to be an anthropologist, and she is a freshman too. I was thinking you two could hang out during this week because she doesn't have any friends here either. What do you think?"

"Oh thank god" was my reaction. "It was going to be so nice to have someone to walk around with."

Hopefully, we will get along, but at this point, I don't care. I'll hang out with anyone to get through these boring presentations.

Erica shook my hand.

"Hi, I'm Erica."

"Hi, I'm Aurora."

"Hey, don't forget. I don't know if you noticed this, but there is a soccer game in a little while and everyone is going to be there. It's going to be so much fun," Julia said.

I gave a surprised look. The soccer game was actually something that I hadn't noticed, and then a feeling of excitement came over me when Julia mentioned it.

"Oh, I hadn't noticed the soccer game on the schedule. Thank you for telling me about it. Is that something you would want to do Erica?" I asked making sure to include my new college girlfriend.

"Oh yeah! I would love to," Erica said with a happy nod.

"Alright kids! I hope you have fun and look out for each other. I have to go do a few things. I also have to meet with a few people. I will catch up with you a little later, okay?"

Before I knew it, Julia had taken off. Julia was such a mom. She seemed so caring when it came to Erica. I guess I was included in her small family now that I was friends with Erica. I could tell now why Julia had taken such an interest in me when she first met me. It looked like Julia had wanted Erica and I to hang out from the beginning.

Julia was completely right. My new BFF Erica and I really got along. We went to the next few events together and having a BFF made even the boring events better. Each boring event gave Erica and I more time to talk amongst ourselves. I learned over the course of a few hours that Erica does in fact want to be an anthropologist. She had already done extensive research on the field of early Greek culture. Erica found out a few things about me, like that I was from Alaska. I also told her about my three brothers. We really did get along as well as two people could. Erica was really easy to talk to.

Things seemed more fun with Erica around. We went to the museum next, and it was exciting. The university had acquired a good number of artifacts. In the history classes, you actually get to handle some of the artifacts once you learn how to. We went to a few other small events, but those events turned out to be kind of boring as well. By the time the soccer game had come around, we still had not seen any sign of Julia. We found out easily where the soccer game was. There was a group of students heading to the field, and Erica and I followed them. They brought us straight to the soccer field. But as the soccer game started, it was a little unorganized. The game started before Erica and I had got a chance to join.

"What should we do?" Erica asked me.

"I think we should just join in," I responded.

We joined the game with no problem; nobody made a big deal about it. The game itself though turned out not to be a lot of fun for either Erica or I.

I guess I was naive to think that things had changed on some level between high school and college with regard to boys. But boys don't get better with age. They get worse and become much more immature. Erica and I both agreed that we would avoid the boys at the school altogether based on what we had seen on the soccer field. The boys on the field acted arrogant and stupid. They were ruthless and didn't even try to let the girls play.

They only focused on chauvinism and competition. The boys only passed the ball to each other and left all the girls out of the game for the most part. I thought this soccer game was supposed to be fun, but the boys didn't make it seem that way. Erica and I left about halfway through the game. There was still no sign of Julia.

"I wonder what happened to Julia?" I asked Erica, concerned.

"Oh, I'm sure she is fine. I don't think she would have liked how this game was going anyways. Stupid boys! We should get something to eat," Erica said.

"Yeah, that's a good idea, but I want to freshen up first. Can I meet you in a little bit?" I asked.

"Okay, let's meet up over by the flagpole, okay?" Erica said.

"Yeah, that sounds good. I will see you in like 45 minutes," I said.

"Sounds good," Erica said as we parted ways.

Chapter 5

Strange Feelings

I went back to my room to freshen up. It only took me about 45 minutes to get ready, and then I dashed to the flag pole. Erica arrived shortly after I did, and we both headed out to get something to eat. We found a place not too far away from the dorms that seemed like a good place to get some food. While we were sitting, I began to feel a weird feeling that suddenly came over me. It was a feeling as though someone was watching me. I suddenly turned toward Erica.

"Erica, I know that we're new friends so I don't want to weird you out, but I feel like someone is watching me. Do you see anyone?" I asked half embarrassed.

Erica didn't seem to mind as she glanced around the room. After looking around for a moment, she seemed to shrug the search off.

"I don't see anyone. Maybe it's just because this place is still new to you," Erica said.

"Maybe," I said. I guess sometimes you get those feelings. After Erica told me that there was probably no one around, I tried to ignore the feeling. But it was still a very strong feeling. The feeling of being watched was hard to shake off. No matter how hard I tried, I just couldn't stop feeling like someone was watching me. I did my best to continue on with the meal.

The rest of the day went well until nightfall came. After all of the organized activities were over, Erica and I got to see a very different side of college. There was a new social order to campus that was not visible during the day. I don't know why I thought that things would be different in real life than they were portrayed in movies.

But when it came to how people act at night on a college campus, the movies were dead-on accurate. Whereas Erica and I had come to college to learn, it appeared that majority of people had come to college to party. There was a lot of drinking and general craziness that Erica and I could see outside of the frat houses.

"Wow! This is crazy isn't it?" I asked Erica.

"Yeah, it is. Do you think we should go?"

"Well, I don't know. Maybe we should walk a little further. I think it's just here that things are crazy. Let's walk around and see if things are better somewhere else."

"Okay," Erica said. It was hard to make out what either one of us was saying. The music sounded so loud, and there was a lot of dancing and drinking. Erica and I walked around. There was no sign of a coffee shop or any poetry readings like I had imagined. It was just a series of drinking and partying.

There was beer everywhere. Even though the competition on the soccer field had seemed bad, it was even worse in the lounges and streets of the campus when it came to drinking. There were shot games, beer games, and every other kind of drinking game known to mankind. There was a lot of making out. Erica and I felt like we didn't belong.

Erica looked at me and said, "Do you want to watch a movie? I have *The Sisterhood of the Traveling Pants* and a bunch of other movies on my computer. It would be better than hanging around here. This seems like a bunch of trouble. It's not what I am about."

"Oh yeah, that sounds good. This isn't what I'm about either," I said, happy that Erica had made that suggestion. "That is one of my favorite movies."

We headed back to Erica's room. Watching a movie was going to give me a chance to unwind. Erica and I relaxed and spent the rest of the evening watching *The Sisterhood of the Traveling Pants*.

At the end of the movie, Erica said half sarcastically, "Well, if that was how the first day went, I can't wait to see how the rest of them go."

"Yeah, me either. I will see you tomorrow," I said with a big smile as I walked out the door.

"Yep, see you tomorrow," Erica said as she closed the door behind me.

I then walked back to my room very exhausted and ready to end my first of college day.

Chapter 6

Bonfire

The rest of the week sort of went like the first day had. Erica and I went from public speaker to public speaker and chose from a list of activities. We tried other sports that were offered as activities, but the result always seemed to be the same whenever we played. The boys were always too competitive, and it wasn't much fun.

On Sunday night, there was a bonfire scheduled. Erica and I decided to attend. I had always liked bonfires. The mystique of ancient fire surrounded by other people all enjoying the same fiery scene was nice. There was usually some good conversation going on too. While Erica and I were there, we started to mingle and had some success with short, quick conversations. People usually talked about what they were planning on doing for their major and where they came from. There was also a lot of random talk about different teachers at the school. Some teachers took it easy on you when it came to assignments, and other ones had overly zealous expectations about work and assignments.

Right in the middle of one of my many conversations I had in front of the bonfire, an odd feeling came over me again. The feeling was like someone was watching me. I quickly turned to Erica.

"Erica, do you remember that feeling I had like someone was watching me earlier in the week when we were eating?"

Erica, who was half distracted by the conversation she was having, turned toward me.

"You mean that feeling you had the first day?"

"Yes, I can't explain it, but it's back," I said.

Erica quickly took a look around. "I don't see anyone. I'm sorry."

"It's okay. Maybe it's just because it's late," I said.

I turned toward the fire so I could think for a moment. The feeling really bothered me, and it was hard to ignore. Both times that I had the feeling, it hadn't seemed like someone was out to get me. Instead, it seemed like someone was just watching me. I had always had a very good ability to feel when someone was watching me. I could usually turn to see who it was, but in this case, I couldn't do that. I couldn't find anybody staring. The feeling of someone watching me had never been this strong before. I guess that was what was bothering me. Who would be staring at me, and why couldn't I see them. I stood there for a few minutes not talking to anyone. Instead, I just stared at the flames as they flickered. I liked how the light of the fire varied and made different colors. It helped me to forget the feeling of being watched. After a few minutes, the feeling of being watched went away. I was able to enjoy the rest of the bonfire.

The fire continued to roar, and I could hear the conversations surrounding the fire echo, the excitement that came from within the fire. As I stared into the flames, it was as though I was lost in thought, forgetting about all of my worries. A little while later, I yawned. I came back to reality and looked at my watch. It was nearly 11:00 pm.

"Wow, it's getting late," I said as I held my watch close to my face. I turned toward Erica.

"Erica, I think I'm going to head in. It's getting late."

"Okay. I think I will too," Erica said. Just as we started to head back in, one of the faculty members stood in front of the fire.

"Students, this concludes Welcome Week. Thank you for coming to all of the events of this week. I hope you had a memorable experience and learned a lot from all of the events we had this week. I look forward to seeing each of you in class. Now if you would mind clearing the area so we may begin cleanup." Then as the announcement concluded, everyone started to clear the area where Erica and I were.

As Erica and I continued to walk, Erica turned toward me.

"So are you ready?" Erica asked in an excited tone.

"Ready for what?" I asked confused.

"Ready for class. It starts tomorrow."

"I guess as ready as I'll ever be."

I really wasn't ready, but I was excited. That feeling of excitement helped me to forget a little more about who or what might have been watching me during the bonfire, but the fact that I had that feeling still bothered me a lot. I couldn't help but think it meant something.

Chapter 7

Semester

I called my mom before I went to my first class. My mom had always done a really good job of trying to get me focused on school. It was a tradition that we had always done. This year was no different. My mom's words of encouragement throughout the years was one of the main reasons that I had done so good in school.

"Don't worry. It is going to be great. You have always done well in school in the past, and this year won't be any different. Show them what you can do, Aurora. I am so proud of you, and I believe in you."

I thought my mom's speech was a bit much for a first day of classes, but it was always nice to hear. It was familiar, and it made me feel at home.

"Thank you mom. I will try," I said back to her.

Talking to my mom made me feel so much better. I had arranged with Erica to meet with me so we could compare schedules. We had met at a bench near a tree, and each of us had our schedules out. We sat and compared schedules. Unfortunately, as we looked over each other's schedule, a sad reality began to reveal itself. We didn't have any classes together, but that was okay.

"It would have been nice to have a friend in class," I told Erica.

I always tried to look at the bright side.

Not having a class together would give me a better chance to focus.

I had four classes on my schedule. It was a full course load. Erica also had full course load.

"Well, at least we can meet up with each other in between class," Erica said.

"Yeah, definitely, and plus we can compare notes later. I will probably have to take the classes you're taking in another semester, and you will probably have to take the classes that I am taking."

I actually was a little sad that Erica wasn't going to be in class with me, but I would make it through the best I could. I hadn't had any friends in any of my classes in high school, and I guess I shouldn't start college off any different. I could tell though that Erica was a little sad. Erica got up from the bench.

"Well, I should get going and so should you. We don't want to be late for our first classes," Erica said trying to hide her sadness.

"Okay, well, I'll see you later Erica. Good luck in class."

"You too," Erica said as she walked toward her first class.

As I walked toward my first class, I looked over my schedule again. My first class for today was English 1, which was an easy one. I gathered up my course book and notebook and went into the class. I looked around for just the right seat, and I sat down. After a few minutes of sitting comfortably in class, I heard a few people talking. An alarm went off in my head as a sudden realization hit me like a rock to the head.

I'm in the wrong class. How could I be in the wrong class?

For as much as I didn't want to believe it, it was true. This was the wrong class. I quickly sprang up from my seat and took a dash for the door. I had to make it to the right class on time. I read the map on the wall and figured out my bearings. I ran in the direction I needed to go. As I got to the correct class, I heard the teacher say "nice" while staring at his watch.

All of the other students were staring at me too as I walked through the door. It wasn't exactly how I had wanted to start my first class of college. In a way, it was nice. The first lesson I learned in college wasn't anything academic. It was that if you are late, the teacher doesn't ask you where you have been or why you are late. The teacher just lets you be late.

I guess that was one of the perks of college. I was there because I wanted to be there. I wasn't there because someone else wanted me to be there. I knew though that for some people, this would be a very bad thing. Other people might try to take advantage of it and never show up to class on time. But for me, for today, it was a nice saving grace. I knew I wouldn't be late a lot. I wasn't getting a hard time about it from the teacher. It made me feel a little better but still a little embarrassed about being late.

I looked toward the ground as I walked in. I didn't want to make eye contact with the teacher because I was late. As I walked by the teacher, I grabbed the handout the teacher handed me and found the only available seat in the class. The seat was about three rows back from the front.

Not too bad, I thought as I sat in my chair. The spot wasn't too close to the front and wasn't too close to the back either. For all intents and purposes, it was the perfect seat. I pulled out a pencil and notebook as the he began to teach the lesson. As the teacher was talking though, I had a hard time focusing completely on what he was saying.

The teacher started to say something about the syllabus, which he presented on PowerPoint. He then explained what to expect from this class throughout the semester. As I looked at the course load, I knew I could handle it. It looked no different than any of the other course schedules I had in high school. As I glanced throughout the class, I saw looks of amazement and horror at all the work the teacher had planned for the semester.

I guess all those years of working hard in high school are paying off.

The teacher continued speaking. I quickly regained my focus.

"Look around you. Every semester, I have one in four students repeat this class. How many of you are repeats?" he asked.

It looked like a quarter of the class had raised their hands. Then I felt more nervous.

"You should be nervous about taking this class. You should pay attention and not make any mistakes. For some of you, this may be your first college class. I want you to know that college is much harder than high school. I expect nothing less than the best quality work. Don't take this class lightly. How you do in this class will set the tone for your whole academic career at this college.

"If there are any grammatical errors or typos, I will hit your paper hard. Don't give me a reason to look for mistakes. Don't give me a reason to fail you. Now, if there aren't any questions about the syllabus, I will let you begin your first assignment," the teacher said as he sat down at his desk and began to go through papers with a red pen.

I looked at my handout and began to follow the syllabus. The English 1 class seemed like it ended shortly after I began to do the first assignment. As I walked out the door, I glanced at the teacher's desk. All of the papers on the teacher's desk were covered in red ink. The sight of all the red ink all over the papers brought back all the feelings of nervousness that I had when I walked in the class. I had a new fear that I was going to fail this class.

I was especially nervous about making a mistake.

I didn't come all the way down here from Alaska to make a mistake.

I decided to put my fears of failing English 1 to the side for now. I wanted to be prepared for my next class. I didn't want a repeat of my first class and be late again. I went back to my room to review notes before my next class. As I walked through the door, my roommate, Jessica, was there hanging out.

"Hey, Aurora, how are you? You look horrified."

"Oh, I'm not doing much. I'm just waiting to go to my next class," I said trying to hide my nervousness.

"Wait, you had your first class, didn't you? You're already nervous, aren't you? I bet you think you're not going to make it."

Jessica had the biggest smile I had ever seen her have the whole time I had known her.

I don't know why she thinks this is funny.

"Don't worry. It gets easier, trust me. Just don't let that first class freak you out. We all have been there. No matter how overwhelming things might seem, Stacey and I will be here to help you through it. Just let me know if you need any help. What class was it?" Jessica asked.

"English 1."

"Oh, English 1! I remember that it was a difficult class. But don't worry, Stacey and I will help you when you need it. Just take a breather and don't let it get to you. I promise, it will get easier. Be brave and enjoy your next class, okay?"

"Okay, I will try."

"Okay, I'm going to leave you alone. But please don't forget, we are here for you." Jessica said and walked out of the room.

I was so thankful Jessica had helped me to be less nervous. I would have been a nervous wreck for my next class if Jessica hadn't talked to me. I sat on my bed and took it easy just like Jessica had said. I found a book that I had been wanting to read and started to read it. It really helped me to calm down and forget about being so nervous. After about an hour, I got my bag and began walking to my next class. My next class was Communications. I managed to get to the right classroom this time. I was sure of it. I looked around at everyone else, and it seemed like the right class.

I also took a moment and looked at the board in front of the classroom. "Welcome to Communications" was written in big writing.

There was no way I was in the wrong class this time.

I was still so nervous about this class though. It was Communications, which could mean only one thing. I was probably going to have to stand in front of the class and talk, which was not something I liked the idea of.

As the teacher made his introductions and gave out his first instructions, the truth quickly came to light. My fear was confirmed: we had to talk in front of the class. It made sense because it was a Communications class after all, but it still took me off guard.

"I want you to come in front of the class, state your name, where you're from, your major, and what you hope to gain from this class," the teacher said as he looked around the class. I must have had something written on my face because the first person he decided to call on for this wonderful assignment was me.

Great, it had to be me! Why does this always happen to me?

I stood up as my heart pounded hard. I found that it was hard to breathe. As I walked up in front of the class, I was sure there were only four people in the class. But somehow when I turned around and looked at the entire class, there were probably thirty-five people.

Where did all of these people come from?

It was a lot of people. I had never really talked in front of a large group of people before. I was so nervous. Luckily, the teacher had written down what he wanted us to say in front of the class. I took a glance back at the board, and then the words sort of came out. At least I thought I had said all of those things that were on the board. The class still looked at me though with anticipation. It gave me an odd feeling as all those eyes stared at me.

"Any time you're ready to start," the teacher said.

I guess, since I was so nervous and my heart was pounding so hard, I must have imagined saying all of those things that were written on the board. I tried again to say what I needed to say. I took a deep breath and then began to speak. But this time, I said what I needed to say.

"Hi, I'm Aurora, and I am from Alaska. My major is..."

Oh God, did I forget my major?

"My major is oceanography. I want to know how the oceans work. From this class, I hope to gain more confidence in public speaking."

I think when I spoke, the words came out quicker than I would have liked. But I had said it, and now I was done talking.

I quickly found my seat and sat down. I could have sworn my face was as white as a ghost, but I don't think anyone was paying attention. At least at the end of my mini speech, I noticed that all of the other students looked at least half as nervous as I had. The teacher came up to the front of the class and clapped his hands.

"Thank you Aurora, that was wonderful. You have such a nice name. I would assume your parents named you after the aurora borealis given that you're from Alaska," the teacher said pleased with himself for making the connection between the two names and where I was from.

"Yes, I believe so," I managed to say back.

"Wonderful! I am glad to have you in my class. I don't want you to worry. You will get better in this class, at public speaking. Everyone in this class is going to speak regularly in front of the whole class. By the end of the semester, all of you will be experts at talking in front of a large audience, or at least you will look like you are experts. Okay, and who is next? You in the back," the teacher said as he pointed to someone behind me.

The next person came up in front of the class looking just as nervous as I had. She gave a similar speech to the one that I had given and then sat down quicker than I had.

I guess I wasn't so unusual in being afraid of talking in public.

A lot of people were nervous. It helped that the teacher taught with such a high amount of energy. His energy level helped make the class a little more bearable. I liked him a lot.

We went through the rest of class with each student doing their introductions. At the end when each student had spoken, the teacher said, "I want you to read chapters 1 to 3. We will discuss these three chapters in our next class. I want everyone to be prepared and ready to talk in front of the class next time. This was just the first day. Over the course of the semester, we will be debating and discussing various subjects in a public forum in front of each other. My goal is to have everyone in this class be a little bit better at talking in front of a large audience. I wish you all the best of luck. I will see you next class."

With the ending of my Communications class, my first day of college had ended as well.

Wow, so that was college!

I went to my room and saw my roommates there hanging out. I kept to myself as best I could for a few moments. I wanted to take a little while and look over my course material I had received. It looked like Communications was going to be an easy class besides the public speaking part. For now, there wasn't much to do in Communications besides reading the first three chapters. I would be able to knock out those chapters easily.

English, on the other hand, was the more daunting of the two classes. I had a big paper due by the end of the semester. The paper needed references in APA format. Every lesson for the whole semester was based on the term paper. As I looked at the overall breakdown of everything, I felt like everything was going to be alright. I had already been writing in APA and MLA format since the beginning of 10th grade. My teachers thought I was advanced enough for learning at higher levels. For the most part, they were right.

I started working on my first writing assignment, which was due in two weeks. About a half an hour later, I got two text messages. One was from Erica and the other from my mom. "How did it go?" my mom wrote. I smiled at this question and then moved on to the other text message.

"Want to get coffee?" Erica wrote. I quickly began to text Erica back.

"Sure, when?" I then went to my contact list and scrolled through my contacts. When I found my mom's name, I called her. I knew that simply writing a text wasn't going to do it for my mom. She wanted details. After a few rings, my mom picked up.

"Hello."

"Hey, mom, how's it going?"

"Well, how did it go? Did you learn anything interesting?" She asked so insistent that every day I would be receiving my PhD.

"Yeah, mom, it's a little different than high school, but it's still the same on some levels. I think it went well."

"Great, remember, do all your homework and pay attention to everything. Alright my dear, I'm sorry, but I have to cut this conversation short. Your brothers are destroying the house. I am really happy that your first day went well Aurora. I will talk to you later. I love you."

"Love you too mom."

That was a quick conversation. Usually the conversations with my mom go on for at least an hour. Oh well, maybe she thinks I'm busy. I looked down at my phone after hanging up on my mom because of another text message I got from Erica.

"Hey, anytime that you want to meet up is good for me. In fact, right now is good for me," Erica wrote.

"Yeah. I'll meet you at the college café," I wrote back and quickly looked for my purse. I found it by my bed and headed out the door.

As I walked toward the café, I could see someone familiar sitting at a table. Erica was already sitting with a cup of coffee. When I looked at the other side of the table, there was another cup of coffee.

Was she sitting with someone else?"

Erica looked at me with a raised eyebrow and then gave me a nod as I came toward her.

"Erica, how's it going?" I asked.

"Hey, Aurora! I ordered you a cup of black coffee just like you liked it the other day. I hope it's okay?"

"Oh yeah, that's fine," I said surprised and stunned that Erica had remembered that detail about me. I took the seat where the coffee was.

"So how was your day?" I asked trying to be really nice.

"Oh, it was a little rough. It really is hard not knowing anyone when you go through these classes. I have good news though that I wanted to tell you," Erica said with a grin.

"Oh, what is that?"

"We have a class together. I changed my schedule when I saw yours. I am taking Western Civilization with you. I thought it would be fun to take it with a friend. Besides, I love this subject. It wasn't on my schedule so I had them change it. Isn't that great?" Erica asked with an excited voice.

"I can't wait! It's going to be so much fun to take a class with you."

Erica and I sat in the café and talked about more details of our day and how much fun things had been. Our conversation went on for another hour. We both enjoyed each other's company a great deal. It was a great stress relief to talk with Erica. In the middle of our conversation, I glanced at my watch and noticed the time.

"Wow, Erica, we have been sitting here a while. I think I should head back and get ready for tomorrow."

"I agree. You can't underestimate the importance of getting a good night's sleep."

"Thank you Erica. I'm glad that you understand."

"Yep, it's my sound philosophy that class is important, and nothing should come before it."

"I couldn't agree more. Well, take care and I will see you later."

We both walked out of the college café, and I began to walk toward my room. Overall, it had been a rather great first day of classes.

If that was how college was going to be, I can't wait to see the rest of it. I already feel smarter.

I quickly got to my room and began to get ready for the next day.

When the next day came, something horrible happened. Even though I had gone to bed early and made all of the right preparations so it wouldn't happen, I had somehow managed to oversleep.

Great, it's only the second day and I was running late.

When I jumped out of my door to run to class, I looked at my watch again. Apparently, I had misread my phone the first time I looked at it. What I thought the screen displayed was 8:00 a.m., but in actuality the screen displayed 6:00 am. I took a deep sigh of relief. I wasn't running late.

I then decided to turn the mistake of waking up early into a positive thing and get breakfast at the cafeteria. The smell of all the good food made my stomach growl as I entered the cafeteria. I chose a nice cheap combo meal for breakfast.

All of the meal choices had my favorite breakfast foods in them. I selected the one with eggs and a nice cup of oatmeal with raisins and honey. I even got a nice cup of green tea with a little bit of milk. By the time I got to class, I was all primed up and ready to go. My first class was Astronomy. I guess Astronomy is one of those subjects that can be either really exciting or really boring. My teacher's name was Mr. Hughes. He, as far as I could tell, was rather dull. It wasn't because he hadn't tried to be exciting. I think instead it was because he was a bit older.

Mr. Hughes used an overhead projector with old star charts as his visual for teaching the class. In addition, he had a very squeaky voice, which was hard to follow at times. I guess he was a world-renowned expert on astronomy, and I was lucky that he was teaching my class. But his lessons seemed a little dull.

"The universe is old and vast. Come with me as we together explore the cosmos," Mr. Hughes said.

As he continued, I realized this class was going to be relaxing. The lights were out. All you could see was the projection of stars and Mr. Hughes's voice. There was no public speaking. I just sat there and soaked it in.

Mr. Hughes wasn't exactly interactive with the class. I started to have questions as he went over the lesson, but he never stopped talking long enough to take any questions. I began to look over my astronomy book for answers. The astronomy book actually helped to clarify a few things. When the lights had finally come on, I looked around and noticed that half of the class had fallen asleep. This didn't seem to bother Mr. Hughes though.

I guess he had gotten used to students falling asleep in his class over the years. I found out later that he had been teaching at the college for almost thirty years and was probably the oldest teacher at the school. When Astronomy finally finished, I thought of having my lunch. I went to the cafeteria and ran into Erica and her sister Julia. I gave them a wave when I saw the two of them. They turned their heads toward me and returned the wave. Then Julia and Erica got up and met me as we all jumped in line for food.

It was at this moment that I started to notice the difference in appearance between Julia and Erica. Julia was tall, slender, and dressed like a model. Erica was shorter and plainly dressed. You could still tell the two were sisters but only because of a few facial features that they shared. Both were pretty, but Julia was absolutely stellar. Julia ate like a model too.

"A salad of course, and ranch dressing on the side," Julia said when asked by the cafeteria worker what she wanted to eat. Erica and I didn't have such dietary tastes. We both got delicious turkey sandwiches instead. We all grabbed a seat next to each other.

"So, how is school going for the two of you? How is class going? I heard you guys have a class together?" Julia asked.

"Oh yeah, we do. We have Western Civilization together, isn't it great?" Erica asked as enthusiastically.

"Oh, that is good! I know you'll do well in that class. It's your favorite subject Erica. I hope you guys have fun," Julia said.

"I hope we do. I don't know much about Western Civilization, but I am looking forward to it," I said trying to join in on the conversation.

"I really think you will enjoy it. Professor Pierce is a really good teacher. He is young, rich, and passionate about Western Civilization. It doesn't hurt that he is kind of cute too," Julia said with a smile. It looked almost as though Julia had a small crush on Mr. Pierce.

"Oh, I can't wait," I said with a smile.

I wasn't as excited about the class in and of itself. I was more excited about having a class with a friend. History had never been my strongest subject. I can't remember anybody who seemed to like history as much as Erica. She really was passionate about this subject. I was glad I was going to take Western Civilization with Erica. She and I soon left Julia and went to Western Civilization class.

As soon as we got to class, Erica could barely contain her excitement. Everyone else on the other hand seemed to stare at Mr. Pierce, mesmerized by his delectable accent and his pronunciation of ancient sites. He really was handsome. I could see what Julia was talking about immediately. Mr. Pierce not only had a nice build to him, like a former football player, but he also seemed so refined like an aristocrat. As Mr. Pierce walked from one side of the room to the other, each of the student's heads moved with him. It was like the class was in some sort of a trance.

I took to the subject material better than I had planned on. Mr. Pierce made history interesting. I guess any teacher can make something interesting if he or she knows how. Mr. Pierce really did know how to make history entertaining. He talked about the romance of the ancient past as if the whole class was going on an ancient adventure.

"The Egyptians were the beginning of civilization as we know it. They were around for so long. They came up with so many good concepts, and you can still see their influences in today's society. Then there were the Greeks. Oh, the Greeks, how I love thee for you have helped all of us to be. Sorry class, a little poetry interruption for my favorite portion of the semester.

"The reason I love the Greeks so much is because they were the first to give us a real civilization of thought and mind and passion. The Greek scholars were the first to refuse to stay locked up somewhere—in an ivory tower—and pluck away at the questions of the universe. Instead, the Greeks chose to experience what life is and go into the deep meaning of things. They are who set the standard for all of modern civilization. Everything from the Renaissance to the latest love romance novel can trace its essence of existence to the mighty empire of Greece. First there was Greece, which led to Rome, and then to everything else.

"We will get into more details about the how and the why later. Are there any questions?"Mr. Pierce asked as he looked out into his class.

Half the class was still dreamy eyed, and I was intrigued. Erica on the other hand did indeed have some questions.

"I think I'll ask him my questions after class. I have too many to ask right now," Erica whispered to me. I glanced at Erica's paper where she had written down something like 15 questions to ask.

Wow, Erica really is into this subject!

I raised my eyebrows and looked at Erica. I couldn't remember the last time I had that many questions about one subject on the first day. Erica was persistent and determined to become an expert in the field of ancient Greek culture.

As Mr. Pierced looked around the class, no other students raised their hands.

"Well, I will be here for a little bit if any of you have questions that you want to ask me in private. I will see you next time."

The class slowly began to shuffle out of the room. I watched Erica wait until most of the students had departed. She then fired her line of questions at Mr. Pierce. By the time she got to the eighth question, Mr. Pierce assured her that we would go into all of her questions by the end of the semester.

"I promise, and if you have questions that I haven't covered by the end of the semester, then I will be happy to answer them," Mr. Pierce finished.

Erica seemed satisfied by this statement.

It seemed Mr. Pierce was amused by Erica and her series of questions. I think most professors would have shooed Erica away after two or three questions. Mr. Pierce had put up with almost all of Erica's questions while still maintaining his debonair appearance.

"Thank you," I said to Mr. Pierce as Erica and I walked out the door.

"I'll see you guys next time in class," Mr. Pierce said as Erica and I walked out the door.

That was how most of the semester went. I would go to class and try to learn as much as I could. The first couple of days had seemed so rough and so different, but as soon as I went to more and more classes, my days seemed to follow a routine almost. It was like I was in high school again except I had my BFF Erica to keep me company. We remained the best of friends throughout the semester. Both Erica and I continued to work hard and keep our schedules clear of distractions.

Soon before either Erica or I realized it, the semester was coming to an end.

CHAPTER 8

AN OPPORTUNITY

One day, I was walking toward the cafeteria to go to lunch with Erica when I found a pamphlet on the ground. I was not a fan of picking up trash, but there was something very different about this pamphlet. It was as though the pamphlet itself was calling to me. I picked it up and gave it a careful look. The pamphlet was from the Oceanography Department. On the back of the pamphlet was the information about a brand new type of lab the college was offering to freshmen.

"Yes," I yelled out as I continued to walk. The description of what this class would entail was everything I had been looking for in a class. The class took trips on a naval research vessel. Students would get to work with animals and help explore modern issues that affect the inner workings of the ocean. It was only open to exceptional students. There was only one drawback to taking this class. If I took it, the school would only allow me enough time to take one other class for the next semester.

That's not that bad of a deal. I could make up for that during another semester by taking extra classes.

This class was too good of an opportunity for me to pass it up.

I continued to walk toward the cafeteria looking for Erica who I expected to already be sitting waiting for me just as she had done all semester. Sure enough as I entered the cafeteria, Erica was sitting at our usual table waiting for me. Erica began to get up and walk toward the beginning of the line to meet me. I was so excited that as I met her in the line, I began to tell her the good news.

"I have something wonderful to tell you. I should wait until we have our food and are sitting before I tell you all the details. I also have something to ask you."

It was hard for me to contain my excitement as we walked through the line and got our food, but I managed. I gave her a very excited look as I got ready to tell her the best news ever.

"Okay, brace yourself Erica. I have an amazing opportunity, and I have to ask you if you want to join me in it."

"Okay, spit it out. What is it?" Erica asked smiling.

Erica hadn't touched her food as she watched me fidget it around in excitement. She just waited for me to talk.

"It's this pamphlet I found Erica. The school is offering a special lab that goes into the ocean and studies mankind's interactions with the oceans. The class also explores how the ocean works. It's everything I had imagined in a class for oceanography. This class is exactly what I was looking for when I applied to come to this college. What do you think?" I said all of this in one breath. Just talking about it made me even more excited.

Erica took a look at the pamphlet for a moment and then said, "I think this program looks great. It's everything you had hoped for like you were saying. Are you going to sign up for it?"

"Don't you mean are we going to sign up for it? I need you with me on this. It will be so much fun, and you'll love it. I know you will. Besides, it's only one semester. There is one catch though. You can only take one other class in addition to the Oceanography class. It's because this class is a little time consuming. At least, that is what the pamphlet says."

Erica sat there for a moment as if she thought about what I had just asked her.

"I will have to think about it. It might set me back on my schedule."

"I would really like you to take this class with me, but if you can't, I understand," I said a little sad.

"I will let you know. I just don't want to rush into a decision about anything this important. I do want to take it though, but I just have to think about it. I will let you know tonight. Do you know what I mean?"

"Yeah, I know what you mean. I really do hope you do end up taking the class with me. It would be so much fun. But if you don't, I really do understand. I am going to take it anyways so don't feel bad if you don't take the class with me. But it would just be so much fun to go on the ship with my BFF and explore the ocean. We can take lots of pictures. Anyways, enough about that! Why don't we go ahead and eat?" I said while staring at food.

"Yeah, I'm starving."

"Me too."

We finished our meals and then went to Western Civilization class for our review for our final. Mr. Pierce was covering every nook and cranny about what we had covered throughout the semester. He was still just as mesmerizing for most of the women in the class as he had been the first day. He still spoke with a refined elegance, but he managed to fill his words with tons of information. Every student in the class had their eyes fixated on him as he spoke.

"And then we have Cleisthenes, the founder of Athenian democracy, which in turn set the stage for most other major forms of democracy. Write that down. Oh, if Cleisthenes hadn't decided one day to just come up with the idea of democracy shortly after a revolt, where would we be today? Don't write that down. It was more of a side note. Okay, I would say that pretty much covers everything. Any other questions?"

The room was silent. Everyone was still jotting down all the review notes. It was a lot of information to review. I myself took five pages of notes just from this one review session. I was glad I did because it was a really good review, especially that note at the end about Cleisthenes. Somehow I had missed that part of the lesson when it was given the first time in class.

Erica looked as fascinated as she always had been by all of the information that Mr. Pierce had put out. Even though I had learned a great deal this semester about things I had never even heard of, it seemed like Erica already knew all of the information Mr. Pierce had put out over the course of the whole semester. This was Erica's major—it was her dream and her passion. It seemed like Erica had even more questions than she had at the beginning of the semester about why things were a certain way throughout history.

Erica was way above anybody else's level of knowledge on this subject. It was almost awe inspiring whenever she talked about history. We walked out of the class and headed to the college café to get coffee for an all-night study session. I was going to review Western Civilization with Erica and study Astronomy, English, and Communications on my own.

I reviewed the notes for Western Civilization with Erica and we both seemed to have a good grasp on the subject. When I was sure that we were ready for tomorrow's finals, I decided to bring up the subject of next semester with Erica.

"So have you made a decision about next semester?" I asked.

Erica turned toward me and put her papers down. Then Erica looked straight at me and smiled.

"I looked over everything, and I realized I had to take the class even though taking it wouldn't help my student career. We are friends, and I think the subject is interesting. I mean it isn't history, but it has an element of adventure that I need in my life. So what I am trying to say is I'm going to do it. I will take the class with you Aurora."

I got up and gave Erica a hug. I was so happy.

"Thank you Erica. I know this class is going to be ten times better with a friend."

"It's what friends do. We stick with each other." Erica said as she glanced at her watch. "It's getting late and I still have to study for my other classes."

"You're right, Erica. I was about to head back to my room anyways. Thank you for all of your help with studying and for agreeing to take the Oceanography class next semester with me. You have made me so happy."

We both finished up our coffee and then got up to head out of the college café. I was tired, but I needed to study for my other classes.

"I'll let you know where sign-ups are for the oceanography lab tomorrow and give you the details on everything," I told Erica as we walked away from each other.

My English final would be in the morning so I needed to begin to study for that. I had to write a comparative paper on the arguments of cloning. It was an in-class paper with no references. I knew I would be able to knock it out easily. It was the one class I was most concerned with. I reviewed all my notes, and then I felt very tired. Probably the most tired I had ever felt. It wasn't just a physical fatigue. I was feeling a mental strain from all of the studying. I looked at my watch and it was late. My brain just couldn't take it anymore. I put my papers away and got ready for bed. As soon as I got to my bed, I just passed out.

When I woke the next morning, I was ready to go. I felt completely refreshed. I was a little nervous remembering everything for the exams, but for the most part, I was ready to ace the exams. I went into my English class. The final started off quicker than I had thought it would. I began to write immediately. I wrote pure arguments for both sides on the subject of cloning. I knew this was going to be one of the topics I could pick from, and I had prepared for my arguments. This proved to be a good idea. It made writing the paper for class so much easier.

When I finished, I felt better about the fact that I had knocked out the hardest class I took this semester with very little trouble.

I hope I did good.

But I didn't have time to think about it. I went on to the Communications class and gave a pretty good speech. The teacher had been right about being more confident when I spoke in front of people. I could now stand in front of a crowd even without anything prepared for what I was going to say—and I could still manage to sound professional. It was so natural now to do public speaking. The words just flowed from me. I gained a lot from my Communications class, and I was sure I passed it with flying colors.

I had found Astronomy throughout the semester to be difficult because I got very little help from Mr. Hughes. I somehow managed to make it through with very few problems. When I went through the exam, it was pretty cut and dry. I was pretty sure, based on how I did on the exam, that I had probably gotten a high B or even a low A. The true accomplishment of Astronomy for me was the fact that I was the only one as far as I could tell who had managed to stay awake throughout the whole semester. I was proud of myself for that.

Then the time for the final for Western Civilization came. It was a breeze. All of the studying Erica and I had done had really paid off. Erica and I were the first ones who finished the test. Sometimes being the first to finish a test can be a bad thing like you rushed through it or something. But I think in this case, being the first to be done was just proof that Erica and I had studied well. I knew that Erica and I had done a really good job studying because everything we had studied was on the test. Overall I was ecstatic. I was worried at the beginning of the semester that I would do badly in this class, but thanks to Erica, I think I managed to pull off an A.

After the finals, I decided to talk to Erica about the next semester.

"I still have to figure out where to sign up for the Oceanography class, but I haven't had any time to find out because we were so busy studying for the exams," I said.

"Okay, let me know. I will be around. I have to hang out with my sister for a little bit."

"Okay, I will find out soon and let you know. Have fun with Julia."

As soon as I walked away from Erica, I couldn't stop thinking about signing up for the class. I decided that now was the time to go find out how to sign up for the class. A feeling of excitement came over me. I decided that the first place I should probably start my search is the administration office. Mrs. Degory will have the answer. When I got to the administration office, I walked right up to the front desk. Fortunately for me, Mrs. Degory was working. She was still hyped up on coffee, which turned out to be in my favor.

"Hi Aurora."

"Hi Mrs. Degory. I was wondering if you could help me. I am trying to sign up for this Oceanography laboratory that I found in a pamphlet. I guess it is a new program."

Mrs. Degory smiled at me and said, "Oh yes, you can sign up for that class. There is a lot of interest in that class though. It's a brand new class that's being offered at the university, and it sounds like a lot of fun so a lot of people want to sign up for it. There are a few spots still open for that class. Do you want me to sign you up?"

Without hesitation, I said, "Yes, yes, please Mrs. Degory."

"Alright, let me just pull you up on the computer." Mrs. Degory began to type quickly on the computer. After a minute, she took her eyes off of the computer screen and focused on me.

"Okay, you're all signed up. Do you have any other questions?"

Mrs. Degory gave me an information card with the starting class date January 21, which was after winter break.

"Yes, Mrs. Degory. I did have one other question. I was wondering if I could sign up my friend?"

Mrs. Degory gave me a stern look like I had released a more serious side of her.

"No. I'm sorry that's not at all possible. School policy doesn't allow me to sign anyone up unless they ask me in person. I'm sorry for the inconvenience, but you can tell your friend to come sign up for the class herself. I would be happy to find a slot for her. She will have to hurry though because those other spots for that class are getting filled quickly. I don't want your friend to miss out on a fun class like that one."

"Alright, Mrs. Degory. I will let her know right away and try to get her over here too sign up. Thank you."

Since texting wasn't allowed inside the administration office, I quickly stepped outside the door of the office to text Erica to come and sign up for the class right now.

"Hey, I need you to come to administration office right now to sign up for the Oceanography laboratory or it might not be available," I texted to Erica. About a half a second later, Erica responded.

"Can't you sign me up?"

"No. I can't, I'm sorry. Mrs. Degory said you had to come down and sign yourself up. It's against school policy for me to sign you up."

"Okay, I'll be right there," Erica text back.

I decided that since Erica was coming, I would just wait at the office for her to arrive.

About three and a half minutes later, I saw Erica running toward the administration office. Erica gave me a glance as she stopped running and began to walk toward the door. I followed her. Erica seemed determined to sign up for the class as she opened the door and ran right over to Mrs. Degory.

"Hi Mrs. Degory."

"Hi Erica" Mrs. Degory replied.

It was always so amazing that Mrs. Degory always knew everyone's name. It always stunned me that someone could have that kind of ability to remember everyone's name at a school this size. Without pause, Erica continued talking.

"Mrs. Degory, I really need to sign up for that class that Aurora just signed up for."

"Oh, are you the friend? Wow, that was quick good job Aurora!" Mrs. Degory said glancing over at me and smiling. "Yes, of course. I can sign you up for that class right now. I still have it pulled up from when Aurora signed up."

Mrs. Degory typed away on the computer. A few clicks of the mouse later and Mrs. Degory looked up from the computer at Erica and said, "Alright, Erica you are all signed up. Here is your schedule for the class."

"Thank you Mrs. Degory," Erica said as she stared at her new schedule. I'm assuming to make sure it was right.

"You're welcome sweetie. If there isn't anything else, I hope you two will take care and have a safe holiday."

"You too," Erica and I said in unison.

As Erica and I walked out of the office, both of us had the biggest smiles on our faces.

"January 21, Erica, January 21. Our adventure begins," I said almost jumping as I walked by Erica.

"I know and I can't wait. Even with all of the finals, I had been thinking about how right this whole thing with taking this class with you is going to be. It is so exciting. I already told my sister and my parents. All of them understand how important it is and are excited for me."

"Oh."

"What's the matter?" Erica asked.

"Well, in all the haste to finish up the semester, with all the studying and everything, I didn't mention that I was taking this class to my mom or even to my aunt."

"Don't worry, you can tell them now. It's better anyways because you are actually signed up. Before, we still didn't know if we were going to take it. Now you know for sure. What are you doing for the break?" Erica asked trying to change the subject.

"Oh, I'm going to stay with my aunt. It will be my first Christmas away from home. I haven't really spent that much time with my aunt and I really need to. I am going to video chat with everyone back home in Alaska too because I know they all miss me there. What are you planning on doing for the holidays?"

"Oh, I'm going home to upstate New York. It is nice there in the winter. It is cold this time of the year, which is good because sometimes here in San Diego, the weather is too perfect. I kind of miss the cold, with the snow and everything."

I didn't feel the same way about the cold. It reminded me of why I left Alaska.

"Well, have fun and let me know how things go. Email or text me, okay, so we can stay in touch throughout the break," I said.

"Okay, you do the same and take care."

"Alright, I will. I should probably get going. I have to go pack. I will see you later hunn," I said to Erica as we gave each other a hug.

"Yep, I will see you later. Take care!"

CHAPTER 9

MEETING UNCLE JASON

I hadn't put any previous thought into what I was going to bring with me to my aunt. I didn't know where to start as I stared at all of my belongings in my room. I took a deep breath and then began to pack. I hadn't planned on coming back to my dorm room during the holidays if I didn't have to. I would have to pack everything I might need for the entire break. Since the school year had begun, I had managed to get some new luggage to replace my horrid green bag.

It was a nice set of luggage from my aunt. It was specifically designed by her for me. It was in a very nice cheetah print and with plenty of room to fit all of my stuff. I loved it. It was one of the nicest gifts I had ever gotten. I was really glad I had new luggage. My old bag just wouldn't have made it. My aunt really did have good fashion sense.

My aunt had started working in banking when she first got to San Diego. Over time, she had managed to sneak out of banking and get into fashion designing. After creating a countless amount of fashion accessories, she opened up her own store in downtown San Diego and more recently in La Jolla. I had seen some of Aunt Carrie's designs on a few of the girls on campus. It always made me happy to see her designs. Just to know that my aunt had designed what others around me were wearing reminded me that if my aunt can make it out of Alaska and be successful, so could I.

I hadn't been to my aunt's house before. Instead I had always chosen to meet her at restaurants or the occasional shopping excursions. I had managed to keep in touch with her for the most part, at least once a week. I had remained busy most of the semester and spent a great deal of time on the campus. When the subject of winter break came up, I had decided I would make up for the lost time with my aunt by seeing if I could spend the break with her. My mom hadn't been too upset about me not coming home, but one of the stipulations was that I had to video chat so everyone could say hi. My aunt on the other hand was ecstatic about the idea.

"I would love for you to spend the holidays with us," Aunt Carrie said. I was excited that I would finally get to see where she lived. I was also very excited to meet her husband for the first time. Aunt Carrie pulled up in a nice coupe, and we drove through San Diego to a place I hadn't been to since I arrived. I actually hadn't been to a lot of places in San Diego. I did see the San Diego Zoo with Erica. I had also gone to the beach twice, but I really got wrapped up in my studies. I spent too much time indoors studying. I was really pale because of it so I was looking forward to catching some good vitamin D from the sun on this vacation.

San Diego was beautiful this time of the year. There was so much going on. People were walking around, shopping, and eating at restaurants. Downtown seemed like a happening spot. My hometown on the other hand was completely different. It was cold and quiet. Most people didn't even leave their houses unless they had to. When I thought about how different this year would be for Christmas than last year had been, I was both sad and happy. I was happy I was here in San Diego, but I was sad that I was away from my family.

I tried not to focus on missing my family too much. I had made my decision to stay in San Diego, and I was going to enjoy myself. As we passed by all of the old Victorian houses, I felt like we were getting closer to Aunt Carrie's house.

Little did I realize that Aunt Carrie basically lives in a mansion of sorts. It was a giant house as I stared at it for the first time. When we finally did get out of the car, I walked into the house through a set of absolutely beautiful French doors. Every room seemed so elegant and so clean. I almost didn't even want to sit on any of the furniture, which were so clean, pressed, and almost untouched.

"Wow," I said.

"You'll be staying upstairs. Let me show you to your room," Aunt Carrie said.

"Okay," I said as I followed Aunt Carrie, still very much in shock at how nice the house looked.

"This is a really nice house," I said still in shock that this was indeed an actual house.

"Thank you," Aunt Carrie said with a smile. We walked up the spiral staircase. She led me into a room that was twice the size of my room back home. My jaw almost dropped.

After being in a room with two other people this last semester, it was amazing to have all of this space to myself.

It was going to be hard to go back to school in January.

Still in amazement. I put my luggage down and started to unpack my stuff. As I was unpacking, my aunt started to talk about dinner.

"Aurora, I am going to take you to one of the best places to eat in San Diego. It is absolutely fabulous. Do you like Italian?"

"Yes, I love it." At this point in the day, I was ready to eat anything. I was absolutely starving.

"Good! We are going to the excellent place in Little Italy to get pizza at the Pizza Grotto. I go there every week with Jason. He's working late tonight so he is going to meet us there. Let me help you finish unpacking, and then we'll go. How does that sound?"

"Alright, that sounds great Aunt Carrie!"

The more time that I spent with Aunt Carrie, the more and more I realized how much she was like my mom. It was strange in a way. I know they are sisters, but Aunt Carrie was like another version of my mom. When I had first met her at the airport, I had thought that she and my mom were completely different. Over the course of a few months, I slowly realized my first impression had been wrong. Aunt Carrie was loving and sweet just like my mom. I was glad that was how she was. It made me feel more at home. It made every second I was with her nice. Even when Aunt Carrie helped me put all of my clothes away, I felt like I was at home putting my clothes away with my mom.

We headed back out to the car and drove to the Pizza Grotto, which was a nice place. It had one of those Italian mobster looks to it. From the first step into the door, a person might feel like he or she had been transported to the Little Italy of New York. Half of the Pizza Grotto was a deli and the other half was a line that went from the front register all the way to the door. Aunt Carrie and I walked past the line and went right into the restaurant.

"Aunt Carrie, aren't we going to wait in line?" I asked half embarrassed that we were cutting in line.

"No, we don't have to. Jason is waiting for us. He already has a table."

I was satisfied by this answer, and we continued to walk passed everyone in line. We met with Uncle Jason who had been waiting there for us.

"Jason, this is Aurora, your niece. Aurora, this is your Uncle Jason."

"It's nice to finally meet you Aurora. All this talk that I have heard about you, and I hadn't even had the pleasure of meeting you before. I am glad we are finally getting the chance to meet." Uncle Jason said as he held out his hand. I returned his gesture by shaking his hand.

"It's nice to meet you too Uncle Jason."

I actually didn't know much about Uncle Jason. I knew that he was some sort of a contractor for some affiliate of the Navy, but I wasn't sure which one. Apparently, he did very well for himself. From my aunt and uncle's house to their clothes and their cars, all of these sounded off their success in life, but when you actually talked to them, you couldn't tell. My aunt and uncle were two of the most down to earth people I had ever met.

We didn't wait long before the waitress came to our table.

"The usual, right?" the waitress said to Aunt Carrie.

"Right, the usual, thank you," my aunt said to the waitress. The waitress automatically knew what we were getting right away and brought it to us starting with an antipasto salad.

"So tell me about college, what is it like? Did you meet any boys?" Uncle Jason asked.

"Oh, it is good. College is great. I am learning a lot. I am trying to keep my romantic life free right now. It helps me to stay focused on school," I said a bit thrown off by the dating question so early in the conversation.

"Good girl," Uncle Jason said. "You stick to that plan. Always plan before you go into relationships. It's the best way. It's like with your aunt and I. We were friends for a year before we started dating. It made the relationship better in the end. We saw marriages fall apart, but ours lasted because it had such a good foundation. I'm so glad we've made it to ten years this year. It's been great every step of the way." Uncle Jason said looking at Aunt Carrie.

"Oh, thank you dear," Aunt Carrie said with a big smile on her face.

Just as the three of us had finished our salads, the pizza came. The pizza looked delicious, and the aroma from it was mouthwatering. It was a thick-crusted pizza. As the first bite entered my mouth, my taste buds tingled. The pizza was the best pizza I had ever had. There was very little talking while the three of us ate the pizza. It was nice because it gave me an opportunity to take in the full experience at the Pizza Grotto.

After we were completely done eating, Uncle Jason said, "Well, I will take care of the bill. You two drive back to the house, and I can meet you there."

"That sounds good," Aunt Carrie said. She and I then took off and went back to the car to drive back to their house.

Chapter 10

Holiday Vacation

As the weeks went on, I settled into my aunt's house and finally got adjusted to it. For the next few weeks, I got to see every mall in San Diego because my Aunt Carrie was determined to spoil me with high-end clothes and jewelry. It was hard to deny her determination. I tried refusing a few times but eventually gave up fighting and just enjoyed being spoiled.

"I had always wanted a daughter. I hope you don't mind," Aunt Carrie would say.

"No, of course not. I don't mind," I would tell her.

We caught a few movies and occasionally dropped into her shop where she inspected and made sure things were running smoothly. Thanksgiving and Christmas both came and went quickly. They were some of the nicest holidays I had ever experienced. I of course made sure that I video chatted with my mom so that she could see that everything was going well. I think it was harder on my mom for me to be away from home for the holidays than it was on me. I could still detect a hint of jealousy in my mom's voice when I talked with her about Aunt Carrie.

In between my video chats with my mom, I overheard her talking with Aunt Carrie. My mom was double checking to see if everything was going alright. I think in a way my mom wanted to remind Aunt Carrie that

I was still my mom's little girl. It didn't seem to affect my aunt very much though. Aunt Carrie still seemed chipper toward me.

Oh well, a little drama is good for the holidays.

I had managed to tell both my mom and my aunt about the oceanography laboratory. They were both so happy for me. It gave me a sense of approval and reassured me that I was doing the right thing by taking the class. We rolled into New Year's Eve, and it was a blast. Aunt Carrie and Uncle Jason threw great parties. Even though I didn't know anyone at the party, I still had fun talking with everyone. There must have been forty people in the house.

After the New Year had started off, Aunt Carrie took the remaining few weeks left before school started to take me shopping again.

"I just want to make sure you have everything you need," Aunt Carrie would say. I just smiled whenever she said that and went along with whatever my aunt wanted to do. I spent most of the time in between shopping thinking about the Oceanography laboratory next semester. I had never been this excited about anything in my life. The closest was when I was accepted into college. It wasn't just the class that I was excited about. I was excited to see Erica too.

I had kept in touch with my BFF Erica the whole time we were away from each other. I knew that seeing her again and taking the Oceanography class would make this semester even better than my first semester had been.

Chapter 11

Second Semester

The semester started out rather nicely. I met Erica at the college café, and we got the schedule for our only other class which was Algebra 1. We were fortunate to be together in that class too. Neither one of us was strong in Math. We had both received an email from the professor stating that the Oceanography class would start at 8:00 a.m. on the *USNS O'Brien*. It was the college's research vessel owned by the Navy. The email also stated that the attire for the class would be jeans, a t-shirt, and shoes that could get dirty. Erica and I wore blue jeans and a red t-shirt. We bought them together so that we would match. We looked like sisters. We arrived on the pier and saw the ship. It was a nice ship. It was much bigger than I had imagined.

It was white and had five crane-looking things running from the front of the ship to the end of it. The ship also had what looked like barrels that had lifeboat on the side of them. The fact that the ship had lifeboats made me feel safe and secure. I hadn't realized that I was nervous about being on ships until I actually got on the ship. Standing on the ship felt a lot like standing on land. But somehow it felt different. It wasn't rocking yet. I had heard stories of how much ships could rock. I was hoping that since this ship was modern, it wouldn't rock too much.

As Erica and I walked onto the ship, we were approached by someone wearing a white uniform with shoulder boards.

"Are you two girls here from the college?" the officer asked with a refined sort of manner about him. He was very professional in his tone and very military in his appearance. There was a certain politeness in the way that he spoke.

"Yes, we are here for the lab, but we are not sure where to go," Erica said in a giddy sort of voice.

I guess Erica had a thing for military men because she looked as though she was flirting with the officer. It didn't faze the officer in the slightest. He pointed toward the front of the ship.

"This ship is big, and I don't want you two to get lost. Here's where I need you to go. They are having all of the students go to the galley. There will be a brief there," the officer said.

"Where do you want us to go?" I said trying to look at where the officer was pointing.

"It's behind that hatch. Walk down the passageway about ten feet. Turn right and keep walking straight until you see a sign that says 'mess decks.' That's where the brief is being held for all the students. Remember stay on the main deck. Don't go up and don't go down any ladder wells. Just keep walking down the passageway until you see the sign for the mess decks."

Both Erica and I had astounded looks of confusion on our faces, neither one of us knew what the officer was talking about.

"Don't worry. You will be okay. If you get lost, just ask someone in the passageway," the officer said.

"What's a passageway, and what's a hatch, and what's a mess decks?" Erica asked laughing at both of our confusion.

"Oh sorry, I forgot that not everyone is familiar with all of this Navy jargon, but you'll get it. Okay, let's try this again. So go through this door, take a right down the hallway, and keep going till you see a sign that says mess decks, that's the eating area like a cafeteria for the ship. Was that more understandable? Do you think you will be okay?" the officer asked with a smile as though he was amused by our confusion.

"Yes, I think we will be okay from here. Thank you," I said to the officer as we walked away from him and entered the maze of the ship.

As Erica and I began to navigate our way through the ship, it turned out that it wasn't as hard as it had sounded. All we had to do was just keep on walking down the hallway till we got to the sign that says "mess decks."

I was glad there was a sign or Erica and I would have been really lost. Everything in this ship looked alike.

There were a lot of wires and white walls. On the walls were signs with numbers, which looked like a glow-in-the-dark sticker. There were a few sailors in blue coveralls, cleaning and talking in the hallway. Ships really are like mazes on the inside. There are all sorts of turns leading to other turns and doors everywhere. It was confusing. I felt like a mouse trying to find some cheese. Hopefully with time, I would learn how to navigate through the ship without getting lost.

Erica and I finally got to the "mess decks" as the sign said. We took a seat in one of the spinning chairs that were bolted to the ground. The tables were all bolted too. There were about twenty other students waiting for the brief to begin. All the students were facing a big television, and everyone looked like they were dressed as comfortably as Erica and I. We waited about twenty minutes for the class to start. Suddenly, two men walked into the mess decks and stood in front of the television. One was older and had a beard, and the other man was younger and very good looking.

"Hey everyone! I'm glad you came out to the ship. Wow! We have a crowd here today, don't we Devon?" the professor said to the cute guy who walked in with him. "I am Professor Burton and this is my assistant, one of the graduate students in Oceanography Department, Devon. Everybody say 'hi' to Devon," Professor Burton said.

"Hi Devon!" everyone said in jumbled unison.

"Hi!" Devon said to the class with a little wave.

Oh, Devon was cute. One of the cutest boys I had ever seen.

"More graduate students will be joining us on future classes. For the first class, I wanted you guys to get to know what being on a ship was like. When we go underway on this ship, you will need to know a few things. This ship goes underway for days at a time. Don't worry about your other classes. This class takes priority at the college, and the other professors know that. Your other professors will give you your assignments that you might miss in light of the fact that this class goes out to sea for days at a time. Just let your other professors know ahead of time when the ship is leaving so they can plan accordingly. Now let's go over safety first and then move on to our schedule."

Devon walked over to a PowerPoint projector and turned it on. He then turned off the front lights to illuminate the screen for the class.

"Thank you Devon," Professor Burton said. Professor Burton then continued on with the briefing. "I am going to make this clear for all of you to understand. Don't mess around while you are on deck. This ship is going to rock, and it's going to roll. I don't need anyone to fall overboard. If you get seasick, get one of the seasick pills from the ship's corpsman. In our first class, we are going to be exploring the concept of runoff and its effects on the environment. I want everyone to meet me outside on deck in about thirty minutes. The ship should be underway by then. This class will last until 4:00 p.m. During our voyages, you will work interactively with the crew of this vessel. Each student will also be responsible for learning some of the instrumentation used during our scientific exploration.

"Your grade will be based on my interpretation of your grasp of the concepts I teach about in relationship to what we see. Each student will also be responsible for writing a term paper on one of the subjects from this semester. With regard to today, I don't want to see anyone get hurt, so watch your step and stay vigilant," Professor Burton said.

Just as Professor Burton finished, I heard a slight rumble, and then I felt the ground start to move a little. After a moment of shaking, everything became calm. There was a whistle that blew on a speaker on the wall, followed by a voice that came on over the loudspeaker.

"Ship's underway, ship's colors," the voice on the loudspeaker said.

"I guess that means we're underway," I said to Erica.

It was a different kind of feeling being underway. The ship would rock a little to the left or sometimes to the right. But I really didn't feel too different being in a ship that was sailing than when I was on land, I didn't even feel sick. Erica didn't take the sea very well though. She threw up immediately. One of the crew members saw Erica throwing up and handed her a couple of salted crackers.

"Here! These will help you not to feel as sick," the crew member said.

I grabbed the crackers from the crew member for Erica and said "thank you." After a few minutes, Erica did feel a little better. At least that was what she told me, but she still had a greenish glow in her face so I knew she was still seasick.

After Erica recuperated a little, we went out to the forecastle. It was there that I saw Devon again. He was helping line handlers pull the rope up that had been keeping the ship tied to the pier. I noticed that he was so built and robust, which I hadn't noticed before. Devon seemed to get along with the crew really well too. After a little while, the class started to convene on deck. Professor Burton stood in front of us.

"Okay class, this is your first assignment. We are going to go right into one of the key forms of science: the scientific method of observation.

Remember, you are trying to limit biases, so I want you to just observe. The ship will be going up and down the coast. I want you to document what you see. Whenever you see something worth taking note of, write the time and a brief description of what you see as it pertains to our topic of runoff.

"Your books describe what runoff is in more detail. But I will tell you briefly that it is pollution. It is debris from water that runs off from the land. It seemed to be having an interaction with the oceans. I want you to observe this interaction, and write it down. Find a comfortable place to sit and get to observing. The class will take a lunch break at noon. Remember, no bias and make your descriptions of what you see detailed. This is the first class you have in this living laboratory, and people are going to be reading what you write. Any questions?" Professor Burton asked as he looked around.

No hands went up.

"Good! Well, in that case, since there are no questions, let us begin," Professor Burton said as the class began to scatter throughout the observation deck to find good seats.

Erica and I found a good spot to sit, right next to the water. Erica and I pulled out pens and paper from our bags and started observing, just like Professor Burton had said. As the ship cruised up the coast, there was a little pollution from what I could see running from the land into the water, but it wasn't a lot. As the ship cruised, there were a number of pockets of runoff that we passed by. I wrote down what I saw and dated it along with the time. I glanced over at Erica. She and the rest of the class were all writing notes at the same time I was.

We must have all seen the same thing.

A few hours passed by and everything seemed to be running smoothly. I glanced over and saw Devon who was standing next to Professor Burton. I somehow got lost as I stared at him for a moment. He's so dreamy. Suddenly Erica kicked my leg. I looked at her sharply.

"I know, Devon's dreamy, isn't he? My sister said he used to be in the Navy, he was a diver, and he used to load bombs onto jets and stuff. But now Devon's studying oceanography. But you got to focus. You don't want to do badly in the first day of this class," Erica whispered.

Erica was right, of course.

"Thanks," I whispered back.

I had to focus. Devon could wait. I tried even harder than I had earlier to focus on everything. One of the crew members started to pass out binoculars to the students. The binoculars helped a great deal to see more details. Around 10:00 a.m., while I was staring through my binoculars, I thought I heard something in the water. It sounded like people talking. I cuffed my ear with my hand to see if I could hear better. I heard several voices all coming from the water.

"Erica, do you hear that?" I asked in a whisper.

"Hear what?"

"That!!!" I said as I pointed at the water. Erica took a look down at the water.

"No. I'm sorry, I don't hear anything."

"Oh, never mind. I must be hearing things," I said not wanting Erica to think I was going crazy. But I could still hear voices, and they were coming from the water.

I decided to try and get closer to the sound. I wanted to see if I could see anything near the sound that I heard. I went closer to the edge of the observation deck, leaning in as far as I could. Suddenly, I felt myself falling. I think I leaned in too far. I felt a surge of fear come over me as I hit the water.

I must of slipped, but how could I have slipped? I must have fallen a good thirty feet.

The fall had happened so fast that I wasn't really sure what had happened. The next thing I knew, I was in the water. To top it off, the ship was moving away from me as I floated in the water.

"Help!!!" I yelled out.

I guess enough people had heard me fall because suddenly a crowd had gathered near where I had fallen from. One person took what looked like a big canister and threw it in the water. Suddenly, a smoke came from the canister, and the ship slowly began to turn. I heard on the loudspeaker the words "Man overboard, man overboard." Then I saw a figure from the observation deck jump into the water. The figure that jumped in the water looked like a rescue swimmer. I could see him swimming toward me. I was still getting farther and farther away from the ship as it floated away from me.

I'm too far for anyone to swim to me, what am I going to do?

I started to panic as I did my best to tread the water. Suddenly, I heard the voices again.

"You fell! You weren't supposed to fall. Why do they always fall in? Don't they know they should be careful," a voice said.

"What?" I asked to the voices.

"Who are you and where are you?" I asked again to the voice.

"She heard us talk. How can that be? How can we understand her?" the voice asked.

"It does not matter how she can understand us. We have to help her, or she won't make it to the ship," a second voice said to the first voice. Then suddenly two dolphins appeared from the water and started coming toward me. The dolphins came right up to me and then waited. I touched one of them and then I heard the voices again.

"Come on, grab on to me so I can save you," the voice said.

It seemed like I was hearing the dolphins talk. I was still in shock from the fall, but I did what I was told by the dolphin. The dolphin took off toward the rescue swimmer, with me holding on. Soon the dolphin arrived at the rescue swimmer and then a voice spoke again.

"Okay, jump off."

"Jump off?" I said confused.

Suddenly, the dolphin stopped. I got off, and the dolphin stuck its head out of the water and stared at me. Its eyes were locked onto mine.

"How could this be?" the voice asked.

Just as I was about to talk back, the dolphin took off.

I didn't have much time to think about what had happened with the dolphins talking because the next thing that I saw was a figure coming right at me. The figure was the rescue swimmer. This rescue swimmer had such an incredible body. His strength was shown in each stroke he made through the water. Even though I was being rescued, I still took the time to notice how he moved.

When I took a second look at the rescue swimmer, I noticed that it was Devon. He came to me, with his chiseled body, at an incredible speed. He was almost as fast as the dolphins. I wasn't too bad of a swimmer, but there was no way that I could have made the swim to the ship from where I was at. Soon Devon came to me. Devon swooped me up and wrapped his arm around my body before I even had a chance to think. Devon had such a grip on me that I couldn't move, but it was a safe feeling to be in his arms. I knew I was in good hands, and I didn't have to worry about anything.

When we got back to the ship, I managed to climb up the ladder that had been lowered down to the water. When I got to the top of the ladder, I took a seat on the observation deck's floor. One of the corpsman came over to me. The corpsman started to check my vital signs. Professor Burton came over to me and started asking me questions.

"What happened? How did you fall? Are you okay?"

I didn't know what to say.

"I guess I just lost my balance," I said in an embarrassed voice.

Professor Burton's tone changed to one of true concern.

"Well, I'm glad you are okay. Next time, let's be careful." With that, Professor Burton went toward some of the crew members of the ship. I suddenly found myself surrounded by the whole class.

"I need everyone to step back and give us some room," The corpsman said. The first person by my side of course had been Erica. Even when everyone else had backed away, Erica remained by me.

"Oh my gosh! I'm so sorry Aurora. I should have seen that you were falling. It happened so fast. I was too focused on observing. I looked away from you for not less than a minute, and before I knew it, you were in the water. It's just a good thing that Devon was there—or you probably would have stayed in the water."

"What do you mean?"

"It was Devon who noticed you had fallen in the water, not me. Devon noticed your fall right away. As soon as you fell, he yelled to the ships helmsman to call man overboard. Then Devon threw that smoke canister into the water and dived in after you, all with one swoop. He did it all within a minute of having them call man overboard. It all happened so fast. I've never seen anyone react that fast to anything. Devon really is your hero," Erica said.

"Wow! I hadn't realized Devon had done all of that."

I looked around for Devon in the crowd. He didn't appear to be anywhere. When I finally got up, I looked around for him again, but I couldn't find him anywhere. I really wanted to thank him for what he had done for me, but Devon was simply not anywhere.

That is really weird. What kind of guy just vanishes after saving someone?

The rest of the class finished gossiping about the incident. They all talked like I couldn't hear them. After a few minutes, things started to quiet down as the class started to go back to where they were sitting before I had fallen in the water. .

I looked around and around for where my notebook was. Erica saw me freaking out as I looked for my notebook. Suddenly she reached in her bag and handed me my notebook.

"Here! I saw that you dropped it on your way down, and I grabbed it for you," Erica said.

"Oh, thank you," I said relieved that even though I had lost all of my dignity by falling in the water, I hadn't lost my precious notebook. For about another two hours, the ship continued to sail down the coast and then it began to pull in.

The whole time after my fall, I had trouble observing in my wet clothes. Fortunately on the way back, one of the sailors felt bad for me and gave me a towel to dry off with. Unfortunately, the towel could not do much for my cell phone. It was already ruined from the fall. But there was something bothering me even more than my cell phone being ruined, or the fact that I had fallen in the water.

Was I going crazy?

The thought kept on ringing through my head as I sat there reviewing the sequence of events leading to my fall. It was those voices that had made me lean over, and it was those same voices that I heard in the water when the dolphins came near me. But I was a rational girl. I had never heard voices before, and I had never talked to animals. But I had never seen a dolphin in real life before.

Could I talk to dolphins? Could that be why I wanted to work with the ocean all of my life?

It was too much to think about for the moment. Erica appeared to be doing some deep thinking of her own. She was probably feeling guilty about my fall though I didn't blame her in any regard. I think that we as people blame ourselves when things happen.

Before I knew it, the ship pulled in. Professor Burton got in front of the class and said, "Students, students, nice job on your first scientific observation study. I want all of you to type up your notes and email them back to me. My email address is in the lesson plan that I handed out. I am very interested in reading all of your papers. Just email them to me by tomorrow. Remember, just type the notes as you wrote them. Don't worry about improving their appearance to impress me, but please make it understandable. There might be other people reviewing what you write, and you will save me from getting a headache if you make it understandable. Alright, our next class will be in the classroom on Wednesday at 8:00 a.m. Don't be late. Alright, you guys are free to leave the ship. Please make sure you gather all of your belongings."

Everyone gathered their belongings and started to go off the ship. Professor Burton greeted each student as they left the ship to bid us farewell. It was nice of him to talk to each student one on one. But I think his intentions were to make sure everyone had made it off the ship. I saw him counting with his lips. As all of the students lined up to leave the ship, Erica and I stood in line. I looked around one last time. Devon was nowhere to be seen. Erica and I were the last ones to pass by Professor Burton.

"Hold on Aurora!" Professor Burton said as we passed by him. He had the look of concern on his face, with his eyebrows slightly raised.

"Are you alright? I mean really alright?"

I wasn't sure what he meant and thought about it for a second. It seemed like Professor Burton was trying to see if I would continue on with the class.

"Yes. I am fine, Professor Burton," I said with a resounding aura of confidence.

I guess my response satisfied his inquiry in some way because Professor Burton got a smile on his face.

"I'm glad to hear that Aurora. I think it's a shame when something like this happens. It is hard on the whole team. You gave me a little scare. I know it's hard to be on the ship for even a little underway. That's why I gave a safety brief. I am so happy that you're okay. The corpsman told me you were not seriously injured. I guess it was a good thing Devon was there when he was, or we might have lost you. That's why I bring him on these things, you know? He's really proven himself in more ways than one. So I will see you in my next class, right? You're not going to drop out on me, are you?" Professor Burton asked.

"No Professor Burton, I wouldn't dream of it. I've been waiting for this class my whole life. I'm not going to let a little fall like that stop me."

"Good. I'm glad to hear it. I will see you in my next class then. Take care now."

"You too, Professor Burton," Erica said as she and I started to turn toward the pier and down the ramp to leave the ship. As I began to walk, an overwhelming feeling came over me. I couldn't let it stand anymore. I had to solve at least one mystery, just for my own peace of mind. So I turned back around, quickly toward Professor Burton.

"Professor Burton," I yelled.

Professor Burton turned toward me, a little startled. I had accidentally interrupted a conversation Professor Burton was having with some of the crew of the ship.

"Yes my dear, how may I help you?"

"Oh, it was just a small thing really. I was just wondering where Devon was? I wanted to thank him in person for rescuing me."

"Oh , I'm sorry. Devon is in the middle of a big project. He made an observation about dolphins' behaviors today that he is trying to document.

It's for his Master's thesis. I will pass along your wish to thank him in person."

"Thank you," I said still unsatisfied with this answer. I knew there was nothing that I could do about it.

I walked off the brow of the ship and caught up with Erica. We both noticed that the bus going back to campus was in the distance and was about to leave.

"Come on Aurora. I think the bus is about to take off," Erica said.

"Yeah, I guess we better run."

Both of us took off running even though I was still a little shaky from the traumatic experience of falling off the ship. Running seemed to help me a lot and made me feel better somehow. I took off at a frantic pace. I guess I didn't want to miss that bus. It was either that, or I was trying to work off some of that frustration I had built up from all of the experiences that had just taken place.

I finally got on the bus and sat next to Erica. She and I sat on the bus for about a minute without talking. Erica had a look on her face like she had something on her mind that she was dying to say. I decided to break the ice by saying something about what had happened just to see if my fall off the ship was what Erica was thinking about.

"Boy, that was some fall, wasn't it Erica? I don't think I've ever fallen that far. It was straight shot into the water. What a way to start a brand new class."

Erica still had a look on her face of concern and worry.

"I don't want to talk about that here on the bus. Can we talk about it later at the college café?" Erica asked with a quiet voice.

I took from Erica's little request that she was trying to be smart. She knew that on a bus, everyone can hear what you're saying even if you whisper.

"Of course," I said as I stared out the window for a minute.

I was bored so I decided to grab my iPod. I was glad that my iPod had been in my bag and didn't fall into the water. Even though I had lost my phone, I still had my iPod. I started to listen to the classics and then floated around my iPod, trying to find a song that matched my mood. I had always had an assortment of music. My mother always said that I was eclectic, which means that I like a lot of different types of music. I had to agree with her. I never liked just one type of music. I always tried to see what was new with music, no matter what the genre was.

Eventually, I turned off my iPod as we arrived at the campus. I didn't want to hear anyone saying anything about the incident, but I knew this was probably unavoidable. All I heard about the fall was a few random comments from different people in the class, asking if I was okay. My response was always "Yes I'm fine, and thanks for asking." It was nice to know that I had so many concerned people in my class, but I suppose they were just being nice.

Erica and I finally made it away from the crowd on the bus and started to take a walk toward the college café. We didn't talk the whole time we were walking. I still had the thought on my mind about the dolphins talking. I knew one thing, I wasn't going to tell anyone in my family about this one.

I mean how could I? It sounded crazy.

We finally got to the college café, and I got a new drink to try—a nice cup of chamomile tea—that I thought would calm me down a little. The college café had labeled it "calming tea." I knew it was only chamomile though, but I hoped a nice cup of this tea would do the trick for calming my nerves after my fall.

When I got the calming tea, it was steaming. I put a little milk and cinnamon on top of it. Then I took a seat. Erica got a cup of decaf coffee and joined me.

We both had taken our usual seats. After a good amount of stirring and waiting, Erica finally said the first words.

"I have to tell you something that's been bothering me since you fell," Erica said.

"Okay Erica. What's bothering you?"

"I feel so horrible that I couldn't stop you from falling and that I hadn't even noticed you falling at first. I know you don't think it's my fault, but I feel like it is. I think that I could have stopped you from falling somehow if I had moved faster or I was looking your way when you began to fall," Erica said almost in tears.

"It's alright. It's not your fault. It was my fault. I fell because I heard...," I stopped myself in mid-sentence.

Perhaps this isn't the time to tell my best friend that I'm going crazy.

Erica carried on.

"No, you don't understand. I still feel so guilty. All this time that we were supposed to be observing and writing down what we saw, after you had come back from falling in the water, I couldn't even think. I kept on visualizing what had happened and how you almost died. So many times in my head, I kept on telling myself that I almost let you down and you could have died. I won't let it happen again, I promise," Erica said in tears.

"Erica!!!" I said putting my hand on her shoulder and looking straight into her eyes.

"Erica, you are my best friend. You have always been there for me since we started this crazy thing called college. You wouldn't have even been on that ship if I hadn't asked you to join me. You are still a good friend, and I should have been more careful, that's all. I will just be more careful next time, okay?"

"Okay, if you promise that you're not mad at me," Erica said, still crying a little bit.

"How could I be mad at you? You are my BFF. I say we talk about something else. Anything else, because you have nothing to worry about. I'm not mad at you."

"Okay," Erica said with a slight smile. I guess she had been thinking about something else but was too afraid to ask me. Erica cleared her throat.

"Since you're not mad at me Aurora, can I ask you one question?" Erica said, a little flustered.

"Go ahead."

"Okay, I was just wondering what did it feel like to have Devon rescue you? It looked so romantic. The way he jumped in like a hero after you."

I smiled a little bit at Erica's question.

"It was nice. I mean, I wouldn't want to fall like that again, but it was so brave of him to rescue me like he did."

Suddenly I felt the feeling of frustration come over me again.

"You know, I really wanted to thank Devon in person, but he wasn't around after I was rescued. Professor Burton said that Devon was writing a paper or something. I think I'm going to find him and tell him on my own. I have to. It's only right. I mean, Devon did rescue me, and I would feel guilty if I didn't thank him in person."

"Oh yeah! I know what you mean. You should give him a thank you."

I guess it was apparent that I had liked Devon.

"Oh, stop it Erica! He would have saved anyone if they were as clumsy as me and fell in the water."

"I don't know Aurora. I think he's been staring at you. I caught him once in the hallway just watching you, but I didn't tell you."

"You saw him doing what?

"He was staring at you in that way. You know the way a guy looks at you when he's infatuated with you."

Had Devon been staring at me? How had he been staring at me without my noticing? Why would he be staring at me? I had never had an admirer before so this was a totally new experience. Or maybe it's something else. It had to be something else. No boy had ever really liked me.

I sipped my tea a little faster now while thinking about this whole situation.

"But if Devon liked me, why hasn't he ever come up to me? Why would he just stare at me? Or give me some sort of sign or something?"

Erica feeling confused.

"I don't know Aurora. It's a little weird, but maybe Devon is just a guy who likes to keep his distance. You know, the kind that we read about as little girls—the kind of guy who has a true sense of deep love. The love you wait for your whole life. I mean, it is nice to think about, isn't it?—that deep kind of romance. An old-fashioned wait period, where he comes up to you when he's ready," Erica said lost in the idea of true romance.

As Erica was talking, a thought came over me.

"Hold on Erica. I have a question. Why didn't you ever mention it to me before? I mean the staring thing. Even if he had been staring at me for a second, it would have been nice to know about it."

Erica leaned back. It seemed like she wasn't ready for the line of questions I was giving her about this whole situation.

"I ahh…I'm not sure why I didn't mention it to you before now. Oh wait! I remember now. It happened when we were doing the deep study session for Western Civilization last semester.

"You always thought someone was watching you anyways. I didn't want you to freak out or get distracted from the finals. I'm really sorry that I didn't tell you before. I didn't mean to keep it from you. I had good intentions. Of course, normally if I saw anybody staring at you, I would let you know, but we were so focused on the exams—and it was so close to the finals. I'm really sorry," Erica said, looking like the end of the world had arrived.

I could tell that Erica was sorry like she had done something really wrong. It was kind of funny. Erica is the rare kind of a person whose emotions are really apparent on her face. She doesn't know how to hide things that she is thinking about like most people do. That was part of the reason why I liked Erica so much. I knew that she was honest and a real friend.

"It's okay Erica, it really is. I'm not mad that you didn't tell me. I was just wondering. I still wonder why Devon hadn't come up to me before if he has such a crush on me. Even after he rescued me, why wouldn't he say anything? I mean, isn't that crazy? I guess I'm probably freaking out about it for no reason, right? Anyways, I'm going to finish this last little sip of my tea, and then I think I should head off. It was such a long and trying day, and I'm still wearing the clothes that I fell into the water with," I said, anxious to stop talking about everything that was going on.

"Yeah, I agree. What a day!" Erica said with a sigh as she copied my actions by raising her cup with both hands and sipping it like it was a bowl of soup. Erica was funny when it came to certain little quarks. She was truly unique and it always helped me to take my mind off whatever was bothering me.

Erica and I grabbed our bags and headed out of the college café. The barista behind the counter had taken a friendship-like relationship with Erica and I. You know the kind of relationship that sometimes happens when you go to a place a lot.

I guess the barista had noticed over time that Erica and I were frequent visitors of the college café and said, "I'll see you two next time. You guys are my best customers."

"Thanks, we'll see you next time too," I replied and waved my hand in a friendly gesture as we walked out the door.

We both began to walk toward our rooms together. When we got to our dorms, I turned toward Erica and gave her a big hug.

"Thanks Erica. I really appreciate everything that you do for me. You are a really good friend," I said just to solidify the fact that we were still friends and that I wasn't mad at her.

"You're welcome. I'll see you tomorrow," Erica said with a smile on her face.

We then parted ways. I walked down the hallway toward my room. I pulled my book bag over to my side to look through the front pocket. I started looking for my keys but didn't find them at first.

Hopefully, I didn't lose them when I fell in the water. Oh wait! Here they are.

I grabbed my room key, and put it into the keyhole. I was ready to go to bed. This after all had been one crazy day, and I was exhausted.

Chapter 12

A Quick Note

When I walked in the door of my room, Jessica was there sitting on the couch. She was wearing an outfit, which gave her a new look. Her long black stockings that reached her knees had a little pink emblem at the top that resembled a bunny. Jessica had changed her hair too. Now she had her hair in two pigtails. She looked a lot like a Japanese anime character.

"Hey sis," Jessica said as I walked into the door.

Over the last few months, we had grown closer. All three of us in the room had learned to appreciate each other more. Now we all called each other sisters. Even when we were in public, we would do this, and people would look at us kind of weird. It was as if we really were related, but it was kind of an inside joke that we didn't really clarify to people. It was nice that Jessica had really warmed up to me. I was glad because I had never really had sisters before but always wanted one.

"What's up sis?" I said as I started walking toward the kitchen.

But just as I got my foot in the door to grab a drink, Jessica said, "Hey, so you didn't tell me you had an admirer?"

How did she know that I had a secret admirer? I just found out about it today. Had Jessica noticed Devon staring at me too? Had Devon watched me more than once? I'll play dumb, and see what's up.

"What do you mean?"

"I mean, the boy who dropped by. You know, the really cute one. The one who works out and has that nice Greek look to him, like the statue of David got up and started walking around and decided he was going to come to college," Jessica said smiling.

I stood there looking at Jessica stunned.

"Devon, Devon was here?" I said in a surprised voice.

"Is that his name? I didn't ask. I was too busy being stunned by his good looks. You know, usually I can't stand the guys around here, but that guy is something else. Nice job! You know how to pick them Aurora," Jessica said.

"What do you mean?" I said, now concerned with what Jessica was saying.

"Oh, it's just that he is so polite, a real gentleman. Not too nice like a pushover, but just nice enough like a very refined gentleman, and he's absolutely an eye candy."

"What did he want?"

"Oh not much! He just asked if you were here. When I told him you weren't, he dropped off this quick note. I put it over there on the table," Jessica said as she pointed at the table.

I walked toward the counter and picked up the nicely folded note. On the front of the note was written in very nice cursive AURORA. I opened it up and it said:

> Aurora.
> I'm sorry that I missed you. I do apologize for not talking to you earlier today after your rescue. Since I didn't get a chance to talk to you earlier, I decided I would drop by to see how you were doing. I would love to apologize in person for not checking up with you immediately after your rescue. I hope to see you soon."
>
> Wishing you the best,
> Devon

Wow! He had wanted to talk. It must have taken him a little while to find out where my room was. Devon must have talked with Mrs. Degory and then came all the way down here. I can't believe I wasn't here when he came. I hope I get to see him tomorrow.

"So what did the letter say?" Jessica asked eagerly awaiting the latest gossip of the hour.

"Oh not much! It was just that he was sorry he had missed me, and he hoped I got to see him soon."

"That was it. Why would he come all the way down here just to write that?" Jessica asked confused.

"Well...," I said with a slight twinge in my voice. "I sort of fell off the ship today during my Oceanography lab. He was probably just checking up on me."

"Well, who is he? I need all the gossip. How do you know him?" Jessica asked as she gestured for me to take a seat on the couch next to her, which I did.

"Well, his name is Devon, and he is a graduate student studying Oceanography. Remember that class that I am taking where we get to go on a ship and find out things about what is going on in the ocean and how everything in the ocean interacts with each other?"

"Yes, I remember. You couldn't stop talking about that class when you got back from break," Jessica said, gesturing to move on.

"Well, Devon is the professor's assistant for the Oceanography laboratory. I sort of fell in the water during class today, and Devon is the one who rescued me."

"Devon rescued you! You mean like actually rescue?"

"Yes. Devon rescued me. He jumped into the water and swam out to save me."

"Wow, yeah I can see it! He looks like the hero type," Jessica said with a smile. "Wow, so you were rescued! I'm glad you're okay. But wait, how did you fall off the ship in the first place? That must have been scary for you."

I wasn't expecting that question. I quickly thought of an answer.

"It's those heavy sea rolls. They really make the ship rock. I somehow fell in after one of the big sea rolls."

"You mean the heavy sea rolls from going around the bay? I've never heard of that, and I've lived here all of my life."

"Oh, I don't know. They said it was a freak thing."

I really didn't like lying to Jessica since we were practically sisters, but I thought telling her about the talking to the dolphins part of my story would sound even crazier than saying there were heavy rolls in the bay. This excuse at least could be blamed on the lack of experience on a ship.

Jessica didn't quiver over the detail of my "heavy rolls in the bay story" for too long. We continued to talk about Devon. It was so funny to see Jessica like this, a hardcore grunge rocker Goth girl talking about boys like a Barbie-obsessed little girl. I suppose that the little girl who obsesses over boys is in all of us, wanting to find that Perfect man. Jessica was no different.

"So Devon must really like you then to come all the way down here to find you?" Jessica asked.

"No. I don't think so. I mean, I think he really would have checked up on anyone if he rescued them. I think he would have rescued anyone who fell in the water," I said still trying to convince myself that Devon wasn't interested in me.

"Well, I don't know. He seemed kind of sad when I said you weren't here, and he made me promise to give you the note that I gave you. It just seemed like he was so disappointed that you hadn't been here."

Well, maybe Devon did like me a little. But it could just be a crush. Yeah, I bet it's just a crush or something like that.

I sat there next to Jessica. I then suddenly took a big yawn. Jessica yawned too.

"Well anyways, Jessica I'll talk to you later. I've had a busy day, and I think I should go to bed."

"Yeah, me too. I was just heading to bed before you came in, but I really wanted to find out about your mystery man, Devon. Keep me updated on what happens with you two. I think you guys would make a cute couple," Jessica said, smiling.

"Oh stop it! I think he's just being nice," I said defensively, blushing a little bit.

"We'll see," Jessica said seeming satisfied that I had blushed a little when she said Devon and I were a cute couple.

Chapter 13

Just Wait and See What Happens

The next day began like any other day at college. I got up and got ready for class. I had chosen to take Algebra as my other class for the semester. It was a good choice. I needed a distraction from the mess that happened yesterday. Math was just difficult enough to let me escape everything for a little bit. Besides, it would give me a chance to run the Devon situation by Erica. I knew Erica would be thrilled by the note Devon had left me.

I got dressed, brushed my teeth, and then grabbed some cereal from the cabinet. After pouring the cereal into the bowl, I grabbed the milk carton from the refrigerator and noticed that we were out of milk. While trying to make as little of a mess as possible, I graciously poured the cereal back in the bag and put the bag back in the box. I'll have to grab something to eat on the way to class. Dry cereal wasn't going to cut it today. But just then I spotted a couple of granola bars in the cabinet and thought these bars will do just fine for breakfast. I grabbed my calculator and put it in my bag with my Math book. Then I headed out the door while eating my granola bars. I reached Algebra and saw Erica waiting for me outside of the classroom. She looked over in my direction as I was walking toward her and began to run over to greet me.

"Hey, Algebra huh? Are you as excited as I am?"

"Oh yeah, loads! It's my worst subject."

"Oh, mine too," Erica said laughing. She started to walk in front of me toward the door to go into the class. I stopped her abruptly by tapping her on the left shoulder.

"Erica, wait! I have something I have to tell you. It's about a certain person from yesterday," I said in a whisper.

Erica quickly turned around.

"You mean Devon?"

"Shhhh!!!!!"

"Oh sorry," Erica said whispering.

"What happened with that guy?" Erica asked, trying to be secretive now by calling Devon "that guy."

"That guy came by my dorm last night and dropped this note off for me." I handed Erica the note, which she read quickly.

"What do you think it means? Do you think it means that guy likes me, or do you think it means he just wanted to see if I was okay?" I asked.

"Oh, he likes you," Erica said with confidence. "Anybody who takes the time to go all the way down to our dorm rooms and find your room likes you for sure. It's just a question of how much he likes you. Besides, I told you he was staring at you before, remember? I guess we'll see when that guy sees you next if anything happens," Erica said handing me back my note.

"Yeah, you're right! No need to squabble over every little detail. I'll just wait and see what happens when I see him again," I said as I looked up and saw Erica heading into class. Erica looked back at me.

"Class is about to start."

I looked at my watch.

"Oh you're right! We better go. We'll talk later about all of this."

I walked toward the door to catch up with Erica. Algebra was taught by a teacher named Mrs. Klee, who was young for a college professor. She began her lesson by staring straight at the class.

"Good morning class. I'm so glad that you are here today. I want to start the class by having everyone here do the following problems on the board. Just grab a pencil and a piece of paper and start working the problems."

There were ten problems on the board. All of the problems didn't seem too difficult. I stared at the board and instantly knew all of the work that had to be done to get the answers to the problems. Then I glanced at Erica. She and the rest of the class had already begun to work out the assignment on their papers. I looked through my bag for my notebook, but I couldn't find it anywhere. Erica glanced over at me and noticed that I was looking for paper. She handed me a couple of sheets from her notebook and then I began to write down what I saw on the board.

I knocked out the first problem quickly. But the second problem proved to be more difficult than I had originally thought. As I began to work out the problem on paper, my mind began to wonder. Then suddenly, I began to think about Devon.

What was it that he wanted? Did Devon really like me?

It was hard to tell if Devon liked me, or if it was some sort of confusion on my part. I mean, wouldn't Devon have rescued anyone if they fell in the water? But I suppose that wasn't the question that was bothering me. I mean, it was bothering me a little, but the real question was, when would I see Devon again? This was an emotionally mixed question. I was excited and nervous at the same time. I was so nervous about seeing him again. My stomach started to get butterflies as I began to daydream. Then with a tap on my paper, I found myself blinking out of my daydreaming state. I glanced toward the tapping. It was Erica. She used her eyes to point toward the front of the class. I looked forward and saw Mrs. Klee staring right at me with her arms crossed with her eyes focused directly on me. I quickly refocused on the Math problems.

I still finished relatively fast even with the distractions. I looked around and noticed that I had in fact finished before all the other students. I had even finished before Erica. I sat in silence, feeling a certain sense of personal satisfaction as I waited for the rest of the class to catch up. Mrs. Klee was staring at me again. She gave me a look as though she was impressed by how fast I had finished the assignment in spite of my daydreaming.

This was the first time that I had ever impressed a Math teacher.

About five minutes later, the other students began to finish. Mrs. Klee continued on with her lesson.

"Very good class. I'm happy to see that everyone here seems to be on the same level. I glanced at your papers as I walked around. Please pass your papers with all of your work up to the front of the class. Before you do, please make sure that all of your papers have your name and which class this is along with the date. I don't like to confuse my classes.

"I have so many classes, and it can be difficult to differentiate between all of them. I want you guys to start going through the first three chapters of the book. We will be covering this in our next class. Do the assignments at the end of the first three chapters, doing only the odd number questions.

When you are done, please show me your work. My email address is on the board. Feel free to write me if you have any questions day or night. I will be happy to help you through your problems. Okay, go ahead and start reading until the end of class."

I opened my massive Math book and began to read the first chapter. It was all about the history of Algebra and rules that you should follow while doing Math problems. A lot of the material in the chapter seemed like a review for me. I slowly lost focus while reading. As I looked around, I realized it was okay to lose focus this time because Mrs. Klee wasn't paying as much attention as she had been at the beginning of class. She was focused on what the class had turned in. I hoped my Math was right. I've had to fight against teachers before about Math all of my life. I didn't want any trouble in college with Math. I just want to pass was the only thought I had as I stared at Mrs. Klee.

I tried to focus on the first chapter by looking at the book again, but slowly as I began to read, I started to think about Devon. I thought about how he looked and tried to figure out what everything meant with hearing the dolphins. I just couldn't get my head clear enough to focus on Math. I went through how I fell in the water, leaving out the weird part about me hearing dolphins talk as much as I could. Every time I thought about talking to dolphins, I thought it was a sign that I was going nuts. Before I knew it, class was over.

"Hey Aurora, do you want to get lunch? It's 'Taco Tuesday' at the cafeteria." Erica asked.

"Oh yeah! That would be awesome."

As we began to walk, I noticed that I stopped thinking about Devon and everything else that was confusing me at the moment. Erica was a good distraction.

"Did you think Math class was hard?" Erica asked.

"No, not as hard as I had imagined it would be surprisingly. Why? Was it hard for you?"

"No. I was just wondering. I had a little trouble with the problems, but I finished it in time. If I need help with Math, can you help me throughout the semester?" Erica asked.

I smiled when she asked me.

"Yes of course. I will always help you Erica. You are my BFF, remember?"

I just hope I don't give Erica the wrong advice with Math. I don't want to be the reason why Erica might do badly in class.

I was already starving when we finally arrived at the cafeteria. The smell of tacos that filled the air made me hungrier. Erica and I quickly got our tacos and took our usual spots. About halfway through my first taco, Erica got up to get a drink, and then I got the feeling again that someone was watching me. The feeling was a lot like I had before when I looked to see if someone was watching me. This time, I felt like the feeling was being projected from behind me. I looked behind me, and there was Devon coming toward me.

Devon didn't walk toward me fast. As he walked, everything seemed to be in slow motion. The first thing I saw was his big beautiful eyes staring right at me. We locked eyes, and I was truly in bliss—the kind of bliss that only happens once. As he and I stared at each other, we got lost in each other's souls—with each second being an eternity in itself. Each motion was like the pounding of my heart. He walked in such a cool, crisp way. His movements were hypnotic. He was absolutely alluring, and for some reason, he was fixated on me.

Out of all of the people in the cafeteria that Devon could be fixated on, he was fixated on me—and I couldn't figure out why. He eventually made it to me. Erica was still off getting a drink and hadn't returned yet. When he finally made it to my table, I noticed that he had no food in his hands, which told me one thing. He was only there to see me.

"May I sit down?" Devon asked with the most graceful pronunciation.

"Yes of course."

He sat down, and then we stared into each other's eyes again. Behind him, a couple of tables down, I could see the outline of Erica sitting down. She sat in a way that Devon didn't seem to notice her. She gestured two thumbs up to me. I shook my head and gave a smile. This caused Devon to turn around to see what I was smiling about. He saw Erica when he turned around and then gave a smile.

"Sorry, that's my friend. She was eating with me right before you came."

"Oh well, I can move if this is her spot," Devon said as he started to get up.

"No, that's okay. She doesn't mind."

As Devon sat back down, it appeared that Erica wasn't the only one in the cafeteria who was staring at us. It was almost as though everyone in the cafeteria was looking at what might be the newest couple on campus. Devon and I didn't notice very much that everyone was staring. It was easy to ignore as I looked at him. He started to talk with a smile on his face.

"So you got my note?" Devon asked.

"Yes, I got your note, but I am a little confused."

"Confused about what?"

"I was confused about what you meant in the note."

Devon gave a confused look.

"Oh and thank you for saving me. I had been wanting to thank you personally when you actually saved me, but you weren't anywhere to be found that day. You are my hero," I said smiling.

"Oh it was nothing. I would have done it for anyone."

"You would have?" I asked with a slight hint of sadness and disappointment in my voice.

"Yes," he said leaning in. "But I'm glad it was you that I got to save," he said as he stretched out his arms and began to hold my hands.

I pulled away. I wasn't ready for this. I wasn't ready for the sudden attention I had just received from him. Nor was I expecting it. He in return pulled away too.

I think I startled him a bit. But the time was not right for him to touch me. It did feel nice for a second to have him touch my arm. But it still took me off guard.

He quickly responded.

"I'm sorry," he said in a calming voice.

"It's okay. It just took me off guard."

"I understand. It wasn't my intention to frighten you or freak you out. I certainly didn't want you to think that I was a stalker or something. I just wanted to check on you and see if you were okay," Devon said. He seemed a bit nervous now like he had made a mistake. I decided perhaps I should change the subject gracefully.

"I really do appreciate you saving me. It was crazy how I fell in, with the rough seas and all."

"Yeah, that was crazy. I didn't even think the seas were that rough though. But that is why you need to be careful on the ship," Devon said.

"How did you learn to save lives like you did? Were you a life guard before or something? I heard that you jumped right in the water like it was nothing."

A big smile came over Devon's face.

"Oh, I've had to swim a time or two before."

"Yeah, but that wasn't some swim. You just jumped in and saved me like it was nothing. Most people wouldn't have the nerve to just jump right in. I guess it's a good thing that you did, or I would still be in the water,"

"You know, I have a confession to make," Devon said.

"What is that?" I asked with a smile.

"I was actually watching you."

"Watching me, what do you mean?"

"I don't know how to explain it. It's kind of funny, but you seem strangely different. I find it hard to take my eyes off of you. I was wondering why you were hanging so far off the ledge anyways. It bothered me when you did that. I think that's why you fell," Devon said.

I was a little embarrassed by this question.

"Oh you know, I thought I saw something in the water and wanted to get a better look at it."

"Well, next time take it easy, okay?"

"Okay. I will. I promise."

"Okay. I'll be watching you," Devon said, half joking while pointing at his eyes with two of his fingers and then pointing at me.

"Ha, ha," I said getting the joke.

Then Devon got up from his chair and said, "Okay, well, I'm glad to see that you're okay. I will talk to you again soon."

"Yeah. I'll see you in class in a few minutes, you'll be there right?"

"Ahh, well, we will see. I only help part time. I am working on a special project. Speaking of which, I need to ask you a few questions later on. Do you want to meet sometime later?"

"What do you mean, like a date?" I asked half shocked because I had never been asked on a date before.

"No, no, nothing like that. It is for my project. I noticed that dolphins came near you when I rescued you. I wanted to document how they interacted with you."

"Oh," I said with a half sigh of relief and a half sigh of disappointment. Then I had a quick realization that I was going to have to tell Devon what happened when I was in the water, which made me very nervous.

"Yeah of course. I would love to tell you what happened. Do you want to talk about it now?

"No, not right now. Later on would be better when I have my computer. I have to write down every detail of what happened. Can we meet later tonight perhaps if you're not doing anything?"

"Yes of course. I would love to give you tonight my account of what happened. What time?" I asked trying to hide my excitement.

"Oh, let's say 8:00 p.m. We'll catch dinner too while we're at it. So don't eat, okay? I know this great place that I think you'll love."

"Okay," I said with a squeaky voice. I cleared my throat. "Yeah, sounds good. Tonight at 8:00 then. Where can I meet you?"

"I'll drop by your place to pick you up."

"Okay, sounds good."

Then Devon got up and left the table. While he was walking, Devon waved at Erica. She waved back and then got up and walked toward the table I was sitting at. Erica was still drinking her drink she had gotten before Devon came. It seemed like she hadn't drank any of it. She had apparently just sat there the whole time and watched the conversation between me and Devon.

When she got to me, she asked, "So what did he say?"

"Oh, not much. He just asked me how I was doing and how I fell in the water."

"That was it?" Erica asked half shocked.

"Yeah, that was pretty much it."

"What do you mean pretty much it? What's with the pretty much part?"

"Oh well, he wants to meet tonight."

"Like a date?" Erica asked.

"No. Devon said it wasn't a date because I asked. He said he wanted to find out what happened with the dolphins."

"Really, he said that? Where are you guys meeting?" Erica asked very inquisitively. I guess she was trying to figure out if my meeting with Devon later tonight was classified as a date.

"Oh, at my place. He is going to come pick me up."

Even as I said he would come pick me up, I knew it sounded more and more like a date. Erica confirmed my beliefs.

"Oh, it's a date," Erica said all giddy. "What dolphins?"

I had forgotten that I hadn't mentioned the dolphins to Erica before. That was the most important part of the whole ordeal. But at this point, there was no need to hide it. I would have to tell Erica about the dolphins rescuing me. But I'll leave the part out about hearing the dolphins speak to me.

"Oh you see, I forgot to tell you. There were these dolphins that came toward me when I fell in the water."

I gave a look at Erica to see if my story sounded believable.

"They came toward you?"

"Oh yeah, right toward me. It was so strange. After I had fallen in the water, I tried to swim back toward the ship, which was moving so fast away from me. Before I knew it, I was really far away from the ship. I started to panic, and then these two dolphins came to me. I held onto them as they swam me back toward the ship. When I got close enough, I jumped off and that's when Devon saved me."

"How come you didn't mention it before?" Erica asked.

"I just forgot to mention it with the whole ordeal. It all happened so fast. I was just happy to be alive."

"How does Devon know about the dolphins?"

"Oh, I'm not sure. He must have seen them when he jumped in the water, I suppose."

"So then what does Devon want to find out from you? I mean, why does he want to talk to you about dolphins tonight?" Erica asked perplexed.

"Devon said it was for some paper he was writing. He said that he needed to document my encounter with the dolphins. It really took me off guard. I really didn't think anyone had even seen the dolphins when they rescued me by the way everyone was going on and on about how Devon had rescued me. I assumed no one had noticed."

"Well, I know I didn't see the dolphins, and I don't think anyone else did either." Then Erica got a big smile again and insisted, "But I think you meeting up with Devon tonight is still considered a date."

I agreed with Erica even though half of me didn't want to believe it. I really didn't need any romantic distractions. I wanted to focus on my studies. I would have to wait and see what happens with Devon. If he was trying to be romantic, then I would be happy and deal with it. But I think if he does like me even if it's just a little, his feelings will fizzle out once he gets to know me.

"Well, it's about time for the next class, isn't it?" Erica said as a reminder to me. I refocused on the moment and glanced at Erica as she looked at her watch.

"Oh yeah, it is," I said.

Erica and I briskly headed into class, trying not to be late.

Chapter 14

It's Not a Date

As everyone headed into class, Professor Burton was waiting anxiously in the front of the class, watching everyone. After a moment, Professor Burton began to talk about our documentation processes and criticized how we wrote—but his criticisms were not said in a negative way. It was a simple critique, but none of what Professor Burton said seemed to matter to me at the moment because I noticed that Devon was not there.

Why wasn't Devon here? I was really hoping that Devon was going to be here.

Class dragged on after my realization that Devon wasn't here. At the end of class, I gathered up my things and walked out with Erica.

"No Devon huh?" Erica asked as we finally got out of the classroom door.

"Nope, no Devon," I said in a voice that sounded half sad.

"It's okay. You still have your date tonight, and it will give you something to ask him."

"What do you mean?" I said.

"You know, you can ask him where he was today in class." Erica said.

That was a good idea.

"Yeah, I will do that, but it's not a date, remember?" I said insistently. But even as I said that it wasn't a date, I didn't believe what I was saying.

"Ahuh, it's not a date, sure. And what are you wearing on this non-date?" Erica asked.

I pointed at my clothes that I had set out for tonight. Erica stared at them in disapproval.

"Oh no! You're not wearing this for the first date, are you? Don't you have anything better?"

"Well, I do have a few things from my aunt, but I haven't really worn them, except for when I bought them with my aunt during the winter break."

"Do you want me to help you pick something out?"

"Yeah, if you want."

I was so thankful that Erica had offered to help me. After arriving at my closet and spending about an hour going through all of the clothes, I realized that I absolutely hated playing dress up. It really did take a lot of effort to look good without looking like you were trying to look good. Finally, Erica and I picked out a good combination.

"That's it, that's the outfit! It doesn't say I'm trying and it doesn't say I'm sloppy either. It's perfect," Erica said smiling as she gave me a complete look over.

Just then a knock came at my door. I looked through the door's security hole to see who it was. Sure enough, it was Devon waiting for me.

"Erica, it's Devon," I whispered.

"Okay, I'll let you out. Have a good date," Erica whispered back, and then I opened the door.

"Devon, it's nice to see you," I said smiling.

"It's nice to see you too," Devon said back. It didn't appear like Devon had dressed up anymore than usual, but he still looked so nice.

"Are you ready to go?" Devon asked.

"Yes, I'm ready," I said as I grabbed my purse. I then shut the door, and we walked to Devon's car. It was a nice car from what I could tell. I really didn't know much about cars.

Chapter 15

First Date?

When we got to the car, Devon opened the door for me. Then Devon got in the car and started driving.

"It's a nice night tonight, isn't it?" Devon asked me.

"Yes, it's nice."

I guess neither one of us had much to say at first because after that quick conversation, the drive was an awkward quiet. About ten minutes into the drive after being on a few freeways that I didn't recognize, I asked Devon a question that I had been trying to gather the courage to ask.

"Where are we going?"

"You'll see," Devon said.

I wasn't sure if I liked this mysterious answer.

"Okay as long as you're not kidnapping me," I said jokingly.

Devon got a quick chuckle from my comment.

"Don't worry, it's a nice place. It will give us a good chance to review everything," Devon said.

"Okay, sounds good," I said, and then there was another moment of silence.

I know there was something I wanted to ask Devon.

I tried to remember as we continued on our drive.

Oh that was it.

"Where were you during class today?" I asked.

"Oh, I was working on my research project. I came up with a new angle that I was trying to pound out. Why? Did you miss me?" Devon asked with a smirk.

"Oh well, I didn't miss you too much. I was just curious about why you weren't there," I said trying to act like I hadn't wondered where he was during the whole time I was in class.

"Oh okay. We're here," Devon said.

The car then began to slow down. There was a sign right next to where we had parked that said Oceanport. I saw the sign but decided to ask where we were anyways.

"Where are we?"

"Oh, this is my favorite Greek place. I thought you would enjoy it. If not, there is a really good pizza place right next to it where we can go to. Do you like Greek food?"

"Yes. I love Greek food," I said.

In truth though, I had never really had Greek food, but I was willing to try anything at least once. We walked through the little outlet of shops. Oceanport was very nice. There was a carousel and a bunch of people shopping and walking around. What made it nice though was the view. Oceanport was right next to the water. You could really see the beauty of San Diego Bay from Oceanport. After a minute of walking, we arrived at the Greek restaurant.

When we walked into the Greek restaurant, a man behind the counter who seemed to know Devon gave him a big wave. Devon waved back.

"What would you like? It's on me," Devon said as he pointed to the menu behind the front counter.

"Ahh, well," I said as I looked at the menu and didn't recognize any of the listed food.

I guess my confusion was transparent on my face because then Devon said, "Is this your first time eating Greek food?"

I smiled when Devon asked me this. I was embarrassed but glad he asked.

"Yes, how could you tell?"

"Just a guess. Can I order for you? Do you like lamb?"

"I've never had it before, but I'll try it," I said smiling as I looked at Devon.

"Okay good," Devon said and smiled.

Then Devon turned toward the man behind the counter and said, "Two Gyro plates please."

"No problem Devon. Anything else?" the man behind the counter asked.

"Yeah, add an extra pita bread and hummus."

Devon then paid, and we sat down to wait for our food.

"This is one of my favorite types of food. I guess it's in my blood," Devon said.

"What do you mean?"

"Oh, I'm Greek."

"Oh cool," I said with a smile and managed to say, "I can't wait to try it."

"I'm glad that you are going to try it. I am surprised that you have never had Greek before. You're in for a treat. This is one of the best Greek places in town."

"Oh well, I guess there aren't a whole lot of Greek places where I'm from," I said.

"Where are you from?"

"Alaska."

Just then the guy from behind the counter yelled "84." Devon looked down at his receipt.

"Oh that's us," Devon said as he got up swiftly and went to go pick up the food.

"Here you go. I hope you enjoy this. Oh, I didn't know what kind of drink you wanted. What kind would you like?" Devon asked showing me an empty cup.

"Um, just water please," I said.

Devon went to go fill up the cup with water while I sat there and watched him. Once the cup was filled, he picked it up and brought it to me.

"Here you go."

"Thanks," I said as I grabbed the cup.

Devon sat down and said, "Shall we begin to eat? I know you're going to love the food."

"Yes, that sounds great," I said as we began to eat. The food was in an excellent arrangement, but I still didn't know what any of it was.

"Okay, so what is all of this?" I asked staring at the plate.

"Oh sorry," Devon said and began to point at my food as he talked. "This is a Greek salad, with olives and feta cheese. This is the lamb that I asked you about, that's a pita, and then here on the side is pita bread and hummus. You are going to want to try the pita bread and hummus first. Trust me."

"Okay," I said as I picked up one of the pita breads. I dipped it into hummus, like a chip in dip and then took a bit. It was really good.

"This is really good," I told Devon.

"Oh wait until you try the rest. You know some people don't like hummus, but most people like it here when they try it. I am glad you liked it. I knew you would," Devon said smiling.

"Yes. I do like it a lot."

I was eager to see how everything else tasted. I started on to the rest of the food. It was all amazing.

"So Devon, how come you didn't make it to class today?"

"Oh, remember I was working on my project?"

"I know, but what is the project that you're working on all about? You were saying that it was about how dolphins interact. What does that mean?"

"Well, it could actually mean a lot of things, but I'm concentrating on something specific. I want to know how dolphins talk," Devon said.

"What do you mean how they talk?"

"Just that, dolphins can talk. They talk just like you and me."

I was in shock.

"But how is that possible?" I asked.

"It has a lot to do with a dolphin's brain size. A dolphin's brain size is very close in size to a human's brain. It's been known for years that dolphins can talk to each other. But no one has really figured out how they talk and what they are saying. I want to unlock the language that they speak. That's why I'm trying to get an account of what you witnessed. I have some recordings that were taken from the ship on the day that you fell in the water. I want to match the video with what you say happened."

"Recordings?"

"Yes, recordings. It's just a standard video recording, and also an audio. The original recording was kind of faint at first, but I increased the volume and tried to wash out a lot of the background stuff on the audio. Then I matched it up with the video. I wrote down what I saw and ran it through the computer."

"What did the computer show you?"

"A few things, here let me show you," Devon said as he pulled out his phone and selected a video player.

"Here you can see a combination of the dolphins swimming and the audio at the same time," Devon said. The video showed just what happened.

"You see, that's you," Devon said as he was pointing at a figure in the water. I was sure it was me as I looked at the video.

"Yep, that's me."

"And here are the dolphins coming toward you. Do you hear how their actions are reflecting their movements?"

"It looks like they're talking," I said.

Oddly enough, I couldn't hear them talking when I watched the video. The dolphins just sounded like dolphins are supposed to sound, with high-pitched squeaking.

Maybe I just imagined the whole thing about them talking when I was in the water. But it seemed so real. How could I have heard the dolphins talk when I was in the water after my fall—but not hear the dolphins talking when I watched the video? I must be losing it.

"So anyways, I just wanted to write down your account of what happened. Do you mind if I record you?"

"No of course not," I responded.

"Good," Devon said and then pulled out of his bag a notebook, a pen, and a tape recorder.

"Alright. I need you to start from the beginning."

"Okay," I said and took a deep breath. "I remember I was sitting there on the deck of the ship. I was writing down my observations, and then I heard something. I'm not sure what it was that I heard. Then I leaned in toward the edge of the deck because I wanted to see what it was that was making the noise. I was hoping I could listen to the sound that I had heard better if I leaned in. Well, I somehow leaned too far and fell. I remember falling, and then I remember looking back after I recovered a little from my fall. I saw the ship floating away from me. The ship was moving far away very quickly. I tried to swim toward the ship as it left me behind.

"I remember seeing fins come out of the water suddenly and thinking they might be sharks. I tried to swim away, but the fins caught up to me. I was afraid and then I realized it was okay because they were dolphins. It looked like the first dolphin looked at the second dolphin and shook its head, and then the first dolphin came toward me and then waited. I grabbed on to the dolphin's fin and then the dolphin started swimming toward the ship."

Devon interrupted me.

"Did you scream or make any noise that might have gotten the dolphin's attention as you were swimming toward the ship?"

"No, not that I recall. I did ask for help though. I was yelling it out toward the ship. Then the dolphins came. I grabbed onto the first one, and it swam me to the ship. As I was being carried toward the ship, I saw you jumping in the water to rescue me."

"So all of this happened really quickly?" Devon asked.

"Yes, but it didn't seem like it was quick while it was happening. Some parts of it seemed like they were in slow motion. Before I knew it, you were saving me. Thank you again by the way. I am so grateful that you jumped in the water when you did."

"No problem," Devon said as he shut off the tape recorder.

"Okay. I think I have everything that I need for my research," Devon said as he put away all of his stuff in his bag and turned toward me.

"Aurora, do you want to take a walk? There is a really nice place near here, and you might enjoy it."

"Yeah. I think I would like that."

"Okay, let's go," Devon said, and we started to walk down a path in front of the Greek restaurant.

"So did you like the Greek food?" Devon asked changing the subject from dolphins back to the here and now.

"Yes, it was great. It was a little different than I was used to, but I liked it a lot."

Devon looked relieved when I said I liked the food. It seemed like he had been worried that I wouldn't like the food. It was sweet of him.

We continued to walk a little further down the path, and then Devon said, "Hey, can we stop by this place? I need to get a hat. I need it for the ship when it goes out. I've been meaning to get one."

"Yeah of course."

Devon and I walked toward a nice little hat shop. Inside there were all sorts of hats. I stood in the corner of the store and watched while he bought his hat. Then we walked out of the store together. He reached into a bag from the hat store. He pulled out a cute light pink beanie.

"Is that the hat you've been meaning to buy?" I asked laughing.

"No silly."

Devon then put the cute beanie on my head. He pulled out and put a blue one on his head as well.

"Thanks," I said.

"I don't want you to get cold next time you're on the ship."

"Thank you. I love it," I said as we continued to walk a little further down the path.

We finally got to this nice beautiful path that was different than the path that we had started on. The path had trees everywhere and was right next to the bay. There were boats on one side of the pathway and the beautiful bay on the other side. The water was calm. We started to walk a little down the new path and then both of us sat on the nice bench that was facing the water.

"Nice night, isn't it?" Devon asked.

"Yes it is."

Then after a minute had passed by, Devon grabbed my hand. At first I wanted to pull away, but I didn't. I let him hold my hand. When Devon held my hand, it felt so nice as we sat there and watched the bay. The moonlight lit the bay, and you could see everything in detail. It had a romantic hue to it, and it was so beautiful.

After about thirty minutes, Devon said, "Well anyways, I think we should head back. It is getting late."

But I didn't want to go. I was having so much fun just sitting there with Devon. He was right though. It was getting late.

"Okay, that sounds good."

We both got up and walked back toward the car holding hands the whole way. When we got to the car, Devon opened the door for me, and I got in.

As we drove off on the way back to my dorm, Devon asked, "I was wondering if you wanted to hang out again?"

"Do you mean like another non-date?" I said jokingly.

"No," Devon said with a chuckle. "A real date, I promise."

"A real date, huh? Okay, sounds good. I think I would like that very much," I said.

Devon gave a boyish grin.

"Okay, how about Friday?"

"Yeah, that sounds good. Friday works for me," I said.

It would be good to go on Friday because it would be the end of the week. I would have plenty of time to catch upon my studies.

"Okay, Friday it is," Devon said.

Before I knew it, we had parked the car and walked back to my dorm room. When we got to my door, Devon let go of my hand.

"Well my dear Aurora, I will see you later. Thank you very much for everything, and I hope you had fun."

"Oh yes, I did have lots of fun. Thank you."

Then Devon leaned into me and gave me a hug. It was a good hug.

"Have a good night," Devon whispered into my ear.

"You too," I whispered back.

It felt so nice even for a moment to be so close to Devon. Then Devon let me go.

"Take care," Devon said.

"You too."

I stumbled around to look for my keys. I found them and opened my door. I gave Devon one last wave goodbye and then closed the door. It had been a long day, but I wanted to text Erica.

"I finished with my date," I texted while smiling.

At this point, there wasn't any use in fighting it. That was, for all accounts and purposes, a date. Maybe it didn't start out as a date, but that was definitely how it ended. I quickly got a text back.

"Oh I want to hear all about it. Can I talk to you tomorrow morning?"

"Yes, I can't wait to talk to you."

"Night," Erica responded.

I couldn't wait to talk to Erica in the morning. I went to bed right after that.

When morning came, I woke up and headed out. I texted Erica asking her where she wanted to meet at.

"The same place we always meet at," Erica responded.

We had arranged to meet at 9 a.m. at the college café. Sure enough, when I arrived at the college café, Erica was there just like she had promised.

"Hi Aurora," Erica said in a happy voice.

"Hi Erica."

Erica had a nice bagel waiting for me.

"Take a seat and tell me all about the awesome date with Devon."

"The date was wonderful," I began.

"Okay, so what happened? I want all the details."

Erica seemed so excited like it had been her who went on a date.

"Well, Devon picked me up, and then we drove to this place that he had planned on taking me. It was a nice little Greek restaurant at Oceanport. I tried some Greek food for the first time in my life. It was really good."

"And did he actually ask you anything about falling in the water?" Erica asked.

"Oh, he did ask me about that. We talked about how I fell in. He showed me a recording with the dolphins and then asked me about what they had done when I fell in the water."

"Dolphins?" Erica asked.

"Yeah, he showed me a video with the dolphins as they came over and rescued me and swam me over to the ship."

"Oh, and then what happened?" Erica asked.

"Well, after we talked about all of the details with the dolphins, Devon asked me if I wanted to go on a walk. I said I would love to."

"Oh, I see," Erica said excitedly.

"Yep, and then we walked by all of these beautiful trees. It was so picturesque and serene. The bay was on one side, and boats were on another. Then we sat on this bench and watched the beautiful bay while he held my hand."

"Oh nice, and then what happened?" Erica asked prying me for details as she raised her eyebrows.

"Nothing happened. It was nice. We just sat there and held hands while watching the beautiful water and looking at each other. I felt so close to him. Even though we didn't do anything but sit, it was wonderful. Then it started getting late so we got up and headed back to the dorm."

"Aww, that's sweet! Did he ask you if you wanted to go out again?" Erica asked.

"Yes, he did ask and I said I would gladly go on a date with him."

"Oh, it sounds like you had a nice little date. I want to hear all about the next one too. Okay? I have to live vicariously through you for now. I hope you don't mind," Erica said.

"It's okay. I don't mind if you live through me. But now I need your opinion. Do you think all of this is going to be a big distraction?"

I asked because I needed a second opinion. Erica thought about it for a moment.

"No. I don't think so. I think you have to follow your heart when the time comes. But just don't let it take up too much of your time. School is still important, but so is this," Erica said.

I was happy to hear Erica say that. It was just what I needed to hear.

"You're right. I don't think this will interfere with my studies. At least I hope it doesn't," I said.

Just then, I felt my stomach rumble from being so hungry.

"Well, let's eat this breakfast. I'm starving," I said as I took a bite out of my bagel.

Chapter 16

Devon

The week passed by quickly and before I knew it, it was Friday. I had managed to knock out most of my assignments and would have plenty of time tonight for my date without having to stress about keeping up with my school work later.

I think Erica was right. I can manage this.

I started to get ready for my date. Stacey was there, and I had mentioned to her earlier that I was going on a date. Stacey had heard sometime during the week about Devon from Jessica. I knew that they had talked about Devon and me a few times. Sometimes when I would walk into the dorm room, I would overhear them chit chatting about Devon and me. It was never anything negative, but Stacey had never actually asked me anything about it directly.

"Stacey, I was wondering if you would help me pick out an outfit."

I had come to terms by now with the fact that I had little to no fashion sense, but I was learning. In the meantime, I didn't want Devon to know that I had no idea what to wear.

"Oh, so you really do have a date?" Stacey asked with a big smile.

"Maybe I do," I said. I didn't mind her asking.

"With who?"

"Do you know who Devon is?"

"Yes. He is that cute graduate student, but…"

"But what?"

"But he doesn't date. I know he's a heartthrob, but honestly, I've known lots of girls who have tried to date him, but he wouldn't go out with any of them. His kind usually stays to themselves from what I've seen," Stacey said. Then there was another pause.

What Stacey had said made me think. Why was he going out with me then? I didn't even want to really think about it. I guess I should feel lucky, but I've seen the girls that Stacey hangs out with. They are the cheerleader types, and all of them know fashion. If he didn't like those types of girls, then why was he talking to me? Why was he going out with me?

Just then as I had got lost in my thoughts, Stacey exclaimed, "I thought you didn't know fashion. You have some nice stuff here. Where did you get all these nice clothes?"

"Oh my aunt. She is into fashion. She has some fashion line or something.

"What is your aunt's name?" Stacey asked

"Carrie Livingston," I said.

"That's your aunt. Oh my gosh! I love her clothes. That explains why you have so many high-end things here. I would love to meet your aunt some time if it's not too much trouble," Stacey said excitedly.

"Of course, I can introduce you later if you would like."

"I would absolutely love that. Anyways, I have good news. I think I've found just the outfit for your date tonight. What do you think?"

I took a look at Stacey's selection.

"It's nice," I said.

It really was nice. Stacey had picked a pink skirt suit. It had black pieces across the board. The black board heels that she had picked out were also nice.

"I think Devon is going to like it. Thank you."

"I hope you have fun on your date Aurora. If you ever need help again, don't forget to ask."

"Okay, thank you. I'll try to remember."

I then went and got dressed. It was almost time for Devon to pick me up so I had to hurry. Because I rushed, I managed to get ready with ten minutes to spare. I took a glance at the mirror and had Stacey take a look and check everything.

"Yep, I was right. You look good."

"Thanks again for your help."

Just then there was someone knocking at the door.

I looked through the security hole, and there was Devon.

"Devon's here!" I whispered to Stacey.

"Okay, have fun," Stacey said again.

"Thank you. I will talk to you later."

I opened the door and saw Devon. Devon looked even better than he had before.

"Hi," I said as I stood in the doorway.

"Hi, are you ready to go?"

"Yes I am."

"Okay, let's go,"

The two of us walked side by side holding hands toward his car. When we got to the car, he opened the door for me like a true gentleman. When we were both in the car, he reached for something. It was a flower broach.

"I hope you like these sort of things. I thought this would look good on you," Devon said.

"Yes I do. Thank you."

He proceeded to lean in to pin the broach on me.

"Do you mind if I…?" he said gesturing the pinning motion.

"Oh no of course. Go right ahead," I said as I moved in closer to Devon as he placed the broach on me. As far as I could tell, the broach looked nice on me. The broach was a star-patterned flower arrangement. It was a bit old-fashioned but still looked nice with my outfit.

"So where are we going?" I asked with an eager voice as we began to drive off.

"Oh now that is a surprise my dear Aurora."

"Okay, well, I can't wait to see."

"Don't worry. I know you'll like it," Devon said as he drove.

We drove away from the college and went through downtown San Diego.

"So how are your studies going? I know the first year of college can be a little tough," Devon said.

"Yeah, it can be a little hectic, but it is moving nicely. I guess once you get used to it, things start to roll. How are your studies going?"

"Oh, they are going good. I will have to show you some of my research sometime. I think you mentioned that you like oceanography. You might like what I am researching."

"I am still confused. What exactly are you studying?"

"Well, I hadn't wanted to tell you before because some people think it's a little crazy."

"Don't worry. I won't think it's crazy."

"Okay, you promise?"

"Yes I promise."

"Okay, I'm trying to figure out how dolphins talk. I mean, I actually think there is a language, and dolphins are crazy smart, so if they do have a language of some sort, then it will give us access to all sorts of knowledge from their perspective."

He seemed so excited when he was telling me. I could see the passion in him when it came to this subject.

"Wow, that is amazing! How did you come up with that idea?" I asked very intrigued.

"Oh well, um…" There was a pause, and then we pulled into a parking lot. "Actually, I will have to tell you that a little later because we're here."

I looked out the window of the car and noticed that we were at a pier so I was a bit confused because it didn't look like a restaurant of any sort. There really wasn't much here. I didn't see any signs of restaurants or anything like that. There were just a few small boats and a stand.

As we got out of the car, Devon escorted me to the stand and said, "Reservation for Devon Karolos."

"Oh yes of course. Please sign here," the man said and handed Devon a paper. Devon signed the paper, and then the man gave Devon a key. The man then brought me and Devon to a nice boat.

"What is this?"

"It's our date, my dear Aurora," Devon said.

We then walked over to the boat and both got in and began to set sail. Devon drove the boat, of course, as I sat and watched him. This was only the second boat that I had ever been on. Devon drove the boat like he had been driving it for years. We pulled into a pier at Coronado where a guy was waiting for us with some bags. The man at the pier handed Devon a paper, and Devon signed it, gave the guy a tip, and took the bags.

"Dinner," Devon said with a smile as he raised the bags a little. "I hope you don't mind. I wanted to surprise you so I ordered for you."

"No. I don't mind."

Then we pulled out from the pier and went further out to sea. When we were far enough out, Devon stopped the boat, and then we just floated. It was calm and the bay was beautiful out here. You could see the downtown skyline. The stars and even the moon added to the scene. The nicest part was it was quiet, and we were alone. There were no distractions in the world. It was just Devon and I. He started to take the food out and set it on a small table. Then we sat at the table and enjoyed the moonlight.

Devon had put on a slow romantic song. It was something that I hadn't heard before, but it didn't matter because it was beautiful.

"Would you like to eat?" Devon asked sitting next to all of the food he had laid out.

"Yes, I would love that."

The food included a lovely salad and spaghetti, with my choice of orange juice or water. I chose the orange juice.

"So tell me my dear, are you impressed?" Devon asked with a smirk.

I smiled.

"Oh yes, it's so nice out here. I like that we can be alone. Thank you for bringing me."

"You're welcome. I actually brought you out here because this is one of my favorite places. It's so quiet out here. It's nice because you can't hear the city, but you can see it. It makes it almost majestic, and the sky is so nice. I love it when it's dark, not too dark, but dark enough to really see the stars. You can really see the stars out here. The stars illuminate so well out here that it's almost hypnotic. It's like staring into forever. It's just a nice place to relax and think about things."

"Yes, it's nice. I can see what you mean. It is like this is our own little world out here," I said staring at the stars.

"So tell me about yourself. I want to know all about you, Aurora."

"Oh well, um…," I said surprised. I had never had anyone take such an interest in me.

"Well, I came from a very small town in Alaska. I had dreamed of leaving Alaska all of my life and that's why I am in college here in San Diego. I want to get a fresh start out of Alaska and study oceanography. I really want to know how the ocean works. What about you?" I asked to return the question. I was actually very excited to finally find out all about Devon.

"Well, there isn't really much to tell. I was in Navy for four years. I was an Aviation Ordnance man and then a Naval Diver for a little bit. While I was in the Navy, I decided to go to college so I got out. Then I worked really hard and got to where I am at now. I am from upstate New York, but I plan on staying here in San Diego. I didn't like it there too much and that's about it," Devon said.

It sounded like he didn't talk about himself very often.

"Wow, that's really nice! What were you saying about dolphins earlier? I thought that was really interesting."

"Oh yeah. I was telling you where I got the idea from, but you have to promise not to think I'm crazy."

"Yep, I promise. I won't think you're crazy."

"Well, it all started when I was little. My family is Greek and comes from some ancient line that was part of an Aphrodite cult. I know that sounds weird, but when I was a kid, I was told all these legends about how Aphrodite could talk to dolphins. Then when I was going to college, I learned a little bit about dolphins and how smart they are. Then one day it hit me. I thought, 'this is it!' This is what I'm meant to do. I'm meant to unlock the language of the dolphins and talk to them, so that I can see what they see and know what they know."

"Wow, you are really passionate about this."

"Yes I am, and it's because we are so close in intelligence to the dolphins. But I don't tell most people about dolphins talking because they would think I was crazy. But I feel like I can trust you. I can, right?" Devon said and gazed at me for a second.

"Yes of course, you can. I won't tell anyone about it. Thank you for trusting me with what you are studying. It means a lot to me."

"Oh, you're welcome. I trust you because I have a good feeling about you. You are different somehow."

Just then as we finished that part of the conversation, fireworks started to go off in the distance.

"Oh, this was part of the reason I brought you out here. I hope you like fireworks," Devon said.

"Oh, I love them."

With that, I sat next to Devon, and we watched the beautiful fireworks display. As one of the fireworks went off, Devon put his arm around my shoulder. Then at the grand finale, as all the fireworks were going off at once, Devon leaned in toward me and gave me a kiss. It was a deep, passionate kiss. It was so good. The kiss lasted for a few minutes, well after the fireworks had finished.

Then we sat there next to each other.

"Did you enjoy the fireworks?" Devon asked me. With every word that came from his mouth, my heart pounded more and more.

"It was so wonderful. Thank you for showing me."

"Oh good! I'm glad you liked it. I really wanted this night to be special. I wanted you to feel special."

I didn't want to spoil the evening, but when Devon said that he wanted to make me feel special, I wanted to know what he thought was so special about me. But I decided not to ask.

"You look so nice under the moonlight," Devon said.

"Thank you," I said not really knowing what else to say. I had never had a guy compliment me so much or treat me this nicely. With each rock of the boat, the night seemed to stand still like we were in a timeless capsule—a magical timeless capsule—as if we were the stars themselves. We turned toward each other and locked eyes. Then Devon kissed me again, but this time it wasn't as long a kiss as the first kiss had been. But after this kiss, I moved away.

"I'm sorry. Did I do something wrong?"

"No. I just don't want to move too fast."

"Don't worry. We won't, I promise," Devon said with the sincerest voice.

"I would never do anything too soon with you and would never force you to do anything. I want this thing that we have—this very magical thing—to not get spoiled by anything. I won't let it," Devon said. A smile came over my face as I heard him say this. It made me feel at home with Devon.

"Thank you," I said.

We waited a few minutes longer holding each other and then Devon asked, "Would you mind if we headed back now? I have some volunteer work to do in the morning, and I don't want to be too tired for it."

"No, I don't mind. That would be fine if we headed back now."

"Thank you," Devon said.

Then Devon drove the ship back to the pier. He turned in the boat keys to the man that we got it from. Then we got to his car. We didn't talk to each other much till we got back to the dorm.

Devon leaned over across his seat toward mine and said, "I had a lot of fun tonight. I was wondering if you wanted to go out again tomorrow night. I wanted to see a movie and thought you might like to join me."

"Yes of course. I would love to!" I said gladly. I was happy that he still wanted to go out with me. Devon then got out of the car and opened the door for me. He grabbed my hand, helped me out of the car, and then held my hand as we walked.

When we arrived at my dorm, Devon leaned in and gave me one final kiss and said, "My dear Aurora, I will see you tomorrow. Thank you for a wonderful night."

"Thank you. I had fun."

"I had fun too. I will see you tomorrow," Devon said.

"See you tomorrow."

I headed into my dorm room. Oddly enough, nobody was up in my room when I walked in. It looked like everyone had suddenly passed out. It was just as well so that I didn't have to tell either one of my roommates about the perfect date. It was mine for right now, and I wanted to keep it just mine, at least until tomorrow. Then I would have to tell everyone about what happened. I headed off to bed, hoping that all of this hadn't been some fantastic dream.

Chapter 17

Romance or Adventure

The next day, Stacey and Erica had both woken up much earlier than me. Stacey came over to me and woke me up.

"Hey sleepy, wake up and come eat breakfast with us. We want to hear about your date," Stacey said with an entirely too excited of a voice for a Saturday morning. I started to get up and headed over to the table.

"So tell us what happened," Stacey said as both she and Jessica watched me start to wake up.

I grabbed a bagel and orange juice, and then said, "Well, it's a bit early, isn't it? Besides, it was just a date." This response didn't satisfy their curiosities.

"Yeah, but how was it? What is Devon like?" Stacey asked.

"Oh, he's nice. He is really sweet. Devon took me on a boat, and we ate dinner under the moonlight. It was so nice. You could see the stars and everything."

"Oh, I'm so jealous," Stacey said with a real sense of truth in her tone as though she was actually jealous.

"You are so lucky Aurora. Are you guys going out again?" Jessica asked.

"Yes, we're going out tonight to the movies in fact."

"Oh that's nice. It is the real test," Stacey said.

"What do you mean?"

"Well, if he goes for the chick flick, then he really cares about what you want. But if he picks the guy adventure fighting type of movie, then he's more about himself than you. It's true about 85% of the time. I read a study about it," Jessica said.

"Huh, well I didn't know that. Well, I will have to see which one he picks then," I said.

I continued to eat my breakfast as talk about my date died down. Besides having an abrupt awaking to find out what my date was all about, my day turned out to be a rather normal day. I just kind of relaxed and called my mom who complained of course about me not spending enough time with my aunt. I didn't mention to my mom that I had met someone. I figured I would save that news if it got more serious between Devon and I.

Before I knew it, it was time for the movies. Devon picked me up, and we went straight to the movie theater. I was excited to see what kind of a movie Devon was going to pick. Sure enough, Devon had selected a romantic film.

"Are you sure?" I asked insisting that we could see whatever movie he wanted to see.

"Yes. I want to see Swan Lake," Devon said.

The movie was the latest romance book turned movie, with twists and turns of ultimate true love around every corner. The funny part was when Devon told me that he wanted to see the movie, I believed him. There wasn't a shred of doubt or resentment in him about wanting to see a romantic movie. We went inside the theater, and he immediately held my hand as we shared popcorn. The movie was good, but the company was better. I found myself distracted by Devon the whole time.

After the movie, Devon asked, "Would you care to take a walk?"

"I would love it Devon."

We began to walk along a nice path. That's what I liked about Devon. He was the right kind of guy. He would talk to me but never too much and rarely about himself. He always let me chime in and say what I thought about things. I tried to be careful not to intrude on his opinion. But it was like we were having magical discussions. Discussions I had never had with anyone else. When we finally reached a bench, it happened. What I thought wouldn't happen this soon did.

"Would you like to sit for a minute?" Devon asked. He looked like he was shaking a little, but I wasn't sure from what.

"Yes of course," I said as we sat down.

Devon turned and locked his eyes on mine and said, "Aurora, I've thought about it. I wanted to know if you wanted to be my girlfriend."

"I would love to be your girlfriend," I said without hesitation.

I was so happy. Devon leaned over and gave me a nice long kiss.

I wasn't sure what being Devon's girlfriend fully meant, but I liked it. The time after that passed without any notice. For the rest of the date, all I could think about was that I was Devon's girlfriend. After that date ended, other dates came. Devon and I started to hang out together a lot. Being together with each other became the new norm. We went to all sorts of places together. We went to almost every restaurant in San Diego. I even introduced him to my aunt and uncle who loved him at once.

Even after all that, life seemed very normal for me and Devon. All of my friends liked us together. Devon and I were a cute couple. Everything was for all intents and purposes perfect. Then something changed.

Chapter 18

Surprise

The day had started like any other. I did my normal routine, and then I ran into Devon. Over the months that we had been going out, Devon liked to take me to different places.

Today was no different, so when Devon asked, "Would you like to go to the aquarium? They have a really nice one here in San Diego. I can get us in to check out the dolphins. I have a surprise if you go."

"Yes, I would love to," I said.

I mean, how I could pass up the aquarium? I had never been to one, and I had always wanted to go. I loved the ocean and an aquarium would give me a chance to see some of the animals that I had always dreamed of seeing. When Devon and I entered the gates of the aquarium, it was like an aquatic Wonderland. There were so many different types of fish and sea animals. Everything was so wonderful.

"I have a surprise for you Aurora," Devon said as we started walking toward one side of the aquarium.

"What surprise?" I said with a smile.

"You'll see," Devon said.

We entered an entrance that said "employees only" on the top of the doorway.

"Devon we can't go in here. It's for employees only."

"Don't worry. I got connections, and this is the surprise. Just follow me."

Devon walked through the entrance like he had been here before, perhaps in one of his volunteer events. It made sense because this place is all about the ocean and that was what Devon was studying. Then I saw them: the most beautiful dolphins I had ever seen. But then after a few moments, I began to hear voices.

It was the same kind of voices that I had heard the day I had fallen off the ship. I had almost forgotten the way the voices sounded. I got scared—scared of what it meant. Was I crazy? I couldn't stand it so I ran out of the room.

"Aurora wait! I want you to see….Where are you going?" Devon said as he turned to see where I had gone.

I ran all the way past the entrance to the employee's only sign and sat on a nearby bench.

Devon followed me and sat next to me and asked, "What's the matter?"

I was embarrassed and scared when Devon asked me.

"I don't want to tell you," I said.

"Why, what's the matter?" Devon kept on asking and asking me.

I started crying. I didn't want my boyfriend after all of this time to think I was crazy. I was so scared of losing everything I had with Devon.

"You can tell me what it is Aurora. I love you," Devon said as he put his arm around my shoulder. After a few minutes, I had to come to terms with it. I had to tell him. He was the one I loved, and I wanted him to know the truth. I looked at him with my tear-filled eyes.

"Do you promise you'll try to understand?" I asked, staring at the ground.

"Yes of course," Devon said. He had such a concerned look on his face.

"Do you remember that day the dolphins saved me?"

"Yes I remember," Devon said.

"Well, on that day I didn't tell you something. Something I wasn't sure of until now."

Then there was a pause.

"You can tell me, I will listen."

"Okay, please don't think I'm crazy. On that day when the dolphins came up to me, I could hear them."

"What do you mean?" Devon asked with a confused look on his face.

"I can hear them talk. I understand the dolphins. I thought I was imagining it. I wanted to forget all about how I could hear them talking. But when I went in the room with you just now and saw the dolphins, I could hear them again. I can hear them talk Devon. The same as you and I are talking right now. Do you think I'm crazy?" I asked still in tears.

"No, I don't think you are going crazy my dear Aurora."

"You don't?" I said surprised.

"No, I don't. I love you Aurora, and I always will. If you say that you can hear dolphins talk, then I believe you."

"Oh thank you. I was so worried that you would leave me."

"I will never leave you. I promise."

"Oh, I love you, Devon," I said as I turned toward him and stared at him.

"I love you too," Devon said and then Devon said in a more cheerful voice. "Well, there is only one way to find out if you can or can't hear dolphins talk."

"What's that?" I asked.

"Let's go test it out inside," Devon said.

"Are you sure?"

"Yes, let's go find out. Who knows, you might actually be able to talk to the dolphins. Wouldn't that be something?" Devon asked excitedly.

"Okay, I'll give it a try," I said, and then we headed back inside.

When we walked in, Devon talked to the dolphin trainers.

"I was wondering if we could have some one-on-one time with the dolphins. My girlfriend is very excited and wants to get the full experience."

"Of course, Devon. You barely have to ask. Just go to the usual training pool. There are a few dolphins doing free swim, and they haven't had their training for the day. You can let your girlfriend help train them, just suit up."

"Are you a good swimmer dear?" the trainer asked me.

"I'm fair," I said.

"Okay good enough. I know Devon will watch out for you. I think the number three-size suit will fit you," the trainer said.

"Thanks," I said as I reached for the number three suit. It was pink and had a nice surf design on it. I went to the changing room and put the pink suit on. It looked good I thought.

"What do you think Devon," I said as I came out from the changing room.

"Looks good honey, you look absolutely great," Devon said as he looked me over. While I had changed, Devon had changed too, and he was wearing a blue wetsuit. We both walked out to the training pool and were given whistles.

"Okay Aurora, let's see if you can hear the dolphins talk," Devon said. He was careful to make sure that no one could hear him say that. Devon blew the whistle, and two dolphins appeared from under the water and came toward us.

The dolphins were moving fast—faster than I had imagined they would. Then a deep, wrenching feeling hit my gut as I saw Devon warm up the dolphins by using a few hand gestures. It was weird—maybe I was crazy. I didn't hear the dolphins talking—not one single word.

"Anything?" Devon asked with an enthusiastic schoolboy-like tone.

"No, nothing yet," I said.

Just as I had said that I hadn't heard anything, I began to hear words coming from the water.

"Who do you think this is?" I heard a voice say. Almost instantaneously, I heard another voice answer back

"Oh that's that one trainer. I'm not sure where he comes from, but he is nice. He's not too crazy with his commands. But I'm not sure who this other one is. There is something different about her."

Just then I saw the dolphins coming over toward me with their mouths wide open and making a high-pitched screech.

"Wow, they are really going at it! Did you catch any of it?"

I was still half amazed at how well Devon had come to terms with my whole ability to talk to dolphins.

"Yes I did," I said.

"Well, what did they say?" Devon asked.

"One of the dolphins asked the other who we were. The other one said they knew who you were and that you were nice, but they didn't know who I was."

"Wow, are you sure you caught all that from the screeching?"

"No, it's as though the screeching doesn't matter that much, at least it didn't seem like it did. The way they talk is based on something else. I don't know. It's like I could hear their thoughts or something."

"Okay Aurora, do you want to try something new with the dolphins?"

"What is that?" I said.

What could he be planning now?

"Well, I have a sort of test to see if the dolphins can understand you better than they can understand most people. You see, we train these dolphins based on trial and error. When they do something we like, we give them a nice spray with this bottle. The problem with it is that it takes a few tries to learn a new trick. We use positive reinforcement. I want to see if you can teach them how to jump out of the water by talking with them faster than I could normally by using positive reinforcement."

"Alright, that doesn't sound too bad," I said.

"Okay good."

"How do you want them to jump?" I asked.

"Anyway you can think of. Be creative. See if you can get them to do a flip. They have been having trouble doing that."

"Okay, should I get in the water?" I asked.

"Yeah, that's fine," Devon said.

I jumped into the water and swam over to the dolphins. They both came over to me eagerly, and then I said, "Can you understand me?"

There was no answer so I asked it again.

"Can you understand me?"

"Yes," one of the dolphins said.

"How can we understand you?" the same dolphin asked.

"I don't know," I said.

"What is your name?" the dolphin asked.

"I am Aurora. What are your names?" I asked.

"I am Isidor and he is Ion," one of the dolphins said.

"Well Isidor and Ion, I was wondering if you wouldn't mind doing a trick for me," I asked in what I think is a polite tone for speaking dolphin.

"Of course, we love to do tricks," Ion said.

"Good. I was wondering if both of you could jump at the same time out of the water and do a flip for me."

"Like this Aurora?" Ion asked and did a flip.

"Yes, that is great," I said and then asked, "Can you both do that?"

"Of course we can," they both said in unison and did a flip at the same time.

The flip was perfectly in unison.

"How did you get them to do that?" Devon asked excitedly.

"I just asked them to," I said.

"And they talked back?" Devon asked.

"Yes," I responded.

"Do you know what this means?" Devon asked.

That I'm not nuts?

"No, not fully. What does it mean?" I asked.

"This means that we can unlock the language of the dolphins. I am so excited," Devon said.

"I can tell."

"Aren't you excited?" Devon asked.

I was actually happy but concerned about what it all meant. I tried to hide my concern though as best I could.

"Yes of course. I'm happy. Do you want me to ask them anything else?" I asked, directing the attention back to Isidor and Ion who were waiting patiently.

"Not for now. You can try to talk more if you want."

"Okay," I said and turned back to the dolphins.

"Nice job, Ion and Isidor. That was perfect. "

"Thank you Aurora. We are glad that you liked it. Do you want us to do anything else?" Isidor asked.

"No, that was it, thank you," I said.

"So we were wondering if you were coming here again anytime soon." Isidor said.

"I'm not sure, but we'll see," I said.

"That would be great," Isidor said.

"Well, it was nice to have talked to you. I will let you go for now. Thank you for performing that trick for me."

"It was nice talking with you too. If you come again, we can do more tricks for you. We are good at them and love to perform," both dolphins said and then went around playing in the pool.

I got out of the pool after that. Devon asked if we could go inside.

"I have to pick up a copy of the tapes from this session," Devon said.

"What tapes?" I asked.

"Oh we're recording this. They record anyways for security, but I will often get a copy for my research. You know, it was amazing. I still can't get over the fact that you can actually talk to them. Was it weird when you talked to them or was it like a normal conversation?" Devon asked.

"It was as normal as me talking to you," I said.

Devon seemed so excited. I could tell I had touched the boy side of him. It was a side I hadn't seen before, and I was happy to see it.

"So where do we go after this?" I asked.

"Well, this was like a pre-experiment. Now I have to figure out a real system for deciphering their language. It might take some time, but I will let you know as soon as I come up with something," Devon said.

"Okay," I said.

Devon then walked out of the room and left me to change while he got his tapes. While I was changing, I started to think.

What could it all mean? What am I supposed to do now? Maybe I should become something besides an oceanographer. But what should I be? I've been given a gift. Maybe I should use it for something.

Just as I had finished changing and getting lost in my thoughts, Devon came back.

"Alright Aurora, you ready to go?" Devon asked.

He was dressed nicely.

"Yeah I'm ready. Where are we going now?"

"Well, I want to take you somewhere nice to eat of course. You didn't think this was the end of our date, did you?" Devon asked.

"No, of course not, but don't you want to do more research or find out what all of this means?"

"Not just yet, my dear. I want to have my date with you. I don't want any of this to interfere with how I feel about you. Besides, I'm hungry," Devon said.

I was happy to hear that. That was the other thing Devon was good at. He helped me not to worry as much. We went on our date, and it was nice. We ate at a restaurant by the bay. For the rest of the evening, Devon and I enjoyed each other's company. I was the happiest I had ever been in my whole life. I couldn't picture myself doing anything else with anyone else. Right in that moment of time, everything was perfect.

Chapter 19

Sometimes Even Breakfast Brings an Opportunity

About a week passed since I had officially confirmed with Devon that I could talk to dolphins. In that time, I hadn't seen much of him. He was busy with research, and I had got busy with school. As I woke up one morning, I suddenly felt like I hadn't seen Erica in a while. I missed her a great deal. I pulled out my phone and sent her a text, "Hey, how's it going? Do you want to hang out?"

"Where?" Erica texted back quickly, which surprised me because it was still early.

"Why not the cafeteria?"

"Sounds good, do you want to meet there now?"

"Yeah."

"Okay, I'll see you there," Erica replied. I was excited. I hadn't seen Erica for a little bit, and it was nice to catch up whenever I could. I walked to the cafeteria, and there was Erica waiting outside.

"Hey Erica, how's it going?"

"Oh I'm good. I've been busy with everything. How have you been?"

"Oh I'll tell you all about it, but first let's get something to eat. I'm starving," I said as my stomach began to grumble.

"Okay, I couldn't agree more. I'm starving too."

We got our food and then took a seat.

"So how are you and Devon?"

"Oh we're good. These days we've been doing a lot of stuff together. I haven't had too much trouble juggling school and my love life, which is good. Do you remember how worried I was? I think there was nothing to worry about all along with love interfering with school. So what have you been up to?"

"Well, I've actually been really busy. It's probably why I haven't been able to see you. I forgot to tell you, I started working at the local museum. One of the professors told me I had a real knack for ancient Greek history and recruited me for his historical team. So I've been busy with that."

I could tell she was really in her element when she was describing the whole thing. I was really happy for her.

"Oh really Erica! You should have told me I know that was your dream. I know you really wanted to work with that kind of stuff. You are so lucky. I wish I had known so I could have visited you at the museum while you were working."

"Yeah, it is awesome. I really get to be hands on with historical stuff. I love to do the restoration of the ancient artifacts and stuff like that. You should come by sometime—you and Devon, that is. I will show you guys everything."

"Yeah, that would be great. I'm sure Devon and I would love that. I will have to ask him. He has been busy this last week. Devon made a discovery that is really helping him with his research project."

I pulled out my phone and texted Devon, "Hey, do you want to check out the museum? Erica is working there and wants to show us some of the artifacts."

I quickly got a text back.

"Yeah, I think that would be cool."

"Hey, I guess Devon and I are in on this adventure. When do you want us to come by?"

"How about tonight? I can show you some new stuff. We just got a new shipment in. It would be great for you guys to come by. Maybe you guys could help unpack some of the stuff. Everyone on the team would love the helping hand."

"Yeah, Devon and I are in. We like this kind of stuff anyways, and I miss you Erica. So of course, we would love to come by tonight."

"Oh great, I can't wait. It's going to be so much fun. Okay, tonight then at 5:00."

"Yep, we'll be there."

"Okay, I will text you where it's at."

"Alright Erica," I said, and we were both very cheerful after that.

"So tell me, how are you and Devon doing besides keeping busy?"

"Oh we are getting closer and closer every day. I think I might be falling in love. But I'm not sure. I like where we are at though in our relationship. We are practically inseparable. I think about him all of the time."

"That's good. I'm really happy for you guys."

Just then Erica took a look at her phone.

"Oh wow, it's almost 2:00! I was supposed to meet up with my professor in a few minutes. Can I take off and see you guys tonight at 5:00?" Erica asked.

"Yeah that's fine. We'll see you at 5:00."

"Yep, 5:00 it is, see you then." Erica said, and then she grabbed her stuff and took off. It seemed like Erica was really in a hurry. I had never seen her rush off so quickly. I was left there to finish my meal alone. I didn't really like to eat alone, but it didn't bother me too much today. I was excited because I get to hang with Erica tonight. I texted Devon and let him know the time that we were all meeting to go to the museum. Then I finished my lunch. I know this was going to be a fun evening.

Chapter 20

Erica and the Museum

Devon came to my room at about 4:30 pm. "So we are going to unpack some ancient stuff?" he asked with an excited tone.

"Yep, that's what Erica said."

"Oh I hope it's that shipment the museum is supposed to get in that I heard about. It's all the Greek findings that were just uncovered. I read a little bit about it. I guess they are finding all sorts of Greek artifacts they have never seen before."

"I don't know. Erica just said it was ancient, but I know Erica has been working with that kind of stuff at the museum so we'll see."

"Well, I hope it is. You know I'm Greek, and it would be cool to unpack some newly uncovered Greek artifacts and to actually touch a piece of history. Maybe I'll see a statue of a relative or something," Devon said smiling.

"Yeah, that would be cool. We should probably get going to make it there by 5:00."

"What time is it now?" Devon's asked.

"Oh it's 4:45. We'd better get going."

"Oh yeah, we definitely don't want to be late for this," Devon said and ran out of the door faster than I did. It only took us five minutes to get to the museum, but it took us about seven minutes to find a good spot to park. So we had about only two minutes to run in before we were late. Devon and I ran into the entrance. Erica was the only one there.

"Oh everyone's late," Erica said as Devon and I caught our breath.

"I'm glad that you guys are here, or I would be here by myself," Erica said as we walked into the door.

"Oh I'm sorry we weren't here sooner. It was hard to find parking," I said.

"Yeah, some people leave their cars here overnight. I forgot to tell you that earlier, sorry. They're not really supposed to but they do. Anyway, it's nice to see you guys."

Just then I realized that I had never really introduced Devon and Erica to each other.

"Erica this is Devon, and Devon this is Erica," I said pointing at both while saying it.

"Hi," they both said in unison.

"I heard you know a lot about history," Devon said to Erica.

"Yes I do, in fact I love it."

"Well, that's awesome! I hope I learn something new tonight. We are both excited you are letting us do this," Devon said.

Erica seemed to like what Devon had said because she got the biggest smile and said, "Well, I hope so too."

"Well Erica, should we start?"

"Yeah, we probably should. I'm sure the others will come soon I hope. Let's start with some of the stuff over here. Remember it's very fragile and very old so we have to be careful. I'll tell you guys where we're going to stack each item."

"Okay sounds good," Devon said. "Hey, what period is this stuff from?"

"Oh well, I didn't know till tonight. They never tell us ahead of time. It's from the golden age of ancient Greece, which is one of my favorite time periods," Erica said.

"Oh wow really," Devon said with a big smile.

"Yes, to be specific, a lot of this stuff is from an Aphrodite cult site that was discovered. They just found it a few months ago. My professor has been going on and on about this exhibit. He was really excited about it, which is why I'm surprised he's not here. Research says that Aphrodite is an odd figure in Greek mythology," Erica said.

"Oh yeah, why is that?" Devon asked.

"Well, she is a figure that historians aren't really sure where she came from. She's not truly Greek. She comes from other cultures, but the Greeks adored her. My professor says that the beliefs about the ancient Greeks have been wrong and that Aphrodite had more of an impact on society than we once realized. Aphrodite was one of the main reasons for everything that we know of as Greek. The subject is still being debated by historians. The university is lucky to get this exhibit," Erica said.

I took a look around while Erica was talking. There was a fair amount of big pallets. In fact, there were about ten pallets full of historical stuff.

Devon carried on the conversation with Erica.

"Did Aurora ever tell you that my family is Greek, and I was raised to know all sorts of things about being Greek? Ever since I was a little boy, my family has been all about pointing out things that are Greek. They went all over the myths and legends with me when I was a child. But one in particular was covered more than the others. Believe it or not, my family was all about Aphrodite back in the day."

"Really?" Erica asked intrigued.

"Yeah really. It's kind of odd that that's what this exhibit is about. My family is one of the foremost authorities on Aphrodite. I chose a different path though," Devon said.

"Why did you do that?"

"Well, I can't say I was as dedicated to the beliefs of my family as they wanted me to be. My family still believes in the legends of Aphrodite. I never understood fully why, but they are passionate about it. I am excited to see if there is anything new here that leans more toward my family's beliefs."

"What do you mean?"

"Well, like I said, I've been looking at this stuff most of my life so I should be able to tell if there is anything new even though I'm just a novice on the subject."

"Well, that would be awesome if we found something new that could offer a new insight," Erica said excitedly.

"Yeah, I hope we find something new."

We started to go through the boxes one by one, starting with the first pallet. The first box had a statue of Aphrodite holding a mirror and walking with Eros.

"Oh yes, I do believe I've seen this before. It's from the late Greek era. Notice how Eros looks like a child," Devon said.

"Oh yeah, I can see it," I said.

"It's a nice piece. Let's put that over here in this corner," Erica said and then we went on to the next item. This item looked like a small statue of Eros.

"Oh this is cute too," I said.

"Yes, this is also from a later period. It's of Eros, and there next to him is Aphrodite. Often times, Eros and Aphrodite are seen together in later statues to associate love with her," Devon said.

"Oh let's put that next to the other statue that we just put away," Erica said.

There were a good number of statues and pictures displaying all sorts of things that were Aphrodite in nature. Then we got to the last pallet. It was wrapped differently and had a seal postmark on it. Erica looked at it with the greatest of intrigue.

"Oh this is it! This is the central piece that I guess caused all the uproar," Erica said.

We opened the box, and it was a beautiful statue. It looked a lot like the other statues that we had looked at previously, but there was one big difference in this statue—Aphrodite was wearing a necklace.

"Well, that is different," Devon said as he stared at the necklace.

"Why is it so different?" Erica asked.

"Well, look at the necklace. Can't you tell?" Devon asked as though it was obvious to everyone. Even Erica looked stumped.

"This necklace is the problem. You see, the necklace is the Greek symbol for love and also for knowledge. Why would the necklace have that on such an early statue of Aphrodite? I think this is perhaps the most ancient statue I've ever seen. Is this really what caused the uproar?" Devon asked.

"I think so," Erica said not so sure of herself.

"Well, I would believe it. Look at this detailed work. Even back then, the craftsmen were good," Devon said. Then he saw something else. It was a crest of some sort. He looked shocked and excited. He stood there just staring at the crest.

"Do you know what this is? This is my family crest. I would know this crest anywhere. It's of my family. This statue is from my family," Devon said almost jumping with excitement.

"May I take a really quick look? I am intrigued by this. I want to use a magnifying glass. It's a trick I learned," Erica said. She took the magnifying glass and did a sweep over the statue.

"I thought I saw something here. Yes, there are little tiny points sticking out, and if I press them here..."

Erica pressed and suddenly a part of the statue came open. What came out was incredibly dusty. Erica grabbed a brush and brushed it off. There was an inscription on it. It was written in ancient Greek.

"I recognize that it's Greek. It's the really old kind. I'm not sure what it says though," Devon said.

"Yeah, I don't recognize it either. It's kind of different."

The item itself was sort of like a tube.

"May I examine it?" Devon asked. Erica seemed reluctant at first but suddenly seemed to change her mind.

"Yes of course, just be careful," Erica said, but as she handed over the tube to Devon, Erica dropped it. The tube hit the ground hard and broke in half. Erica let out a big scream. I gasped and Devon stood there stunned. All three of us couldn't believe we had busted something so old and valuable. We all braced ourselves for a minute.

Then Devon bent down and picked up the pieces that were scattered on the floor and placed them all on the nearest table.

"Well, it doesn't look that bad, and I think we may have discovered something by dropping that," Devon said to Erica who had her eyes covered by her hands in horror from dropping the tube. Erica brought her hands down from over her eyes and walked over to see what was left of the ancient artifact.

When we got closer to the artifact, Devon had been right. It didn't look that bad. I had originally thought it might have busted into a million pieces, but it hadn't. It was more like two pieces.

"You see this," Devon began. "It's like this is a canister that holds something, and if we brush this away gently…"

Devon grabbed the brush and brushed away a few pieces of the dirt grain that surrounded one of the bigger pieces.

"You see, this is something like a scroll. Do you mind if I try to remove it?" Devon asked.

"Well, I guess we can't do too much more damage. Now I am really curious about what it is. Go ahead," Erica said.

Devon took the greatest amount of care to remove the item from the canister.

"It's a scroll," Devon said.

"Does it open up?" I asked staring at it. It had a tannish sort of outside and an even lighter color paper-like leather on the inside. It looked very old.

"Yes, I believe I can open it."

Devon took the greatest of care to open up the scroll. For as old as it was, it actually opened up very nicely. But again, it was written in ancient Greek.

"Well, I guess we will have to wait for someone to translate it," Erica said. "I think I can ask the professor to get his ancient language expert up here by tomorrow."

"Look, I don't think this can wait till tomorrow. I have to know now what this says now," Devon said.

"But why?" I asked.

"It's my family crest. This scroll means something. I have to know what it means." Just then Devon opened up his cell phone and scrolled through his contacts. He pushed the call button and put his phone up to his ear.

"Who are you calling Devon?" I asked.

"My uncle."

Devon waited a minute while Erica and I watched him.

"Hi Uncle Arnot. I'm sorry for calling you so late. I was wondering if you could take a look at an ancient Greek text for me."

There was a pause for a second as the other person answered him.

"Okay great! I will send you a picture of it. Okay then, talk to you in a few. Thanks. Bye."

Devon hung up the phone and turned on the camera on his phone. Devon quickly took two pictures: one of the seal and one of the scrolls with the text and then sent the pictures to his uncle.

A few minutes passed, and then Erica got very anxious and said, "What do you think is taking so long Devon?"

"Well, sometimes these things take time. It is a very old script, but my uncle is good. He will figure out the translation. You'll see," Devon said. Just then Devon's phone rang.

"Uncle, what's going on? What did you find out? Wait! I want to put you on speaker so everyone here can hear you," Devon said and then put his phone on speaker.

"Devon, can you hear me?" Uncle Arnot said.

"Yes Uncle, I can hear you. Go ahead."

"Okay, this is a very ancient Greek script—very, very ancient. I think the most ancient I've seen. I've only seen a few texts that were from this period so that's how I know it's ancient. Okay, now to what is says. That first piece you have, the seal, it says roughly: for her that will come in my place. The other scroll says something along the lines of 'the one who is great and made changes will come forth again and will speak the language of knowledge.' Devon, do you know what this means?"

"No Uncle. I'm not sure."

"This is from the old legends of our family. It's from the followers of Aphrodite," Uncle Arnot said.

"But Uncle, I thought those were just legends. I just thought my dad was trying to get me to go to sleep. I didn't think that they were real."

"Oh they're real, at least some elements of them are real. There is always some element of truth in every legend. Was there anything else that you need me to look at?" Uncle Arnot asked.

"No Uncle. I think that we are good for now. Thank you for translating that, and I'm sorry to have bugged you so late."

"Anytime Devon, anytime. Have fun on your adventure."

"Thank you. I will," Devon said.

Devon ended the call, and then there was a moment of silence as everyone gathered their thoughts.

"Well, what does this mean?" Erica asked.

"I'm not sure, but I know it does change things for me," Devon said.

"How does it change things?" I asked.

"Because maybe those legends are true. At least some of them."

"What legends are you talking about?" Erica asked.

"Well, there is a legend my dad used to tell me about Aphrodite. This is a little different than what you might have learned in school about her. It's a legend about a woman, not a goddess."

"A woman?" Erica asked.

"I've never heard anything about that, and I've done a lot of research on the subject. I studied all of the Greek gods, and Aphrodite has always been a goddess in every legend that I have read," Erica said.

"Well, Aphrodite is not really Greek. She comes from other cultures. In fact, she was adopted by the Greeks who created the legend that we know of today. But there is another secret legend that has been passed down in my family from generation to generation about Aphrodite. The legend goes something like this. There was a village where peaceful people lived. But one day, a warrior clan came and destroyed the village and all that lived in it.

"But one woman named Aphrodite escaped by jumping into the water. While Aphrodite jumped into the water, warriors came after her. She yelled for help, and dolphins came and took her away before the warriors could get to her. Then the dolphins took her to a secret place and taught her great knowledge they had learned. They taught her about love and how the world works. Then Aphrodite came to a new village where she fell in love and wrote a book that contained all the secrets she had learned from the dolphins. The book was considered sacred and was shown throughout Greece. Many people used the book of great knowledge to explore new ideas. As the knowledge spread, Aphrodite was considered by some to be godlike. But the book was lost a very long time ago. The only thing that remained of the legend to most Greeks was that Aphrodite was a goddess," Devon said.

"If we could find that book, it would really change things for history," Erica said intrigued.

"That's true, it really would. But for now, we will have to go with what we have here," Devon said.

"But what do you think the scroll meant, by language of knowledge?" I asked. It was kind of odd that I was so fixated on that one phrase, but I couldn't stop thinking about it.

"I'm not sure, but I hope it's revealed to us with time. I'm just glad this proves that my family isn't completely crazy," Devon said.

Just then a janitor walked in.

"Will you be needing some assistance in cleaning up?" the janitor asked,

Erica looked at her watch.

"Oh wow, it's getting late! No, I think we have it, but thank you," Erica said back to the janitor who didn't hesitate to leave. All of us started to pick up all of the trash from the unpacking.

Just as we were finishing up our cleanup efforts, Erica turned to Devon and me and said, "Well guys, thank you so much for coming. I'm really glad you came. If you hadn't, I would have been doing all this unpacking myself, and I probably wouldn't have found the scroll of Aphrodite."

"Oh no problem Erica. It was fun," I said.

"Yes, it was so much fun. I am so glad I came here tonight. I think it changed my life. I am going to put this into my research efforts. I will also find out if I can find more about the whereabouts of that book from my family records. My uncle might know a thing or two about it too."

"That would be great. I will tell the professor. Hopefully, it will make him less mad about us breaking something. I hope you guys have a good night," Erica said.

"You too, Erica," Devon and I said.

Then the three of us walked out the door and parted ways. Devon and I went to his car, and Erica went the other way.

We were both tired from the unpacking.

"Do you want to hang out for a little bit?" Devon asked.

"Oh Devon, I don't think so. I am so tired. Maybe I should head to bed," I said.

"Oh okay, that's fine Aurora. I will miss you though, but I understand. It has been a long day. I will see you tomorrow."

"I'll miss you too."

When we got in front of my room, Devon dropped me off. I gave him a kiss goodnight and then went to bed without hesitation. But I had trouble sleeping because I kept thinking about all of this new information. It was a bit much to take in. I eventually fell asleep. It wasn't a good sleep though. I started to have weird dreams. I dreamed that I was floating. I saw images of Aphrodite and the dolphins like they were all intertwined. It was strange and left me wondering what all of it meant.

Chapter 21

An Unexpected Visit

The next morning, I woke up and was still really tired. I thought about going to school for a few minutes and then decided I needed a day off. After all this new information, I just needed time to take it all in. I picked up my phone and saw an email from my aunt asking me about how things were going so I decided to call her and ask her if she wanted to hang out. I hadn't talked with my aunt in a little bit so I was a little excited to catch up. The phone began to ring.

"Hello," a voice answered, it was my Aunt Carrie.

"Hey Aunt Carrie! How are you?" I asked.

"Aurora, I'm so happy to hear from you. I am good, how are you?"

"Oh I'm good. I just decided to skip school today and wanted to know if you wanted to hang out."

"Oh yeah, I would love to hang out. Actually, I've been meaning to call you. I have a surprise."

"A surprise?" I said.

"Yeah, a surprise! There is someone from your neck of the woods that is here visiting."

"Who is it?" I asked, trying not to sound too awkward.

"Well, I said it was a surprise." My aunt went on, "You have to drop by and find out. I think you're going to be happy. Your surprise is going to be here later on this morning. Your mom made me promise not to tell you until your surprise arrives, but since you called, I'm having a hard time resisting. Apparently, he is here just to see you."

"Okay, I will be right over. I'm glad that you told me. I was hoping that we could have lunch today and maybe go somewhere," I said a little excited and nervous at the same time about who might be visiting and why. I just couldn't imagine who would fly all the way from Alaska just to come and see me. I mean, it was like a fourteen-hour plane ride that would cost at least $1,200.

"Alright, I will see you soon," Aunt Carrie said.

"Yes, I'll see you soon," I said.

"Great, see you then, bye."

"Bye," I said and then I hung up the phone. Then I texted Devon.

"Hey Devon! I'm going to hang out with my aunt today. I'm still tired from last night and decided to skip classes. I will see you later on. I hope you're having a good day. I love you."

I soon got a text back from Devon. "I will always love you. Have fun and be safe."

I put my phone away after that. I checked to make sure I had my bus pass. I got on the bus and began my journey on the bus system. It was a beautiful day out.

After transferring a few times through the San Diego bus system, I finally got to my aunt's house. It was just as big as I remembered. I walked up the long drive way, and as soon as I reached the door, I rang the doorbell. There was no answer so I tried again and again. I pulled out my cell phone to call my aunt. I had got a text message from her that I hadn't noticed.

"Hey Aurora! I went to go pick up your surprise. I'll be back in a few." The message was from about 30 minutes ago.

"Alright, I'm at your house so I'll wait for you," I texted back.

I decided to take a seat while I waited. While I sat waiting, I felt a cool breeze hit me as the morning sun slowly rose over the distance. There was a nice cloud cover that was big enough to give me temporary shade every now and then, which complemented the breeze very well.

I didn't have to wait long. I soon saw my aunt's car pull up. Then I saw who Aunt Carrie was talking about. It was Andrew. But what was Andrew doing here? I walked up to the car as both Andrew and my aunt got out of it. After my aunt gave me a hug, I then walked over to Andrew.

"Hi Aurora," Andrew said.

"Hi," I said back.

It was a bit of an awkward moment on my side. I couldn't stop asking myself why Andrew was here. As I stood in front of him, I had nothing to say.

"Alright kids, let's go inside," my aunt said. My aunt then opened her front door, and we all headed inside.

"Okay, you kids probably have some catching up to do so I'm going to let you guys hang out for a minute and then we can all go to the museum. How does that sound?"

"Sounds good," I said.

Andrew and I then headed into the living room and sat down.

"Andrew, I haven't seen you in a few years. What brings you all the way down here to San Diego?"

"Well, I had some business to take care of with my dad's company," Andrew said.

"Oh really! All the way down here?" I asked relieved that Andrew had in fact not come all the way down to San Diego just to see me.

"Yeah, it's the fish business, you know. We've become global over the last few years and made our way down here to San Diego recently. My dad asked if I wanted to go to San Diego so I jumped at the chance because I knew it would give me an opportunity to come visit my old friend Aurora."

"Oh wow, that's really cool! How did you know that I was down here?"

"Oh well, through your mom of course. I actually went to your house to see you a few months ago, but when I got there, your mom told me you were down here going to college. So when I found out I was coming to San Diego, I called your mom who then called your aunt. They decided to let it be a surprise. So, surprise!"

"Well, it really is nice to see someone from home. I haven't been home in over a year. But why were you coming to see me a few months ago?"

"Well, I was just thinking about the good old days in high school so I thought I would pay you a visit. I was actually kind of sad that you were gone. So how do you like college?" Andrew asked trying to change the subject.

"Oh college is good. I like it a lot. I like studying stuff about the ocean. I am learning a lot of new and interesting things."

"Oh that's great! What are your plans after college?"

"Well, I still want to be an oceanographer I think, but I might be leaning toward undecided for the moment until I learn more about things. College really has a way of opening your mind."

"Well I guess that's the point, isn't it? To explore new horizons. Then after college, are you going to move back home in Alaska or are you staying down here?" Andrew asked.

"Oh I'm staying down here for sure. It's too nice here in San Diego," I said with a chuckle.

"Well, I can't argue with you there. It is really nice here," Andrew said and then there was a pause in our conversation. It was one of those awkward times when you are talking and then the conversation kind of runs dry. So we just sat there. I think both of us were trying to find something new to talk about. Then just as it looked like Andrew was about to say something, Aunt Carrie came into the room.

"Hey you kids, ready to go?"

"Yes Aunt Carrie, we're ready to rock and roll," I said.

Andrew and I then got up and all of us headed out to the car.

"Okay guys, when we get to Balboa Park, I have to check out the photography museum. One of the photographers used my cheetah fashion in several of his pictures, and I was invited to go check it out. Then we can walk around and check out the other stuff. How does that sound?"

"Sounds good, Mrs. Livingston," Andrew said, and I nodded my head in agreement.

The museum where we went to was very nice. The architecture was so alluring. There was something about the feel of it. It was like the whole complex was one giant piece of art.

"Do you see over there?" my aunt asked as she pointed to somewhere on the left. "That is the San Diego Zoo. It's a part of Balboa Park, and it's really nice. I will have to take you later Aurora. You would love it. Over here is the theater," Aunt Carrie said as she continued to drive toward a parking lot.

"I think we will find parking in this section," Aunt Carrie said.

After driving around in a few circles, we finally managed to find a spot. It seemed very busy at Balboa Park.

"Wow, there are a lot of people here today," I said.

"Yes there is. Everyone is here to see the exhibit that we are going to. The photographer has followers from all around the world. So I am not surprised that it's busy. I'm glad we found a spot that was kind of close," my aunt said.

"Yep that was kind of lucky that we found a spot within walking distance with everyone here," I said jokingly as we continued to walk.

We walked through a set of giant doors that led to the entrance of the museum. There were such beautiful pictures everywhere. We walked through the museum's entrance. It was so incredibly quiet—even quieter than other museums I had been to. There were a lot of people inside the museum walking around. For as busy as it had seemed in the parking lot, it seemed just as busy in the museum.

About halfway through the photography portion of the museum, we finally reached a place with pillars. Among the pillars on the walls there were a series of photos.

My aunt turned to me and Andrew, and she said in a whisper, "These are the pictures I was telling you about. I recognize them from the photographer's name."

There were several ladies staring at the photographs. When they saw my aunt, they all came up to her and started to talk. All the ladies seemed to really like my aunt.

"Wow, your Aunt Carrie seems to be famous," Andrew said.

"Yeah, she is pretty famous with this fashion stuff. I don't know too much about it, but all the girls at school love her."

"Wow, that is really cool," Andrew said.

We started to look at the photos. The photographer had done such a good job of blending the beauty of the model with the fashion. It was almost mystical in the way it appeared. I could tell instantly what the big deal was about. It was true and utter beauty. There wasn't anything else like it. I was very happy for my aunt. She seemed most at home when people were talking to her about fashion. Now her work was immortalized in a piece of artwork. After a while, my aunt had managed to get away from her crowd of fans, and we got to finish walking around the museum. Before I knew it, it was lunchtime.

"Do you guys want to get a bite to eat?"

"Yes I would love to eat, Mrs. Livingston," Andrew said.

"Yeah Aunt Carrie, I'm starving," I said.

With that, we got some hamburgers at a nice stand in the park. As I finished my meal, I turned toward my aunt.

"Thank you for the lunch and for taking me to see the very nice photographs. They were so wonderful," I said.

"You're welcome Aurora. I am glad that you liked them. Andrew, did you like the photos?" Aunt Carrie asked.

"Mrs. Livingston, the photographs were absolutely breathtaking. Thank you for bringing me to see them. It made my trip to San Diego much more enjoyable. We don't have stuff like this in Alaska, do we Aurora?"

"No, no we don't," I said and smiled.

"Well, I guess then that is it for the park today, unless there was some other place you kids want to go around here," my aunt asked.

"No, I think I'm good for now. It will be nice to just relax for the rest of the day," I said.

"Yeah and I should get back to meet up with some of my father's business associates," Andrew said.

"So we are all in agreement that we should go back," my aunt said.

With that, we all headed back and got to the car. Then my aunt started to drive.

"I'm really glad that you guys came to see the exhibit with me. I was so amazed at how many people liked the pictures. I was a bit nervous when the ladies first approached me about taking the photos. I was worried that they might not come out right. But I was glad that they did turn out as good as they did," Aunt Carrie said.

"Yeah Aunt Carrie. They really did turn out nice."

"Now your fashion will live on through art," Andrew said.

My aunt got a big smile on her face.

"You know, I was thinking something along those very lines. It is nice that future generations can look at this art and see what kind of things I created. That's what I was discussing with one of the ladies that I met in the museum. It's a pleasing thought," my aunt said as she continued to drive.

Soon we were back at my aunt's house.

"Mrs. Livingston, I am so sorry, but I have to be leaving now. Thank you so much for picking me up at the airport and being such a gracious host. It was a pleasure meeting you," Andrew said.

"It was nice meeting you too. Next time you are in town Andrew, you will have to stay longer and meet my husband."

"Yes that would be great! I would love that," Andrew said.

"Won't you need a ride?" I asked.

"No. I already texted to have a car come and pick me up. I didn't want to have to inconvenience your aunt any more than I already have."

"Oh you haven't inconvenienced me. Next time, let me drive you, I insist. I love to drive around in my car," my aunt said.

"Okay, if you insist. Aurora, I was wondering if I could give you a ride." Andrew asked.

I paused for a second and thought about it. I really didn't see the harm in going with Andrew.

"Yes that would be nice," I said and then shortly after that, the car arrived. It was a black limousine. When the driver parked, he got out of the car and opened the door for Andrew and me, and we both got in. I turned around to my aunt before the car started driving away.

"Thank you so much again. I had so much fun," I said.

"Yep, no problem Aurora. Call me, and we will do this again."

Then Aunt Carrie turned around and went into her house as Andrew and I drove off.

Chapter 22

Unwanted Affection is Never a Good Thing

After driving for a minute, Andrew said, "So where are you heading to?"

"Back to the college," I said.

"Oh okay," Andrew said, and then he turned to the driver. "I need you to drive us to the college first to drop off my guest before we go to the meeting."

"Yes sir," the driver said back to Andrew.

Then there were a few minutes pause in the conversation. It was as though Andrew was trying to figure out what he wanted to stay. I tried to ignore this by looking out the window. He leaned toward me. We were sitting across from each other. Then he took a deep breath and looked me into the eyes.

"Aurora, I don't know how to say what I'm about to say, but I have to say it," Andrew said.

"Okay," I said taking a deep breath, half scared about what it could be that Andrew was about to say.

"Aurora, I love you," Andrew said in a serious tone.

"You love me?" I repeated back to him in a tone of shock.

"Yes I love you. It is why I went to go see you a few months ago. I had made up my mind then that I love you. There is no other way around it. I can't stop thinking about you. You are the one that is meant for me," Andrew said. He stared straight into my eyes.

I couldn't stand it so I looked away in shock.

"What do you mean you love me? We didn't even go out in high school, and I have a boyfriend," I said.

"I know. I heard when I talked to your mom, but I don't like it. I don't know much about him, but I have trouble picturing you with anyone else."

I suddenly felt the sudden urge to leave. I was furious. If Andrew knew that I had a boyfriend, why the act? Why would he go through the day acting like he was my friend just to turn around and spring this on me? I was speechless and in shock.

"Well, how do you feel about me?" Andrew asked.

I paused for a moment.

"I'm sorry if I have ever misled you Andrew. We were friends in high school, and that is all that we have ever been. I don't know where you got the idea that we were anything else. I know this seems cruel, but I don't want you to think that we are anything more than friends. I have a boyfriend that I love. I really, really do love him with all of my heart. I hope that you can understand that."

Andrew now had his head turned away, and his eyes were looking at the ground. He had water surrounding his eyes like he was about to cry, but he wasn't crying yet. Andrew didn't say a word and just sat there stunned. Then Andrew spoke.

"But doesn't my coming down here prove how much I love you. I came all this way to tell you in person before I lost you forever. Can't I change your mind a little?" Andrew asked.

"No Andrew. I'm sorry, but it isn't going to happen. I know in time you will accept that. I think I'm going to get out of the car here. I don't want this to continue. I can walk," I said angrily.

"No, I don't want you to go. I understand that you are in love with your boyfriend, but I don't want you to get out of the car. I will take you to your college. But I want you to know that if you change your mind, I will always be here for you," Andrew said with a tone of desperation.

"Thank you, and I really am sorry," I said.

"Don't worry about it. It was a nice trip down here anyways. I am happy I got to hang out with you."

"Yep, it was fun hanging out until you pulled this," I said still angry. There wasn't any talking for the rest of the ride to the college. Before I knew it, we were at the college.

"Alright, this is good. I'll get out here," I said to the driver. The limo stopped.

"Thanks again Andrew," I said, trying to hide how angry I was.

"No problem. I will talk to you again soon," Andrew said.

"Yep take care," I said with sarcasm as I walked away from the limo fast. With that, I walked out and left the nightmare day behind me. It was a shame that it had started out to be such a nice day, until Andrew pulled that number in the car and told me that he loved me. What would possess him to say that and to travel all the way down here? I couldn't stop shaking my head at how ridiculous the whole thing seemed.

The first thought that came to me as I started to walk was to tell Devon about it. The whole thing had just upset me so much. I would have to find Devon as soon as I could to tell him what had happened. I knew that was the only way I would feel less angry about it. I pulled out my phone.

"Devon I'm back at the college, and I have to talk to you," I texted to Devon.

I got a text back.

"Okay, where do you want to meet? Are you okay?"

"Can you meet me at the Central Courtyard?"

"See you in five minutes."

"Okay, see you then."

I headed over to the Central Courtyard and found a bench and waited. Before I knew it, Devon was there in the courtyard coming toward me. He had such a concerned look on his face.

"What's the matter, my love? I rushed over here as fast as I could," Devon said as he was running toward me.

"I'm sorry to have bothered you, but something just happened to me. I wanted to stay honest with you and tell you about it," I said.

Devon took a seat.

"What is it? Whatever it is, it's okay," Devon said.

I took a deep breath and looked at Devon.

"Okay, I don't want you to be mad but something happened today," I said.

"Okay, go ahead and tell me," Devon said as he braced himself.

"Well, when I went to go hang out with my Aunt Carrie, there was a friend of mine from Alaska named Andrew who had flown down here to see me. We all hanged out at the museum. A photographer had taken really nice pictures of some of my aunt's fashion and made an exhibit out of it. After we were done seeing the exhibit, Andrew offered to drive me back here to the college. On the way over here, Andrew told me that he loved me. I told him I have a boyfriend and that he didn't have a chance, but I don't think he understood completely. The whole thing made me furious. I just don't ever want to lose you, so I wanted to make sure you know everything that goes on in my life."

Without a breath in between finishing my story, Devon held my hand and said, "Don't worry, I'm not mad. I'm glad that you told me. You will never lose me. Is the guy gone?"

"Yes, he's leaving today, I think."

"Okay good. I didn't want to have to beat him up or anything," Devon said half joking and half serious.

"Oh I'm so happy that you're not mad. I thought you might have been. It makes me feel so much better because I just don't ever want to lose you. I'm sorry I interrupted you. So what are you up too my love?"

"I'm doing research on our next experiment. This one will be for establishing direct communication with the dolphins," Devon said.

"Yeah, what do you have planned for us?"

"Well, it's still in the works so I can't tell you the details yet, but it's going to be good. We are going to be going out to sea. We are going to confront the dolphins in their natural habitat," Devon said.

"Their natural habitat! But how are you going to find out where the dolphins are? The ocean is so huge," I asked.

"That's what I'm researching. We are going to go out in the morning. I am still arranging it all. I will let you know when things are more certain my dear," Devon said.

"Okay, but no crazy surprises, okay?"

"Don't worry, I won't make it too crazy," Devon said laughing. Then Devon got up.

"Okay, well I have to get going. I have to tie everything together and make sure all the arrangements are good for tomorrow. You're going to be okay, right?" Devon asked, looking me straight into the eyes to double check my emotions.

"Yeah, I'll be okay. I feel a lot better now that I have talked to you. I am just happy you're not mad. I love you," I said as I pressed my lips together. Devon leaned in and said, "I love you too, always and forever." Then he gave me a kiss.

"I'll see you tomorrow. I will text you tonight to let you know what's going on," Devon said as he was walking away.

"Okay, I'll wait for the text, my love," I yelled back.

I felt so much better because I had talked to Devon. That's one of the things that I loved about him. I could tell him anything, and no matter what it was, he always made me feel better. I got up and decided to hang out in the student lounge for a change.

I went to the student lounge, which was nice and quiet. The TV was on and my favorite movie was playing so I decided to watch. The chairs in the lounge were so comfortable. Before I knew it, I had fallen asleep. I woke up about four hours later. I looked down at my phone, and it was late now.

"9:00 pm," I said shaking my head to wake up.

I don't know how I slept this long.

I saw that I had a text message too.

"Tomorrow I'll drop by your room at 7 a.m. to pick you up. Wear shorts, it's supposed to be a hot day tomorrow," Devon said.

"Okay," I texted back.

The text had been enough to wake me up. I had spent enough time in the lounge so I got up and went to my room. Even though I had fallen asleep for four hours, I was still really tired. I guess this day had been emotionally draining. Whenever that happens, I feel the most exhausted. There was no fighting it. I decided to go to bed so that I would be recharged for the next day.

Chapter 23

Dream Chapter

As soon as I laid down on my bed, I fell asleep. I could feel myself beginning to dream. It was hard to know at first if I was dreaming, but I soon realized that I was indeed in a dream—a dream that I was walking through a large building, a building that was like the Parthenon. There were many white pillars. As I passed the white pillars, I walked toward a large statue of a figure. It was of a woman. When I got up to the statue, I heard something starting to come from the other side of the room at me. It was a dolphin swimming in the air. Afterward, a bunch of other dolphins flew by me. Then I suddenly woke up with a gasp.

That was weird.

I looked at my cell phone. It was 5:30 am. I quickly got up. I knew that Devon was going to be here soon so I got ready as fast as I could. Before I knew it, it was already 7:00 am. There was a knock at the door. I opened the door, and it was Devon.

"Aurora my love, are you ready to go?"

"Hi honey! I love you too. Yep, I'm ready. Let's get going," I said and with that, we headed out the door and got to Devon's car. I could feel my anticipation growing as we approached where we were going.

"Alright Aurora, are you ready to hear the plan?" Devon asked while we were driving.

"Yes go ahead. I'm ready."

"Alright, we're going to track one of the dolphins that we've been monitoring at the research center. It should be with other dolphins. Then you and I are going to jump in and scuba dive with the dolphins."

"But I've never went scuba diving," I said concerned.

"It's okay. I'll show you, and we're not going very deep. You will be okay."

"Okay," I said reassured. I knew that Devon would never put me in harm's way.

We soon got to the boat. There was someone in the boat waiting for us.

"This is it," Devon said pointing to the boat. I glanced in the back at the figure.

"And who is that?" I asked Devon after glancing at the figure in the background.

"This is George. George, this is Aurora, my girlfriend."

George put his hand out to shake mine. He was a skinny guy with glasses and a big head of curly hair.

"George is our tech at the research center. You're one of the best trackers of aquatic signals that we have, aren't you George?" Devon asked.

George grinned when Devon said that.

"Yeah I am. I suppose," George said.

I smiled at him and said, "Well, I'm glad you're here then."

"Thank you. It's nice to meet you," George said and continued to smile as he went back to his work.

Devon soon went to work as well. He jumped right up and ran to the other side of the ship, leaving me unsure of what to do now. Devon quickly came back to me after a second.

"Sorry Aurora. I didn't mean to leave you. I have to start getting the ship ready to set sail. Can you just wait here?" Devon asked and then ran off again before I could answer.

I guess Devon was in some sort of sailing mode again. I sat down on a nearby bench. Before I knew it, the ship began to cast off and was in the bay heading out. George went to his computer station. I was curious about what George was doing and went over to him.

"So how does all off this tracking stuff work anyways George?"

"Do you know anything about how animals are tracked in the wild?" George asked.

I shook my head no.

"Well, that's okay. It's all based on tracking technology that we've had for years. It's your basic animal tracking system. We insert the tracker in the dolphin right before we release it back into the ocean. Sometimes we use radio signals to track the animals, other times we can use satellites. I personally like the satellites a little better," George said.

"Why?" I asked intrigued.

"Well, the radio transmitter is not as reliable. They used to use it a lot back in the day. But we have to have almost get line of sight for the radio transmitter to work. The satellite transmitters are way better anyways. Their range is so much greater. We can use any number of satellites around the world to pinpoint exactly where the dolphins are," George said.

"And are you tracking any now?" I asked.

"Yes, I'm tracking a few animals right now—some whales, some seals, some killer whales. Here you see these little red blips, those are our dolphins that we are going to track today," George said.

"Wow, so each one of these blips represents an animal?"

"Yes, they each represent an animal that was released into the wild. A lot of the animals will end up on the beach hurt and stuff, and so there is an effort to rehabilitate their health. Then when they're ready to be released back into the wild, we release them and then track them. Most of the time, we track the animals just to see their migration patterns. Fortunately for us, this doubles as a way for us to track down individual dolphins," George said smiling. You could really see that George was passionate about tracking animals.

"Don't they have to track down these animals a lot?"

"No, not a whole lot. That's why we like the satellite system. Back in the day, to get the data on the animal's migration patterns, we would have to find the animal and extract the animal's information manually. Now we can gather all of the information remotely," George said.

"Wow, that is really awesome."

"Yeah, it is really awesome. That's why I love my job. Let me show you something else," George said as he put his hands on the screen.

"This is us you see. Do you see these little blips on the screen?" George asked as he pointed to several other blips.

"Yes," I said as I looked at what George was pointing at.

"Well, those blips are what we're after. These are two dolphins that we released into the wild a few months ago. Now watch this," George said and zoomed in on the dolphins.

The graphics on the screen were incredible. The background was a full-scale picture of what it looked like under the water. The image showed what the dolphins looked like in the water and where they were swimming. It actually looked like I was watching a dolphin swimming up close.

"You see, we can actually watch the dolphin. The sensor that we placed in the dolphin is so advanced that it gives us a direct representation of how the dolphin appears. This isn't a real image of the dolphin like if this was being filmed with a camera. It's a calculated rough estimate of how the dolphin may look. You see this, here in the corner?" George asked.

"Yes," I said as I moved closer to look at the screen.

"This is a reading of the dolphin's health. If I press this reverse button here, I can follow the path this dolphin has taken all the way back to when the dolphins were first released into the wild," George said.

"I just can't believe it. This is so cool," I said amazed.

"Yeah it is. You know, in a couple of years, we won't even have to put the tracker in the dolphins. With the way technology is going, soon we'll be able to tell where all living things in the ocean are just by using satellites. That's why Devon's research is so important to the school," George said.

"Why do you say that?" I asked intrigued.

"Because with Devon's work, if he can unlock some sort of language, then it will open up so many doors for science. We will be able to get a firsthand account of what happens down there. Can you imagine what the dolphins would tell us? It could open up so many doors for the world."

"Did Devon tell you what we are doing today?" I asked curious if George knew about my special talent.

"No, but knowing Devon, it's something good. Devon made promises to everyone that he is close to finding the answer. He wouldn't say that if he hadn't figured out something. But he hasn't told anyone what it is that he has found. I personally can't wait for his research to succeed. A lot of us at the university really believe in Devon and what he is trying to do. It's like getting the last piece of a giant puzzle."

"Wow, I hope he did find something," I said with a smile. "Thank you for showing me all of this. I think this stuff is so cool. I want to work with this kind of stuff soon when I get out of college."

"Well, if you have any questions later on, just let me know. I will be happy to teach you how to use this equipment."

"Thank you, I really appreciate that." Just then Devon's voice was projected toward us.

"Aurora!" Devon yelled.

"I'm over here," I yelled back to Devon.

"Hey! I need to have a safety brief with you and review how to use some of this equipment," Devon said.

"Okay hun," I said as I got up from George's computer station. "Thanks again George for showing your awesome equipment."

"No problem, any time. I'll just stay here being cool," George said as he went back to staring at the computer screen.

I met Devon who opened a door to an area where all of the scuba stuff had been set up.

"Okay, I just wanted to go over some of this stuff with you. Do you remember when we went scuba diving before?" Devon asked.

"Yeah I remember," I said.

I mean, who could forget the scuba date? I was new to the whole experience of scuba diving, and it was in a pool. It had all been new and exciting to me. All of this scuba stuff was fun. It still scared me a little, but I didn't want to tell Devon that.

"Okay, here we have weights, boots size 9, fins, and your air regulator system made super easy for you, and there's even a nice computer to go with it. Okay now, there is a new feature made special for this kind of an expedition. Our masks have a screen interface that is directly linked to the computer on the boat. The computer can see what we can, and we can see some things that are displayed from the computer.

"We will be able to see things like interactive topical information. The masks can also display your direction, water temperature, and what's in the area like whales. All of this extra stuff is going to make this dive super easy. What do you think?" Devon asked.

I only caught the highlights of the whole briefing because when Devon is really into something, he speaks really fast.

"I think I caught most of that. How do the radios work?" I asked.

"You strap those around your throat just like on our date. The vibrations from your voice going through your throat are picked up and sent to the other radio. I checked, and they work so if you have any questions while we're down there, just say something. Also, if we have to come up for any reason, we will have to come up slowly so we don't get poisoned from Bernoulli's, okay? Alright, so as soon as we see the dolphins, we're going to suit up. Any other questions?" Devon asked.

None had come to mind at that moment.

"No, I don't have any questions, but if I think of any, I will let you know," I said.

"Okay, sounds good," Devon said with a smile.

"Alright Aurora, I have to drive the boat. If you want, you can stay here, or you can just relax in the galley and get some tea. I made sure they had your favorites. I think there is some food stored in the cupboards, if you're a little hungry. I'm not sure how long this is going to be. We could be coasting for a little bit," Devon said.

"Alright, well I suppose I could just take a seat and relax for a little while if you will be okay without me," I said trying to sound as sweet and sincere as possible.

"Yes of course my dear. I will be okay. I will come get you when we're close," Devon said.

"Okay, sounds good," I said as I leaned in and gave Devon a kiss. Then I started to head down to the galley. The boat was now rocking a lot as we began to speed up. The rocking made me a little sick. George saw me in the galley.

"Getting sick, huh? You should try an orange for the seasickness, or you could try resting. Just sit down and try to take a nap. When you wake up, you will feel a lot better," George said.

"Well, with all of this rocking, I think I would almost try anything. Do you have an orange?" I said about to throw up.

George looked but didn't seem to find anything at first. Then he brought something to me.

"Here is some orange juice, and there is a nice couch," George said as he handed me the juice which I gulped down in one sip. I hadn't drunk that much, but it seemed to help a little. I still felt sea sick though. The boat just continued to rock and rock and rock. No matter what I tried, I couldn't get over the rocking. I went to the couch to lay down.

"Here, try these crackers," George said.

"Thank you," I said.

"No problem, we have all been there before," George said as he headed back to his computer station.

I don't know whether it was the rocking or maybe the crackers or the juice, but I soon found myself falling asleep. As I slept, I began to have an odd dream. I was walking through the ocean, and there were white pillars and seaweed. The pillars were fallen on top of each other like they had collapsed. Then the dream shifted, and I was in another place where there was an incredible blue—such a deep blue. As I walked through the blue, a voice could be heard faintly that called in a whisper, "Auuuurrrooorrrraaaaa," and then the voice called again, "Auuuuurrrrrrrooooorrrraaaaa." Then the blue illumination let up a little, and everything got a little darker luminescent shade of blue. Then a dolphin appeared. Then more dolphins appeared all together. As I stared at the dolphins, I could see that there were thousands of them all around me.

Then one dolphin came closer to me and said, "Come to us. Wake up! Wake up!"

"Where?" I asked.

"Come to us," the dolphin said again. Then I started to hear another voice as all the dolphins began to fade away.

"Wake up! Wake up!" George said.

"What?" I said startled and surprised that I was now looking at George.

"We're here. We are about three minutes away from some dolphins. Are you feeling better?" George asked.

I actually felt a lot better.

"Wow, I feel great! Thank you for the suggestion. That nap really did do the trick and make me feel better," I said.

"No problem. Um, I think Devon wanted you so you guys can start to suit up," George said.

"Oh yeah, thank you," I said as I walked over to the area where Devon had put the gear.

"Are you ready?" Devon asked.

"Well uh, I'm not sure, but we'll see how it goes," I said.

"Okay, I don't want you to be nervous. I need you to be totally relaxed and aware of everything that is going on around you. Remember when you're down there, I will always be right next to you, just in case anything goes wrong, okay?" Devon said.

He then handed me my wetsuit.

"There is a changing room over there," Devon said. I was still a little modest about changing around Devon. I walked into the changing room and put on the wetsuit. I quickly came out.

"How do I look?" I asked.

"My dear, you always look breathtaking. How do you feel? Do you feel like you are about to change history for all of humankind?"

I looked dumbfounded.

"I hadn't really thought of what we were doing was historical. I always thought of it as significant, but not historical," I said.

"Well, if I am right about the dolphins, then what we are doing right now is history. It's historical on the grandest scale, like when Neil

Armstrong went on the moon for the first time. We are going to change the world. Are you ready?" Devon asked again.

I had started to put on the rest of the gear and was just finishing when Devon had finished his little statement about what we're doing being historical.

"Yes, I just have to put on my flippers. Can you help me? You know, I always have trouble with the flippers," I asked in a helpless kind of way.

"Yes of course. I will help you with that," Devon said as he looked around for a minute.

"Here, sit in this chair," Devon said as he pulled out a chair.

I sat down and then Devon grabbed the flippers and put them on my feet. I took a deep breath knowing that I was almost ready to go in the water.

"Okay, let's grab the rest of this stuff and head over to where we're going to jump in," Devon said.

We grabbed all of the other equipment and then headed over to an open area on the deck where there was a removable rope fence. The oxygen tanks that were full of breathable air were set up in this area and waiting for us. When we arrived at the oxygen tanks, Devon grabbed the first one and placed it on my back and then put one on himself too. It weighed more than I had remembered.

Finally, we put the masks on. Devon then pushed a button on the top of my mask. The mask suddenly lit up like it had been activated. It started to highlight all the information about the layout of the ocean floor and where the dolphins were.

"So the dolphins are over there?" I asked pointing to the area where I saw the dolphins on the screen.

"Yes they are," George said from the background still at his computer station.

"Okay, are you ready to jump in?" Devon asked.

I took a deep breath. I was still a little apprehensive about the whole thing. I wasn't sure if it was because I was going into the deep or if it was because of the supposed historical significance of what we were doing—or the fact that it would all be caught on tape—but whatever it was, it made me apprehensive. I just want things to go well.

"Yes, I'm ready," I said with a voice of confidence.

"Okay, I'll jump in first and then you can follow Aurora."

Devon looked so confident and sure of himself. I wish I could be like that.

Devon jumped in while I stepped up to the ledge. He swam out of the way so I could jump in. I closed my eyes and jumped. I was in the water before I knew it. He pointed down and gave me thumbs up as if he was asking if we were ready to go down. I understood this gesture and nodded my head in agreement, and we both headed down.

The first sight I saw was a breathtaking blue—it was calm and serene. It was everything I had imagined. The ocean was clear like glass. There were fish everywhere. Then I saw two dolphins coming toward us on the screen, but I couldn't see them yet. They were still too far away.

Devon pushed down on his microphone wrapped around his neck.

"Let's go this way. You see how it is on the screen. We should follow that."

I pushed down on my microphone. "Okay, sounds good," I said.

"Let me know if you hear anything from the dolphins."

"I will," still trying to get used to the microphone around my neck.

As we began to swim toward the dolphins on the screen, there were two distinct blips. The 3D map imaging made it easy to navigate at first, but it was hard to see some of the stuff in front of me. I reached up to see if I could shut it off. The map part turned off, and I continued to swim.

"Anything?" Devon asked

"No, not yet," I said.

Just as Devon asked that, I heard some voices muffled in the background.

"Hello, hello, who is that?"

I looked around to see where the voices were coming from. It was like the muffled voices were coming from my head. I then remembered that they were the same kind of voices I had heard on a previous occasion. I could absolutely hear a dolphin.

"I'm over here," I said back to the voice. Then I put my hands on the microphone.

"Devon, Devon, I heard a voice and answered it."

Devon turned toward me.

"Okay, let me know what happens."

Soon I saw a dolphin appear.

"Are you the one?" the dolphin asked.

"The one, what do you mean?" I asked.

"The one who can hear us, the one that can understand dolphins."

"I can understand you, but I don't know what you mean by 'the one'."

"The one that was prophesied long ago. Don't you know the legend?"

"No, I'm just a girl. I can talk to you, but I don't know about any legend."

"That's odd that you don't know the legend, but I don't have time to tell it to you now. I am Lyra, and you must come with me."

I turned to Devon.

"Devon, the dolphin wants us to go with him."

"I didn't even hear you talk to him," Devon said surprised.

"The dolphin talked, I promise, and he said we have to go with him," I said.

"Okay, let's go," Devon said.

"We will follow you Lyra," I said.

"Okay, keep up. I will try to move slower for you. What was your name, Oh Great One?" Lyra asked.

"I am Aurora," I said.

"Aurora, the chosen one. Very well follow me my lady," Lyra said as we began to swim.

Soon we arrived at a small rock formation and then something happened. I'm not sure what it was, but it was like a bright light that flashed from the ground. Then it was like I wasn't in a dive suit anymore. It was like I was just breathing normally as if I was breathing air under the water.

"What's going on?" I asked startled as I turned to Lyra.

"We are going somewhere," Lyra said.

I turned to look at Devon to see if he was alright, but Devon wasn't there.

"Where is Devon?" I demanded.

"Is that the other human who was with you, my lady?" Lyra asked.

"Yes it is," I said.

"Oh, he will be fine. He just can't go where we're going," Lyra said.

"But where are we going?"

I didn't feel panicked. I felt calm, but I was still worried because Devon had just vanished. In fact, the whole ocean seemed different now.

"We are going to my home. Don't worry about the other human, you will see him again. But you have to go to where I am from. You see, my lady, it was prophesied a long time ago that you would come to my home, and we have been waiting for you," Lyra said.

"But what do you mean you have been waiting?" I asked confused.

"I have spoken too much already, my Lady Aurora. We must make haste," Lyra said as he began to swim away.

Chapter 24

Antilla, the City of Dolphins

L yra turned around toward me and saw that I wasn't moving. "I promise you that you will see the other human again, but you must come with me. There is not a moment to lose. Antilla is awaiting our arrival. You can almost see it in the distance," Lyra said bobbing his head to point toward what looked like some distant star.

Right now, the water was a majestic deep blue. The water however felt as much like water as it did like air. I could see in the distance a shimmer of light. It was the only brightness in the deep void of blue. As we continued to swim, the light became brighter and brighter.

It was almost a golden light. As we approached, I began to make out several white pillars—the same pillars that had been in my dream—and a large set of stairs. At the top of the stairs was a large archway. All of it shimmered like gold. Swimming among the pillars, there appeared to be a bunch of dolphins. There were more dolphins than I had ever imagined could gather in one place. There were hundreds of dolphins that were all looking at me as Lyra and I moved through the city. I stopped in a gaze. It was so remarkable that I almost couldn't believe what I was seeing.

"My Lady Aurora, we must continue to move. They are waiting for you," Lyra said.

I glanced at Lyra.

"Who is waiting for me?"

"They are," Lyra said and then I saw it.

I saw the stadium. It was so massive and looked like it was full of thousands of dolphins. My heart fell as I saw the sight. It looked so beautiful. We approached the central location. As we came closer, I could see the central stage in the middle of all of the dolphins. All the dolphins in the stadium started to stare in my direction as Lyra and I swam through the stadium. I could hear the sound of thousands of whispers all at once.

Then a very large dolphin approached us. He glanced at me and then said to Lyra, "Is it she? Is it the chosen one from the prophecy?"

"It is, my lord," Lyra said to the strange dolphin.

"I am Kaitos, my dear," the dolphin said.

"I am Aurora."

"We know, my dear," Kaitos said and then faced the crowd and began to speak loudly.

"Children, children of Antilla, let me speak. The great prophecy is upon us. As you know, there was a prediction of a time when one of the land dwellers would come and join us for the unity and peace of our two worlds. Behold, I give you Aurora, the chosen one," Kaitos said and pointed at me. The crowd cheered and awed at hearing this news.

I had no idea what was going on. I wish someone had explained to me what was going on so I would have a better understanding of why all the dolphins were so happy. But no one explained it, so I just stood there in awe at the incredible site of all of the dolphins. Kaitos turned toward the crowd and raised his fins.

"Let all who hear me know the time is now. We must be vigilant and wait. For those of you who have had your doubts, let the doubts be gone. For this day has arrived. Follow through and continue on our journey. Stick to the way of our kind, and soon peace will exist," Kaitos said to the crowd.

Kaitos then took a bow and the crowd roared again. After a moment of cheering, Kaitos looked up again.

"Thank you, now gather your thoughts for soon we will dine in a feast of celebration for the promised day has arrived," Kaitos said.

With that, Kaitos took off from the stage. Then Lyra shook his head up and down and said to follow Kaitos. We followed Kaitos until we arrived at a beautiful area. There were all sorts of sea and land plants, and beautiful fish swimming through the water. It was one of the most beautiful gardens

I had ever seen. When we finally stopped, a beautiful yellow fish swam past my head.

I was in amazement when the fish swam by me because, like I said before, it didn't feel like water. It didn't feel like the weightlessness of being in water. As I stood there, it felt like I was on land breathing air. But the dolphins and fish swam like they were in water. Kaitos came close toward me.

"Aurora, it is so nice to finally meet you. I was told as a child that I would be the one to greet the chosen one as she came into Antilla. Until this day came, I still had my doubts, but here you are, just as the prophecy foretold. Are you ready to take on your duties as the Great Uniter?"

I could feel the confused look that had come over my face as I heard all of this.

"I'm sorry, but I don't know anything about any of this. One moment I thought I was crazy because I could hear dolphins talking, and now you're telling me that I am some sort of a chosen one. That I am destined to unite two different worlds," I said flustered in my speech.

"You mean, you don't know anything about any of this?" Kaitos asked with a dolphin's version of a shocked look on his face.

I guess in all the years that Kaitos had been thinking about whatever this prophecy thing was, it never once crossed his mind that the Great Uniter herself would not know what was going on. Kaitos got quiet for a second. He then swam back in forth in a pacing fashion.

"My lord, what are we to do?" Lyra asked.

"Patience Lyra, I am thinking," Kaitos said.

A moment later, Kaitos turned his head toward me and stared in my direction but didn't say anything. Then a dolphin came through the entrance of the garden.

"You called, my lord?" the dolphin with a female voice said.

"Yes, yes, I did Sadira," Kaitos said and then turned toward me.

"Aurora, this is Sadira. She is our most talented storyteller and teacher. Sadira will teach you all that you need to know. She is very knowledgeable and will answer any of your questions. I would love to teach you myself. Trust me, nothing else in life would give me more pleasure than to teach the Great Uniter, but my duties as leader of Antilla will be distracting me today because of the feast and a few other things. I hope you don't mind, my Lady Aurora," Kaitos said. There seemed to be a surprising tone of deep respect that I could hear as Kaitos spoke to me.

I had never experienced it before, and it made me smile.

"Of course, that would be fine to have Sadira teach me. I have so many questions to ask," I said.

"Good. I am glad. Well, I must be off. I will see you at the feast. Before I forget to tell you, Lyra is your protector. He was chosen from birth to protect you. He has been training all his life. Guard her well Lyra."

"I will, my lord," Lyra said.

"Very good. Well, I must be off," Kaitos said as he took off, swimming extremely fast.

"Well, what would you like to know, my Lady Aurora?"

"Tell me everything," I said.

Sadira took a deep breath.

"How do I start? There is so much."

"Why don't you start with the story of Aphrodite," Lyra said.

"Yes, that is a good idea, but first, we must get to a better venue. Please follow me," Sadira said as she began to swim.

"My lady, if you would like, you may grab onto me," Lyra said.

"Thank you," I said and then grabbed onto Lyra's fin. It felt a little different than the last time I had held onto a dolphin. It seemed like Lyra was flying as we took off. I instantly loved holding onto Lyra. It made me feel like I was flying. After a few moments of following Sadira, we soon stopped at a meadow where there was a bright glowing crystal. Sadira turned toward me.

"Let me begin with the beginning. Early on, the first dolphins came here. This wonderful place was created as a paradise. It is our escape from the dark. This is the light. The first dolphins here realized what they had with this place and swore to always protect it and preserve it. The first dolphins also created Antilla, the city that you see. It was where dolphins would come and learn and contemplate the meaning of life and the meaning of all things in the world. In the early days of Antilla, there were many schools of thought, and this civilization flourished. No one was sure how it existed, but everyone knew how to come here. It was the first kingdom. Then soon after, other kingdoms of dolphins came and spread throughout the world. Every kingdom was of greatness, and everyone was at peace," Sadira said.

Suddenly, I saw the crystal glowing and all the area around me began to fade in and out. It was like you were tuning in on a radio station. Then I saw it: a simple void of blue nothingness, just like the one that Lyra and I had passed through before we got here. I slowly began to make out a few objects. I could tell they were dolphins, and there were dozens of them. What I was looking at didn't seem like a screen. It was more like some 3D projection. But I still didn't know how any of it was possible. It looked like it was all coming from the crystal as if the crystal had some sort of power of projection, like it was a super computer.

"What you see here is our first record we have. This is where the dolphins came together for the first time to create this place," Sadira said.

The dolphins were moving so fast, swimming up and down, and then they stopped and looked at each other. You could not hear what they were saying, but soon they began to spread themselves out over a very large distance—and then their heads began to glow. Then a foundation of the city began to form, and the walls and the pillars stood straight up.

"You see here is the birth of Antilla," Sadira said. I watched in amazement. "I must be dreaming," I thought. Soon the city began to look like the Antilla that I had seen with Lyra. Then the projection changed—it was like transcendence through space—to a new scene that showed dolphins. The dolphins were all gathered together.

"Brothers and sisters," one of the dolphins yelled as all of the dolphins faced the dolphin that was speaking.

"Brothers and sisters, let this place that we have built be a place of paradise, a place where our kind can come and be in peace and escape the world that we live in. Let this place be the light in this dark world we live in. Let us finish it," the dolphin said. Then the dolphins came close together, and their heads began to glow again. Then the city began to glow in iconic shimmering gold.

"Now, let me show you the legend of Aphrodite. You have heard this name before, correct?" Sadira asked.

"Yes I have, a little. We consider her to be a goddess where I come from," I said surprised to hear the name Aphrodite from Sadira.

"Well, let me tell you the legend that we know of here. During the time of great knowledge, there was a school that taught all dolphins," Sadira said. Suddenly, there was a fading, and the scene of building Antilla disappeared. Then a new scene appeared that showed large dolphins and smaller dolphins.

"This is one of the schools. These are the children, and these are the teachers. There was a great teacher at this time called Naos. Naos was one of the great thinkers of his time. He explored the universe farther than any of us have been able to, then and now," Sadira said. The scene centered around one dolphin that looked older than the rest.

"Naos was also one of the great teachers of the school of thought. Naos taught about philosophy and science and defensive strategy to all of his students. Many students who learned from him went on to do great things. Once there was one student who did better than all of the other students had ever done. That student was Algorab. Algorab could see as far as Naos into the workings of the universe. Naos recognized this talent in Algorab, and selected Algorab to be his successor. Naos began to teach Algorab all of the secrets he had learned about the universe," Sadira said.

I saw the older dolphin Naos selecting Algorab and taking him to a place where Naos showed Algorab different stars. Then I could see Algorab began to get older and larger.

"Soon Algorab began to grow older and began to wander on his own, going deep into thought about the secrets of the universe. One day Algorab began to question Naos," Sadira said.

"But Lord Naos, is there not a way for us to go on land? Should dolphins not dominate land like they do the oceans?" Algorab asked.

"No, there is no way to be on land. We don't exist in that world. Just as things on land don't exist in ours," Naos said to Algorab.

Algorab turned toward Naos.

"But my lord, doesn't all of the world exist for dolphins? Is it not our right to dominate land as well as water?" Algorab asked Naos.

"It is not our place to dominate the world. There must be a harmony among our two worlds. I never want you to ask me that again. You must follow the ways that I have taught you," Naos said angrily.

"I understand, my lord," Algorab said as he looked at the ground and then swam away.

Algorab seemed mad. The scenes seemed to follow Algorab as he swam through the blue.

"Algorab swam to look for answers. The answer that Naos had given him did not satisfy his desire to rule land as well as water. Algorab went to the surface and began to swim and look to the heavens. As he was swimming, Algorab saw something new that Naos had not taught him before. After analyzing what it was, Algorab realized that it was man, a creature from land. Algorab stared and stared at the men as they fished. Finally, Algorab had found the answer he was looking for to how to dominate land, and swam back to Naos," Sadira said.

"My lord, I have found the answer," Algorab said.

"The answer to what Algorab?" Naos asked.

"The answer to how to rule the land. It is possible to rule the land. We can rule through the use of humans," Algorab said and then there was a pause. Naos paced back and forth, and there was silence. Then Naos took a deep breath.

"Mankind is our ally. I have looked and studied the universe for most of my life, and I have seen into the future. I know many secrets, and I have taught you some. But I tell you this now. Mankind will rise in knowledge and grow. With our help, one day their civilization will equal ours. We will live in peace with man. They don't exist to be conquered by dolphins. They must not be touched. Do you understand?" Naos said as he stared directly at Algorab.

"But…," Algorab said with a pause of frustration.

"I understand, my lord," Algorab said with a bow and then swam off.

"But there was corruption in Algorab's heart. Algorab saw the humans not like others did. He saw the humans as a useful tool and as a potential threat to all dolphins. He began to find other dolphins that he could influence to join him in his quest to turn humans into a conquered species," Sadira said.

"We will conquer them, and then control the sea and the land. Naos must be wrong. This is the destiny of dolphins. I know it is. I will prove him wrong," Algorab said to himself.

"Algorab then began to discover a new power," Sadira said as the crystal showed Algorab going to the top of the ocean. Algorab approached a fishing vessel and stared at it. As Algorab stared at the fishing vessel, he closed his eyes and the wind began to move and the waves began to crash into the boat. The boat began to move toward the land. The crew tried to move frantically around the ship to stop it from crashing, but it was useless. The ship went aground, and then Algorab smiled.

"Algorab had figured out how he would stop man from being in the ocean. He had a power that hadn't existed before. Soon he taught his followers the same power he had discovered. He gathered himself and his thoughts on a new plan. If he had the power to control the ocean, then that meant he could truly wage war: a war against dolphins and a war against man. The incident with the boat and the fishermen would be the first, but it wouldn't be the last. Algorab commanded his troops and under his rule with their new weapon—the power of controlling the oceans—Algorab and his followers waged war with mankind first. They started bringing about terrible storms—storms that caused ships to hit rocks and sink. Mankind was powerless against this force, because they could not tell where it came from.

"Soon the other dolphins that weren't a part of Algorab's following saw what Algorab and his followers were doing. The dolphins tried to stop Algorab from harming the humans. Humans were a new species, and it had to be protected. The dolphins from long ago had decided that mankind would be protected, and the idea that a dolphin would bring harm to the humans was terrifying to most dolphins.

"The whole concept of war had never occurred among dolphins before. War was something new. It was a time of danger. The first attack on dolphins occurred shortly after the attack of the human ships had occurred. An investigative party was sent to investigate what was happening with the humans. Reports had been made about humans being stranded on sea, and some ships being sunk into the ocean," Sadira said.

"My Lord Naos, a strange occurrence is happening among the humans," one dolphin said to Naos.

"Send out dolphins to investigate what has happened. We must protect the humans," Naos said.

"And with that, the first group of dolphins went to find out what had happened to the humans. The investigative team found man everywhere.

"Then they saw it. It was Algorab with the other dolphins. At their first appearance, the investigative party had thought that Algorab had just come to investigate like all of the other dolphins. But soon the investigative party was attacked by Algorab, and they realized that there had been treachery among the dolphins. Out of all of the dolphins that went among the investigative party, only one dolphin survived the attack. That dolphin went back to Antilla to warn the others of Algorab. The other dolphins of Antilla were frightened. When Naos found out about the attack, he wasn't sure what the fighting was about, but Naos became infuriated," Sadira said.

"Who was it that was leading them? Was it one of the other dolphin tribes?" Naos asked the lone survivor.

"No, my lord. I'm sorry but it was Algorab," the survivor said. Naos became even more furious.

"How could my student, my successor, do this? We shall defend ourselves and the humans. We shall protect Antilla from any attack," Naos turned toward another dolphin.

"Gather up all the dolphins. If Algorab wants to battle, then we shall battle," Naos said.

"All the dolphins that were left in Antilla went toward Algorab and his followers to fight the attack head on. But Algorab and his followers fought back and quickly began to win," Sadira said.

"You will never destroy Antilla," Naos said.

"I'm not trying to destroy Antilla. I'm just trying to make our kind better," Algorab said.

"How is this better?" Naos said.

Algorab looked around. He could see what the two sides were doing to each other.

"I don't know," Algorab said and gave a sign to his followers, and his followers retreated. Naos turned toward one of the other dolphins.

"Gather all the dolphins together. We must pray for salvation. It is the only chance we have now," Naos said.

"But my Lord Naos, Algorab has retreated, You have won the battle," the dolphin said.

"No, I fear we will lose the war. The next attack will be soon. Gather up everyone, it's our only chance," Naos said again.

The dolphin went to spread the word about the great gathering. Soon all the dolphins came together. Naos stood in the middle of them.

"Brothers and sisters, children of Antilla, I need you to pray with me. We are in a time of great trouble. It is a time our kind has never faced before, and we need to pray for help to come. In the ancient times when difficult times were upon our kind, they would pray for help. We shall do that now," Naos said.

With that, all the dolphins formed a circle and closed their eyes. All of Antilla began to glow like a giant beacon.

Chapter 25

Aphrodite

In a small village, a woman dropped a cup. She was a beautiful woman. "This is Aphrodite. During the great turmoil, prayers would be answered by her," Sadira said.

"Oh, I'm sorry," Aphrodite said as she bent down to pick up the cup she dropped. But she was beat at picking up the cup by the man who was next to her. He had grabbed the cup first. The man smiled and handed the cup back to Aphrodite.

"Thank you. I don't know what went wrong with me," Aphrodite said confused.

"It's okay," the man said.

The man turned away from Aphrodite and turned back toward the storekeeper.

"So you were saying?" the storekeeper asked.

"Well, I was just saying how interesting it was that the ships seem to be hitting land lately. No one can explain why," the man said.

"Yes, that is interesting, and there is no sign of a monster or anything along those lines. I think we haven't seen the end of this. The God of the sea must really be angered," the storekeeper said.

The man nodded his head in agreement as the storekeeper said this. Aphrodite heard every word that was spoken. Aphrodite turned toward Quill, her friend.

"Quill, it's like my dreams," Aphrodite whispered.

"What dreams?" Quill asked.

"Oh yeah, I forgot to tell you I've been having these strange dreams about forces in the water. I'm not sure what the forces are, but in my dream, they have been doing something to the water—changing it somehow," Aphrodite said.

Quill looked at Aphrodite and blinked, and shook her head.

"Oh Aphrodite, you must keep your head clear. That man there talking to the storekeeper, I hear, is looking for a woman. I think he might be right for you."

"Quill, this is no time for that. There are bigger things to be taken care of. I've had this conversation with you before. I'm not looking for anyone. I am going to live alone the rest of my life," Aphrodite said as she started to pick up things in the store and straighten them up.

"No Aphrodite, you're not. You're going to find a man and have a family. It's how it's done. It's not right for you to want to be alone the rest of your life," Quill said unsatisfied that Aphrodite had pushed her to the side again on this issue.

"Look Aphrodite, you have to listen. How can you live without love? Every woman needs love in her life. Just give it some thought, okay? This guy is a good match for you. He's successful, and he's looking for a woman. Promise me, you'll give it a thought," Quill said.

Aphrodite turned toward Quill and took a deep breath.

"Of course I will Quill. You know me. Sometimes I just forget how important love is," Aphrodite said with a sad look.

Satisfied with this, Quill walked away.

"Quill just doesn't get it. I'm happy alone," Aphrodite said to herself. Then Aphrodite continued to straighten the store. It was a nice little clothing store. The store was one of the first of its kind. People would come and trade for the latest type of clothing. It was the only place that would hire a woman. So there Aphrodite was, straightening clothes and making the store look overly neat.

That is why the storekeeper liked her so much. Aphrodite seemed to care. As Aphrodite continued to straighten up, she heard something and looked over. The man who had been talking to the storekeeper was about to leave. As he started to walk out the door, the man stopped. The man seemed to be taking a moment to stare at Aphrodite. He smiled as Aphrodite glanced his way. Aphrodite returned the smile. Then the man walked out the door. The storekeeper walked over toward Aphrodite.

"Aphrodite, that man was asking about you," the storekeeper said with a giant smile.

Aphrodite just stood where she was and remained silent.

"Aphrodite, would you mind getting an old man some water from the well?" the storekeeper asked.

"Yes of course," Aphrodite said as she grabbed the pail and headed out to get some water.

As Aphrodite walked out the door, the man stood next to his horse preparing his packet. It looked as though he was going to go on a long trip. But in the middle of the man's packing, the man stopped when he saw Aphrodite again.

"Do you live here?" the man asked Aphrodite.

"Yes I do," Aphrodite said shocked that the man had actually talked to her.

"Well then, I will definitely be back. I will return in a week, will you be here?"

"Yes I will. I work in that shop where you were in, and I live close by."

"And you have no man? I mean, you are not taken?" the man asked smiling.

"No, I'm not taken," Aphrodite said smiling back.

"Good. I will call on you later, my lady," the man said and jumped on his horse. Aphrodite stared at him as he galloped away.

"Maybe Quill was right. He might be the one," Aphrodite said aloud as she watched the man gallop away.

Then a sudden vision rushed over Aphrodite. It was a vision of spirits gathering in water. The spirits were together praying and chanting. Then there was a spirit that looked like an evil dolphin, and then there was destruction. Then Aphrodite saw a vision of herself going toward the water. Aphrodite did not know what any of it meant. She tried to ignore it.

As she walked toward the well and got the water, Aphrodite then returned to the store.

"Here you go," Aphrodite said as she handed the storekeeper the cup of water.

"Oh thank you," the storekeeper said pleased as he took the cup.

"Aphrodite my dear, we are closing the store for the rest of the day. I must rest. Take the rest of the day off and enjoy yourself."

"Oh thank you," Aphrodite said.

She grabbed her bag and started to head out the door.

"Have a good day. I will see you tomorrow first thing," the storekeeper said.

"You too," Aphrodite said back to the storekeeper as she started to walk out the door. Since it was so early, Aphrodite decided to take a walk along the beach. It was what she always did when she needed to think. She soon arrived at the beach and began to walk along the sand. It was so calm and serene. She found a spot that was free of rocks and took a seat. After a few minutes, she began to hear a faint cry for help. She thought it sounded like a child.

Aphrodite jumped up and went toward the water. Then the water started to react and move around her like a swirl. Then something like a bubble surrounded her. She was shocked and tried to escape but couldn't. She started to cry, but as she cried and panicked, a calm voice came from somewhere and talked to her.

"Calm down my child. You must relax. You are needed," the voice said.

Aphrodite felt the sudden urge to relax and didn't cry anymore. The bubble that Aphrodite was in then began to travel through the water.

Aphrodite took a seat as best as she could. She was in a bubble—at least it seemed like a bubble. The bubble didn't go very far but instead just began to spin with Aphrodite inside it. It was clear, and she could see all around her. Then the bubble stopped, and she suddenly felt very tired and soon fell asleep. When she awoke, Aphrodite was walking through the water. Aphrodite seemed confused. She looked around and saw a light ahead of her. She then felt the sudden urge to move toward the light so she did. As she walked and walked toward the light, she realized that she was approaching a shining city. This city was unlike anything that she had ever seen. It shimmered and seemed like it was made out of gold.

There was a beacon of shining light that Aphrodite saw in the distance. It was blue like a jewel. As Aphrodite left the bubble, she walked toward the blue jewel being surrounded by dolphins as if she was strangely attracted to it. She had never seen so many dolphins. Naos looked up and saw Aphrodite for the first time. A feeling of relief came over him.

"Could it be? Is this what was destined to happen? Surely, one of the humans would come to be our savior. Of course, it must be true for you are here. What is your name my dear?" Naos asked Aphrodite.

Aphrodite had never seen a dolphin before and never heard an animal talk, but after everything that she had just been through, she wasn't too shocked.

"I am Aphrodite," she said and took a bow.

"Aphrodite, yes. Aphrodite, the savior, you are here to save us, thank you," Naos said.

"Save you? How can I save you, and from what?" Aphrodite asked in a stunned tone.

"My dear, I don't know how you might save us, but it must be so. You would not be here if it wasn't what is meant to happen. We will wait till things reveal themselves. In the meantime, welcome to Antilla and enjoy our hospitality," Naos said and then turned toward all of the dolphins.

"Behold, this is your savior Antilla. She will rescue us when the time is right. Welcome her as our guest and show her our ways," Naos said.

With that, all of the dolphins came up to Aphrodite and surrounded her. Aphrodite could see all of their faces. It was a look of fear and hope at the same time. She could not say no, though she didn't understand fully why she was there or what she was saving the dolphins from.

"I will stay and learn," Aphrodite said. Then there was cheering from the crowd at this news. It was a loud cheer from all around the city.

In the distance, outside of Antilla, there wasn't any celebrating going on. Algorab and his forces gathered together in a meeting place. Algorab and his followers had created a new realm outside of Antilla. In this realm, they were able to do new things—things dolphins had never done before. At least that's what they thought. Algorab was the greatest of them all. He instructed and taught his followers the art of controlling water.

"Water is what we live in. It is our right to control it, and if you listen to me, I will show you how to control it with your mind," Algorab said to all of those that followed him. Algorab and his forces continued to train. They learned the art of controlling water.

Back in Antilla, there was nothing to do but wait and learn, which was exactly what Aphrodite did. She still wasn't sure why she was there, but she knew it must be destiny. After all of the dolphins were gone, Aphrodite was left alone in the city. She thought that it was unlike anything that mankind had ever created. It was a flawless city. All of the structures were beyond smooth. They were like glass, but they glowed like gold. There was another thing Aphrodite had noticed. Even though it seemed as though she was breathing air, the dolphins floated through the air like they were swimming.

"Wow, this place is strange!" Aphrodite said aloud. She continued to walk and then ran into Naos.

"Hello Aphrodite," Naos said.

"Hello, I'm sorry I don't know what your name is."

"I am Naos, the leader of the dolphins. I am here to teach you our ways. Come with me, and we will learn together," Naos said.

Aphrodite and Naos then began to walk. As they walked, a strange hue surrounded Naos and Aphrodite.

Time passed quickly as Naos trained Aphrodite. In what seemed like months had taken place, Aphrodite learned all that Naos knew. Then Naos turned to Aphrodite after all of her training had been complete.

"My dear, take what I have taught you and use it to save us. You are our last hope," Naos said to Aphrodite.

"I will do my best Naos. You have taught me so much."

Aphrodite then decided to take a walk to think about what to do next. It was like a spiritual walk. She thought about everything that she had learned. She was still unsure if she could fight Algorab, who she learned was the mortal enemy of Antilla. Aphrodite wanted to be the one she needed to be, but she still wasn't sure if she could be that person.

Aphrodite continued to walk until she reached a strange path. The path glowed a pink luminescent color. Aphrodite had never seen this path before. She walked down it until she was far away from Antilla. Then a flash appeared, and there was a dolphin that she had not seen before.

"Who are you?" Aphrodite asked.

The dolphin did not talk, but instead, came closer and glowed as it stared at Aphrodite as if to analyze Aphrodite for a few minutes.

"Who are you?" Aphrodite asked again.

"I am the mighty Phe."

"Who?"

"My dear, I am here to help you on your path. Long ago, your arrival was prophesied. You must fulfill your destiny and save Antilla," Phe said.

"But mighty Phe, I don't know how to do that. I learned all that Naos could teach me, but I still don't know if it is enough to defend against Algorab," Aphrodite said.

Phe began to laugh.

"My dear, you will save them. You have a deeper power than all the powers known to dolphins, and that is why you are here. Long ago, when the ancients saw you coming, they created something that would help you to uncover your power," Phe said and shook his head up and down.

A glowing amulet then came from out of nowhere.

"Here my dear is the key to your power. You must learn to use it wisely for you are the only one that can use it. There will be only one another that will be able to wield its power. Contained within the amulet is a great power that will destroy evil when used against it."

The necklace floated over and went around Aphrodite's neck. When it went on her neck, the necklace glowed with a shining deep blue light like a blue fire. Aphrodite felt alive for the first time in her life—like life had not existed before this moment. She suddenly knew that she had the power to defeat Algorab.

"This necklace can never come off of you. This necklace is now alive and bonded to you, and you are bonded to it. Therefore, it cannot be removed. Its power can only be used by you as long as you are alive," Phe said.

Aphrodite looked at the necklace again. The blue slowly dimmed down in brightness and then became the color of a blue sapphire. The sapphire was surrounded by two dolphins and had a gold symbol over the stone.

"Have you understood everything I have told you?" Phe asked

"Yes mighty Phe, I have, thank you," Aphrodite said.

"Go on your way then and fulfill your destiny."

"Mighty Phe, what if I need further guidance. What if I still can't do the job I am destined to do?"

"You will my dear. It is your destiny and must happen," Phe said and then disappeared.

The path then glowed a pink luminescence again. Aphrodite began to walk down the path, back to where she had started walking. At the end of the path, Naos was waiting for her.

"Did you have a good walk Aphrodite?" Naos asked smiling.

"Yes I did Naos. I feel better now," Aphrodite said.

"That is good because I fear the time is at hand. The time to fulfill your destiny will be soon. Come and join us as we celebrate on this late hour with a sort of feast and prayer," Naos said and pointed toward the left.

Aphrodite took the hint and began to walk. They soon arrived at a banquet. There was all manner of fish available. For Aphrodite, there were wine and all the foods that she was used to.

"We specifically prepared this food for you. We read your mind and found out what sort of things you liked from where you are from. I hope that you are most pleased," Naos said.

Aphrodite looked at all of the foods she saw and was most delighted. They were all her favorite foods. Then Aphrodite realized that the whole time she had been in Antilla, she had not eaten once.

"How is it that I have been here all of this time and not eaten?" Aphrodite asked.

"Time is very different here. It stops and starts at our leisure. We are timeless in this place. When I was training you, it seemed like months had passed, but it was actually only a few minutes. Do you understand?" Naos asked.

"Yes I do, I think," Aphrodite said and began to eat.

There was also a fair amount of chitchat and music in the background. It was music of the ocean, and it was very calming. Then after everyone had been eating and chatting for a little bit, Naos stood in front of everyone.

"My children, I fear the time is upon us. You know of the enemy that is out there, that wishes to defeat us and destroy all that we hold dear. You must defend this place, even until the last of us is swimming.

Everyone must fight or all will be lost. I leave you for the rest of the evening to reflect and pray for you might not get the chance to later. Good luck tomorrow."

Then Naos was quiet and the whole banquet began to quiet down and slowly everyone left to be alone. When Aphrodite was alone, she found her way back to where she was to sleep for the evening.

It was a nice little house that had been created for her. It looked different than all other houses. It seemed special. Aphrodite soon came over her nerves about the next day and quickly fell asleep. She slept more soundly than she had ever slept before. Time went by quickly while Aphrodite slept, and soon the sound of trumpets rang as the dolphins on watch sounded off the invasion. There were dolphins everywhere in sight—all a part of Algorab's forces. His forces seemed to have tripled, and they were being violent. They began to tear the city apart. Algorab's forces moved the buildings apart brick by brick and pushed the bricks into oblivion. Any dolphins that tried to resist were pushed into oblivion as well.

Soon a few of the dolphins wearing a white dressing arrived with Naos. They began to push Algorab and his forces back toward oblivion. Some of Algorab's forces began to fall into cliff and began to be sucked away into the unknown. Algorab came and went toward Naos and pushed him close to the cliff.

"Now Aphrodite, it is time for you to do what you have to. Save Antilla and all that is left," Naos yelled.

Aphrodite ran toward the battle as fast as she had ever run. Then Aphrodite stood, stared, and tried to use the mind techniques that Naos had taught her, but Algorab's forces came toward Aphrodite and were not stopping.

Aphrodite feared that she would die. She had already seen so many dolphins die. Then suddenly in the panic of the situation, Aphrodite suddenly thought of that man she had met at the store. Aphrodite thought of how much she would miss him if she died, and how sorry she was that she hadn't been there for his return. Deep down inside, Aphrodite had such strong feelings for him that it might be considered love. With that thought of love—that ever so slight thought of the possibility of love—suddenly became amplified into a million fold of the power that it once was. A shining shimmer of blue suddenly spewed from the amulet that had been given to Aphrodite. That amulet power stopped and froze Algorab and all of his followers.

Naos and his forces were able to move, but all that Aphrodite wanted to remain paralyzed and frozen stayed frozen.

"Are you able to hold them like that?" Naos asked.

"Yes I believe so. My power seems to be holding them," Aphrodite said with a calm voice.

Aphrodite wasn't even struggling to hold them. Naos swam through the crowds of dolphins until he arrived to Algorab. Then Naos spoke loudly so that all could hear.

"You have tried to destroy the good and light of the world, and now you have failed. You are forever banished from Antilla, and you may never return," Naos said to Algorab.

Then Naos reached out his fin and then a slight ball of light came from Algorab. It was thrown into oblivion, and then Algorab said, "I will return one way or another—either I will return or someone like me. I won't be the last to threaten Antilla, mark my words. I will destroy Antilla one day," Algorab said and took a bow and then vanished and was never heard from again.

Naos turned toward the other dolphins that made up Algorab's forces.

"I will give all of you a second chance. If any of you ever do anything like this again, I will banish you too. Now go back and be a part of our society and all will be forgiven," Naos said and then he turned to all of the dolphins.

"Brothers and sisters! Today our way of life has been tested and was almost destroyed. All was almost lost, but through hope and love, we were saved.

Remember this day, and remember that a human named Aphrodite saved us from ourselves. From this day forward, she shall be worshiped as sacred, and all of her kind will be protected. Now let us rebuild Antilla and have peace."

Naos stopped talking and turned toward Aphrodite.

"Thank you my dear, you have saved us all," Naos said.

"You're welcome," Aphrodite said and then let the other dolphins that she had been holding go. The dolphins all swam back with the other dolphins.

Then Aphrodite turned toward Naos and said, "Naos, great and mighty! I think it is time for me to go."

"Go? Where would you go?" Naos asked shocked.

"Naos, I must go back to my kind. It is time. My purpose here has been fulfilled. Now I must help my kind," Aphrodite said and began to walk away.

"I understand Aphrodite, and I hope one day you will return," Naos said.

"You have taught me so much, but I must follow my heart, and my heart is with my people."

"I understand, but if at any time you wish to return to Antilla, you may. Once you have found this place, you can always find it again."

"Thank you," Aphrodite said and with that, walked away.

"Aphrodite returned to her home. She went on to shape human society and make it what it is today. Over time, she fell in love with the man that she had left in the beginning. Some considered her a goddess among your kind, but she was never a goddess. She was a woman. After she changed your society and found her love, she left it.

"From the moment she left Antilla, she thought her place was with the dolphins. That is where she lived out the rest of her days, among us. Aphrodite was unable to bring the man that she had loved to Antilla so she left her heart partially with him and the rest of her heart stayed with us. Before Aphrodite died, she made a prediction that another one like her would come and would make her heart complete again by taking her spot among the dolphins.

"That is why you are so celebrated Aurora, because you are her chosen successor. You are here to complete her heart," Sadira said and then suddenly it seemed like we went out of the memory projection, and we were back in present-day Antilla.

Suddenly there was a shudder among Lyra, Sadira, and I as though we had all just been a part of the most spectacular dream together. It was absolutely amazing.

"Do you understand now what your purpose is?" Lyra asked me in a very determined voice.

"Yes I do believe so. I must protect your people and mine. But you must forgive me, it is still a lot to take in," I said.

Sadira started moving away from the crystal. The crystal went dark, and then Sadira said, "It is okay my lady. It will come, just give it time to sink in. No one here expects you to fully feel the power that is within you yet, but you must know it is there. It was felt by all the dolphins the very second that you entered Antilla. There was an omniscient presence that each dolphin felt. You represent the power of two worlds, and that is what makes you so important. Now we really must go back to the celebration. It will most likely be beginning soon," Sadira said and pointed as though I was supposed to go first.

Chapter 26

A Heart Complete

Luckily, Lyra jumped in front of me and started to swim. "Follow me my Lady Aurora, I shall show you the way," Lyra said. We began to move, and as we did, a light of essence started to come toward us. I wasn't sure if we were moving or if all of Antilla was moving toward us, but we soon arrived at our destination.

There were thousands of dolphins present. It was the largest display of any gathering that I had ever seen. In fact, the whole feast was set in an ancient Greek amphitheater. I was lead to the center of the amphitheater where my table was. There was only one chair there that looked like a throne, and I could see all of the dolphins from it. Beside me at the table was Kaitos.

"Aurora welcome, we haven't begun yet. You will be at my table, or should I say I will be at your table, for tonight is your night. Please take a seat in the chair of Aphrodite," Kaitos said and gestured for me to sit in the very amazing chair. It was embossed with scenery of clams and dolphins and an intertwined embossment of the battle of Antilla that I had seen with Sadira. It was very well made. When I sat in the chair, the figures began to move, and the whole chair seemed to light up. Then Kaitos began to speak to the thousands of dolphins that were there.

"Antilla, our Lady Aurora has arrived. Tonight we have come to celebrate the completion of the heart. As you know from the legends, it was said that one day the heart would be complete once more. That time is now. Aurora, the new Aphrodite, has arrived. Bring forth the gift."

Suddenly a box came floating in the water toward my table. It too was crested in a similar design to that of the throne. When the box arrived at the table, it opened up, and the necklace I had seen on Aphrodite was here in front of me.

"My dear Aurora. This necklace was worn by Aphrodite, and it is to be only worn by her successor. You are her successor. With the graciousness of Antilla, I do humbly request that you accept this gift on our behalf. Is it your heart's desire to receive this gift?" Kaitos asked and looked at me as though I was supposed to know the answer.

"Yes of course," I managed to say loudly so everyone could hear me.

"Excellent," Kaitos said, and then the necklace came toward me and went around my neck. Then Kaitos spoke loudly.

"From this day forward, you must keep this necklace on you. It is to be used for good, and never evil, through the power of love. You must use it to protect Antilla and your world. Now Antilla, join me in welcoming Aurora as our protector," Kaitos said and started to cheer.

There was a loud cheering from all of the dolphins. Then there was a celebration. It was the largest party that I had ever been to. I managed to see a few familiar faces. Lyra and Sadira both came toward me.

"Are you having fun?" Sadira asked as I sat in my chair and watched the celebration.

"I am now," I said and the party continued on. After about thirty minutes of talking, I finally decided to ask the question that had been perplexing my mind for a little while.

"Sadira, I have a question, and I don't think anyone else will know the answer."

Sadira smiled. "Go ahead, you can ask me anything, my lady."

"What's next?"

"What do you mean?" Sadira asked.

"What is next for me? I mean, I can't stay here forever, can I?"

"It's hard to say. It is actually up to you," Sadira said.

"What do you mean?" I asked perplexed.

"This place is not a prison. There are a lot of mysteries to it, and no one really knows how it exists. But one thing is certain, you can leave anytime you wish. You just have to desire it," Sadira said.

There was a pause as I thought about what Sadira said. Then Lyra turned after hearing what Sadira and I had talked about.

"Perhaps there's a reason you haven't left yet. You must be waiting for something, my Lady Aurora," Lyra said.

What Lyra had said had a lot of truth to it. I was waiting. I wanted to see what was going to happen with everything, but now that the celebration and ceremony were over, I think it might be time to go back to reality."

"How can I return to reality? I mean, how do I go back to where I am from?" I asked Sadira.

"My dear Aurora, no one can tell you how to go back. You actually have to figure it out for yourself. It is different for everyone. You just have to think of something you miss badly enough from the other place, and you will go back," Sadira said.

I decided to try not to think about what Sadira said until after the party was over, but it was hard. The party continued on. It was an intense celebration. Eventually, the celebration was over, and I was left thinking about it. Those that had been at the party soon left, and I was left there alone. It seemed like I was thinking about everything that I missed all at once. I tried to focus on just one thing that I missed. Then I suddenly thought about Devon.

I began to imagine how he looked when I first left. I pictured him with the biggest smile when we set out to communicate with the dolphins. Then suddenly there was a flash, and I was back into my scuba gear and there was Devon staring at me.

Chapter 27

Unexplainable

I nodded my head in agreement after Devon said "Let's go up." We slowly began our way back up toward the breathable air.

It was hard to believe that after all of this time, I was still in my scuba gear. We soon arrived back into breathable air, and then we got back into the boat. Devon ran over toward the computer as soon as his feet touched the deck.

"What happened? Where did that dolphin go? It was like he just vanished," Devon said.

"Don't you want to know where I've been? How come you don't seem the least bit worried about me?" I asked in a frustrated voice.

"What are you talking about? I had my eyes on you the whole time. You were with the dolphin one second, and the next second the dolphin was gone. I think it is best that we head back up to see the video and figure out what happened," Devon said.

Then Devon stopped looking at the computer and came up to me.

"You act like you've been gone for months. Where did you get that necklace from?" Devon asked with a perplexed look as he put his hand on the necklace. I backed away a little. Something in me wanted to protect the necklace.

"Devon, I don't know how to tell you this, but something happened when we were in the water. It was something that I am having trouble coming to grips with myself," I said and then paused. I suddenly felt the need to take a deep breath. I did and then continued to talk.

"Can I tell you what happened?"

Devon continued to look at his equipment. He didn't even look at me. I waited and stared. For the first time since I had known Devon, I became very mad at him. Devon was for all accounts and purposes ignoring me. I couldn't stand it.

"Devon, are you going to look at me? Don't you want to know what I've been through?" I asked.

Devon just continued to go over all of the data that had been collected.

"Devon!!!" I yelled.

"Yes Aurora, just give me a minute," Devon said seemingly trying to shrug me off. This infuriated me. I walked off.

"Let me know when you're ready to listen," I said and walked toward the small galley. George was in the galley and getting a drink.

"Had fun in the water, huh?" George asked.

"I guess you could say that," I said and sat there about to cry.

"Hey, can I make you something? We do have a few things here to drink. It's not a bad galley. Nope, not too bad at all," George said as he started to look through the cupboards.

"Yeah, I think I would like that. Do you have any tea?" I asked trying to ignore what had just happened with Devon and me.

"Yeah, I got some Earl Grey here. But I'm going to have to nuke it, is that cool?"

"Yeah, that's cool," I said and sat there trapped back in my thoughts.

I still can't believe Devon. Why didn't he want to listen to me? What just happened was a great thing. It was a life-changing thing and I wanted to share it with him. I had missed him so much while I was gone, but he didn't even pay attention to me just now. Devon cared more about that equipment than about me. I still didn't know how I could have only been gone for a moment when I was actually gone for what seemed like a couple of weeks.

"Here is your tea. Cream or sugar?" George asked.

"Just a little cream."

George handed me the tea.

"Thank you, I really appreciate it."

Just then Devon walked in.

"Dude, you look in shock. Did you have a good time out there? What did you find out?" George asked Devon.

"We'll see George. I'm not sure yet, but something cool did happen. I will tell you about it later," Devon said as he stared at me.

"George, would you give Aurora and me a minute?"

"Sure," George said giving a smirk and then walked off.

I stirred my tea. I didn't want to look right at Devon just yet. I was still really mad at him. But Devon always knew how to get me to warm up, and it was hard to stay mad. Devon sat on the other side of the table.

"Aurora, I'm sorry that I ignored you. I was so focused on looking at the computer and trying to figure out what happened with that dolphin that I neglected you. I'm sorry. Won't you forgive me?"

I glanced at Devon. He had such heartfelt puppy dog eyes.

"I can't stay mad at you," I said and smiled.

Devon leaned in and gave me a kiss, then everything was good.

"So tell me, what was it you were talking about?"

"Well, it can wait. Why don't you tell me what you found out."

Devon smiled.

"Well, it is really weird. If you look at the data, I mean, there really isn't much there. But what is there shows us in the water with the dolphin one second. The next second, there is no dolphin, like the dolphin just vanished. It is too weird. I have looked at all of the data, and I can't figure it out. All of the instruments were working properly, and it's impossible to explain," Devon said and then focused his eyes again on me.

"So what were you going to say my dear?"

"Well, I had a different experience. It was life changing," I said.

"What do you mean? It was just like all of the other times that we have went. Oh wait, I know what you mean. Swimming with the dolphin was life changing, right? I mean, I can't believe that you actually talked to one in the wild. I just am having trouble putting it on paper. I mean, think of the implications. I think if we run a few more tests, we will be able to prove without a shadow of a doubt that you are actually communicating with the dolphins.

"Mark my words on this day, we have experienced something momentous. It is almost like they are aliens—and this is the first encounter—but it is all happening right here on this planet. Isn't it amazing? I'm sorry Aurora. I couldn't contain myself. This moment means so much to me. It's what I've been dreaming all my life. I'm so glad I have you to share it with me. You are the reason we have this moment too. It is like the best bonus ever. What were you going to say my dear? I keep interrupting you and I'm sorry," Devon said.

I was now having trouble coming up with the words to say what I wanted. It was so difficult to discuss this with Devon right now. He was so wrapped up in all of his little projects for the communication between the dolphins and humans. But I wanted to tell him so bad. I mean, think of all that I had just went through. But I couldn't deny the man that I love from experiencing the happiest moment I think I have seen from him since we got together. I just couldn't spoil it for him. I decided to keep him in the dark for now. I would reveal to him all that had happened in time. I put on a big smile and looked like the happiest woman on earth.

Devon came close to me. I was still sitting with my tea. Devon came right up and got on his knees and placed himself in front of my face. Then he held my hands and leaned in putting his eyes right in front of mine.

"Aurora, I love you so much. Thank you," Devon said and leaned in to give me a kiss.

I kissed back and then that was it. There wasn't much said after that. I couldn't and wouldn't spoil it for him. He had to be happy.

I will tell him what happened when we get back.

Then after Devon released my lips, he got up.

"Aurora, I want you to enjoy your tea. I have to go back to my research. I really need to figure out what happened to that dolphin. They don't just vanish like that. I think I might consult someone when we get back. In the meantime, I need to analyze the tapes. I will be at my computer for a little while if you need me," Devon said.

"Okay, I will be here," I said and let him go.

Telling Devon about my whole experience was going to be a lot harder than I had thought it was going to be. I just hope that I would have the courage later.

Devon left and was at his computer the rest of the time that we were out to sea. We soon pulled back in San Diego. It was always good to be back, especially for me. Even though this little cruise had been a day, it really did seem like a few weeks. I smelled the sweet air, and everything looked breathtaking. I stood on deck and watched as we pulled in. George was steering. He really was a master of steering.

"Aurora, come here," George yelled to me.

I ran over to him.

"Do you want to steer?" George asked.

"Oh, I don't know," I said and smiled.

"Okay, that's fine. I just thought I would offer. We should be in a few minutes."

"Okay, I think I'm going to wait out on deck," I said.

"Okay," George said without taking his eyes off the sea.

Then I went back out on deck. I loved to watch the city as we began to pull in. From a distance, things seemed so serene. We pulled in within minutes. Then just as we pulled in, Devon came out.

"Any luck?" I asked trying to be nice.

"No. If I wasn't there, I would think there was something wrong with the instruments, but I was there and I remember the dolphin disappearing just like on the video. Don't you remember that?"

I was taken off guard and wasn't sure what to say.

"No, I'm sorry. I'm having trouble with the whole thing. It all happened so fast." I was lying of course, but I think I said it with enough confidence to where Devon believed me.

"Well, I will have to look over it a few more times before I give up," Devon said and then looked out at the pier.

"This really is a nice view," Devon said as he put his arm around me. It was in that moment that I probably should have told Devon what had happened, but I didn't. It came down to me not wanting to take away from the moment. Now a new question started to build in me.

Why was I so protective of the whole story about my journey?

Instead of talking, I just stared at everything with Devon. It was a good moment. It was our time. Right now, there was no person on earth who could interrupt it.

That is, no person but George who immediately started yelling at us when we got next to the pier.

"Grab the line and toss it around the davit to secure us!" George yelled out. I didn't know what he was talking about, but Devon seemed to go back to his Navy days, because he jumped fast right to the rope and threw it around the davit. Devon then secured the rope really tight.

"Good job honey," I said.

Devon gave me a smile.

"Okay hun, I have to get all of my equipment ready. We're not going to be able to carry it all off in one swoop. George and I are going to have to take off most of it. Would you mind going to get the truck so that we can pack it up?" Devon asked and handed me the keys.

"Of course my dear. I would do anything for you," I said, and Devon smiled.

Devon went toward his equipment and started to pack. I took a flying leap onto the pier and started walking toward the truck. I got into the truck and put my seatbelt on and turned the engine on.

Though the truck looked a lot like something I might have driven in Alaska, it was now something that I wasn't used to. At least, it was an automatic. It was just the sheer size that I wasn't used to. I drove off and went toward the pier where Devon and George were waiting for me. I parked and got out of the truck.

"Here you go. It's not my style," I said and smiled as I handed the keys off to Devon.

"Thanks. You looked cute driving it though," Devon said.

Devon and George loaded up the truck with equipment. I just waited. All of the equipment was a little on the heavy side. After they were done loading, George said, "Hey, I'm going to get going. Thanks for everything."

"No problem George. We'll see you next time," Devon said.

George walked off and it was just Devon and me.

"Well, let's go hun. I have to drop this stuff off to the college, and then we can return to our lives."

We headed into the truck and drove off.

Chapter 28

There's a Surprise Over Every Hill

We drove into the college area and approached the campus. It was a lovely scene. The trees were the perfect kind of green, and there was a slight wind. The campus itself didn't appear to be too busy today. It was serene and peaceful.

It probably would have been an ideal picture for the website of the school. You know the kind of picture the school puts on the website to try to convince future students that they should attend the college. We drove up the driveway right in front of the research building. Devon put the truck in park.

"Okay Aurora, we're here. Can you help me unload?" Devon asked in the sweetest voice.

I had to help him of course. I couldn't just sit by and let him do all of the work.

"Of course I will," I said and we both got out of the car. All of the equipment wasn't as heavy as it had appeared. We actually managed to unload the truck in only a few minutes.

"Hey, I have to try and look at this data on the better computer inside the research center. Would you mind if I took a look really quick, and then I have somewhere special that I wanted to take you?"

"Yeah sure, that sounds good," I said as Devon went toward his computer in the office.

"Okay, so like five minutes?" Devon said as he was walking.

"Five minutes, huh? Okay, we'll see," I said with a smile. I knew better, but it didn't matter too much.

"No really, time me. Watch only five minutes," Devon said again, and I took a look at my watch.

"Okay go! You got five minutes."

Devon shook his head and smiled. I took a seat on a chair. With these research things Devon does, sometimes it's good to be involved with him every step of the way. Other times like now, when Devon was too focused, it was best to just wait for him to do what he needs to do. No less than a half an hour had gone by before Devon finally came back.

"Five minutes huh," I said with a smile. Devon smiled back.

"Okay, okay, you got me. It wasn't five minutes. Sorry, I still can't figure this thing out. It makes no sense, but I'm not going to worry about it now. We have a date, right?"

"Right, but please, if I can freshen up a little bit," I said.

"Yeah. I'll drop you off at your room, and then we can meet up in an hour. How does that sound?" Devon asked.

"Sounds good."

We got to the room in five actual minutes, and then I asked, "Where are we going on the date?"

"Oh, it's a surprise so dress informally, okay?"

"Okay, I'll text you when I'm ready."

"Okay, sounds good. See you in an hour or so. Love you."

"Love you too, Devon."

I walked toward my room. I opened the door and walked in. My room was nice and quiet. It all looked the same as it had before. It actually started to feel more and more like all of the stuff with dolphins hadn't really happened.

Had I just imagined it all?

The longer I was away from the water, the more it seemed to be a dream. Maybe I had dreamed the whole thing up. Oh well, it wasn't what I wanted to concentrate on right now. I had a date I had to go to, and that was what I wanted to focus on for right now.

It only took a little bit of time to get ready and be beautiful. As I stared in my closet, I thought about what to wear. Since the days that I started to date Devon, I had gotten a lot better at the art of dressing up without really dressing up—to be informal but still look spectacular. I pulled a nice little black dress from the closet, and then I took a shower, put on some makeup, and gave myself a spray with Devon's favorite perfume. Then I got dressed and went up to the tall mirror. I wanted to make sure I looked completely awesome. I took a good look.

Yes I do believe I look good. Now, time for the date.

I picked up my phone to text Devon.

"Okay hun, I'm ready," I texted him and got a text back quickly.

"Knock, knock," Devon wrote.

"Knock, knock?" I said aloud perplexed. Then I heard a knock on the door right behind me. I laughed and looked through the security hole. It was Devon. I began to unbolt the door, and then I opened it.

"You're funny Dev," I said and he smiled.

"Wow! When you say freshen up, you mean it. You look wonderful. Are you ready to go?"

"Yes I am," I said grabbing my purse. I was super excited. I closed the door and locked it. Devon grabbed my hand, and we began to walk toward his car. We both walked to the passenger side. Then Devon opened the door for me.

"My lady," Devon said as he took a bow.

"Why, thank you," I said.

One thing about Devon was that he sure did know how to keep things romantic. Even after all of these months, when he was in date mode, he never failed to make it a date. It made any girl feel beautiful inside. After I was sitting for a few moments, I turned toward Devon who was still adjusting himself in his seat.

"Where are we going?" I asked again.

"My dear Aurora, it is a secret. I was going to blindfold you, but I thought it might make you nauseous on the drive, and people might think I was kidnapping you."

That comment made me smile. Devon knew me so well. I loved surprises.

"Don't worry. I promise I won't disappoint you," Devon said.

There wasn't a lot of talking on the way there. I still had that feeling that the day had been a lot longer than just a day, like I hadn't even been with Devon for months, but everything was coming back. I must have gone in a daydream-like state while we were driving because before I knew it, we were there.

"We're here," Devon jumped out of the car and opened my door.

I stepped out of the car and looked around. It was an open field with a hill. In front of the hill there were a bunch of cars parked. Besides all of the cars there, it didn't seem like there was anything here.

"Ha ha Devon, I know you wanted to be alone, but this is really alone. Where are we?"

"You have to trust me," Devon said as he grabbed my hand. We began to walk up the hill. When we reached the top, I saw it.

"See, I told you to trust me," Devon said.

I was speechless. It was a movie theatre, an outside movie theatre. It was not a drive-in. There were blankets laid out and a screen, and there were people all around. I had never been to one of these before. In fact, I had never even heard of this kind of a theatre.

"Where did you find out about this?" I asked.

Devon just smiled as we walked up to a cashier.

"Two please."

The cashier responded, "Two, absolutely, that will be twenty dollars."

Devon reached into his wallet and handed the cashier a twenty. The cashier handed Devon two tickets and a blanket.

"Where did you hear about this place?" I asked again anxious.

"I have my ways," Devon said as we walked toward an open spot among the crowd of people. The spot that we found was a nice open spot that was not too far away from the center.

"Wow, this is lovely!" I said.

"Have you ever been to one of these before?" Devon asked.

"No I haven't, this is a first. What movie is playing?"

"Well, it is one of my favorites—a classic, in fact, that I wanted to share with you. It's *The Wizard of Oz*."

"*The Wizard of Oz?*" I said.

Devon spoke sheepishly now as though he had done something wrong.

"You don't like this movie?"

"No, I do. I'm just surprised this is one of your favorite movies."

"Oh it is. It's one of the best. I love the whole story, and when I heard that it was going to be played on the big screen, I knew it would make the most wonderful date for me and the love of my life."

I smiled and leaned in to give Devon a kiss. Devon returned the gesture, and we locked our passionate lips for a minute. I loved it when he called me the love of his life. It made me feel so tingly inside. As we were kissing, the necklace glowed a slight glow of blue. It wasn't a blinding shine, but it was enough for Devon to notice.

"Wow, that is glowing! Where did you say you got it from?" Devon said as he picked up the amulet portion of the necklace.

"Well I…," I began to say but the words didn't seem to want to come out. I was still unsure about my explanation. I didn't want Devon to think I was crazy.

"It was just something that I picked up somewhere," I said as Devon continued to look at it.

"It really is blue. It is the deepest darkest kind of blue that I have ever seen. It is spectacular. It suits you so well—the most beautiful necklace for the most beautiful lady."

"Oh thank you so much, Devon," I said with half a smile. I wanted to tell Devon the truth so bad, but I stopped myself each time. After another moment, the movie began to play. Devon let go of the pendant and grabbed my hand. We were sitting wrapped into each other, and we cuddled. I loved it. I loved being close to Devon—so close that we were almost one. Devon had his arm around my back, and he held me the whole time. We watched as Dorothy went through her adventures in Oz.

It was a good escape from all of the questions and things that had come up today. I loved this movie. I had never seen it on the big screen. This movie was meant for the big screen. It was so bright and vivid. It was amazing, and it was so nice to see with Devon. When the movie finally ended, we got up and gathered our blanket. Devon returned the blanket to the front just like all of the other couples did. Then we walked holding hands toward the car.

"Would you like to get something to eat?" Devon asked.

"Yes of course, I'm starving."

"Well, it is late so there's not much open, but I know this place where we can go."

"Sounds good," I said as we got to the car and started to drive.

"I really liked the movie Devon," I said.

"I'm glad that you liked it. I had never seen it on the big screen like that, and it was really nice," Devon said with a smile.

"Yeah, it was really nice. It was so bright and beautiful."

We continued to drive and then eventually got to San Diego's Old Town. I love Old Town. It always has a nice feel to it. All the times that I've been there, I felt like I was experiencing a part of history. We arrived at one of the restaurants that was open late.

Devon walked inside the restaurant and asked, "Are you still open?"

"Yes we are. Will it just be the two of you?"

"Yes, just the two of us."

"Very good, let me show you to your table," the man said as he grabbed some menus and took us to a table. We sat and began to look at the menu. I quickly found something that I wanted to eat.

Devon then called the waiter over. After the waiter left with our orders, Devon began to talk.

"You know, I am really excited about how all of the research has been going with the dolphins."

"I know you are Devon, and I am too. I know it's your dream to figure out the dolphin's language," I said encouraging him.

"It really is. I just know it's there. I can feel it. This last encounter makes me want it more and more. I think you're the key. I really do. I think there's something there when the dolphins see you. They see what I see, which is something amazing," Devon said with a smile.

"Oh you're good, I love you too," I said to Devon and smiled.

Then the food came. Before I knew it, we were back at the car.

"That was good meal. We should come here again some time," I said to Devon.

"Yep, it was good—a good finish to a good date," Devon said smiling as we walked toward his car. Devon opened the door. I got in and then we drove to my room. When we finally arrived at my room, we stopped at the front of the door.

"I had the most amazing night with you my dear. I'm glad that we found time to do this. I know I've been so busy with everything for a while, but I still love going out with you and I love being with you. I just wanted you to know that," Devon said and then leaned in for a kiss.

I returned the kiss. It was a deep long kiss, the kind that will make your heart stop. Then we stopped kissing. Devon pulled away as if that was it. Then Devon looked at my lips and kissed me quickly one more time and said, "Alright dear, I love you, and I will see you soon."

"Love you too Devon," I said and opened the door. Devon gave one last wave goodbye. I returned the wave as I slowly closed the door.

"Wow!" I said aloud. It really was a great date, and I was completely and utterly happy, at least for that moment. Then I glanced at the time.

"It's really late." I knew I should get to bed. After this day, I needed some sleep. I was happy and extremely exhausted so I headed to bed.

Chapter 29

Alone in Thought

The next morning I woke up and instantly remembered the weird feeling that I had about Antilla. Was it real or was I making up the whole thing? Then it hit me. I should talk to Erica. It seemed like after everything else, that I hadn't seen Erica in forever. I grabbed my phone, which was about to die because I had forgotten to plug it in last night. I plugged it in quickly and texted Erica.

"Hey do you want to hang out?"

"Yeah I would love to, do you want to meet at our spot?" Erica quickly texted me.

"Yes of course."

"Okay when?"

"How about in a half an hour?" I glanced at my watch.

"See you there," Erica wrote.

I got all of my stuff and started to get ready. I just barely got ready in a half an hour and rushed out the door. I made it in just enough time to get to the College Café where Erica amazingly was waiting for me. This time though Erica didn't have a drink waiting for me. It was funny because it seemed like each time I had met Erica at the College Café she always had a drink waiting for me.

"Hi Erica."

"Hi Aurora, I'm sorry I didn't get a chance to order you a drink. I just got here," Erica said.

"Oh it's okay, it was just the first time you hadn't got my drink. It's actually kind of funny. What would you like to drink Erica?"

Erica, looking stunned, said, "Café latte please."

I went up to the coffee bar and ordered.

"Café latté and an Earl Grey tea."

"No problem," a voice from the back said. "That will be five dollars."

I reached into my pocket and pulled out a five. A moment later the drinks came, and I grabbed them.

"Thank you."

I walked over to where the cream and milk were. I poured a good portion of milk into my tea with some cinnamon and a drop of honey.

"Here you go, Erica."

"Thank you so much," Erica said and then took a sip of her coffee.

"So what have you been up too?"

Erica was taken aback by the question.

"Well you know the usual. I have been busy with my studies. I've actually started a revolutionary new study on the after effects of the Hellenistic period, as it affects modern Western Civilization. I'm hoping that soon I will have a few answers that historians have been wondering about for decades," Erica said in such a quick roll-out, that it seemed like she didn't need coffee. She was already hyped up on the idea of history.

"Wow that was a lot of information for one statement Erica. I guess that you have been busy,"

Erica smiled at my approval of what she had been doing and leaned toward me.

"So what have you been up too," she said with a smirk implying that there was more than education going on in my life.

"What do you mean, Erica?" I asked with a girlish laugh.

"Oh you know with Devon. I mean has your relationship gone anywhere new? Are things going good with you two? Is there a future? And how is everything else going?"

I had forgotten that I hadn't been keeping my best friend up to date on my social life for some time.

"Oh Erica, well, it has actually been going really well between Devon and I. Really, I can't complain. Devon is so romantic, he is my dream man. Everything else has, well, I guess it has been going okay. Devon and I have been working on that little project for talking to dolphins, and it has been taking up a lot of our time. Each time that we go and do something on the dolphin project, it's like a date. I am really happy," I said with a look of refrain on my face.

"What's wrong?" Erica asked.

"Oh, it's nothing really. I have just been perplexed about something."

"Oh, what is it?"

I still didn't know how to bring it up, and then it suddenly came to me. "What do you know about alternate realities?"

I got a very weird and strange look from Erica.

"Alternate realities are a bit strange, aren't they," Erica said smiling.

"Well, yes the concept is a little weird, but do you know anything about them?"

"Well I don't know a lot about them. I think the concept is kinda cool. I mean, science provides us with a lot of possible evidence to suggest that other forms of reality might exist within our plane. But actual evidence has not really been found to suggest that there might be any other realities within our dimension," Erica said.

A new look of confusion was now apparent all over my face. "Erica would you mind maybe speaking in more plain terms?"

Erica made a big smile.

"Well in plain terms, I believe another reality could exist within ours, but I'm still a skeptic on the whole matter. At least until I see some further evidence on it. Why do you ask? How did all of this come up?"

Now I really wasn't sure if I should tell Erica the truth. I mean she knew a lot on the subject of alternate realities, and she was my friend—but I still wasn't sure if she would understand. I think Erica might be a little too logical for this.

"Well no particular reason, it was just something that I read that made me wonder about alternate realities. You are one of my best sources of information Erica. You really do know so much about everything. I wish I was as smart as you."

Erica gave another very big smile.

"Well I do try. I wish I was as beautiful as you," Erica said complimenting me back.

I smiled at that.

"Oh really you're too funny, I'm not that beautiful."

"Oh yes, you are. I bet if you weren't dating Devon, you would have all sorts of guys trying to ask you out."

I made an even bigger smile when Erica said that, almost blushing a little.

"Oh come on Erica, I can't believe anyone thinks I'm that beautiful. But thank you."

"No really, you are like the Aphrodite of campus. I'm really surprised you haven't noticed. Since you've walked in the College Café today, all the guys started staring at you," Erica said and smiled.

"Well it doesn't matter too much, they will just have to stare, because I have found my Devon and that's all I need," I said with a modest smile.

"Is it that serious?"

"Yes I think it is. I mean we both seem like we are in love as far as I can tell," I said.

"Well, that's good. I think you two are cute together."

"Me too."

Then we both began to giggle. It was just like old times with Erica, like we had never stopped talking for what seemed like months. But it was still hard on me. I didn't know what I was going to do about the Antilla situation. I mean, who could I go to about Antilla, as if it were real when in reality I might be just a part of my subconscious?

It could just be a figment in my imagination I guess. Now I know how Dorothy felt after she left Oz. At least I didn't have to think about a talking scarecrow, and at the moment, I was pretty sure I could talk to dolphins—but that too seemed a little outrageous to believe. I would have to be alone on this whole Antilla thing. At least I had one piece of evidence that made me feel better. I had the necklace around my neck. I still hadn't taken it off since I received it. I mean since I had gotten out of the water with Devon. Just then Erica glanced at my necklace.

"Wow, that's nice. I have never seen you with that necklace before. Is it a gift from Devon?"

I didn't know what to say at first but something came to me.

"Yeah it was something like that."

"Wow, that Devon is so spontaneous, you really are lucky."

"Thank you,"

"Wow, look at that. It's been almost forty-five minutes."

"Wow time has flown by. I hadn't noticed. Do you have to be somewhere?"

"Well, umm actually…umm…I have to actually get ready for class. It will be in a little bit, but I don't want to leave. I have really missed you, and I enjoyed catching up with you," Erica said.

"Oh no, Erica. I don't mind. I know how busy you get, and I don't want you to be late on my account."

"Thank you so much, Aurora. You always were my best friend. Can we meet again soon? I like to keep up to date on you and Devon."

"Absolutely, I'm just sad that we hadn't met up before this. We really must make more time for each other outside of class."

"I agree," Erica said as she gathered up her stuff.

"Well then, I will be off. Thank you so much for the café latte. It really means a lot. I will see you again soon."

"Oh yes, definitely, I will see you again soon. Text me, okay, or call me. We can meet up anytime," as I walked towards Erica and gave her the biggest hug.

I was left with my tea alone, to wallow in my thoughts for a bit. I gulped up my last bit of tea and decided to drink another. I went up to the counter and waited in line. After waiting behind two people, I finally got up to the front.

"What can I get you?"

"An answer," I said aloud, without realizing it.

"What was that?" the barista asked with a laugh.

"Oh nothing. I would like another Earl Grey please," I said.

"No problem, that will be $2.50."

"Here you go," I said and handed him three dollars.

"Thank you, your tea will be ready shortly." The barista handed me 50 cents which I placed into the tip container.

"Thanks."

After about five minutes of waiting, I was handed my tea. I grabbed it and then sat down again. I had a fair amount of thinking to do.

I mean what was I going to do about this whole problem? When do you declare yourself to be crazy?

I pulled out my phone and typed in: "How do you know if you're going crazy?"

A bunch of pages popped up. I found one that seemed to match what I was talking about. "How to tell if you're going crazy or insane" I clicked on it and read it. I began to worry instantly at the things I saw. I saw things about losing it and not being able to tell what reality is what.

"Wow that seems to describe me," I said in whisper and then read down a little further in the article. The article said crazy people don't know their going crazy so if you are reading this for yourself, you're probably not going crazy. I blew a sigh of relief.

I don't know how reliable this article was, but at least it made me feel better. I guess I wasn't going crazy. At least no more than someone that has a dream and wanted it to be real. As far as the necklace, I must have found it somewhere. I mean I know I thought I got it when I went to Antilla, but who knows, that was probably just a dream. A very real dream. I'm not sure what's going on with that, but the other thing about Antilla and a dolphin society just seems too crazy. Just then I looked at my watch, and another hour had passed.

"Wow it is getting late," I said. I knew I couldn't spend all day at the College Café. I gathered up my stuff and started to head out.

"Well see you later," the barista said.

"Yep see you later," I said and walked out.

"I think I'll check out what my roommates are up too," I said aloud and headed back to my room. When I got to my room, my roommates were inside. I could hear them before I even got through the door. I grabbed my key and opened the door.

"Hey Aurora," Jessica said.

"Hey guys, how it is going?"

"Hey Aurora, what have you been up too. We haven't seen you in a few days. We keep missing each other," Stacey said.

"Well it has been a little while, hasn't it," I said.

I stepped further into the room and took a seat on the couch next to Stacey.

"So I was just talking about you, Aurora," Stacey said.

I raised my eyebrows when she said this.

"What were you talking about?"

"Well I was just talking with my friends, you know the ones that are really into fashion, and they were asking me what your Aunt Carrie was like, then I realized that after all of this time of having the coolest roommate ever, I still hadn't met your Aunt Carrie," Stacey said.

"Well that's true, she doesn't come by campus a whole lot. She is busy, you know, as am I."

"Well, I know you are busy. I can see that from your tireless studies and social escapades," Stacey said.

Jessica gave a laugh at this, I guess there was a joke or something I wasn't catching.

"What do you mean social escapades?" I asked.

"Well it's nothing, I just noticed that you and Devon seem to be very serious, that's all."

"Oh I see, and what's wrong with that?" I asked.

"Nothing, nothing at all. It is just rare to be in such a solid relationship during your first couple years of college, that's all. We are very happy for you though, Devon is a real catch. Anyways, so back to the subject of your Aunt Carrie, would it be possible for me to meet her. I just have so many questions that I would like to ask her. It would really mean the world to me to meet her."

"Well I suppose I could give her a phone call, and see what she is up to, and if she can meet us for lunch or something," I said.

"Oh that would make you the greatest roommate ever," Stacey said

"Hey!" Jessica said jokingly.

"No offense," Stacey said defensively smiling.

Jessica smiled back.

I began to search my contacts looking for my Aunt Carrie. I soon found her and pressed call on my phone. The phone ran through all of the rings and then went to voicemail.

"Shoot she didn't answer. Let me try again one more time," I said and pushed call again. The phone rang and rang and then a voice came from the other side.

"Hello," Aunt Carrie said.

"Hello Aunt Carrie, how are you?"

"Well I am doing good," Aunt Carrie said sounding as cheery as I had remembered. There was a slight pause before she continued to talk.

"How are you? What's up?" Aunt Carrie said quickly.

"Not much, I was just calling to say hi. I was wondering if you wanted to have lunch. One of my friends is dying to meet you. She is a big fan of your work."

"Oh well, of course, but I'm only free for dinner. Is that okay?"

"Is dinner tonight alright?" I asked Stacey.

"Yes, yes, yes," Stacey replied, leaping with joy.

"Yes, Aunt Carrie, that would be great."

"Okay, see you guys at 8. I will come pick you up."

"Yep, see you tonight at 8. I can't wait."

"I can't wait either," Aunt Carrie said and then hung up.

"So what did she say? Did she say anything else?" Stacey said in such an excited stupor. She had her hands together, right next to me. I guess she had been there the whole time to try and hear what my Aunt was saying on the phone.

"Well she said that she couldn't wait to meet you," I said.

"Did she really say that?" Stacey asked.

"Well, not in so many words. I mean she pretty much said it when she said that you could come with us tonight. I think you will like my Aunt Carrie, and I know that my Aunt Carrie is going to like you. You guys have a lot in common."

"Well, I have been meaning to ask you for months now, but something always seems to come up. Your Aunt Carrie is just simply amazing. I can't wait to meet her. Okay so when do you want to meet up to go out tonight. You know in case one of us wants to leave or what not. It's noon right now," Stacey asked.

I wasn't sure what to say.

"Well I guess since we are being picked up at eight, we might as well be ready by seven," I said.

"Okay that sounds good. Seven it is. Now if you'll excuse me, I have to buy something to wear. I have looked through my closet, and I haven't found anything to wear that will be suitable for meeting your Aunt Carrie. It has to be spectacular and glamorous," Stacey said, and with that, she ran outside.

Stacey ran so fast out the door I barely saw her leave. I looked at Jessica.

"Oh don't worry. Stacey has been telling me for months she was going to do that. She is so excited," Jessica said.

"Well, I am glad she is excited. I don't know what I am going to do with myself in the meantime," I said.

"Well, don't you have to catch up on class or something?" Jessica asked.

"No. I have actually been doing a good job at keeping up my studies. I am ahead on all of my classes. It was a good idea though. Did you want to hang out?"

"No, I can't. I'm so sorry. I do appreciate the offer, but I can't because I have this giant paper that's due tomorrow. I am only halfway through it. I put it off till the last minute, and now I will have to rush to finish it," Jessica said.

"Oh," I said with a very sad voice, and then I paused.

"Oh, are you going to be okay, Aurora? I mean do you have another plan for today? I hope that I didn't put a dent in your plans," Jessica said as she continued to talk about the paper.

"It's okay, Jessica. I really do understand, and yes don't worry, I will find something to do, I promise. You should get back to your paper. I will see you later on."

"Okay, I will see you later." Jessica said.

I began to walk into my part of the room, but suddenly I remembered that I hadn't invited Jessica to come with us tonight—and that is considered rude. I turned towards Jessica.

"Jessica."

Jessica quickly turned towards me again.

"Jessica, would you like to come tonight? I know that you have your paper, but you might need a break later," I said and waited for a response.

Jessica thought and thought about it. It looked like she was going through all of her emotions at once. "Well I will keep an open mind, but I am pretty sure I will be working on my paper tonight."

"Well suit yourself, just remember that it is good to get a breather every now and then," I said and then continued to walk into my room. Or at least what I called my room. It was still an open space so the section that was my room was actually just my bed. At this point in the day, I realized that I was pretty tired. I looked at my watch again. I had more than enough time to go ahead and take a nap. I got onto my bed and laid down. I quickly fell asleep. When I woke up, it was 6:30 pm.

"What the heck" I said as I stared at my cell phone and realized I had slept the day away. I hate it when I sleep the day away. Even though I enjoy the rest, it always feels like such a waste of a day. I heard the door begin to open. It was Stacey in some nice new clothes.

"Wow, don't you look spiffy," I said as Stacey came through.

"Do you like it? Do you think your Aunt will like it?"

"Well, I think it really does look good. I am almost positive that my Aunt will be impressed by your outfit. Besides she doesn't know you like I do. I will vouch for you. I mean you are one of the most knowledgeable people that I have ever met when it comes to fashion,"

I glanced in the mirror to look at myself. Yes, I was indeed a mess. I looked through the closet to try and find something that might be suitable for tonight.

Nothing too formal, nothing too light. Oh here, it was the perfect outfit, it is just right. After I put it on I walked over to Stacey.

"How do I look?" I asked.

"You look good. You always look good," Stacey said.

I smiled and didn't say anything after that. Even though I didn't believe that I was beautiful, I realized it was best not to argue with people about it. I just nodded and shook my head. Then I looked at the time. It was fifteen minutes away from when my Aunt was supposed to arrive. Just then there was a knock at the door. I looked through the security hole and realized quickly that it was my Aunt Carrie. I opened the door.

"Well, are we ready?" Aunt Carrie asked.

"Almost," I said.

Just then Stacey came over towards me.

"Umm, Aunt Carrie," I said to get my Aunt's attention, which was currently focused on the rest of the room. "Ummm, Aunt Carrie," I said again, and then Aunt Carrie turned towards me.

"Yes," she said as she stared at Stacey and Me.

"This is my friend and roommate, Stacey."

Aunt Carrie put out her hand in a friendly gesture. "Hey, I am Carrie Livingston, Aurora's Aunt."

Stacey grabbed her hand and smiled, "Hi, it is so nice to meet you."

My Aunt smiled at this.

"It is so nice to meet you too. I hear that you are a big fan of mine, is that true?"

"Yes, it is. In fact before we go, I was wondering if you wouldn't mind taking a picture with me?"

Aunt Carrie gave a slightly thrown off look at the request. I don't believe she was expecting that. But Aunt Carrie covered it up well. I could barely tell that she was in the state of shock, but that was mostly because I knew my Aunt.

"Of course I would love to take a picture with you."

Before she could finish the sentence, Stacey was handing her camera to me. I held up the camera to my face.

"Alright, get ready to say cheese."

My Aunt and Stacey said cheese at the same time. The picture came out nice.

"Here you go, I hope you like it," I said to Stacey.

"Yes, I love it. Thank you so much," Stacey said to me and Aunt Carrie at the same time.

"Not a problem," my Aunt said as she grabbed her purse which she had placed on the ground. "Alright well, are you guys ready to get some dinner? I am positively starving."

"Yes, we are," I said as I grabbed my purse. Stacey followed suit and grabbed her purse. We all started to walk out the door. I locked up the room behind us, and then we all walked towards my Aunt's Bentley.

"New car?" I asked.

"No, no. I've had it for a little while. It is one of your Uncle's. Mine is in the shop being checked out," Aunt Carrie said.

"Oh I see," I said as we all began to get into the car.

"Alright everyone buckle up," Aunt Carrie.

"So Stacey, tell me what is it that you want to do with your life?" my Aunt asked while she drove.

"Well honestly, Mrs. Livingston I am not sure, but I think I want to be more like you. I want to open up a fashion line. I want to be successful and not have to compromise about anything," Stacey said, hoping her answers were good enough.

"Well first, you can call me Aunt Carrie, and second, it takes a lot of work to get to where I am at. Don't let anyone tell you that you can't be successful. You can be successful in anything you want to do. You just have to want it bad enough. You have to know how to get it, and you have to come up with a plan for how to get it. You need to make what you want happen for you. Nothing is just given to you in this business. At least that's what I have always believed, and that has been the main reason why I have been so successful. I don't let anyone change my vision. How could they know how it's supposed to be? It's my vision, not theirs right?" Aunt Carrie said looking for confirmation.

"Right," I said and Stacey followed with a quick "Right."

Stacey seemed to be taking in everything that my Aunt Carrie was saying, but it seemed like a bit much to talk about before we ate. I decided to change the subject.

"So where are we going to eat?" I asked.

"Well, we are going to one of my favorite spots. It's a real wonder of San Diego. But it is a surprise," Aunt Carrie said.

"Okay, I'll be surprised then," I said, smiling and leaning back into my seat.

Before I knew it, we had arrived at a parking spot.

"We're here," my Aunt said as she finished her parallel parking. We all got out of the car.

"Okay, well that is your surprise," my Aunt said and pointed at a little place on the corner. It was a nice looking restaurant called The City D. It had good lighting, and it looked like a New York Deli. We walked in, and the first thing I saw was some delicious pastries. There were cookies and cakes of all sorts.

"The hostess is a friend of mine," Aunt Carrie said as we approached her.

"Carrie how nice of you to join us this evening, and who is this that you have with you?"

"Oh, well this is my niece, Aurora, and this is her friend, Stacey. I brought them here for a good time," Aunt Carrie said. The hostess got a big smile on her face.

"Well, I'm Saundra, and I hope that we don't disappoint. Is it just you three ladies this evening?" Saundra asked.

"Yes, it is just us this evening," Aunt Carrie said.

"Excellent, come this way please."

"Here you are," Saundra said as she pointed towards a booth.

It was a nice booth. It was black and had one of those old school music choice listings, the kind where you can look through the songs and pick one by putting a quarter—all from the comfort of your seat. It was cute. We all scooted into the booth. Then Saundra handed us all our menus.

"Alright your waiter will be with you in a minute. Nice talking with you, Carrie. Maybe sometime soon we can do lunch?" Saundra asked.

"Yes of course."

I began to look over the menu. There were so many selections. I saw an eggplant sandwich. I had never had that before. So I decided I would go with that. The waiter came up to the table.

"Can I get you guys something to drink?"

"Why yes, I would like water with a lemon," Aunt Carrie said.

"Excellent and you?" the waiter asked pointing at Stacey.

"Same."

"Excellent and you?"

"I will have water, but no lemon please," I said.

"Yes of course. Okay I will have those drinks for you in just a minute, while you decide what you would like to eat," the waiter said.

"Actually I think that we are ready to order now," Aunt Carrie said as she turned towards Stacey and me to see if we were ready. We both shook our heads yes.

"Yes, we are ready, I will have the Chicken Cesar Salad please," Aunt Carrie said.

"Yes of course," the waiter said as he scribbled down the order, and then the waiter lifted his head up and gestured to Stacey.

"I will have the same," Stacey said and smiled.

"Very good and you miss?"

"I will have an eggplant sandwich."

"Okay I will have your orders ready shortly."

Within a minute, the waiter was gone, and we were at the time in any meal when you wait. I looked over at Stacey, and she seemed so nervous. Like she was around a celebrity, and she didn't know what to do. I decided to break the ice.

"So what have you been up to lately Aunt Carrie?"

"Well, not much. I have my new line of clothing out. It is the latest in animal print. It is a combination of animal and autumn colors, and the blend is superior to anything out there. We have been working for months on it. I finally just finished my final approval the other day."

"Wow," Stacey said.

"Oh, would you like to see? I have a few pictures here on my phone," Aunt Carrie said as she reached for her purse. She quickly had the pictures up in no time. Aunt Carrie showed me and then she showed Stacey.

"Wow, these are really nice, Aunt Carrie. I think they are really going to do good. They look so different," I said.

"Thank you, we are supposed to be hitting New York for the first time with it this next month. My agent said I have a real shot at making it big in the fashion industry, you know, finally go global with my local fashion techniques. So that people all around the world can see who I am. I won't be limited to just here in California," Aunt Carrie said.

"Wow, I am so happy for you Aunt Carrie, and Uncle Jason must be taking this really well," I said.

Aunt Carrie suddenly had a sad look on her face.

"What's a matter Aunt Carrie?" I asked.

"Well it's nothing."

"No, really tell me. You can trust us," I said.

"Well Uncle Jason and I have been going through a lot of stuff, with all of my extended hours at work, I have been neglecting him a little bit," my Aunt said as she looked so sad.

"Don't worry. I know that as soon as I go to New York for the fashion release, things will get better between us. You will see," Aunt Carrie said with a glimmer of hope in her eyes. She quickly recovered though, and after a minute, she didn't look sad and turned the conversation to me.

"Let's talk about something else. How are things going between you and umm…."

"DEVON!!!!!!" Stacey blurted out.

"That's it, Devon. How are you and Devon doing?"

"Well we are actually doing really well. I know a lot of people probably think that we have the perfect relationship, but Devon and I really do have a perfect relationship. Devon is everything I could ever hope for out of a man," I said.

"Well that is good. I mean out of the few times that I have seen you and Devon, you too seem really happy." A sort of sly smile came over her.

"So have you heard anything about your friend Andrew?" Aunt Carrie asked.

"Well, actually, no I haven't. Why?" I said, surprised to hear his name being brought up.

"No reason, I was just wondering. Your mom was talking about him. Andrew is making big moves in the world. His dad is leaving him the company, and his dad has already let him start making key decisions in the company's future. I know that Andrew always had his eyes on you, and that is why I was asking."

"Oh Aunt Carrie, I am really happy with Devon. Andrew will find someone else. He doesn't need me," I said.

"Well, I just thought it was worth mentioning. Your mom told me about it, and it sparked my interest. That's all. I am really pleased that you and Devon are happy, and I hope things stay that way," Aunt Carrie said.

"Well I do too, and I am really happy. I can promise you. Devon and I are inseparable. I mean he does get busy, but I think of him all of the time, and I am sure that he thinks of me all of the time. I do hope the best for Andrew though, and it's great that he's making big moves in the world. But I have what I want in a guy."

Just as I finished saying that, our meal came.

"Your meals are here," the waiter said as he handed out each dish.

"Thank you," Aunt Carrie said to the waiter.

"You're welcome, ma'am. Will there be anything else?"

"Nothing for now, thank you," Aunt Carrie responded. The waiter gathered up his tray and walked off. Aunt Carrie gave me a slight look and then focused on Stacey.

"So Stacey, tell me, what are your plans for fashion? What are you and your friends saying about my work?" Aunt Carrie asked.

Looking practically tickled, Stacey began to talk all about Aunt Carrie.

"Well my friends and I think you are great..."

Suddenly I found myself in another place. I couldn't focus on the conversation at the table anymore. I started to think about what my Aunt Carrie had said. There was something about Andrew, something that bothered me about him gaining power. I mean he was a nice guy, but it gave me a feeling like there was something not right about the whole thing. I guess I got very deep into my thoughts because before I knew it, the meal was over, and we were leaving. The three of us got into the car, and Aunt Carrie once again focused on me.

"Well this was a very nice get together girls. Aurora, you will have to call me soon so that you and I and Devon can get to know each other better. I know you are in love with him. I was once a young girl too. It would be really nice for him to know that we like him. Please pass on to him that we should get together. Can you do that for me?"

"Oh yes of course I can, Aunt Carrie. I would be happy too. I will call you soon," I said as she continued to drive. We eventually got back to my room, and Stacey and I got out of the car.

"Hey girls, it was fun. I hope you have a safe night," Aunt Carrie said as we departed the car.

"Yes, yes, it was fun. Thank you for dinner. I will talk to you later. Be safe I love you," I said to Aunt Carrie.

"Thank you, you have really changed my opinion and viewpoint on fashion. I love it even more now. Take care, and it was nice meeting you," Stacey said.

"Did you have fun, Stacey? Was it everything that you had hoped for?" I asked.

"Yes, it was everything I had dreamed of. I can't wait to tell all the other girls that I had dinner with Carrie Livingston. They are going to be so jealous. Please let me know if you need anything. I really do owe you one," Stacey said.

"Don't worry about it. I had to catch up with Aunt Carrie anyways. I had focused so much on everything else going on in my life that I had forgot about her."

When we arrived at the door, Devon was there. Stacey walked inside the room as I turned toward Devon.

"Aurora I'm glad I ran into you. We have to talk," Devon said in a frantic voice.

I didn't like the way he said that. Why did he have to say it like that?

A million thoughts ran through my head, and my heart skipped two beats.

Chapter 30

Devon Left

I was really concerned and asked, "Devon, what is it?"

"I have to leave. I have to go today. I'm sorry," Devon said, as he put his hands on my shoulder. Devon stared straight into my eyes.

"I love you, Aurora. I don't want you to ever forget that," Devon said.

I began to cry.

"Why are you leaving?" I asked.

"Don't cry Aurora. I didn't mean to upset you. I'm leaving because my grandpa died. I have to go to Greece. I'll be gone for two weeks," Devon said as he came in close to me and gave me a hug.

"Don't cry. I'm sad too. I'm so sad that my grandpa died. It doesn't seem real. He was such an important part of my life, and now he's gone."

I stopped crying.

"I thought you were going to break up with me."

"No, I just found out about my Grandpa and wanted to come and tell you that I had to leave. I'm sorry I didn't mean for you to think that I was breaking up with you. I will never do that to you. I love you too much. Our love is eternal. I want you to keep in contact with me while I'm gone. I don't know how practical it will be though. Where my grandpa is from, is a bit out there in Greece, but I will do my best to call you. My plane leaves in four hours. I have my stuff packed, and I'm waiting for the cab to come. I want you to promise me that you will take care of yourself while I'm gone," Devon said as he wiped a tear from my face.

"Yes of course, I love you too, and I will miss you so bad," I said as I went in for a kiss.

Devon kissed me with a deep passionate kiss. The kind of kiss that makes everything seem alright. Devon then looked me in the eyes.

"Two weeks okay. Just two weeks," Devon said as he looked in the distance.

"Oh my cab is here. I have to go," Devon said as he grabbed his bag.

"Can I walk with you to the cab?"

"Yes please," Devon said. When we got to the cab, Devon put his bag in the car and then gave me another hug.

"Okay, well, I have to go. I don't want to leave, but I have to take care of this—and if I keep staring at your eyes, I will never leave. I love you."

I got the hint. I knew this was hard for both of us. We had never really been apart ever since we had started dating. But I knew Devon had to go.

"I love you too. Okay I am going to walk back to my room. I will see you in two weeks."

As I was walking, I never looked back. It made me too sad. When I got up to my room, I looked down, and Devon was gone. I shrugged my shoulders and let out a sigh. I knew I was going to miss him so much. My heart was halfway broken, but I knew this feeling was only temporary. I went inside and made some tea. When I was done with the tea, I was still sad. I yawned.

"Well I guess I should go to bed," I said aloud, and soon I was sound asleep.

I woke up the next day with a new outlook. I was a little sad, but I wasn't as sad as I had been. I walked into the common space. Jessica and Stacey were there, talking amongst themselves. I ignored them for the moment, though. I was sad. I decided to think about school. I looked at my schedule I had posted. Then it hit me. I had to focus on school. I had spent too much time thinking about everything else. I had to focus on school. It would keep me distracted from being sad. The rest of the day was beginning to look better already, with my new outlook on life. I took a sigh of relief, then I smiled. I read something next to the schedule.

"I'm too blessed to be stressed," I read aloud. That was exactly what I needed to read. I ate my breakfast and pulled out my phone to check my email. I was eager to see if Devon had sent me a message. I wanted to know if he had made it safe to Greece. I read a single line message from Devon.

"Hey, I made it halfway to Greece, and just wanted you to know I was okay," the message said.

I was glad that he had wrote me. It made me a lot happier than I was when I first woke up. I guess without realizing it, I had been really worried about Devon.

"I'm glad that you are doing good on your trip. Please write me whenever get a chance, love you." I replied and put my phone away.

I took another shrug. I was happy, but I wasn't absolutely happy. I still had a lot of doubts. I decided I wanted to call someone I've learned to trust. I would call my mom. I hadn't talked to her in a while, and it would be good to hear her voice.

I went to class and had a hard time focusing the whole time. When class was finally over, I had an open schedule for the remaining part of the day. I decided I really should call my mom. I found a nice place under the tree and looked through my contacts. I found my mom in my contact list. I pushed call, and then I let the phone ring. Soon there was an answer.

"Hello," my mom said.

"Hi mom, how's it going? This is Aurora."

"Aurora, hey hun, how's it going?"

"Oh not much, mom, I just wanted to say hi."

"Oh hi. I miss you. How is school? How is everything?"

"Yeah mom, I'm doing okay. You know the average. I try to focus on school, and I try to keep up with everything. It's just a lot mom."

My mom began to laugh a little.

"I know, dear. You just have to keep at it. I believe in you. I always have, and I always will. So does everyone else here. We are so proud of you. Just don't give up. I know that studies can be tough. But you will make it through. Just remember that we all believe in you. Now on to more pleasant things. How are you and Devon doing?"

"Oh, you know, mom, the same. I love him, but we are taking it slow. We're not going to rush anything. Our love is still strong."

"That's good that you're not moving too fast. I want you to still stay young. I want you to enjoy your life. I know you have to focus on school but don't forget to have some relax time okay."

"Okay mom, I will try to relax." I laughed.

"And how are my brothers?"

"Oh they're good. They're all still in school right now. Do you know who I ran into the other day?"

"Who, Andrew?"

"Well, yes it was Andrew. But how did you know that."

"Well I had dinner with Aunt Carrie last night, and she actually mentioned him. I wondered why she was asking about Andrew, and she told me that you had run into him. But mom, I'm not interested in him no matter how successful he is," I blurted out, half-angry about the whole thing.

"That isn't what I meant. I talked to your Aunt, and I think that she misunderstood me. See, Andrew came by, and he was asking about you, but I told him about Devon and how happy you two were with each other."

"I told him about Devon before," I said.

"Yes, he said that you had told him about Devon, but he was still asking me about you."

"I know that he has feelings for me, but I don't feel that way about him. I love Devon."

"I know, I know you love Devon. I just mentioned it to your Aunt in case she ran into you. I never hear from you—and not much happens up here. I talked with your Aunt Carrie, and I just mentioned it because I thought it was interesting that for as successful as Andrew seems to be becoming, he still remembers my little girl."

"Well, did he seem heartbroken?"

"A little but then he started to talk more about his business, and that seems to be where the focus of the conversation went. I promised him I would tell you 'hi' from him next time I talked with you. So here I am telling you."

"Well tell him I said 'hi' back next time you see him but don't let him think that I'm interested because I'm not. Okay mom?"

"Okay, Aurora I won't. Oh dear I have to go. I have an appointment in a forty-five minutes, and I have to drive to meet them. Can I talk with you a little later?"

"Yeah, of course, mom, I love you."

"Love you too," mom replied and the conversation was over.

I looked at my watch and it was already 9 p.m.

"Well it is getting a little late" I said aloud as I yawned. "I guess I better get to bed."

There wasn't anyone to hear me say that, but I guess it helps me to feel more at home when I talk. Even if there isn't anyone there to listen. I went to bed and went immediately into a deep sleep.

Chapter 31

Illusions of My Reality

What seemed like right after I closed my eyes, I was suddenly back. I had been transported back to Antilla. All the doubts that I had about Antilla being fake were gone. I walked around the structures. I touched the pillars. I walked around the whole city, but there was just one problem. There were no dolphins.

There was nothing here. There was definitely something wrong. It was just like I had remembered it. It was so real, and yet there was no one to talk to. Surely this place was a figment of my imagination. Or was it? How could a place that seemed so real, so much more real than any dream, be fake? I yelled out for anyone to hear me.

"Hello," I yelled out. There was no response.

"Hello," I yelled again, but still there was still no response.

What was I going to do? I was stuck. I decided I would take a look around again. This place was so familiar. It was just like I remembered it. Every facet and every little detail. There was marble everywhere. As I walked, I could feel the realism of it all, but as I walked through the pillars—and saw all of the pictures of scenes of battles of the past—there was no one here. Not even the faintest noise.

"Hello!" I yelled out.

"Hello!" I yelled again, but there was still no answer.

I could hear my voice echo through the entire complex. After walking for several minutes, I finally reached the central place where I had received my necklace. The place was so real, but where was everyone? Where did all of the dolphins go? I had given very little thought to the actual dolphins of Antilla, that is until now. And now I couldn't stop thinking of Lyra and Sadira.

They were my friends here, and yet they were gone. How could they be gone? I now had two very different feelings in my heart. I felt a great sigh of relief that at least this place, this place which is Antilla, seems so real. But at the same time, there's no one here. How could this be? There was another feeling of confusion accompanied by doubt that came over me. After walking around for what seemed like another thirty minutes, I heard nothing and saw no one. I finally decided that I would take a seat and figure all this out.

I found a nice seat near a stage in a part of Antilla that I didn't remember from before.

"How could this be real? How could I possibly be imagining all of this? I must be going crazy," I said aloud.

Just then I heard laughing in the background. It was a little child. There was a constant "HAHAHAHA" from a loud voice. The voice seemed to be coming from not just one direction, but all directions. I took a look every way that I could. But I couldn't see where the voice was coming from.

"Hello…" I yelled, but the laughing continued.

"Hello!" I yelled again. Then the laughing became quieted down. Then I heard a new sound coming from one side. It was now the sound of a little girl.

"Hello," I yelled, as I walked towards the little girl.

The little girl stared at me for a second as I approached her, and then she began to run in the opposite direction of me. I began to walk fast to chase her. The girl started to walk faster. So I began to run. Then the girl began to run too. Before I knew it, the girl was out of sight. I ran and ran to the last place that I saw her. When I got to the place where the girl had been, she was gone. I didn't see her anywhere. I looked, and looked, and then I heard the laughing again. This time it was at the top of a stairs leading to a second floor.

"Hello, I don't want to hurt you," I yelled as I walked up the stairs.

When I got to the top of the stairs, the little girl was there.

"Hello," I said.

The little girl turned toward me and just stared at me again—and then pointed towards a picture behind me. I turned around to look at the picture. The picture was of Aphrodite. I turned back around, and the girl was gone again.

"Hello," I yelled out. But there was no answer, and now I was alone again. I turned around to look at the picture of Aphrodite. I looked at it closely. It was actually a collage of different pictures. In each one, Aphrodite was pictured with the necklace I was wearing.

"What does this mean?" I said as I looked at the pictures.

"Why would I be shown this and then left without an explanation? What was going on?"

Now the feeling of confusion completely consumed me. I closed my eyes and rubbed them. I was frustrated. When I opened my eyes, I was back in my room. I had been asleep. Now I was in shock.

Had all of it been a crazy dream?

The only evidence that I ever had of Antilla was this necklace.

It was all that I could hold. It served as a constant reminder that all of it had not just been a dream. The necklace was all that I could use to continue on. Now it seems that it really was just a dream. I took a big yawn.

What time is it?

I glanced at my watch. It was four a.m.

"Wow, too early," I said aloud in a whisper. It was early; there was no doubt about it. I laid back down. It wasn't time to get up. I laid there in bed, but I wasn't asleep. It was a lot to take in. All of this stuff that was happening...was still so unfamiliar to me. This resounding doubt. The place I went in my dream, Antilla. It seemed so real, but it couldn't be.

How could some place like that exist? How could talking dolphins be real? How could I be the chosen one? The one that would unite the worlds.

I thought about how real Antilla seemed in my dream. Then I just laid there in my bed. It was impossible to sleep, and it was impossible to move. The hours passed, and I laid there. I could hear noises all throughout the building. Then I heard my roommates eating breakfast. I slowly got up out of bed, and walked to the kitchen.

Chapter 32

Feeling Better

Stacey nudged me up with, "Hey sleepy."

"Hey," I said back. I grabbed some cereal and sat down. As I poured the cereal into the bowl, I thought about what I might do today. Both Erica and Stacey were talking amongst themselves, but it was as though I could barely hear them. I heard them mumbling and that was about it. I ate my cereal and carried on as if everything was normal. Then I saw a picture of Devon on the refrigerator.

"What do you think?" Stacey asked. Apparently Stacey had been talking to me, and I hadn't even realized it.

"Sorry, can you say that again?" I asked.

"Do you want to go out with us? We are going shopping."

"Yeah sure, I don't have anything planned for this morning."

I hadn't really thought about it when I answered yes. We all finished our breakfast and then headed out. We arrived at one of those outside malls. I hadn't been to a mall in a while. I wasn't sure what I wanted, but the atmosphere was good. It was going to give me a good chance to get my mind off of things. All three of us walked around together, and things seemed good.

"I have to get a blouse," Jessica said. We stopped at one of the cute stores where there was a big selection.

"So what's up with you?" Stacey asked.

"Oh what do you mean?" I said with a surprised tone.

"Well, you're not acting like yourself. You haven't seemed like yourself for a little while."

I put on a smile and looked back, sort of trying to avoid this conversation. The last thing I wanted anyone to do was notice that I was having all sorts of doubts. I guess I hadn't dedicated too much time trying to hide my emotional state from the people around me.

"Well, nothing really," I said quickly. This response didn't ease anybody's mind.

"Oh come on! I know you pretty well by now. I can tell when something is up, and Jessica and I have both talked about it. Something is definitely up with you," Stacey said.

I shrugged my shoulders and looked at the ground.

"Really, there isn't anything," I said.

"How are things with you and Devon?" Stacey asked.

"Well, they are good. It's just that…"

"Oh that's it! It must be Devon. I can tell by how you said that. Tell me all about it, what did he do?" Stacey asked.

"Well, he didn't actually do anything. He's just gone."

"He's gone! Oh I'm so sorry. We had no idea you guys broke up," Stacey said shocked.

"No, no, nothing like that," I quickly shot back.

"Devon had to go on a trip. We are still doing good, but he is gone right now, and I miss him."

"Oh well, that's what we're here for. You need to lean on us. I know that it can be hard when people that we love are gone, but don't worry, it's going to be alright. How long is he going to be gone for?" Stacey asked.

"Oh, only two weeks."

"Oh see, only two weeks, that's nothing. You know what you should do?" Stacey asked.

"What's that?"

"You should plan out a really nice date for Devon when he comes back. You know, really welcome him home. How come Devon left for this trip?" Stacey asked.

"Oh well, his grandpa died."

"Oh that is so sad. In fact, that is horrible. How did his grandpa die?" Jessica asked from the background. I guess she had been listening.

"Well I don't know. It all happened so suddenly," I said. "There hadn't been much of an explanation. It was just one second Devon told me that he was leaving, and then the next second he was gone. The worst part is that he can't communicate with me that much. Where Devon went probably has bad reception."

"Well it's okay. Just be there for him when he comes back—and yes, you should definitely do that date thing like Stacey was saying. If I hear any deals, I will let you know," Jessica said.

"Oh thank you, Jessica and Stacey! You two are such good friends," I said as we continued to shop.

Then I got a text from Erica.

"Hey give me a call," the text said.

I was surprised by that because it was different for Erica to write that. I looked up her number under the contacts and called her. Erica picked up her phone after a few rings.

"Hello, Aurora," Erica said.

"Hey Erica! What's up?"

"Hey, not much. I just wanted to know if you wanted to hang out with me. There is this extra credit thing I have to do. I wanted to see if you wanted to come with me."

"Yeah sure, what is it?"

"Well, it's nothing much. It's just a historical video. It's showing at the science center, and it's an IMAX movie."

"Oh yeah, for you Erica I would watch anything," I said and laughed.

"Oh I'm so glad Aurora. I was worried I would have to go by myself. Does Devon want to come?" Erica asked.

"No, he's not here. It's just you and me. What time will it be shown?"

"6:30."

"Okay, I'll meet you at five at the coffee shop, and we can go to the movies from there."

"Yeah sounds good, see you then."

"What's up?" Stacey asked as I put the phone down.

"Oh nothing, it was just Erica. We're going to one of those documentaries at the IMAX tonight."

"Oh how cool! I've been wanting to go to one of those. I just like the size of the screen. Can I come too?" Stacey asked.

"Oh and me too please! I need the extra credit for my history class," Jessica said. I thought about it for a moment.

"Yeah, I'm sure that Erica would love the extra company. I don't think you guys have ever hung out with Erica before. I have to warn you though, this movie might be a little on the boring side."

"Oh we like boring! It will be fun," Stacey said.

After that, we all had big smiles on our faces. We continued to walk around the mall shopping. Before I knew it, hours had passed. It was time to meet up with Erica.

"Well, it's getting to be about that time," I said to Stacey and Jessica.

"Oh, what time are we meeting with Erica?" Stacey asked.

"Oh, like five," I said.

It was almost 4:30.

"Oh we better go then so that we can be on time," Jessica said with a determined voice.

She had a real sense of urgency in her voice. I guess Jessica didn't want to miss out on her extra credit. We drove away from the mall and back to the college to meet up with Erica. When we parked, we walked up close to where we were meeting Erica. She saw us and began to wave. We all waved back.

"Hey, what's up Erica?" I asked as we got closer.

"Not much, I'm just ready to go check out this cool movie. It's all about history, and I can't wait," Erica said.

"We can't wait either Erica," I said as I turned my head toward Stacey and Jessica.

"Erica, do you know my roommates, Stacey and Jessica?"

"Oh no, I don't think I've had the pleasure. Hi, I'm Erica," as she had her hand out.

"Hi, I'm Jessica," as she shook Erica's hands.

"Hi, I'm Stacey," as Erica moved toward her.

"Erica, I'm sorry I didn't ask, but I didn't think that you would mind them tagging along. Stacey and Erica really wanted to check out the video with us so I told them they could come."

Erica smiled.

"No, no, I don't mind. The more the merrier. I'm glad to see there are others who are also interested in history. It is going to be a good movie, you wait and see. History isn't as boring as everyone thinks it is. This movie is all about Western Civilization. It's my passion, you know. I think it's going to be enlightening."

"Well, should we be off then? The movie will be starting in a little while," I said.

"Yeah, we should go. It will be coming up soon," Jessica said, and we all began to walk.

"Can we take my car?" Stacey asked eagerly.

"Yeah that sounds great, right guys?" I asked.

"Yeah," Jessica and Erica said at the same time.

"Looks like we're all going with you," I said.

We all got into Stacey's car and drove to the IMAX theater. When we got to the theater, there were a lot of posters displayed for different movies, which were mostly science movies. All of us got a student discount of course, which was good. Any chance to save money is always a good thing.

"What is the name of this movie?" Stacey asked.

"In Search of Greek Gods and Goddesses," Erica said.

"This movie is all about tracing back the steps of the Greek gods, with this guy George Tramain. He and his team have found new evidence about the Greek gods, and he is retracing their steps. It's so awesome," Erica said enthusiastically.

I could tell there was something in her voice that made me think Erica might like this guy a little too much. It was like a crush or something. We all walked up to the ticket booth.

"Hi, can I have four for *In Search of Greek Gods?*" Erica asked.

"Yes, absolutely," the guy behind the counter said as he began to ring us up.

"Oh can we have a student discount with that please?" I said as we all waved our student IDs.

"Yes, no problem, that will be twenty dollars," the man said.

Everyone reached into their purses.

"I've got it girls. This movie is on me," Erica said as she paid the man for the tickets.

"Oh thank you Erica, that was really nice of you," I said.

"Yeah thank you so much, that was really nice," Stacey said. Jessica followed with a "thank you, you didn't have to."

"Oh no problem. It is my pleasure. I wanted to treat you guys because I'm so happy to see others who are as fascinated with history as me."

We all walked into the theater and sat down. The screen was really big. IMAX theaters were always big. I never got over the reaction that I had when I first entered one for the first time. The screen just seems like it stretches forever. It's so incredible. It makes you feel like you're actually inside the movie. Shortly after we all got situated, the lights went dim, and the movie began to play. The movie started with classical adventure history music. Then the host George Tramain came on.

"Hi, I'm George Tramain, join me as we uncover the truth behind the Greek gods. Were they real? What proof do we have? My team and I have found new historical evidence to support their existence. I leave the conclusion up to you."

George Tramain continued on, and then the movie started to really take off. The movie zoomed in and began to go over all of the old Greek myths—the ones you hear about a lot—from Zeus to Olympia. The movie went over all of the major characters. Then George Tramain got to Aphrodite. There was a statue of Aphrodite riding the dolphins that George Tramain was standing in front of.

"And here we have the great Aphrodite—the most mysterious of all the Greek gods. She is the goddess of love. Her origins are not entirely Greek, but she was adopted by the Greeks wholeheartedly. And my team has found what we believe to be the best evidence of the Greek gods' true existence."

George Tramain pulled out a very old book.

"This book is very exciting for me and my team. It is the main reason we made this whole movie. When we first uncovered this book, it gave me goose bumps. This book has what may be the greatest evidence for the Greek gods' existence—and here, right here is where it begins."

The scene shifted to an old sleepy Greek town.

"Here in Cythera is where Aphrodite is from, according to this very ancient text. You see, in the ancient days, there weren't many books. The Greeks simply didn't write down a lot of stuff. I have an expert with me here, Doctor Rupert Hoover. He is an expert in ancient documents.

"Doctor, what can you tell me about this book?" George Tramain asked.

"This book is extremely rare. After careful analysis, I believe this book is genuine."

"Thank you Doctor," George Tramain said and then turned toward his left. "And now we have an expert in ancient Greek."

George Tramain didn't even have to say the name—it was Devon's Uncle Arnot.

"What can you tell us about this book?"

Devon's uncle took a look at the book.

"Well, after examining this document thoroughly, I can tell you that it changes the whole perception on Greek philosophy. It is so different from all other documents we have on the ancient belief system of the Greeks. Where did you find it?" Devon's uncle asked.

A look of horror came over George Tramain as if he wasn't expecting that question.

"Well, I was just going to cover that. We found this book in an older part of this town. One of the crew members of my team discovered it in a used-book store. As you can tell from the book's appearance, we knew it was old. But little did we realize what it would contain."

George Tramain now picked up the book.

"Thank you Dr. Katris," George Tramain said.

"No problem," Devon's uncle said.

"Next, we're going to discover this secret text. What are its ancient mysteries? We will uncover what has been discovered from it. Hopefully by the end of this documentary, we will have answers," George Tramain said.

That was how the documentary played out. George Tramain went from place to place following the lost book of Aphrodite to the tee. Then finally, the conclusion came.

"Well, it is hard to say if I believe this book. I mean, the book itself seems to have a lot of credibility. All the sites in the book are there. But who can really tell the truth? Your guess is as good as mine. There is some evidence that we have discovered together, but the rest of this book's secrets will just have to remain a mystery for now. This is George Tramain signing off for *In Search of Greek Gods*. See you next time."

Shortly after that, there was an analog at the very end of the film that said: "Shortly after the filming of this episode, the lost book of Aphrodite was stolen and has not been recovered. Authorities are on the lookout."

The four of us read this in amazement—it was hard to imagine that someone would steal such an important artifact. Soon the screen showed the credits, and then we all got up from our seats and headed out.

Erica turned toward me.

"What did you think?"

"It was good," I said.

"Oh I'm glad that you liked it, but what did you think at the end about how the book was stolen?" Erica asked.

Jessica and Stacey had overheard the conversation.

"Yeah, that part was crazy, after all that they found from that one book to have it stolen—the lost book is lost forever," Stacey said.

"Yeah, I think George Tramain should have made copies or something," Jessica said.

"Oh, you know how these shows are, they like to add extra drama for effect," Erica said.

Watching the movie didn't help distract me though. I thought it would have put my mind at ease a little, but it simply didn't. I now had even more doubts in my head. Even though I tried to escape my doubt about the dolphins and Antilla, it seemed to be coming at me head on. Now I wasn't sure what to do. My frustration was apparent on my face I'm sure. When we got into the car to drive back to campus, Erica turned toward me.

"Are you okay? Do you want to get coffee?" Erica asked.

"No. I think I need to get some sleep. I think when we get back, I am going to head back to my room. You guys should go ahead," I said.

"Okay," Erica said as we drove toward the college. When we got to the college, we all began to get out of the car. All I could think about was getting back to my room to get some sleep.

"Alright, well, I hope you feel better. Take care and get some sleep."

"You too," I said as the three of them headed to the college café.

I headed to my room. When I got to my room, I sat down, took a deep breath, and thought about how frustrating the whole situation was. I knew what I had to do, and it weighed heavily on me. But I suppose I had known for some time that the necklace had to come off. It was the last thing keeping this little fantasy alive, and I couldn't live with so much doubt.

I slowly looked in the mirror. There it was—the necklace. Even though I had never taken it off, I had barely even noticed it around my neck. I took a deep breath and closed my eyes. Before I knew it, the necklace was off. I placed it in the jewelry box that I had set aside. After I took the necklace off, I quickly decided I wouldn't wear it again. It didn't feel great to have the necklace off. It made me feel kind of empty inside. It was like my heart had been removed. It was an odd feeling.

"I have to do this," I said aloud as I closed my eyes to get used to the feeling. I suddenly felt extremely tired.

Chapter 33

An Unexpected Lesson

I decided to go to sleep. My heart felt heavy. I hoped that the sleep would help me to feel better. But it was hard to fall asleep. Eventually after fighting it, I fell asleep—and that's when it happened. Without knowing how, or why, I was back in Antilla. But this time, the little girl that I had seen before led me into a room. After I entered the room, I was led down to a hallway that I hadn't been before in my dreams. The little girl looked at me and then ran away. I followed her. Before I knew it, I was back in my room.

The little girl had run to where my necklace was in my room. I hadn't woken up; I was still dreaming. The little girl opened the box and showed me the necklace. As I stared at the necklace, the blue from it shined brightly. The glow hit me like a bolt of lightning. I opened my eyes suddenly. I was in the room alone, and I was almost 100% sure that I was awake. I walked over to the necklace. I picked it up, and then something happened.

It was a glowing sensation that seemed to resonate throughout my whole body. Then I stood face-to-face in front of someone I had thought I had only imagined. I stood in front of Aphrodite herself. I stood still for a moment and felt as though I couldn't move. I don't know if it was because I was in utter shock, or if Aphrodite had some sort of control over me, but I stood there motionless.

"Hello Aurora, I have been watching you for some time. Why did you take the necklace off?"

I stood there in front of Aphrodite and didn't know how to answer that question.

"Who are you?" I asked even though I knew the answer.

"Aurora, I know you know who I am. I have been watching over you ever since you put on this necklace. So please let me ask you again. Why did you take the necklace off?"

I closed my eyes and started chanting.

"This isn't happening, this isn't happening. Wake up Aurora, wake up, wake up." I closed my eyes and reopened them.

I wasn't dreaming.

Aphrodite came up to me and tapped me on the shoulder. I opened my eyes. That tap that came from Aphrodite felt eerily real.

"Let's start again. I am Aphrodite as you might have guessed, and I am not a dream. Now please, I have to know why did you take the necklace off." Aphrodite asked again.

I took a big gulp. I wasn't sure how to even start to answer the question. I just said whatever came to my mind first.

"I have a lot of doubts. I can't believe that any of this is real. I can barely believe that you're real, and you are standing right in front of me," I blurted out and almost began to cry.

"Why are you crying?" Aphrodite asked.

"Yes because I'm going insane. I know it now, and that sucks because my life is going to be ruined because of it," I said and began to cry.

Aphrodite gave me a hug and wiped the tear from my eyes.

"My dear sweet Aurora, first you're not going crazy, and second, your life is hanging in the balance. But it will be okay. Let me help you. I want to guide you. I want to teach you the ways," Aphrodite said as she had a very large smile and a look of confidence on her face. Aphrodite reminded me of my mom whenever she would try to make me feel better.

I slowly stopped crying.

"I'm only asking why you took off the necklace. Don't you remember what the dolphins told you? You should never take the necklace off; it is for your protection, remember?" Aphrodite asked.

I felt confused.

"How did you know what the dolphins told me? I can barely remember that. How could you possibly know that?" I asked.

"Well, I was there actually. I have been with you ever since you began to wear the necklace. I live within the necklace," Aphrodite said.

"But how can you live inside the necklace? That's impossible," I asked even though I was getting used to the impossible.

"Well, it's what you would call magic. A part of my soul is contained in the necklace for you because you were chosen to unite the worlds. I foretold it long ago that you would come—and on that day that I predicted your coming, I vowed that I would find a way to be there to guide you. Here I am my dear Aurora," Aphrodite said.

I was now in utter shock.

"I don't know what to say," I said.

"There is nothing to say. I am here to help. You do want my help, don't you?" Aphrodite asked.

The question resonated loud within my head. As much as I needed help, I wasn't sure this was the answer I was looking for. It seemed like it was adding more craziness to an already extremely odd and incredible situation. Aphrodite focused in on me again.

"Let me put it to you this way Aurora. I am going to help you. You need my help, and there is way too much riding on this situation for me not to help you," Aphrodite said.

"Well, what do you mean?" I asked to clarify.

"You are not getting it, are you, Aurora? There is more than just your confusion that we have to consider. The world is relying on you to figure this out—and that is why I am here. I have come to help you find your way. Okay, so let's move on. I know that you have been having trouble. Let's talk about it. What is the problem?" Aphrodite asked.

I thought about it for a minute. I guess I hadn't thought about what exactly the problem was.

"I guess, I think I'm going crazy, and that seems to be a problem."

"Exactly, self-doubt is holding you back. I sensed this. Why do you think you're going crazy?" Aphrodite asked.

I suddenly felt like I was in front of a psychologist with the way Aphrodite was asking me questions. But the way things were going, I might as well be in front of an actual psychologist—being treated for having some sort of mental breakdown.

"I guess my biggest problem is that I'm having trouble believing that all of this stuff is really happening. I just can't believe this is happening to me. Since I can't believe it, I certainly can't tell anyone else about it. I mean

I can't prove any of this is true to anyone if I did tell them. So why would they believe me?" I asked.

A small laugh came from Aphrodite as she put her hand on my shoulder.

"You see, now you are thinking. So what we need to do is find some way to show everyone that you are telling the truth. I mean you don't want to show just anyone about all of this—at least not yet. You should try to keep this a secret for right now. But you do want to show a few people that you can trust for support. So what can you do that will prove that you are not lying?" Aphrodite asked as she stared at me while thinking. It seemed like she was searching for the answer.

"I know! I could show them you," I blurted out.

"Oh dear, as flattering as that is, they really would think that you were crazy because you are the only one that can see me. I was thinking about really helping out with something you need. I am going to help you by showing you how to use your powers," Aphrodite said.

At this point, any new information that I found out no longer led to shock, but I still couldn't believe the word.

"Powers?" I said as if the word was as foreign to me as the concept of me becoming an astronaut. "What powers?" I asked.

"Oh we have a lot to learn, don't we my dear? You have contained within you certain powers. They have always been in you. You have probably just never noticed. But in this place, we will find out what they are together."

I looked around. I hadn't taken a good look at where we were. I was originally only focused about Aphrodite. We weren't in my room anymore. Now we were somehow somewhere new. This place was different. It was quiet and had a bluish tint to it.

"What is this place?" I asked.

"This place is our place. It is a place where you and I can come to talk or explore new things. It is a place of your mind and of mine. We are united here. I know you may have always felt like you are normal, Aurora. It's understandable, but there is something very different about you. You are one of the rarest types of people in this world. There are only two in human history that have ever existed. Those two people are you and I—and this is our sanctuary," Aphrodite said and pointed to my head.

"What is up here in your mind comes from down here in your heart," Aphrodite said as she pointed to my heart. "Do you understand?"

"A little, but I still don't understand what are we. Are we aliens or something?"

"We are the salvation. I need you to just try and understand. I promise you the rest of the answers will come with time, okay?" Aphrodite said.

"Okay, I will try," I said.

"Okay good, now our powers come from pure love. Love is the greatest thought, feeling, and purpose in life. It is what moves us. It is what binds us, and it is what the mind works off of. Love is the source of your power. When you find the one you love, the power takes over. It is the reason why you can talk to the dolphins. That much is the same between us. Your other powers might be different from mine, but there should be some that are the same.

"So with that in mind, let's try out a power that you should be able to do. That way you can show people that you trust so they will believe you and not think that you are crazy."

Aphrodite closed her eyes, and then our scene changed like we had been teleported to a different place. We were now in front of a bay. It was incredible for a place that was not real to look and feel the way that it felt. Even the smells were right.

"Okay, I need you to walk," Aphrodite said.

"Where?" I asked.

Aphrodite pointed toward the bay.

"Like into the water?" I asked.

Aphrodite shook her head.

"No, I need you to walk on the water," Aphrodite said.

"I don't think that is possible," I said.

"Oh it's possible," Aphrodite said and walked out onto the water.

It looked like one of the most graceful walks I had ever seen. It wasn't like a ship floating. Aphrodite's walk was like the most graceful ballet dancer performing in front of me. It wasn't even a struggle for Aphrodite to stay above the water. It was amazing. I felt my jaw drop as I watched Aphrodite walk. As Aphrodite walked on the water, she had such a look of confidence. It was the confidence that I had only seen in nature when an animal knows it's in its element, like a duck in the water.

"Alright, now you try. Do you still doubt me?" Aphrodite asked.

"Okay, here goes nothing," I said.

I began to walk, but as soon as I got to the water, I broke the surface. I could feel my foot glide right through the water and hit the bottom of the bay. My failure was met with water splashing. Aphrodite shook her head in disappointment.

"You are thinking about how things usually are. You are not using your love. Clear your head. Don't think about what you know to be true. Think about what needs to be true. Think about your love, what is his name?" Aphrodite asked.

"Devon."

"Devon, yes, think of Devon and that you have to walk on this water. Don't have any doubt that you can walk on the water. Replace the doubt with thoughts of your love for Devon."

I closed my eyes and thought of Devon, and began to take a few steps. I still broke through the surface of the water. I walked back to the shoreline and closed my eyes again. I took a deep breath and thought of walking with Devon on top of the water. I imagined us holding hands like we did on our first date. I remembered the love I felt on that night. It was like no other feeling in the world. It was the feeling of absolute bliss.

As I raised my foot to place it on top of the water, I visualized Devon putting his foot next to mine. We held hands the whole way. I continued to hold the thought of Devon. I blocked out any doubt and any other thoughts. All I thought about was walking on top of that water. As my foot was placed on the water, I prepared for it to break through the water again.

But instead of feeling the bottom of the bay like I had previously, I felt the air brush over the top of my foot. I took a few steps.

"Am I actually walking on top of the water?" I asked myself. It was like I was walking on concrete.

"You did it, Aurora," Aphrodite said.

I opened my eyes and looked down. I could see fish below me. I could see through the water as if I was on top of a glass. There was a circle around me that formed on the surface of the water. Even though the water around the circle looked extremely rough and chopping, the water in the circle was calm and had ripples like I was looking through a window. It was like all of the serenity pictures that I had seen. I felt like I was in absolute bliss like how my love for Devon made me feel.

"Wow, I don't know if I could get used to this," I said as I leaned in to get a closer look at the fish. Right when I got my head close to the surface of the water, I fell through.

"Oh Aurora, you broke the thought of Devon. You lost focus. You must never stop thinking of your love. It is easier for you to use your powers in this place when our minds are together. But out in the real world, it is a little harder. You must always focus on your heart and your love, or you won't be able to use your powers. Do you understand?"

"Yes," I said.

"Okay good, now let's try it again," Aphrodite said.

I walked back to the shoreline and closed my eyes. Then I pictured Devon again and walked on the water. It was there again—the feeling of bliss. I could walk on water just like before.

"Yes," I said, feeling proud of myself.

I began to sink a little into the water so I quickly started to think about Devon again. Within an instant, I was back on top of the water. My ability to walk on the water renewed my faith. It made me believe that I wasn't going crazy—it finally made me feel right again.

"Now Aurora, come toward me, won't you?" Aphrodite asked.

I walked toward Aphrodite who was out in the middle of the water. I made it out about twenty feet.

"That was good Aurora. Let's see if you can do it a little faster. Let's race," Aphrodite said.

"Race to where?" I asked.

Suddenly an island appeared about a mile away on my left side.

"Oh, how about to there," Aphrodite said and pointed to the island.

"Okay sounds…," I began to say but before I could finish, Aphrodite had taken off.

"Too slow!!!" Aphrodite said as she ran past me.

I took off after her, but Aphrodite was fast. I tried hard to concentrate on Devon while running on the surface. It was beginning to get easier and easier. The water literally cleared a path for me. Where the water had been rough, the water became smooth. I soon made it to the other side of the water where the island was. Aphrodite was there waiting for me.

"Not bad," Aphrodite said smiling.

"Thank you," I said as I breathed heavily. I breathed in and out just like all of those times that I had done before when I ran.

"Why are you breathing so heavy?" Aphrodite asked.

"Well, I'm trying to catch my breath."

"Oh well, in this place, you don't need to do that, try it," Aphrodite said. I stopped breathing heavily. Aphrodite was right. I wasn't out of breath.

"Wow," I said.

"Trust me, it gets better. Now Aurora, it's time for something else that is very important—your next lesson. Will you walk with me?"

"Yes," I said.

We walked a little ways out toward a spectacular garden, which had two rows on each side. The garden looked very Greek with its pillars and statues. On the other side of the garden was a palace. There were green bushes and flowers everywhere. There was a pool in between the two sides. Aphrodite and I walked toward the end of the pool. There was a very nice white bench where Aphrodite sat down.

"Come and sit here next to me, my dear Aurora."

I quickly sat down, and then we stared at each other for a moment. Then Aphrodite began to speak.

"I'm sorry. I don't mean to stare at you. I just can't believe that you have finally arrived. All of this time of waiting and wondering, now you are finally here to fulfill the prophecy. I know someone like me shouldn't be this excited, but I really am. This is a wonderful time that we are living in. You don't even realize it, do you?" Aphrodite asked.

"Well, I had some idea but...," I began to say and then paused and looked at Aphrodite again. "Um I guess I hadn't realized it."

"Well, it really is the time of times, my dear Aurora. You are the link between our world and theirs. I don't want you to fold under the pressure. The weight and the significance of it all might seem daunting at times. But just remember, one step at a time, okay? Now with regard to your powers, you did a very good job for your first lesson. How do you feel about it?"

"Well, good actually," I said.

"Good, I am glad to hear it, but there isn't a moment to waste. Your second lesson must begin. I will teach you how to summon Antilla. I understand that you have been having some trouble with that—and it is very understandable.

"The dolphins don't understand how hard this is for us. It is like second nature for them. But don't worry, I will teach you," Aphrodite said.

For the first time, I felt like someone completely understood what I needed, and it made me very happy. It had been entirely too hard for me to summon Antilla myself. If I had been able to, maybe I wouldn't have felt as crazy.

"Thank you," I said.

"Alright then, the first thing I need you to remember is that Antilla is not really a place—at least not a physical place. It does exist though, but what I mean is that you can always go there, no matter where you are at. You don't have to be in the water. Do you understand?" Aphrodite asked.

"I understand, I think," I said.

"Good, okay now, do you remember how the dolphins said that once you have been to Antilla, you can always go back?" Aphrodite asked.

I searched my memory banks for that.

"Yes, I do."

"Okay good, that is half the battle. Now I need you to visualize Antilla. Not your Antilla but instead the actual Antilla—the place where you received the necklace will do. Can you visualize it? Can you remember the sounds and all of the dolphins?"

"I will try," I said as I closed my eyes.

I had a clear visualization of Antilla. I could see the theater where everyone had gathered and where I had received the necklace. I opened my eyes.

"Yes, I can see it. I can remember it."

"Okay good. Now I need you to remember as much detail as you can. The more detail, the better. It will make this easier so just keep that in mind when you do this," Aphrodite said.

I nodded my head showing that I understood.

"Good, now the next thing necessary for you to go to Antilla is the ancient symbol. You may have seen it before," Aphrodite said as she raised up her hands. Her hands were touching each other tip to tip and were bent in a way that resembled a heart.

"Can you do this symbol with your hands?" Aphrodite asked.

I raised up my hands and made a heart shape

"Like this?" I asked.

"Yes, just like that. Do you know this symbol?" Aphrodite asked pleased.

"Yes I do," I said with a smile. "It's a symbolic heart."

"No, like most things you will find, it is more than it appears. This is my symbol. What you saw was probably a variation of me doing this. Doing this symbol is our greatest display of our power. It represents the heart and love. It symbolizes the essence of love. That is why it is such a powerful symbol. Never use this symbol in vain. Never abuse it. It must be used for good just like all of your powers. Do you understand?" Aphrodite asked.

"Yes, I understand."

"Good, now raise your hands to your face while visualizing Antilla and your love—always visualize Devon." Aphrodite raised her hands to her head. I did the same.

"Now bring your hands to your heart while thinking about Antilla and Devon," Aphrodite said.

I did and nothing happened.

"Nothing happened," I said.

"Yes I know. It was a practice run. Let's try it again. But this time, have your eyes closed. Don't focus on me, focus on Antilla and Devon," Aphrodite said.

"Okay," I said and closed my eyes and took a deep breath.

My heart was pounding as I began to picture Devon in every detail. I thought of everything about him. Then I pictured Devon in Antilla waiting for me. He was waving. I rose up my hands like Aphrodite had shown me and then lowered my hands to my heart. A giant opening appeared in front of us. I opened my eyes. I could see Antilla—the real Antilla. There were dolphins swimming back and forth.

"Is that really Antilla? I thought we would actually be transported into Antilla," I said.

"No, it doesn't work that way. But this is indeed Antilla that you see. This is a window that you see before you. You can normally step through it, but while you are in this place, you cannot go to Antilla. When you are in this place with me, you cannot step through to another window. You must wait till you are back in your world. Do you understand?" Aphrodite asked as she looked at me.

"Yes I understand."

"But you will always have the power to see Antilla no matter where you are," Aphrodite said and smiled.

"But how will I go to Antilla once I am back in the real world?"

"Oh that is easy, once you have the window in front of you like we just did—just jump through it. But remember, you are the only one who can go through the window. You must never try to bring anyone else through it."

"But why?"

"Mankind is not ready for it. Antilla is just for us. Once mankind is ready to go to Antilla, they will be able to. But for now, you must serve as its messenger. You must make the other humans understand what Antilla is. You must make them believe. That is why you and you alone have been given this gift. Do you understand?" Aphrodite asked.

"Not fully," I said.

"Well don't worry. Your purpose will be understood better as time goes on. For now that completes our lesson. I think it's time for you to go back to your world. Remember, do not take the necklace off. I will always be here to guide you and teach you. Do not show off your powers to just anyone. Only use them to prove to those closest to you that you are telling the truth. I will talk with you again soon. If you need anything, I will be there with you," Aphrodite said.

Aphrodite began to fade and eventually disappear. Antilla began to fade as well. Soon I was back in my room holding the necklace, which I quickly put on.

Chapter 34

Devon Returns

I said aloud to the necklace, "I will never take you off." I was so glad that I finally had some answers. But now the question remained: what to do next now that I could prove I wasn't crazy. While I was thinking about it, I got a message on my phone from Devon.

"I'm coming back tomorrow. Don't worry about picking me up. I've already arranged to be picked up at the airport. I can't wait to see you," the message said.

"I can't wait to see you either. I love you," I wrote back.

My heart beat fast from the excitement. Devon was coming back. This is great news. I thought he would be gone longer. After all of the stuff that just happened with Aphrodite, this was the best news that I could have hoped to hear. I would finally be able to prove I wasn't crazy, and I could finally tell Devon everything that has been going on. I thought of telling Erica too. The three of us would be able to figure out how to handle everything.

"But I can't tell anyone else," I said aloud and smiled.

For the first time in a little while, things began to feel like they were going to be okay. I texted Erica.

"Do you want to meet Devon with me tomorrow? He's coming back."

I had a big smile on my face from the excitement of the thought of Devon coming home. I got a quick response back.

"Yes of course, I would love to."

"Great! I will work out the details with you later," I wrote back.

I faced the ultimate question of where would I show Devon and Erica that I could walk on water. Without even thinking about it, I had lost all sense of time. It was mid-afternoon already.

I had slept all morning so I had a lot of catching up to do. I walked around excitedly. I had missed Devon so much while he was gone. I hadn't been able to really talk to him so I was so utterly and fantastically excited. I started to go over what outfit I might wear tomorrow. Then I realized I wasn't sure what time Devon was coming so I grabbed my phone and texted Devon.

"Devon, I was just wondering what time you would be back tomorrow."

I got an instant response back so I thought that he must finally be getting a good signal.

"I'll be back around two, love you," Devon wrote.

I looked over my closet and stared at what seemed like an endless option of outfits. Then without knowing how or why I saw it, I found the perfect outfit. It was a white long-sleeved shirt, with long arms and a nice overlay.

My heart beat fast just thinking about the fact that soon Devon would be back. I looked in the mirror and realized that my hair was not nearly as nice as my outfit.

"Maybe I should call Erica and get my hair done," I began to think as I pulled my hair up.

"Hey Erica, want to go get your hair done?" I texted.

"Yeah, I would love to. I'll see you in a moment," Erica wrote.

"What do you mean?" But as soon as I sent the text, there was a knock on the door.

I looked through the security hole. It was Erica. I quickly opened the door.

"Erica, I'm so happy and surprised to see you."

Erica smiled when I said that.

"I'm surprised at myself too because I don't normally want to do this kind of girly thing. I was actually coming over toward your room to ask you if you wanted to. As soon as you had mentioned that Devon was coming, it seemed like the right thing to do. But you texted me first."

"Oh that's too funny," I said and grabbed my purse.

"Well, do you even know where we can get our hair done? I usually just do it myself," I said.

"There is a place near here called Sally's that seemed to be nice."

"Okay Sally's it is," I said and off we both went to Sally's, a small salon that had about six chairs and two hairstylists. There was also a place to get your nails done.

"Hi, is this your first time here?" one of the hairstylists asked as Erica and I walked in.

"Yes, this is our first time," I said.

"Well, what can we do for you?"

"Well, I'm trying to look nice for my boyfriend. He is coming back from being out of town for a while. I wanted to surprise him by looking great," I said.

"Yeah and I just want to tag along and look nice," Erica said.

"Oh of course, of course, and what style would you like?" the hairstylist asked as she gave me a look over.

"Well actually, we never do this sort of thing so we have no idea. We just want to look good," I said.

"Okay, I think we will do a chignon. That will give you the great look that you're looking for. How does that sound?"

"Okay, I don't know much about this sort of stuff so if you think it is going to look good, then I trust you," I said and smiled.

"Me too," Erica said.

"Okay, two chignons coming up. Please each of you take a chair."

We both walked over to the chairs. Then the two hairstylists went to work on shampooing our hair. Eventually after an hour or so, the hairstylists were done.

"How do you like it?" my hairstylist asked.

I took a good look at it in the mirror.

"Oh it looks very nice," I said as I put my hand up to my hair.

"I hope that it looks good for my date tomorrow," I said.

My hairstylist had a look of concern on her face.

"Is there something the matter?" I asked.

"Oh well, it is more of a concern. I didn't know this was for a date tomorrow," the hairstylist said.

"Oh well, is that a problem? Do you think it will still look good for tomorrow?" I asked.

"Yes, I think it might be fine, but I don't want you to look bad. It could become bad by tomorrow. I know this date is very special for you."

The hairstylist looked like she was in deep thought. She took a stark look at my hair and then said, "I have it. I don't normally do this, but if you want to, you can drop by tomorrow, and I can touch it up a bit. You know—fix any areas that might have gone astray over the night. It will be free of charge of course. What do you say to that?"

"Wow, thank you! That would be so nice if you could do that. This is a very important date, and I need to look my best. I'm sorry I didn't say that it was for tomorrow. I don't normally get my hair done like this most of the time. I usually just put my hair together myself. I will be coming by early tomorrow. What time do you open?"

"Oh we open at eight a.m."

"Eight sounds good. What was your name by the way? You guys don't wear name tags," I said.

"Oh, we don't wear name tags because it's so impersonal. I'm Deb and that is Barbara. I always try to help people out. I want my clients to look the best that they can look. That's my job, and I'm good at it. Speaking of which, I have been staring at your nails. Would you like a manicure?"

I glanced at my nails, and then I looked at Deb's. I could see that mine were definitely missing that nice little spark that gives your hands a good glow.

"Yes of course, I would love a nice manicure. What did you have in mind?" I asked, trusting that Deb would not steer me in the wrong direction.

"Oh well, just take a seat over here at the nail salon, and we will fix you up," Deb said. She began to scrub my fingers and go through all of the rough spots. Just then Erica walked over with her new hair.

"Wow, it looks really nice!" I said.

It really did bring out the beauty of Erica.

"Do you really think so?" Erica asked smiling.

Deb perked right up.

"Yes, it really does look nice. I can see a difference. Nice job Barbara. You gave her the full treatment," Deb said.

"Oh thank you! Are you getting your nails done too?" Erica asked as she glanced down at her nails.

"You know, I think I could use a good nail improvement session too," Erica said.

Barbara perked right up.

"Yes of course. Please take a seat," Barbara said and then she went right to work on Erica's nails. After about a half an hour, we were both done with the manicures.

"Do you want me to do your feet too?" Deb asked.

I glanced at my feet. Sure enough, they needed work too.

"Yeah, I think we will both take a pedicure too."

Erica smiled and nodded her head. Erica and I were both having fun. We both felt like beauty queens. After another half an hour, we were all done. We both looked spectacular.

"You look awesome," Erica said to me.

"You too," I said and smiled.

"Okay well that about finishes it. Can I ring you up over here?" Deb said.

Erica smiled and looked at me and said, "I got it."

I of course put up a fight.

"No, I got it. You get the next one."

Erica was already paying and then walked back over to me.

"Thank you, but you didn't have to," I said.

"No, I wanted to. It's my treat."

"Well thank you, but lunch is on me, okay?"

"Sounds good," Erica said and we both began to walk out of the door.

"Well, see you guys again soon. See you tomorrow, Aurora," Deb said with a wink.

"Tomorrow at eight. I will see you then. Thanks again."

We both waved good-bye, and Deb and Barbara waved back. Then we were on our way off to get some lunch somewhere. But where we would get lunch I wasn't sure.

"What do you feel like eating?" I asked Erica.

"I don't know. Maybe we could go to a place where we could find some simple sandwiches," Erica said. After walking around the shopping complex for a few minutes, we found a quaint little sandwich shop.

"How does this look? It's something new and simple," I said.

"Looks exactly what I was hoping for," Erica said.

We both sat down at a table. While waiting, a bunch of guys kept on checking out Erica and me. It was nice to have someone besides Erica approve my new look—it gave me a good feeling inside.

"I think they're staring at us," Erica said as she bobbed her head toward a group of boys. Before I had time to respond, the waiter arrived.

"Hello ladies, what can I get you? Have you had a chance to look at the menu?"

"Oh well, I haven't looked at the menu yet, but I think I already know what I want," I said.

"Okay, go ahead," the waiter said as he stood with a pen and paper.

"Well, I would like a turkey sandwich."

"Yes of course, a turkey sandwich and to drink?" the waiter asked while looking at Erica.

"Oh just a water," I said.

"Excellent and for you miss?"

Erica smiled and stared back at the waiter who still hadn't taken his eyes off of her.

"Well, I think I'll have the same."

"Okay excellent, your food will be coming right up."

Erica had the biggest smile on her face.

"Wow Erica, looks like you have an admirer," I said.

Erica blushed a little. It was hard to see her blush if you didn't know her. Erica seemed to have a way of hiding her emotions.

"He is cute," Erica said with a smile.

"So are you excited about seeing Devon tomorrow?" she asked trying to casually change the subject.

"Well, I am actually so excited it's hard to describe. Thank you so much for saying that you would meet Devon with me. I know it might be a little weird, but I think right before Devon comes, I will be on pins and needles. I need someone to be there with me to wait. I miss him so bad."

"Yes I know," Erica said and smiled. Just as we were finishing up that part of the conversation, the waiter brought our drinks.

"Is there anything else that I can get you?" the waiter asked, looking at both of us, but mostly glancing at Erica.

"Well no, I don't think so," I said.

"Well, if there is anything, please let me know. Your sandwiches should be ready soon."

"Wow Erica, I really think the waiter likes you," I said again.

"Well thank you, but no boy really likes me too much. That's why I focus so much on my studies. I mean, it actually works out good because then there are fewer distractions that way. I still don't know how you do it—focus on school and on Devon, I mean," Erica said.

"Well, it is hard, Erica, but I make it work. I mean, it takes time, but you get used to it. Do you know what I mean? I wouldn't have it any other way. Devon is the love of my life. He is my heart and soul. I think I would do anything for him," I said without even thinking about it. I had almost gone into another subject.

I wanted to wait in telling Devon and Erica at the same time about my powers and about Antilla. That was the real reason I wanted Erica there tomorrow. It would be when I would tell them both.

"Well, I am jealous, but really happy for you," Erica said.

"Well, don't worry. I know you will find someone one day, you just have to give guys a chance. You have to have a little faith. You just never know," I said.

Just as I finished saying that, the waiter came with our food.

"Oh I think that is our food," Erica said and smiled.

"Here you go," the waiter said.

"Thank you," Erica and I said.

"You're very welcome. Is there anything else I can get you?"

"No, I think we are good," Erica said smiling.

"Well, I will be over here if you need me. Enjoy your meals," the waiter said with a giant smile. He backed away and walked toward the kitchen. We ate our meals with very little talking. It was nice to just relax and enjoy things.

"How was your sandwich?" I asked.

"Oh, it was good. How was yours?" Erica asked.

"Oh good. It was just like I imagined it would be," I said.

When both of our plates were empty, the waiter came back.

"Well, can I offer you ladies any dessert?"

I looked at Erica. She smiled and shook her head no.

"No, I think that we are good, thank you."

"Oh you're welcome. I hope you enjoyed the sandwiches."

"Yes I did," Erica said.

"Oh I'm so glad to hear it. Well, I will get you your check."

"Sounds good," I said.

The waiter walked off to grab the check.

"Well, he is really nice," Erica said.

I smiled and gave a little chuckle.

"He's cute too," I said.

Erica smiled and closed her eyes for a second in embarrassment. The waiter came back with the biggest smile.

"Well, you ladies have a good day. Don't worry about the check. This one is on me," the waiter said.

"Really?" I said in shock.

"Yes, it's my treat. It's not every day that two beautiful ladies walk in here," the waiter said.

"Oh well, thank you very much. What's your name?" I asked.

"Oh, it's Mike," he said still smiling.

Erica looked happy. Mike was still staring at her.

"Well I hope I see you ladies in here again soon," Mike said.

"Yes, we will be back for sure," Erica said.

"Awesome, I will see you then," Mike said and walked toward the front register. Erica and I gathered up our things and headed toward the door. As we were leaving, Erica turned toward Mike. It looked like she was trying to get up the courage to say something.

"Can you wait a minute," Erica said to me.

"Of course," I said.

Erica walked toward Mike.

"Hey, did you want to hang out sometime?" Erica asked.

Mike seemed so surprised that he almost jumped.

"Yeah, I would love that, when?" Mike asked.

"I don't know, but I can give you my number so you can call me later. We can talk about it," Erica said.

Mike handed her a piece of paper and a pen. Erica wrote her name and number and gave it to Mike.

"Call me, okay?" Erica said.

"I will," Mike said happily.

"You promise?" Erica asked.

"I promise," Mike said with the biggest smile.

"Okay, talk to you later," Erica said as we walked out of the restaurant.

"Wow Erica, I didn't know you had it in you," I said.

"You underestimate me. I know how to go after what I want when I want to." I smiled when Erica said that.

We both headed back to the dorm, which was quiet when we got there. Erica glanced at her watch, but before she could say anything, I spoke up.

"Well Erica, it looks like it might be a good time for me to head in. I want to catch up on my sleep to get ready for tomorrow."

"Oh yeah, sounds good. Thank you for hanging out with me. It was fun. I will see you tomorrow," Erica said.

"Yeah, I'll see you tomorrow," I said, and then we both walked to our separate dorm rooms. When I got to my dorm room, it was empty.

"I guess Stacey and Jessica are out," I said as I looked around the room. I then got ready for bed. While getting ready for bed, my phone rang.

"I can't wait to see you tomorrow. I'm getting ready to get on the plane now. See you soon. Love you," Devon wrote.

"Love you too. I can't wait to see you," I text back.

Then I laid down and eventually passed out after a few minutes.

When I woke up, I got the shock of my life. My hair as predicted did not stay nice. It was an utter mess. It was worse than if I had never got my hair done at all. I glanced at my watch—it was eight a.m.

"Plenty of time," I said and got ready to head out. When I arrived at the salon, Deb was shaking her head.

"I told you it might get messed up," Deb said with a smile.

"Yeah I know, I know. Can you fix it?"

"Of course, take a seat," Deb said as she began to work on my hair. After only ten minutes, it looked as good as it had yesterday.

"So are you nervous?" Deb asked.

"No, just excited," I said.

"That's good," Deb said as she made the last adjustment.

"There—what do you think?" Deb asked as she handed me the mirror.

"My hair looks great. Thank you. I don't know what I would have done without you," I said. Deb smiled.

"Don't worry. I just wanted you to be confident with your hair. If you need anything else, please feel free to come by. It was nice helping you and your friend."

"Well thank you," I said as I glanced at my watch.

"Well Deb, I'm taking off. I will see you next time. Sorry I can't stay and chat. I still have a lot to do."

"Don't worry, I understand. Good luck."

"Thanks, I'm going to need it," I said and walked out the door.

It was still early in the morning, and Devon wasn't supposed to be back till two this afternoon so I really didn't know what I was going to do with my time. I took out my phone and stared at a picture I had of Devon and me. It was my favorite picture—it was from one of our first dates. It always made me feel better. I stared at the picture for a minute, and then the anticipation and excitement built up in me.

It really didn't matter if I was away from Devon for an hour, a day, a week, or a year. The feeling was always the same. Devon was my other half—he really did complete me. When he was away, I felt like half of my heart was gone. I got excited when I think about seeing him. It took away my sadness, and today I would see him. I went back to the dorm and sent a text to Erica.

"Erica, do you want to hang out with me till Devon gets here. We could get coffee or something."

"Yep, on my way out now. I will meet you at the college café."

When I read that, I ran out the door and headed for the coffee shop. I was going to beat Erica for a change. I got to the college café, and Erica wasn't there yet.

"Yes," I said excitedly, "I had beat Erica."

Right after I walked in though, Erica walked in as well.

"Well, I guess I only beat you by a second," I said.

Erica laughed.

"Yeah you beat me, ha ha ha," Erica said.

We both got our usual drinks and then grabbed a seat.

"So guess who called me?" Erica asked with a smile.

I looked astonished.

"No, did he—the guy from the restaurant?" I said.

"Yes, yes, he did," Erica said still smiling.

"Really, and did you guys hit it off?"

"Yes, he is great to talk to—a real listener–at least he seems that way. We talked for about fifteen minutes. Mike asked me out, and I said yes."

"Wow, that is **great**! When are you guys going on your first date?"

"Well, that is the thing. It's tonight, and I'm a little nervous."

"Oh, don't be nervous. Remember, you're just getting to know him. Don't worry about anything else, okay? The rest will fall into place if it's meant to be," I said reassuring her.

"Okay, I will try to keep that in mind. I just hope that it goes well."

"Just have fun, and let me know how it goes."

"I will fill you in on all of the details tomorrow. So when does Devon come in again?"

"Well, he said around two, and it seems like so far away, but I am so excited. It is only ten, and I just can't wait."

"Don't worry, Devon will be here soon," Erica said.

We continued to talk for the next few hours. Before we knew it, it was already one p.m. Then I got a text from Devon.

"I'm here, where are you my love?"

"We are at the coffee shop." I wrote and soon I received the next text.

"See you in a min," Devon said.

"He's on his way," I told Erica.

My heart was pounding hard and fast. I kept on staring out the window looking for Devon. Erica did the same.

"Do you see him?" I asked Erica.

"No, do you?" Erica asked.

"No, I don't. Oh, where is he?" I asked aloud. Just then a noise came from behind me.

"Madam, these are for you," the voice said. I could smell the scent of sweetness as flowers were placed on the table. I turned fully around, and my heart dropped.

"Devon!" I exclaimed.

I jumped up and gave him a hug. I was in tears. I was so happy to see him. Devon looked happy, but he wasn't crying like me.

"I missed you," Devon said as we hugged. Then Devon gave me a deep, passionate kiss. It felt so good. I closed my eyes. It was just like I had imagined. My heart was whole again in that moment. I forgot everything around me. I could have stayed in that moment forever. When our lips finally weren't pressed against each other, my lips were quivering. My eyes locked onto his.

"I love you," I said.

Devon peered into my soul and said, "I love you too."

My heart beat with all of the joy that was in my soul. We were complete in that single moment, and nothing could be more wonderful. Just then Devon turned toward Erica.

"Erica, it's nice to see you," Devon said.

"Hi Devon, welcome back."

Erica had remained quiet in our moment of passion. She had given us our moment, and I was grateful for that.

"Nice flowers," Erica said.

"Yes, I love them, thank you so much," I said to Devon.

"You're welcome my love. You should have seen all of the jealous looks I was getting when I walked around with them. But I knew that my love had to have flowers," Devon said.

"Well thank you, they are beautiful," I said.

I continued to wrap my arm around Devon's waist. Devon looked at Erica and me.

"Well, do you ladies want to get something to eat? I'm starving. I've only ate Greek food the last couple of days," Devon said.

"Yeah of course, what would you like to eat my love?" I asked.

"Oh I think at this point anything American. Maybe a nice hamburger or pizza or something."

"Okay, well let's go. I'm starving," Erica said and started heading out the door. I grabbed the flowers and smelled them again with my eyes closed. Devon leaned into me.

"I'm glad that you like them," Devon said and smiled.

I smiled too and said, "I love them. They are the second best present I've received today."

"Oh yeah, what's the first?" Devon asked smiling.

"You," I said and smiled.

Devon laughed when I said that.

"So burgers are cool right?" Devon asked.

"Yep, whatever you want dear," I said.

"Yep, sounds good," Erica said.

We all hopped into the car and drove off.

Erica drove. She seemed to know the exact place to go. We got to a hamburger place that had all sorts of gourmet burgers. We all selected our favorite burgers and took a seat. As soon as the food came, Devon had the biggest smile on his face.

"Oh I think I'm going to enjoy this," Devon said as the burger came near his mouth. We all ate without saying much after that. It was nice to see Devon happy. In fact, it was nice just to see Devon, period. I smiled as I watched him.

"So how is your family? Did everything go well while you were there with all of the arrangements and everything?" I asked.

Devon wiped off his mouth and then began to speak.

"Well, it was hard. My grandpa had died before I got there. So when I got there, the whole family was sad. Everyone was crying. It was hard to see my grandpa in the coffin. But it was good to see relatives that I hadn't seen in a while. It was good just to talk about him. It was important to remember all of the good things. I actually got to talk to the whole family," Devon said and then paused.

"Oh it must have been hard. I haven't been to any funerals before, but I know that they can be very emotional," Erica said.

"Yeah it was. It is hard to describe. When I stood in front of my family and tried to talk, I couldn't. Words could not express how I felt. Even now, it's hard to talk about it, but I am glad that I went. I needed the closure. I am glad that it is behind me now. I did miss you so much my love. I thought about you all the time when I was away," Devon said.

I smiled.

"I missed you too," I said.

I took a deep breath. There was a pause in talking. It was like I was trying to figure out what to do next. My heart began to beat fast as I thought about it. I knew that now was the time to tell Erica and Devon—and that made it hard for me to breathe. I looked at Erica and Devon.

Chapter 35

Trust

Devon and Erica looked surprised as I announced, "Guys, I have to change the subject. I have something important that I have to show both of you."

"What is it?" Erica asked.

"Yeah, what is it?" Devon asked. There was a pause.

"I have a secret to show both of you. It is something that I feel I can trust the both of you with. I can't show you here though. We have to go somewhere private," I said.

Devon looked at me—locking his eyes on mine.

"Is it that thing that we discovered about your abilities?" Devon asked.

"Yeah, it's something like that, but it is something completely new."

"Okay no problem. Let me just pay for this meal, and then we can head out," Devon said as he got up and went up to the front register.

Erica looked at me surprised.

"What is this all about?"

"Well, it's just a secret I have been hiding from you two for a little while, but it is time for me to tell you both. I was going to show you earlier, but it wasn't time. I wanted to wait till both of you were here because I only want to show this once."

"Show what?" Erica asked confused.

"You will see Erica—you just have to trust me," I said, turning my head so that Erica wouldn't talk anymore about it. My body sign was loud and clear. Erica didn't ask anymore. I felt a sort of new excitement and nervousness at the same time. I wanted to tell Erica for so long about my secret, but it was just too hard.

"I just hope that this goes well so that Erica can understand what I have been going through," I thought. I wasn't even sure where I was going to reveal the secret—but I knew the longer I waited, the harder it would get. Devon came back.

"Okay, are you ladies ready to go?" Devon asked.

Erica jumped up in an excited manner.

"Yes, let's go," Erica said.

"Yep, I'm ready," I said, and with that, we all got into the car.

"Okay, so where did you want to go?" Devon asked me.

"Well, all I need is some water," I said.

Devon thought for a moment.

"Okay, I know a place," Devon said.

Devon began to drive while Erica sat in the back bewildered. She remained quiet and just watched as Devon drove into the unknown. We soon arrived at our destination.

"Here we are!" Devon said and pointed to a building.

"What is this?" I asked.

Devon smiled.

"My dear, that is your water you requested. Don't worry, I know the owners. Nobody is going to be here," Devon said. I stared at the building. It was an indoor pool, as far as I could tell, and it was closed.

"But how are we going to get in?" I asked.

"You just leave that up to me. You and Erica have to wait here for a moment," Devon said as he got out of the car and walked toward the building. Devon stood there staring at the building for a moment, and then he reached down and picked up something on the ground.

Soon Devon came back and knocked on the window of the car.

"Okay, we're in. I found the hideaway key. Come on."

Devon gestured for us to get out of the car. We all started walking toward the building. Devon pulled out the key he had found.

"I used to be a lifeguard here so I know the owners. This is the spare key that I have had to use sometimes to get in. No one will bother us here," Devon said as he opened the door and let us in.

"I'm relieved to hear that," I said.

We all walked through the door. The pool was very nice. It was an Olympic pool. I had seen a few Olympic pools in my lifetime, but none was as nice as this one.

"I hope that you don't need a suit," Devon said with a smile.

"No, hopefully not," I said.

We all walked toward the water.

"Okay, pay attention."

As Erica and Devon both watched, I threw my shoes off of my feet and closed my eyes. I tried to do what Aphrodite had taught me. I took a deep breath.

"What are you going to do?" Devon asked.

"You'll see," I said with my eyes closed.

I began to walk toward the water.

When I got to the edge, Devon yelled. "What are you doing?"

I guess the lifeguard in him kicked in. I ignored Devon and continued to walk. I concentrated so hard. I tried to remember what Aphrodite had said: make the world as it has to be, not as it is. Walking on the water felt as real in this world as it had felt in the world Aphrodite and I had trained in. I walked and walked and walked. Devon and Erica didn't say anything. They both just stood there in amazement. I walked all the way across the pool. It felt like I was walking on concrete the whole time. Then I stepped out of the pool on the other side. Devon and Erica both ran over to me.

"How is this possible, my dear? How did you walk on the water?"

I closed my eyes and took a deep breath.

"Well, now that I have your attention, let's sit and I will tell you everything," I said. We all sat on the bleachers and then I began to talk.

"I am able to do this because I have powers," I said.

"What sort of powers?" Devon asked.

"How long have you been able to do this?" Erica asked.

"Well actually, walking on the water—that actually just started. But it all falls back to me being able to talk with dolphins—and this is the only power I have so far," I said.

"What?" Devon said confused.

"What do you mean you can talk to dolphins? That's not possible," Erica said. Devon turned in my defense.

"No, that is true, she can talk to dolphins. I have been doing research with Aurora on it. Aurora knows their language, and now I guess she can walk on water too," Devon said shaking his head in disbelief.

"But how?" Erica asked.

"Well it all began that day I fell in the water and heard dolphins' voices. You remember, Erica? It was the first day of our class. Then this last time when Devon and I went out to do research, I tried to communicate with dolphins as a part of an experiment. Do you remember that Devon?"

"Yes of course, I do—that dolphin just disappeared right in front of both of us. But what does that have to do with this?" Devon asked.

"Everything Devon—it has everything to do with this. I have been trying to tell both of you all of this time that things have changed for me. Something happened that day, Devon. I disappeared too, but you didn't see it because it happened so fast. I wanted to tell both of you, but I thought you guys would think I was crazy. I even thought I was going crazy myself. In fact, this whole thing has been unbelievable, and if it weren't true, and if it weren't happening to me, then I wouldn't believe any of it. But it is all completely and utterly true. I need your help and support," I said.

"Well you have it. I definitely believe you. It's kind of hard to argue with walking on water," Devon said.

"Yes that goes for me too. Even though I don't understand it completely, you have my support," Erica said.

"Thank you, but there is something else that happened on that day I tried to contact the dolphins. I went somewhere with that dolphin. I went to a dolphin city called Antilla—a city where dolphins live together. They talked to me."

Devon and Erica looked like they were in extreme shock. They were both speechless as I paused.

"Well, what did they say to you when you went?" Devon asked.

I chuckled.

"They actually had a lot to say. The dolphins told me that all of this was my destiny, and that I was chosen to unite their world and ours. It was hard to understand at first, but I am beginning to understand it better now."

"So let me get this straight, the dolphins have a society, and they want you to tell mankind about them. Then we will have some sort of united society?" Erica asked.

"Yes, that's the gist of it," I said.

"But why you and why now?" Devon asked.

"I don't know, but there is more to the story. There was another woman who came before me. She was able to do the things I can do—and her name was Aphrodite."

"Aphrodite, the love goddess?" Erica asked.

"Yes, the love goddess. She learned from the dolphins and gave the knowledge to mankind. It's one of the main reasons the Greeks were so successful. Now it is my job to continue the legacy. I have to help both societies. It is my job to reveal the truth to humankind—the truth that we are not alone in the universe. There's been an alternate society among us the whole time," I said.

"Wait, so when you say you can talk to the dolphins, you mean you can really talk with them? Like you are talking to Devon and me?"

"Well, that is one way of looking at it. It is different, and it is a lot to describe," I said.

"I understand you completely, my dear. My next question though, is where do we go from here? What do you need us to help you with?"

Devon asked as though the situation was no longer a shock and was just a new reality for him. Devon seemed so sure of himself.

"Well, I don't know where we go from here. I hadn't thought past the moment of telling you guys. I had to tell you two all of this so you could support me. I had to find some way to have you believe me. You both do believe me, right?" I asked just to make sure again.

"Yes, yes, we both believe you, my love," Devon said.

"Yep, I believe you. This is the coolest thing I've ever heard of. Wherever we go from here, I'll be there for you," Erica said.

"I'm so glad to hear it, but I don't know where we go from here. I guess we will have to wait and see what happens. Hopefully, time will tell us what the next step is."

Then we all got up from the bleachers. Erica looked at her watch.

"Oh dear," Erica said.

"What is it?" Devon asked.

I looked at my watch.

"Oh you have your date," I said.

"Yes but I...," Erica began to say.

"No, you need to go on your date. We all need to continue with our lives as they were before we found out all of this new information, okay?"

Devon turned to my side.

"Yes, you're right. We all must continue our lives as they are. I can drop you off so you can make it to your date on time," Devon said.

"Oh thank you," Erica said relieved.

We all then exited the pool.

"Thank you for bringing us here," I said to Devon.

"Thank you for trusting us. You know you can always tell us anything no matter what it is. We won't tell anyone," Devon said.

"Yes I know, but I almost didn't believe it myself," I said with a smile.

It was so nice to finally get all of the weight off of my shoulders. Now I had support, I felt like I could do anything. We all got to the car and got in.

"I'm going to drop you off at the college, okay?" Devon said to Erica.

"Sounds good," Erica said.

Then Devon turned toward me.

"And you and I have a date that we need to go to," Devon said with a smile. I began to refocus as I remembered how happy I was that Devon was home.

Chapter 36

It's a Nice Evening for a Picnic

I blurted out to Devon, "I need to change."

"No, I think you are perfect the way you are," Devon said.

Maybe it was that I didn't have a secret anymore, or maybe it was something else, but when Devon said that, it made me feel beautiful all over. I smiled as we all headed back to the college. When we arrived, Devon stopped the car and let Erica out.

"Have fun on your date," I said.

"Thank you, I will try," Erica said right before she ran off toward her room.

"Now where are we going?" I asked.

"Well, that is still a surprise, but I think you're going to like it."

"Okay, but it better be good," I said jokingly.

"Well, it won't be me walking on water or anything, but I will try," Devon said jokingly.

"Oh stop it, you," I said back.

It was nice that we were able to joke about it. It made everything seem more normal somehow. Devon continued to drive until we arrived somewhere I had never been before.

"Where are we?" I asked.

"This is a place I've never brought you to before. I thought we could take a walk," Devon said as we got out of the car.

It was a nice quiet place. There were trees everywhere. It was absolutely beautiful. Devon grabbed my hand. As we walked, there was a silence. It was the kind of silence that only two people who are in love can share. When you're in love, you don't always have to talk—sometimes breathing with each other is enough. We continued to walk for an hour holding hands. I hadn't noticed it at first, but Devon had a bag with him.

"Here's the spot," Devon said as he looked at an open spot. As I looked around, I had the absolute feeling that we were alone. Devon opened the bag and pulled out a blanket and a cooler.

"I brought dinner," Devon said.

He put the blanket on the ground. We sat together, and Devon passed a sandwich to me.

"I got you your favorite, a turkey sandwich," Devon said.

"When did you have time to do this?" I asked.

"I have my ways," Devon said with a smile.

We sat together trying to forget everything. The sun began to set while the wind gave a slight blow. It felt good as the air moved over my body ever so slightly. Right where we were sitting was the perfect spot to watch the sun set over the horizon like a golden crisp that touched everything. It made everything look elegant.

"I wanted to bring you here to watch this It's beautiful, isn't it?" Devon asked.

"Yes, it's so beautiful. I'm so happy that you brought me here. I love picnics, and I've never been on a sunset picnic before."

"This is my first one too," Devon said and leaned in toward my cheek.

"I wanted to show you this sunset in this place because of the way the sun lights up everything and makes the whole world glisten with a resonating beauty. That is how I feel about you. You light up everything in my life. You touch every part of my existence, and you are my everything. I want you to know that I will always love you," Devon said.

I was speechless. I never thought I could hear something so wonderful be said about me. But then I had a concern.

"But Devon, what about all of this stuff happening—all the changes? It's what worries me. With everything going on, what does it mean for us? It's going to be hard for us to have a normal life," I said.

Devon brought his face close to mine and stared straight into my eyes.

"I don't want a normal, dull life. I like the way things are with us. I wouldn't change a thing about it, and I don't want you to want any changes. What we have is perfect, and I wouldn't have it any other way," Devon said.

Then he kissed me.

"Devon, I love you."

"I love you too, Aurora."

We held each other until the sunset. When the sun set, Devon turned to me.

"I will always be here for you," Devon said.

I closed my eyes.

"Thank you Devon," I said in a whisper.

Then we got up. Devon grabbed the blanket and the bag. We began to walk back holding hands the whole way.

Chapter 37

An Emergency Can Change Everything

It had been a couple of days since Devon had come home. Even after the big secret was revealed to Erica and Devon, things were like they had always been. Devon made it a point every day to come and see me after school at the library where he had been doing his research for his thesis.

"Just one kiss," Devon would whisper when he saw me as he lifted his eyes from his computer. I would always lean in and say "I love you" and give him a kiss. Then Devon would go back to work. I would usually sit close to Devon and do my school work. We were inseparable just like we had always been. One day when I walked into the library, I followed the usual routine. I spotted Devon enthralled in his work. I crept up to him. But I didn't make it past three steps before Devon spotted me. We locked eyes as I walked toward him. Then Devon said again, "just one kiss." I smiled and jokingly kissed him on the forehead.

"Ha ha," Devon whispered back, and then I leaned in for the real kiss. It always seemed like a release from everything every time we kissed. I loved to kiss Devon.

"Okay, I'll be over here studying," I whispered to Devon.

"Hey, let's go out for dinner tonight," Devon whispered with a smile.

"Okay, sounds good."

I sat down in a chair right across from Devon's table. I didn't want to distract him too much. I opened my books and went to work. Just as I was about to begin to study, I got a text message. I glanced at it.

"Something has come up, and I need you here right now. This can't wait," my Aunt Carrie said.

I got up abruptly and walked out of the library to call my Aunt Carrie to find out what all of this was about. Devon saw me leave and followed me. When I arrived outside, I called my Aunt Carrie, but there was no answer.

"Come on," I said in a frustrated voice.

Devon came up to me.

"What is it? What happened? I saw you back there, and you looked worried," Devon asked.

"I am worried. My aunt just sent me a text saying some emergency came up but didn't say what it was," I said while trying to call my Aunt Carrie again.

"Do you want me to take you over to your aunt? I have the car," Devon asked.

"Yes, would you? I am really worried. Something must be terribly wrong."

"Yes, of course," Devon said.

We both ran inside and grabbed our stuff. We then headed back out and jumped into the car. I tried to call again but still there was no answer.

"She's not answering her phone," I said to Devon still frustrated.

My heart was pounding fast.

"Maybe you should try texting her again," Devon said.

"I will try," I said as I texted again.

"Is everything okay?"

I got a quick response text back.

"No, I need you here right now," the text message said. I quickly texted back.

"On my way!"

On the way to my aunt's house, there was a silence as Devon drove. Devon wasn't driving faster than the speed limit, but at times it seemed like it.

"Slow down," I reminded him.

"Sorry," Devon said as he continued to drive.

"I just want everything to be okay with your family," Devon said.

This seemed to be having an incredible effect on Devon.

"I just want everything to be okay too," I said.

We soon arrived at my aunt's house. Even from a distance, I could see a different car in the driveway. I didn't see my aunt's nor my uncle's car. I looked again.

I know this car somehow, I know it.

It was hard to figure out whose car it was with all of the other scenarios racing through my head from the strange text message from my aunt. Then it hit me like a rock to the head.

Andrew was here, but why?

"I wonder whose limo that is," Devon asked.

"I think that it's Andrew's," I said.

"Who is Andrew?"

"He is my friend from back home. He is frequently in San Diego. His family and my family are old-time friends. I'm wondering what all of this is about," I said suspiciously.

"Well, there is only one way to find out," Devon said.

We both got out of the car. I was getting more nervous with each step as we approached the stairs. There was so much running through my head, and it appeared to be the same for Devon too. Whenever some sort of emergency happened, and you only have a little information, every scenario could run through your head. It was always like that for me. I guess it was like that for Devon too.

We got to the door, and Devon rang the doorbell. No less than two tries later, the door swung open. It was Andrew. Walking behind him down the hallway was my uncle.

"Come in, Aurora and Devon," my Uncle Jason said.

As we both walked in, I turned toward my uncle.

"Uncle Jason, what is the matter?" I asked.

"Well dear, umm," Uncle Jason began to say and then stopped.

"Come into this room. I need all of us to sit down for this," Uncle Jason said.

We ran into the living room. I took a seat as fast as I could. Soon my uncle and everyone else took a seat too. The anticipation was killing me.

"Okay Uncle Jason, we are sitting now, what's up?"

Uncle Jason began to talk.

"Well my dear, I'm having a hard time telling you this, but your brother George was in a horrible accident. It's really bad. He might not make it much longer," Uncle Jason said.

The news was horrifying. I couldn't believe what I was hearing.

"What do you mean he might not make it much longer?" I asked insistently.

"Just that we don't know how much time he has left. He was hit really hard, and nobody knows by what. George was out in the middle of nowhere, and now he's in critical condition. Your friend Andrew has offered to fly you back on his private jet," Uncle Jason said.

"Is this true?" I asked.

"Yes it is true, every word of it. I received a message from my dad asking me to try to get you home as soon as I could. I didn't get many more details than that about your brother George. So I came to see your aunt and uncle because I didn't know where to find you these days, and I remembered where they lived. I figured they were my best bet at finding you," Andrew said.

I took a pause to let it all sink in for a moment. I fought crying or acting hysterical. This was the worst news I had ever heard. I felt like my heart had been ripped out. I knew that the only course of action was to go home as fast as I could.

"Okay, well I guess I'm going with you then," I said as I turned to Andrew.

Devon turned toward me.

"I will take care of all of your classes. I can persuade your teachers to let you make up the work," Devon said to me.

Devon took a sharp turn toward Andrew.

"You will take care of my Aurora, won't you?" Devon asked staring straight at Andrew. It seemed like Devon didn't like Andrew very much.

Andrew put out his hand to shake Devon's, and the two shook hands.

"Don't worry. I will take good care of Aurora. We are old friends, and you have nothing to worry about."

Then Andrew turned toward me.

"Aurora, we really must get going. I want to get to Alaska as soon as possible," Andrew said.

"Yes of course," I said as I ran over to Devon and gave him a hug.

"I love you," I said to Devon.

"I love you too. Take care of yourself and call me when you get there or I will be worried sick about you. Wish your brother well for me. I will be praying for him," Devon said.

"I will," I said.

We quickly walked out the door and into Andrew's limo. Then I turned around. It suddenly hit me that I hadn't seen Aunt Carrie.

"Where is Aunt Carrie?" I asked Uncle Jason.

"She is getting ready with everything. She has to clear a few things at her work. She said she would meet you in Alaska," Uncle Jason said.

"Okay," I said as I waved good-bye to Devon.

Devon ran over and gave me a final kiss.

"Remember I love you," Devon said.

"I love you too, always and forever," I said.

The car drove off. I was left with nothing but the feeling of utter sadness, and at the same time, a resounding feeling of utter worry. Originally, I didn't know what to worry about. Now that I knew, I feared the worst. I cared so much about my brother George. On the way to the airport, I just sat there in silence and worry. The only real thought that ran through my head was that I needed to get to Alaska.

Chapter 38

In a Rush

We arrived right in front of the jet so all we had to do was jump out of the car and go onto the jet. There was no checkpoint with security or anything.

"Where is security?" I asked.

"Oh, I bypass that. In these emergency situations, I don't bother with the trivial things," Andrew said.

"Oh thank you, I really do appreciate this. You don't know what it means to me. My brother means everything to me," I said.

"Yes, I do know what it means to you. Remember, your brother George is my friend too," Andrew said.

It made me feel better to know that I had a friend who would be there for me like Andrew. He really seemed a lot different from the last time I had seen him. Andrew had connections. Every person we passed seemed to know who Andrew was.

"I guess you're pretty important around here," I said.

"I try," Andrew said with a smile.

We got on the jet. As we walked, I saw the most amazing cabin layout. This jet was fully loaded and was one of the most amazing things I had ever seen. But even as I sat there and appreciated being surrounded by luxury, I couldn't help but worry about George.

"I'm so worried about George," I said to Andrew as I broke into tears. Andrew gave a smile and looked me in the eyes.

"It's going to be alright Aurora. We are going to get there fast and see your brother in time. This jet is crazy fast. Do you like it? I just got it. It is the fastest jet available on the market today," Andrew said.

"Yeah, it's really nice. I am glad that it goes fast," I said trying to appear impressed, but it wasn't enough of a distraction for me not to worry.

"Don't worry, it will be okay. I need to go to the front and make the final arrangements," Andrew said. Then Andrew glanced over at a couple of very comfortable looking chairs.

"Why don't you take a seat over there? I will send someone to get you a drink or something," Andrew said as he pointed to the chairs.

"Okay," I said as I walked over to the chairs.

"I'll just take a seat then and try to relax," I said as I sat down and laid my head back.

Andrew walked toward the front of the plane. No less than three minutes later, one of the crew members came up to me.

"Miss, Andrew asked me to come and see if there was anything I could get you. We have an assortment of beverages—anything from wine to juice to water," the flight attendant said.

I sat up.

"Well, do you have a water maybe and some pretzels?" I asked with a smile.

"Yes of course," the crew member said.

She walked over to a bar behind me and then came back.

"Here are your pretzels and your water, Miss...," the crew member said.

"Oh, it's Aurora."

"Yes of course, Miss Aurora. Is there anything else that you need?" The crew member placed the pretzels and water on a table next to my chair.

"Is there anything else that I can get you, Miss Aurora?" the crew member asked again.

"No, that will be all, thank you," I said.

The crew member walked off. I was left to lay my head back. I tried not to worry as much. Andrew returned shortly after that.

"Well, we will be leaving soon. I talked with the pilots, and they think we will be there in four to five hours if the weather stays clear," Andrew said.

"Wow, that is fast," I said surprised.

"I told you this jet was fast. It's top of the line. I may not be good at a lot of things, but I'm good at buying jets," Andrew said with a certain look of satisfaction on his face.

"I wanted to thank you again. If you hadn't come and offered me a ride back home when you did, I don't know if I would be there even half this fast. So thank you so much," I said.

"Yes of course, remember, you and I go way back. We are old friends. George is an old friend, too. I would do anything for my friends," Andrew said with a serious tone.

"Thank you, you are a good friend," I said somewhat relaxed.

"Yes, you should relax and not worry about anything for now. We are all going to be okay," Andrew said.

I didn't argue with what he had said. I was tired from all the worrying. I couldn't do anything more than I had already done. I laid back my head and tried to take a nap. I quickly dozed off.

Chapter 39

Other Intentions

A noise woke me up. Without opening my eyes, I listened trying to maintain a level of relaxation.

"Yes sir, we are on track to Japan as we speak. The weather is remaining clear, and we will arrive on time," a figure said.

I couldn't see the figure because my eyes were still closed.

"Very good, continue on and remember, no announcements. I don't want to wake anyone up," Andrew said trying to keep his voice down.

"Yes sir, of course," the figure said.

The figure walked away quickly toward the front of the jet. I opened my eyes and an instant rush of anger went over my whole body.

"Where are we going?" I said confronting Andrew head on.

He undoubtedly heard from the tone of my voice that I was angry.

"Oh, you're awake? Did you have a good nap?" Andrew asked in a joyful tone.

"Where are we going? What about George? Why would we go to Japan?" I asked still mad.

"Okay, you caught me," Andrew said.

Andrew now had a sneaky smile—a smile I hadn't seen before from him. I sat up completely in my chair.

"You caught me, so I have to confess now. It was something I was going to do at the end of the flight, but it's spoiled now. First off, before I begin, I know that you are going to be mad at me. You may think all of this is crazy, but it was the only way, and for that I am truly sorry," Andrew said in a very apologetic voice.

I was still furious.

"What are you talking about?" I said almost screaming every word out of my mouth.

"Well, first off, a confession. There is nothing wrong with George, so you don't have to worry about him. That was a rouse, I'm afraid. The second thing is that I love you Aurora, and I always have," Andrew said.

I never thought so much anger could be contained within one person. But for a split second, my blood boiled from the anger that I felt.

"Where are we going? What do you mean that there is nothing wrong with George? Was this all a big lie?" I screamed.

Andrew grabbed his drink and drank the rest of whatever he was drinking.

"Well, yes, it was a big lie. I have no idea how your brother is, but I am sure he is fine. But I had to do something Aurora. I had to get you on this jet. I knew you would do anything for your brother—even fly to Alaska at the drop of a hat if you thought he was in trouble. I had to give us one last chance. Sometimes in life everything comes down to doing one crazy thing that sets up the rest of your life. I had to do something. I had to tell you how I felt, but I knew that you wouldn't listen to me unless I showed you the extra effort," Andrew said.

"This isn't happening," I said.

But it was. I couldn't go anywhere because I was on a jet. Whatever Andrew's plan was, it was working. I was trapped in a cage that was going hundreds of miles per hour.

"Are you going to hurt me?" I asked scared.

"No Aurora. Oh God, please don't think that. I would never hurt you. I know that I probably have no chance with you at all right now. I know that you're in love and that I can't separate you and Devon. I missed my chance to be with you so many times before, but I couldn't live my life without telling you how I felt. I'm sorry to have scared you, but I don't see any other way. I hope you believe me when I say that you mean more to me than almost anything else in this world.

You are the reason why even after my dad started to be successful and tried to move me to a better school, I fought to stay in the same school.

I wanted to be with you. I didn't care about anything else even though I never let you know that I loved you all of these years. I have loved you and no one else," Andrew said.

The anger slowly left my body. I was not naturally an angry person. I started to reason with myself—I couldn't leave, I was on the plane, and there was nowhere to go. A more logical side of me suddenly took over. I could appreciate the fact that Andrew cared for me, but I had no idea why he had to lie about it.

"So why am I here?" I asked pretending to be interested.

"Well, Aurora, I put on this big show for three reasons. One was to tell you how I really felt. The second reason was to see if there was even the smallest chance that you might choose me over Devon. There isn't, is there?" Andrew asked as he paused and leaned in.

I gave him another pissed off look.

"Okay, I'll take that as a no. The third reason was to offer you a job," Andrew said.

"A job!?"

"Yes that's what I said, a job."

I looked perplexed and amazed. How is it even remotely possible that Andrew could be offering me a job after lying to me and having me fly halfway across the world by basically kidnapping me? Was he serious? Did he really think I would even consider it? I sat there and stared at Andrew.

I wanted to scream at him and tell him that I never want to see him again. But I couldn't bring myself to do it. I couldn't break his heart even though he had done all of this stuff to me. Andrew was right—I had known him a long time, and I couldn't get over that fact. I closed my eyes and shook my head. Then I opened my eyes and smiled at Andrew. I said the first words that came to me.

"So what is this job?" I asked with a smile, trying to pretend that I was enthusiastic.

Andrew got a big grin on his face like he had achieved some personal goal.

"Well, it is a job for you and for Devon. I have been following your career at college a little while. Your mom told me that you and Devon both wanted to work with the ocean. She also said that you're doing research on how to make the oceans better. So that's why I know you will love this job I am offering you. You see, it just so happens that my dad's company spearheads the top organization involved in the study and research concerning all oceanographic areas."

"Your dad's company?" I asked.

"Yes, my dad's company has started a research foundation that has a sole mission of researching the oceans and finding better ways to protect them. I want to give you and Devon top jobs. That is why we are going to Japan," Andrew said.

My anger switched completely to curiosity..

"Why Japan?" I asked.

"Japan is where my dad's company set up the research facility. If you choose not to work there, I will understand, of course, but I wanted you to see it. I knew that you would never agree to go with me without a little push. I've been meaning to tell you for some time how I felt about you. I really couldn't live the rest of my life without telling you how I felt. I'm sorry I caused you so much trouble. That was never my intention, and I hope you will forgive me," Andrew said.

I took a deep hard look at Andrew. He didn't seem like a bad guy. Andrew seemed like the Andrew I had always known—an overall good guy—but I could not condone what he had done. Devon was probably worried sick. I slowly cleared my throat to talk, but Andrew talked before I had a chance.

"Aurora, I know all of this is hard, but for now, I hope you will forgive me for bringing you here and for everything else. I'm not asking you to forgive me for good—at least forgive me long enough to come and look at the facility, and then you can decide whether you want to work for me and my father—or not. I will understand if you never want to talk to me again."

I smiled.

"Only on one condition," I said.

"Yes of course, anything you want."

"I have to call Devon and tell him I'm okay when we land."

"Yes of course, as soon as we land, you can call him. I have no problem with that," Andrew said.

Just as Andrew finished speaking, the pilot came up to Andrew.

"Sir, we are nearly forty-five minutes away from Japan," the pilot said.

"You have done very well in making this run to Japan in excellent time. Keep up the good work," Andrew told the pilot.

"Thank you sir," the pilot said and walked away. Andrew then turned to me.

"So we are agreed then? You will call Devon upon our landing, and then I will take you to the research institute. Then shortly after that, I will take you back to San Diego," Andrew said and raised his glass.

"To our adventure," Andrew said as he stared at me.

"And straight back?" I said verifying.

I just wanted to hear it one more time.

"Yes, straight back," Andrew said as he continued to raise his glass.

I raised up mine.

"To our adventure," I said and our glasses clicked.

Chapter 40

Even the Grandest of Ideas Can Have a Dark Side

We departed the jet shortly after it landed. A couple of men in suits came up to Andrew as we walked down the steps of the jet.

"Sir, your car is this way," a man in a suit said.

"Very good. Aurora, will you come with me this way? I have arranged for a car to drive us to the research facility," Andrew said.

We walked toward the car and got in. Then Andrew handed me a cell phone.

"Please call Devon. We don't want him worrying," Andrew said.

"Oh, thank you," I said and grabbed the phone.

"There is no country code. I have it set to America so just call the area code, phone number, and that's all," Andrew said.

"Okay," I said as I began to dial.

I pressed call, and the phone began to ring. It only rang twice and went to Devon's voice mail. I tried to call again—and still the same thing, no answer. I just decided to leave a message. I had to let Devon know that I was alright. I began to speak low into the phone so Andrew could not hear what I was saying.

"Devon, I'm okay. I will explain everything later to you, but I wanted you to know that everything is okay. It was a misunderstanding. I will be back in San Diego later this evening. I love you so much, and I will talk to you later. Oh and if you get this message, call me back so I know that you got it." I ended the call.

"Thank you," I said as I handed the phone back to Andrew.

"No problem," Andrew said as we continued on. After thirty minutes, we arrived at the research institute. Andrew looked out the window.

"You see that Aurora?" Andrew asked as he pointed out toward a large structure. I looked and saw a facility that was near the water. It was white and very modern-looking. It had a pier with boats.

"That is the research institute," Andrew said.

"Wow, that is nice," I said as I stared at it. The institute was very large and impressive.

"Oh yeah, if you think that is good, wait till you see the inside," Andrew said. Just then Andrew's phone rang. My heart skipped a beat.

I hope it's Devon calling Andrew's phone back.

Andrew answered and talked with a voice that was too low for me to hear. After two minutes of talking, Andrew got off the phone.

"Well Aurora, I have more good news," Andrew said.

"What's that?"

"My dad is waiting for us at the research institute," Andrew said.

"Waiting for us?" I asked surprised.

"Yes, waiting for us. I had mentioned that I was bringing you here today, and my dad must want to show off or something. Anyways, he wants to see you when we arrive at the institute. I hope that's okay."

"Yes of course, that is fine. I would love to see your dad."

Just as I finished my statement, we pulled up to the research institute. When I took my first step out of the car, I saw a grand view of the modern facility. Everything about the building looked new and wonderful. As we walked toward the front door, I saw the sign on the top of the building. "Oceanographic Research and Preservation Institute. It's our job to save the oceans. If we don't, who else will?"

I read it aloud, and Andrew watched me.

"Nice right?" Andrew asked.

"Yes, it's very nice," I said as we began to walk through the door.

The inside of the building was so beautiful. I was so impressed that I almost lost my breath. There were massive amounts of incredible light shining through from the side glass, which was inlaid with stained glass ocean scenes. The sun shined through the stained glass, and the light hit the adjacent wall and projected each scene like a projector showing a movie.

The whole scene was alive and vivid like the ocean itself. The giant spiral staircase was a wonder. It circled around from the top floor down to the bottom floor like a giant elegant earring. It was breathtaking.

As I followed the staircase with my eyes to the top, I saw a figure that I thought I recognized from my past. Andrew recognized him immediately. Andrew waved, and the figure waved back and walked toward us. It was Andrew's dad. He was dressed in what looked like a fine black suit. Andrew walked up to him and shook his dad's hand.

"Ahh, I remember this girl. Little Aurora, how are you? How is your family? I haven't seen you or them in ages," Andrew's dad said as he walked toward me.

Andrew's dad put out his hand to shake mine. I put out my hand in return and gave him a handshake.

"They are good and back in Alaska."

"Good, good, it's a good place, very rugged. I miss it a lot. It's been so long since I've taken a vacation back there. I really should drop by and say 'hi' to everyone. So I guess Andrew finally dragged you all the way over here. Andrew has been talking about doing this for months. Where is your boyfriend? Andrew said you both would come and check things out."

Suddenly Andrew interrupted.

"Well dad, it's a long story, but he wasn't able to make it."

I rolled my eyes slightly as Andrew said that.

"Ahh, well at least we got you here, Aurora. I really hope you enjoy my institute. Please let me know if you both need anything. This place is my dream—and Aurora, I would love for you and your boyfriend to be a part of it," Andrew's dad said.

Then he turned to face Andrew.

"Hey, I have a swell idea. Why don't the three of us have lunch after you check things out? We have a great dining facility here that I have been meaning to eat at," Andrew's dad said.

"Well, I don't know, dad," Andrew began to say, but I quickly interrupted.

"We would love too," I said with enthusiasm.

"Excellent—lunch at let's say, three then?"

"Yes, three is fine," Andrew said.

Andrew's dad had a smile on his face.

"Well, I have to get going. I have a meeting to get to. I'm kind of a big deal around here," Andrew's dad said with a chuckle.

He walked up the stairs waving back at Andrew and me. We waved back. Andrew turned toward me.

"Well, shall we check things out?"

"After you," I said as I used my hand to gesture for Andrew to lead the way.

As we walked, Andrew began to spout out facts about the facility.

"Our facility is one of the forefronts in research on the interactions between mankind and the ocean. We are finding what we can do to conserve our oceans for future generations," Andrew began to say as we were walking. The institute was huge.

"We have every species at this facility that you could imagine. Each animal has its own research team—and then we have the grand masterpiece. It is what I wanted to show you most of all," Andrew said as we approached a double door.

"Are you ready?"

"Yes," I said as Andrew opened the door.

"This, Aurora, is a mini ocean," Andrew said.

It was the largest tank I had ever seen. It was the size of three football fields.

"Wow!" I said in absolute amazement.

It was hard to describe the sheer size of this tank. It seemed to go on forever.

"Anything that we can't do through computer simulation or observation in the ocean is found here. This is the largest tank in the world. It's crazy to maintain, but we are learning so much here about the oceans. We can put anything in this tank, and we observe and document. This is just one side of the facility—the other side is all about observing the actual ocean. We have five ships and two submarines. Each vessel has a team of scientists who go out to see what is happening in the oceans. But you see, there is a problem. That is why I need yours and Devon's help," Andrew said.

"My help? What could you need my help for? I haven't even finished college," I said a little intimidated by the whole scene.

"Well, that's the thing. We only have one facility so we are limited to only one region. I want to put a facility like this on each coastline, starting with one in California. This is the first modern effort to see what effects man is having on the ocean, and what we can do to change it. We are the first generation that has the knowledge to do something about what is happening in the oceans.

My dad and I want to start the major effort to save the oceans. We want future generations to enjoy the ocean like we do today. So Aurora, won't you help me? Won't you be a part of this effort to save the oceans?"

"Well, with everything that you have shown me, how could I say no? I can't of course speak for Devon, but I think I would love to work at a place like this. I mean, it has everything that you could want from a research facility," I said.

"Good, I'm so glad that you said that. I knew you would agree," Andrew said smiling.

Andrew had the biggest grin I had ever seen on him. We walked around the aquarium portion of the institute for hours. Then we approached another portion of the institute.

"And here is the research sector of the institute."

There were scientists in white lab coats everywhere. Andrew walked up to one of the scientists.

"Hi, I was just showing off the facility to my friend. Can you tell us some of the stuff you guys do here?" Andrew asked the technician.

"Oh yes, of course, I would love to. We do a fair amount of research here—anything on the interaction between species to the interaction of man. We cover communication and pretty much anything you can think of when it comes to ocean research. If there is a study of the ocean going on, chances are we are doing it," the technician said and smiled and then went back to work.

"See, was I right or was I right? We cover everything," Andrew said and then we entered a hallway.

Andrew looked at his watch.

"Well, it seems it's just about three. We should meet up with my dad."

"Sounds good," I said in agreement.

We began to walk down a different hallway. After about a minute of walking, I began to hear a faint cry. I stopped to listen to it better.

"Help," a faint voice said.

Then I heard a second voice yelling, "help."

Chapter 41

The Truth

As I cuffed my hands over my ears to get a better listen, I said to Andrew, "Do you hear that?"

"Hear what?" Andrew asked.

"Someone is calling for help," I said and began to walk forward, trying to hear the cries better.

As we walked, the yells for help got louder and louder. My heart began to beat fast. I was afraid for what those cries meant.

"I don't hear anything," Andrew said.

"I hear it, I swear, someone is crying for help!" I said to Andrew and continued to walk toward the cries.

Eventually we reached a double door. I put my ear up to the door and listened. The cries continued to get louder.

"I can hear cries on the other side of the door," I said.

"I still don't hear anything."

"Well, either I'm going crazy, or someone needs my help. Either way, I am going through these doors," I said and walked through the door.

I could feel my heart beating fast, and my legs began to shake. The cries were so loud. How could Andrew not hear them? When I went through the double door, I entered a long hallway. The cries continued over and over again.

There was a door at the end of the hallway. I turned around to see Andrew. He still acted like he couldn't hear the cries as he walked reluctantly behind me.

"Are you coming?" I asked Andrew.

"I guess, but I don't understand."

"That makes two of us. You really can't hear that?"

"No I can't, but if you can, I will follow so you don't get into any trouble," Andrew said.

I opened the door at the end of the hallway leading us to a staircase. The yells for help got louder and louder. It was as if someone was being tortured. The stairs led to a dark hallway, which had a small round window that lighted up the hallway a little. This was the scariest thing I had ever seen—but I had to do something to help. I was so scared. I looked at Andrew again. He had to hear the cries by now.

"Anything?"

"No, I'm sorry. I have never seen this part of the facility. I thought I knew all about this place," Andrew said fascinated by his surroundings.

But this was no time to be fascinated. I just shook my head.

"What is this place?" Andrew asked.

He now seemed as shocked as I was.

"I don't know, but what I do know is that someone in there needs our help," I said.

There were other voices on the other side of the door now. They made sounds—like mumbling.

"I hear voices now," Andrew said.

We walked up cautiously to the door. I took a look through the circular window. There were men with lab coats on. I cautiously opened the door. No one turned to look at us coming through the door. Then I heard the scream again.

"Help!"

I looked at where the sound came from—it was a dolphin. There was a bunch of surgical tools around. Then I saw another dolphin that was cut open. Its fins had been removed. I couldn't contain myself.

"What are you doing," I yelled.

I ran over to a lab technician with a knife in his hands about to cut into one of the other dolphins. I pushed the knife out of the technician's hand.

"What are you two doing down here?" one of the men with lab coats asked.

Andrew stood there and stared at the guy.

"Who are you? And what is this place? This institute is supposed to save the ocean. What are you doing? Does this look like you are saving the ocean? This is a massacre," Andrew said.

"No, this is research," the man said. Then he did a gesture toward a couple of other technicians. The other technicians came toward Andrew and me.

"You can't be here," the lead technician said.

"I can be wherever I want. I own this institute," Andrew said.

The technician took a look at Andrew.

"No you don't, your father does. Why don't you ask him about this research that we're doing. He knows about it. It's important for your company," the lead technician said.

"My father?" Andrew said shocked.

"Yes, your father—this is his project. Speaking of which, how did you find this place? It was top secret," the lead technician said.

I tried to communicate to the dolphin trying to ignore everything else, but there was just so much blood.

"Hi, I'm Aurora," I said to the dolphin.

The dolphin turned its head and looked at me.

"Aurora, please help me. The other dolphin just got chopped up. Please don't let them do that to me," the dolphin pleaded.

Behind me I could hear a dolphin's last cries for life and then nothing. My heart beat fast, and I turned to the dolphin next to me.

"I will stop them," I said and turned to Andrew.

"They are chopping up these dolphins, we have to stop them," I said to Andrew.

"How do you know that?" the technician said.

Just then a technician came from behind a computer.

"Boss," the computer technician said as he came over to the main technician. The computer technician leaned in and whispered something to the main technician's ear and pointed at me. Then the computer technician went back to the computer.

"So you can talk to dolphins, can you?"

"What is he talking about Aurora?" Andrew asked.

"Grab her," the lead technician said and gestured for his men to grab me. Andrew tried to stop them, but they overpowered him.

"You can't do this. This isn't right. What are you doing to Aurora," Andrew said.

"We can do this, and I don't answer to you," the lead technician said.

Then the two other technicians tied me down.

"You are going to help us unlock the secret to this dolphin language," the lead technician said to me.

"No, I won't help you," I said.

"I'm going to give you one last chance. Stop this now. I order you!" Andrew yelled.

"I can do whatever I want. I have approval directly from your father. If you don't like it, take it up with him," the lead technician said.

"I'm going to get help," Andrew said and then ran off.

"Where are you going," I yelled as Andrew closed the door.

I was alone with the technicians. I was so scared. The dolphin turned to me.

"I'm sorry," the dolphin said.

"It's okay," I said as I lay tied up.

The lead technician turned toward one of the other technicians.

"Go get the boss," he said.

The other technician ran through the door. Then the lead technician came over to me.

"Let's move her into the other facility," he said and then I was blindfolded. I was taken to a white room that had a tank with dolphins in it.

"Help us," the dolphins said in unison.

"I will try," I said as my necklace began to glow.

"I wish Devon and Aphrodite were here," I thought as I sat there waiting. I tried but I couldn't get out of the knots that I was tied in. One of the technicians came over to me and put a helmet on my head.

"Okay, you're going to help us with a little mystery we've been having. We can't figure out why our code for communicating with the dolphins isn't working. Now talk to the dolphins," the lead technician said.

But I didn't say anything—I wouldn't and I couldn't. I just sat there and didn't think about anything.

The lead technician soon got frustrated because I wasn't playing along.

"Well, if we leave her here long enough, she will talk. We will have the key we've been looking for. Leave her, and I'll get the boss myself," the lead technician said.

The dolphins somehow sensed that they shouldn't talk so they didn't—and I didn't say anything either. There was an utter silence. I knew that they were after something, and it didn't seem right to give it to them. I saw what they did to the other dolphins, and I wasn't going to let that happen again.

I just sat there and thought about Devon, Andrew, and Aphrodite. I didn't talk to the dolphins at all. I sat there for about thirty minutes, and then one of the technicians came over to me.

"Come on, just say something to the dolphins, and we'll let you go," the technician said.

"No," I said and stared at the wall.

Then just as I said that, the lights went out.

Chapter 42

Saved

In the darkness, there was an absolute silence of fear that could be felt coming from the technicians. One of them yelled, "Get the lights." There was a sound of a struggle as the technicians tried to turn on the lights. The light switch flickered up and down, but the lights didn't come back on. I struggled to get out of the ropes that were holding me. I wasn't going to let the confusion of this moment go to waste. Then one of the technicians yelled.

"Hey, what is…"

There was a loud thump, and it was like one of the technicians fell to the ground. Then I heard a second body go to the ground, and then a third. Then the lights came back on.

"Look who I found," Andrew said.

I looked behind me.

"Devon!" I exclaimed. "But how are you here right now?"

"There's no time for that Aurora, we will explain it on the go," Andrew said.

Andrew and Devon untied me. I got up, wrapped my arms around Devon, and gave him a kiss.

"Thank you, I was so scared."

I let go of Devon, and we all headed for the door.

"Come on," Andrew said.

"But what about the dolphins?" I asked remembering that we had to save them.

"The dolphins?" Devon asked.

"Yeah, this institute is torturing dolphins so they can crack some code for communicating with the dolphins. That is why they had me tied up. The institute was trying to use me to crack the language code of the dolphins," I said.

Devon went over to one of the technician.

"Where is the code?" Devon asked as he grabbed the technician.

The guy looking afraid for his life pointed to one of the computers. Devon went to the computer and started typing.

After a moment of typing Devon said, "This is amazing—they have cracked the code for communicating with dolphins. This is exactly what I have been trying to figure out with my research. But we can't let them have it," Devon said as he pulled out a thumb drive.

"Devon, what are you going to do?"

"I'm going to copy their code, and then I'm going to destroy the copy they have. It will only take a moment," Devon said as he typed frantically.

Two minutes later, Devon pushed the final key.

"There, the code is destroyed. Now let's go," Devon said.

"Wait, but we have to free the dolphins."

"We will, follow me," Andrew said.

Devon and I followed Andrew into the room where the dolphins were being held captive.

"Here, help me get these dolphins into these carts, Devon."

The two worked hard and picked up the dolphins and put each one into a cart. There were four dolphins total in the room. I looked over at the one that had lost its fins. It lay motionless. I put my hand on it. I didn't feel any life come from it. The dolphin was dead.

"I'm sorry," I whispered to the dead corpse as I cried a little. I was so sad that we weren't able to save that one.

"Aurora, we have to go," Devon said.

We all began to go down the hallway, each pushing a cart with a dolphin. Andrew stopped suddenly and looked frantically.

"There must be an elevator somewhere around here. Ahh, here," Andrew said as we walked fast.

Andrew pressed the button to open the elevator, and we all went in. The elevator roared up to the top level. It opened up right into the aquarium where the other dolphins were being held. We walked out of the elevator and then wheeled the dolphins over to the tank.

"Here, give me a hand pushing the dolphins in," Andrew said.

Devon assisted Andrew in putting each dolphin back into the water.

"Andrew, we have to let the dolphins into the ocean. We can't let them be tortured anymore. We can't let anymore of them die," I pleaded.

"I know Aurora, but there is only one problem. The tank goes right into the ocean, but the only way to open the floodgates as fast as we need them to be open is by pushing the emergency release. One person has to push on this side while someone else pushes on the other side. It normally wouldn't be a problem, but we won't be able to sneak over to the other side of the tank without getting caught—and we don't have time. We will have to leave and get help from outside and then sneak back in," Andrew said.

"No, we can't leave without letting those dolphins out!" I yelled.

"I am a good swimmer. I can swim to the other side, push it open, and then make my way back," Devon said.

"No, that won't work. There's no time for that, and you will never make it back. There is only one way," I said.

I began to concentrate. Devon looked like he knew what I was thinking. Devon put his arms on my shoulder and then looked into my eyes.

"Are you sure?" Devon asked.

"Yes, it's the only way. I can't let the dolphins die," I said.

"I can't lose you Aurora. I love you too much," Devon said.

"You won't ever lose me," I said.

My heart beat fast. As I stared at Devon's eyes, I could feel my necklace glow. I could feel the power I needed to walk on the water. I climbed up the ladder and then took the first few steps across the water. Andrew stood in disbelief.

"How is this...?" Andrew began to ask.

"I'll tell you later," Devon said.

I ran to the other side of the floodgates. When I got to the other end, I looked for some sort of a release button, but I didn't find it.

"Where is the release button?" I yelled back to Andrew. Andrew was still in a state of shock but managed to yell back.

"It's on the other side—there are two buttons. There is a green button on top and a red button on the bottom. Push the green button. It should begin to open the gates and allow the water to go out."

"Okay," I said and ran over to the button.

"Okay, are you ready?" I asked Andrew.

"Ready!"

"Okay, go!" I said.

We pushed the green button, and the gates began to open. The water began to rush out.

"Okay run back!" Devon yelled. I didn't have much time. The water quickly began to rush out. I began to sprint. The water rushed out a little faster at first, but as the gate opened more and more, the water rushed out at an accelerated rate. It became almost a dangerous speed for me to run across. I soon lost my balance and fell down just as I got to the other side of the tank. I held onto the ledge as I tried to get my feet in a more stable position, but it was hard because of the rushing water. Just then I saw the dolphins as they swam out of the gates. There were dozens of them heading out to the freedom of the bay. I saw some dolphins struggle to go against the current. The dolphins came up to me.

"We will help you Aurora because you helped us," the dolphins said. Just as I was about to get carried away by the water, the dolphins gave me the push I needed to get over the ledge.

"Thank you," I said to the dolphins as soon as I got over the ledge to safety.

"No, thank you Aurora. Your kindness will be known among my kind," one of the dolphins said.

Then they all swam out of the floodgates. Just as the dolphins swam off, Devon came up to me and hugged me.

"I got you my love."

We had a moment of silence as we held each other. Then Andrew came over to us.

"Yes, bring the car around to the front," Andrew said instructing the driver on his phone.

Andrew turned toward us.

"Sorry to interrupt, but we probably just set off every alarm in this place. My dad is going to be pissed. We better take off," Andrew said.

We all ran till we saw the car pulling up. We opened the door and jumped in as the car did a rolling stop.

"Go!" Andrew yelled to the driver.

"Go where?" the driver asked confused.

"Just go, I don't care, drive straight till I tell you to stop."

There were at least fifty employees coming at us, but before they got to us, the car drove off in a panicking speed. In the background, you could see that the giant doors of the massive aquarium were opened fully, and all the water had rushed out into the bay.

"Thank you," I said to Devon and to Andrew.

Then I turned to Devon.

"Now, can you please tell me, how did you get here?"

"Well, when you left to go to Alaska, your Aunt Carrie came in the room and said that she had talked to your mom, and George was fine. So I assumed the worst that Andrew had kidnapped you," Devon said and turned toward Andrew.

"Don't think this is over about you kidnapping my girlfriend," Devon said with a tone of anger, and then continued to talk with me.

"So when I realized that you had been kidnapped, I did some research on the Internet and realized where Andrew was taking you. I called a friend, and he got me here fast," Devon said.

"It was a good thing too because when I went to go get help, I found him in the lobby—and before he had a chance to kill me, I told him what had happened," Andrew said.

"Yep, and I knew I had to help. I had to save you. I'm so glad you're okay," Devon said.

"I'm so glad you came," I said.

I turned toward Andrew.

"But Andrew, didn't you know that your dad's company was doing that to dolphins," I said.

"Aurora, I had no idea. I swear," Andrew said.

Just then Andrew's phone began to ring.

"Oh, it's my dad," Andrew said and answered the phone, placing it on speaker.

"Where are you?" Andrew's dad asked.

"I'm leaving, dad," Andrew said.

"No, you're not. You're going to help me clean up this mess you created," Andrew's dad said angrily.

"No, I'm not, dad. What you're doing is evil. You are torturing dolphins, and I won't be a part of it. That's not what I signed up for."

"Andrew, this is business. Come back now, and I will explain it to you."

Just then Andrew hung up the phone.

"I'm not going back," Andrew said.

"Take us to the airport," Andrew told the driver.

Andrew turned toward Devon and me.

"I'm taking you back to San Diego as promised Aurora. I'm really sorry for all of this," Andrew said.

Devon still looked mad and wouldn't look at Andrew.

"Thank you Andrew," I said.

Then there was silence as we drove to the airport.

Chapter 43

Normal Again

We soon arrived at San Diego. We got off the jet and began to walk down the flight line. Andrew caught up to us.

"Wait, wait. I just wanted to tell you again that I really am sorry Devon. I'm going to work hard to make it up to you, I promise—but I have a lot of battles I have to fight right now between my dad and his company. But as a start, I wanted to offer my car to take you two back to wherever it is that you want to go today," Andrew said.

"Okay, I guess," Devon said.

I turned toward Andrew.

"Thank you, and good luck with your dad and everything. I hope it all works out in the end—and thank you for your help back there. It won't be forgotten," I said.

Devon and I walked toward the car. I leaned in toward Devon.

"Devon, where do you want to go?" I asked, trying to feel like now we could be normal. Just for this moment after everything, I just wanted things to be normal again.

"I think after all of this, I just want to go somewhere quiet and forget everything for today," Devon said.

"Let's go some place nice," I said.

We got into the car.

"Where to?" the driver asked.

"Some place nice," Devon said, trying to crack a joke and ease the mood a little.

I could see the driver smile.

"I think I know just the place sir," the driver said, and we drove off.

The car stopped at a very nice park. It had a nice view of the bay.

"Let's go watch the sunset," I said to Devon smiling.

"I would love nothing more," Devon said back.

We got out of the car, and Devon grabbed my hand.

"I'm not going to let you go again. I've never been so worried and scared in my whole life. I don't know what I would do if I ever lost you," Devon said.

"I never want to lose you either," I said and leaned in for a kiss.

We walked a little and then sat down on a bench at the end of the path.

We held each other as we watched the sun begin to set. The sky was a beautiful pink blended with a hint of blue. It was a breathtaking moment. In that timeless moment, I couldn't picture anything more perfect. I truly believe that we were the two happiest people on earth. I turned to Devon.

"I love you," Devon said.

"I love you too, always and forever," I said as we sat there holding hands.

When the sun was just barely breaking into the water, a little girl came up to the edge of the cliff where we were sitting.

"Look, mommy, look!" the little girl said to her mom as she pointed. I looked at where she was pointing. In the distance, I saw it—a scene that had never been seen before. There were thousands of dolphins all coming toward the shore. Devon could see it too.

"I don't think it's over," Devon said.

I knew in my heart he was right.

"I don't think it will ever be over," I said as I gazed out watching the dolphins with Devon, knowing that our lives were truly changed forever.

About the Author

MATTHEW JENKINS

Matthew Jenkins is a graduate of Southern Illinois University with a B. S in Workforce Education, and a Masters in Human Resource Management from National University in San Diego.

He has served in the Navy since 2001 and has lived in San Diego during his service. Previous to that, Matthew lived in Elmira Heights New York.

This is his first published work.

CPSIA information can be obtained
at www.ICGtesting.com
Printed in the USA
FSOW01n0453250915
11490FS